PRAISE FOR

The Kindness of Strangers

"A moving novel about the ways in which healing can occur after a child's sexual abuse; Kittle's clear prose gives a luminous quality to her story of thriving against the odds."   —*People*

"[A] heartbreaking story [that] encompasses fear, fury, and loyalty. . . . Thanks to the author's exceptionally fluent narrative skill, [this] novel . . . becomes utterly compelling. . . . Kittle unfurls her tale with absolute devotion."   —*Kirkus Reviews*

"Unselfishness is at the heart of this most memorable, compelling novel of survival. Kittle's careful character development and depiction of a loving family situation, along with the variety of statistics offered, help make this tale hard to put down. Although it is a grim, disturbing study of abuse, the conversational style and vividly drawn characters render it a moving portrait of how we heal. Recommended for all public libraries."   —*Library Journal*

"Kittle crafts a disturbing but compelling story line, as Sarah, Nate, and Jordan uncover and come to terms with the horror in alternating chapters. . . . Though the movement is toward healing, there are bumpy roads ahead for everybody in this . . . gripping read."
—*Publishers Weekly*

"Katrina Kittle has written a wonderfully moving but distressful book, which is hard to put down but harder still to forget. . . . The story is disturbing but is well written in descriptive prose."
Star Press

"The story is a brisk, lively, intelligent page-turner that gives the proper payoff and never lets readers doubt that they're in capable storytelling hands."   —*Dayton Daily News*

About the Author

KATRINA KITTLE is the author of *Traveling Light* and *Two Truths and a Lie*. She helped found the All Children's Theater in Washington Township, Ohio, and teaches theater and English to middle schoolers at the Miami Valley School in Dayton, where she lives. Chapters from this novel earned her an Ohio Arts Council grant.

THE KINDNESS

OF

STRANGERS

Katrina Kittle

HARPER  PERENNIAL

NEW YORK • LONDON • TORONTO • SYDNEY

HARPER ● PERENNIAL

A hardcover edition of this book was published in 2006 by William Morrow, an imprint of HarperCollins Publishers

HarperCollins books may be purchased for educational, business, or sales promotional use. For information please write: Special Markets Department, HarperCollins Publishers, 10 East 53rd Street, New York, NY 10022.

First Harper Perennial edition published 2007.

Designed by Jeffrey Pennington

The Library of Congress has catalogued the hardcover edition as follows:

Kittle, Katrina.
    The kindness of strangers : a novel / Katrina Kittle.—1st ed.
        p. cm.
    ISBN-13: 978-0-06-056474-2
    ISBN-10: 0-06-056474-1 (acid-free paper)
    1. Boys—Fiction. 2. Secrecy—Fiction. 3. Suburban life—Fiction. 4. Foster home care—Fiction. I. Title.

PS3561.I864K56 2006
813'.54—dc22
                                                      2005049103

ISBN: 978-0-06-056478-0 (pbk.)
ISBN-10: 0-06-056478-4 (pbk.)

07 08 09 10 11 ❖/RRD 20 19 18 17 16 15 14 13 12

For Monica, Rick, and Amy Jia Schiffler

Beside a well, one does not thirst.
Beside a sister, one does not despair.

—CHINESE PROVERB

Danny

Danny wondered if people looked at his family and knew. Did it show?

Sitting there, in his childhood home, hours before the wedding, he was astounded they'd all come so far. He looked back and remembered a time he'd never dreamed there'd be a scene like this.

He wondered if anyone else looked at them and still thought, *My God, it's amazing.*

He knew that his family still thought it. And that's what he loved about them. On days like this one, or on their graduations or holidays, they sometimes caught one another's eyes and it was there. That sparkle of "we did it, didn't we?" This light of how lucky they were.

Danny loved the days when they remembered that.

Because they didn't always. They couldn't. He knew that it went against human nature to truly savor every moment and continually remain aware of all they had to be grateful for. They couldn't *live* like that. They'd never get anything done. There wasn't always time to savor every damn little thing, like electricity, or your car starting, or the shipment of specialty cheeses arriving on time. He thought about how much effort and energy it would consume to perpetually relish everything. It wasn't practical.

But he thought his family did it more than most.

And with good reason.

His favorite days were when he knew they were all doing it at the same time.

The bustle here in his mother's kitchen gave him a rush. Mom looked great, but he was careful not to tell her too many times. He'd finally convinced her to color her gray hairs, and he didn't want to make too big a deal out of being so obviously right; he just grinned every time someone else told her, "You look fabulous, Sarah."

Danny had already taken off his tux jacket and tucked a cloth napkin into his shirt as an apron. He envied how Mom could stir up the brown-sugar frosting and never get a drop or a splatter on her ivory dress. It was so like her to make the cake herself. Danny had told her he would do it—she had a ton of other things to worry about today—but, as usual, she tried to do everything. At least she was letting them all help, even though that added to the chaos. She'd embraced the frantic quality of the day and turned it into a party instead of a hassle. She caught his eye and laughed, then dipped her finger into the melted butter and brown sugar she stirred. She closed her eyes to express her approval.

Danny's brothers stood nearby, looking like movie stars in their tuxes, eating the scraps of the buttermilk chocolate cake Danny had trimmed off. They laughed at something, and Danny tilted his head and studied them; his brothers looked as different as two members of a family could look.

Most of the time Danny forgot to remember. But today that was impossible.

Odd things brought it all back to him. Sometimes the triggers were obvious, but occasionally they surprised him—the scent of a swimming pool, the sight of a flowering dogwood, a glimpse of a black-and-white cat, the sound of his laser printer, police in uniform, or a blond woman wearing pink.

Today it was everyone taking pictures. The flashes and the video cameras reminded him. They always had, since the discovery on that rainy, cold day twelve years ago.

Twelve years. Damn. Sometimes the memory seemed so recent it could still make the panic thicken in Danny's chest. Other times it was difficult for the man he was now to recognize the boy he had been then. But Danny couldn't pose for a picture, or have someone film him, without remembering it all.

"That summer," his family called it. Even though it started in the spring, in April. Or "that year." If they just said "that summer" or "that year," they all know what it meant. Anything else would be specific: "the summer that Nate left for med school," or "that summer I was sous-chef at Arriba Arriba in Manhattan." But if someone just said "that summer," the rest of them knew what was meant.

Danny didn't believe that everything happened for a reason. He refused to believe it. He hated that image of a God, of a world. Too many things were just petty and mean if he looked at them that way. But in college he'd studied a bit about reincarnation in a comparative-religions class. Some people who believed in reincarnation thought that there was a place somewhere, a place they couldn't ever recognize in this world, from which they chose the path of their lives on earth.

Danny pondered that when he encountered certain people or contemplated his family's history. If it were true, what made some people choose a remedial, cush life and others choose an advanced-placement course? What would have made his family *choose* the shock, the betrayal, the heartache? He wished he understood it.

On days like this, he felt he got a little closer. Knowing everything he knew now, seeing how it had turned out so far, from this better place, he thought he'd choose this life again. He really thought he would.

"Ready with the raspberry?" Mom asked.

Danny opened the raspberry preserves he'd canned himself. Certain items held a family history. A jar of raspberry preserves was bound to set off a family story.

Danny knew he loved the family stories more than anyone else did. Everyone else would complain and cry out, "Not again!" but Danny adored them, longed for them, and secretly devised ways to get them started.

He spread the raspberry preserves between the three layers of dense chocolate cake. When served with homemade vanilla ice cream, this cake was, as Mom called it, "just about as close to culinary ecstasy as is possible." This cake had been his father's favorite, and so it touched Danny that it had been requested for today. Thinking about his dad reminded Danny of a family story. An old one. One that used to be told at all the weddings, the Thanksgivings, the bar mitzvahs, and the birthdays. Always on Danny's birthday. At Danny's expense. Before, back before Dad had died, Danny was embarrassed when the story was told. But now he sometimes asked his mom to tell it.

He'd been very small. Four, maybe five. And he'd been playing by himself in the backyard of this very house. Mom and Dad loved to tell how Danny came running into the house and shouted, "Did you know that when you jump, both your feet come off the ground?"

Everyone thought it was so cute and dumb, but really, to Danny, it had been a scary moment and an amazing realization. He had seen his shadow against the garage. He had jumped into the air and had seen this space between his body and the grass. Against the white wall of the garage, he saw himself floating, not connected to anything.

What kept you from floating away?

Dad had told him about gravity, but it was Mom who listened to Danny explain his fear and who hugged him and said, "I'll keep you from floating away. There's a connection between us, even though you can't see it. You'll always be connected to us."

When Danny used to think about his father dead, he sometimes thought of a shadow floating. Dad was like Danny's own shadow. Danny couldn't really touch it, and it was sometimes really hard to see, but it was always there. Danny knew it. He couldn't lose it.

And that was family. That was the feeling of safety.

And so even though he used to be embarrassed when they told that story, now he liked it. That story was a connection, too. It connected everyone who told it to each other.

But that story was from Before.

There were new stories. The stories of After.

And the story of how Before became After.

The story of how they became who they were now.

CHAPTER ONE

Sarah

Whenever Sarah thought back to that morning twelve years ago, she remembered the chick.

She cracked open an egg, but instead of a yolk, a bloody chick embryo fell into the bowl. She stared at its alien eyes and gaping mouth, and the hair rose on her arms and neck. The maimed chick felt important somehow, a sign of how bleak and bad things had become. Sarah sensed that this was an omen, but she couldn't imagine for what or how to prepare herself.

The chick—in addition to giving Sarah second thoughts about buying free-range eggs at the local farmers' market—made her remember the robin's nest she'd found the day before in the apple tree. There had been four eggs, pale and delicate, like the sugardough decorations on the wedding cakes she was known for.

Sarah looked at the chick in the bowl and wanted to make sure the robin eggs were all right. She knew that this need was irrational—her sons were expecting breakfast, it was typical springtime in Ohio with the rain running in sheets down the window, and the robin certainly didn't require her assistance. Sarah knew she had more pressing things to focus on—she had to cater Thai red seafood curry for twelve today, she needed to start production on a wedding cake, and she was supposed to be developing recipes for a "salads as whole meals" spread for *Food & Wine,* whose deadline was rapidly approaching. Sarah mentally inventoried these obligations, but she slipped out the back door anyway. She jogged across the sodden ground and stepped onto the bench under the tree. At the sight of Sarah's gigantic head, the mother robin shrieked and fluttered to a higher branch. Sarah peered down at the nest, dry and cozy even in this downpour, and the eggs that, to her relief, still sat there like jewels. Four perfect eggs. Nothing but promise and potential ahead of them.

She'd once felt that way about her own family.

The eggs and that contorted chick reminded Sarah of the sappy assignment she'd been given in her grief support group two years ago, back when Roy, her husband, died. The counselor had told her to find three things each morning for which she felt grateful. The counselor told her not to count her two children—they were "givens."

The robin screeched at her in urgent, one-note cries, and Sarah tried to think of *something* that inspired gratitude. Weariness and regret weighed her down, but she stubbornly shoved them away. She could do it, damn it; she could come up with three blessings. She scanned the yard, appraising it, as if it were a property she'd never seen. She looked at the old sandbox the boys used to play in and at her garden, its recently tilled earth as dark as Black Forest cake. One of these days, if the rain ever stopped, she would plant.

The mother robin hopped to a lower branch and continued the staccato warnings. Sarah felt bad prolonging the bird's worry, so she stepped down from the bench. As she did, she reached for a branch, for balance, and in a flash the robin dove at her. Sarah jerked her hand away, but not before she felt the stab of beak and the surge of adrenaline at the attack. The robin flew one more swipe at Sarah before settling defiantly back onto her nest. Sarah examined the wound. A drop of blood welled on the back of her hand but washed away in the rain. More blood rose from the tiny puncture when she clenched her fist. The entire hand throbbed, and the slight pain felt almost good. This was pain from outside, not from within. And not only did her hand ache, but she shivered, aware of how wet and cold she was, skin tight with goose bumps, nipples erect. *She felt something.* She was alive.

There. That was a blessing. She looked up at the tree, wanting to thank the bird for this sensation. This apple tree belonged to her younger son, Danny, who was eleven. Roy and Sarah had planted trees for both sons, in the ancient tradition that the branches from the trees would later be used for the chuppahs at their weddings. Danny used to be as sweet and cheerful as the tree's early-April bloom, but a crab apple tree might have suited him better lately. He'd changed. They'd all changed. And Sarah didn't know how to stop it, how to go back to the family they'd been before.

Sarah walked across the yard, through the rain, to Nate's dogwood tree and touched the trunk. This tree was planted nearly seventeen years ago. Now it stood taller than Nate.

Thank God, Nate's suspension from school was over—that would be the second blessing of the day. He'd already been suspended twice this year for truancy; once more and he'd be expelled. Actually, this was the second for which he'd been *caught*. She knew he'd skipped more than that, because she'd seen him in the middle of a school day. Once, visiting Roy's grave at Temple Israel cemetery, she'd been outraged to see someone sitting on Roy's stone, smoking, but when she recognized Nate, she'd slunk away before he saw her. She'd never told him she'd seen him there, never scolded him for cutting class. And from the cigarette butts that accumulated at the grave, she knew he went frequently. She never mentioned the butts, for fear he'd cover his tracks, and she took comfort in knowing some small thing about his life. Plus, her approval of the visits might make him stop. Everything she said to Nate these days seemed only to insult and anger him. That's why she was making his favorite burritos this morning. She hoped they could be a peace offering.

The back door opened, and Nate stood at the screen. "What are you *doing*? You've been standing out there forever."

Sarah laughed. An excitement rippled through her, a vaguely familiar sensation—of looking *forward*—and she wished she could articulate it to Nate but decided not to bother. He stood and stared at her as she came back into the kitchen and grabbed a dish towel to dry her hair and dab at her soaked clothes. Her heart caught, as she realized afresh she now had to look up to face him. His green eyes, so like his father's, met hers, then darted away, a blush obscuring his freckles. He had the same straight, gingerbread-brown hair as his father, too. Danny had inherited Sarah's thick, black curls.

Nate poured himself some coffee. He took his cup and the paper into the living room, spreading the paper on the coffee table.

After changing into dry clothes and putting a Band-Aid on the back of her hand, Sarah returned to the kitchen. This huge room painted ripe-tomato red was the only modern and completely renovated room in the old house. She and Roy had knocked out a wall and combined the existing kitchen with a downstairs bedroom. It was state-of-the-art, with two wide, blue marble-topped kitchen islands—both with sinks—two industrial-size refrigerators, double ovens, and a walk-in floor-to-ceiling pantry.

Remembering the damaged chick, Sarah opened six other eggs and inspected their yolks before whisking them. She rolled homemade salsa, scrambled eggs, and cheese into flour tortillas and garnished them with avocado slices.

"Here." She handed Nate his plate in the living room.

He wrinkled his nose. "Eggs?" he asked, as if she'd handed them to him raw.

"There's bagels or cereal if you don't want it." She tried to keep her voice light, her buoyant new sense of purpose already waning.

Danny came in, yawning, his wiry black curls poking up like porcupine quills. She ruffled his hair and set a plate for him on one of the kitchen islands. "Burritos? Cool," he said, and began to eat standing up. She reveled in his grin, a sign that the day was at least beginning on a bright note, and in the fact that she could still make him happy.

Sarah leaned in the doorway, where she could see both the kitchen and living room, and sipped her coffee. Nate skimmed through the sports section, eating the offensive eggs after all. Sarah didn't want any eggs herself, still unsettled by the baby bird she'd found, its gnarled claws reaching up to her like little hands.

She missed Roy all the time, but the mornings were when she missed him the most. Mornings when he'd been home to eat with the kids had always been minor celebrations, with stacks of pancakes or waffles, bad jokes, and wild stories from the ER where he worked. She reached out and touched the bright walls he'd helped her paint. She'd actually taken a tomato with her to match the paint. She and Roy had made a ritual of bringing a salt shaker out to the garden each summer to eat the first ready tomato off the vine. She remembered kissing him, with the tangy juice still on their lips.

That's enough, she told herself. *No point in going there.* She left the door frame and walked back into the kitchen, where Danny still stood. He held open his vocabulary workbook with his left hand and ate with his right.

Sarah touched his arm. "Sit down and eat your breakfast."

He puffed air through his lips. "I gotta study. I get extra credit on the test today if I can use these in sentences."

"I'll help," she said, "but sit down at least." He did. The words were fairly simple, although she tried to put herself back into a fifth-grade mind. "Review." "Deceive." "Salvage." She looked over his shoulder at the remaining list.

" 'Epiphany'? That's a hard one." She checked the cover of his workbook, skeptical that it could be a fifth-grade text. Oakhaven, an affluent suburb of Dayton, was known for its excellent schools, but she often felt frustrated that Danny seemed to be challenged too much and Nate not at all. "Can you think of a sentence for 'epiphany'?"

"I don't have to know that one. Only the smart kids have to know the ones with stars."

Sarah swallowed. "You're a smart kid."

Danny shook his head. "I'm in Track Three. The retards. Only the Track One kids have to know 'epiffle' . . . whatever that word you said was."

An ache unfurled through Sarah's rib cage, as if she'd pressed a bruise. Of her two boys, Danny was the more obviously affected by Roy's death. In the last two years, he'd lost all confidence, all sense of himself. And in the last two weeks, he'd apparently lost his best friend at school, too. And he didn't have that many friends to start with. "You are not a 'retard,' Danny. I don't want to hear you say that again."

He lifted one shoulder and dropped his head back over his workbook.

"Did you get *your* assignments?" she asked Nate, crossing to the doorway again.

"Yup." He didn't look up from the paper. "There's a chemistry test I can't make up, but I have, like, a hundred and five percent on every other assignment in that class, so I'll still get an A in there, I bet. I'm going to Mackenzie's, and she's gonna help me catch up before practice tonight."

A weight spread across Sarah's shoulders. *Why, why, why* did he have to do this? "No, Nate. You know the new rule." He turned to her with that look on his face. The look she saw at least ten times a day. The look one might give a person who wasn't just insane but who also reeked of body odor and spoke with her mouth full of rotten food.

He snapped the sports section closed and dropped it on the coffee table. "Why not?"

"Her parents aren't home until ten."

"I thought that rule was about Tony!"

"No. It's about you. I don't need to trust Tony." She managed not to raise her voice, but heat burned in her cheeks. He knew all this already; why did he insist on making her the villain over and over again?

"Who's Tony?" Danny asked.

"So I can't go anywhere? I'm still grounded?"

"Don't act like this is some brand-new thing I just made up." Nate wouldn't have dreamed of pulling this crap if his father were still here, even though Roy had rarely handled the kids' discipline. He was gone too often, even before he was gone for good, and they'd grown used to that fact, as all doctors' families do. But there had never seemed to *be* any discipline problems when he was still here. Everything seemed fun and adventurous then. Without him Sarah was just a nag. She felt like a mean, haggard harpy. She took a deep breath. "As we discussed after your court date, you can't be at a friend's house without adult supervision for a month. At least. If you keep—"

"Look, Mackenzie doesn't even like Tony, okay? He won't be there."

"Which Tony?" Danny asked. "Tony Harrigan?"

"Well, good for Mackenzie. I like her even more for not liking Tony. But you still—"

"Tony Harrigan?" Danny repeated.

"Yes, Tony Harrigan!" Sarah snapped. "What other Tony do we know?" Danny looked crestfallen, and she immediately felt guilty. She breathed deep again. "Please don't interrupt, Danny. You know that makes me crazy."

"Is Tony who you skipped class with?" Danny asked Nate.

"That's a lie!" Nate yelled at Sarah, as if she'd said it. "He wasn't with me. I was by myself. But you don't care. You just decided you hated him after his party. You always make these sweeping generalizations about people based on zero facts."

"Okay. This discussion is over," Sarah said. She couldn't say any more, or she'd be yelling, too, and if she did that, she felt she would have lost.

"This *sucks!*" Nate bumped the table as he stood, slopping his coffee. Sarah entertained a brief fantasy of hurling the coffee cup at his head. He stomped upstairs.

She looked at Danny, who still held his vocabulary book open. "Oh," he said. "Tony had that party, right? The party where Nate got . . . where the police brought Nate home?"

Sarah paused and sighed. She was so tired. Danny knew that story; there was no reason for him to ask. She tried to remind herself to be patient, but this new habit of asking questions he already knew the answer to made Sarah wild. "Yes," she said, forcing a neutral tone. "You know that party was at Tony's house. Now, finish your breakfast, sweetie."

Danny nodded happily. How could he be happy when he'd just been screeched at? When every morning began with this friction and nastiness in the house? Is that all he wanted—a reaction from her, any reaction? She had to do better, she had to get it together.

She shook her head as she poured more coffee. She told herself those things every morning.

Nate had gotten trashed at Tony's party on one of Sarah's rare evenings of solitude since Roy's death. Danny had been spending the night at his friend Jordan's house. Sarah had sunk up to her chin in a bubble bath and drunk three vodkas with cranberry juice in a row. She'd thought of Roy without her customary anger—anger that infuriated her further with its irrationality. It wasn't as if he'd gotten cancer *on purpose.* She'd even managed to think of him without crying. That made her bold, and she ventured into memories that warmed her with a heat quite different from the bathwater and steamed walls. She'd allowed her hands to slip beneath the bubbles when the police had banged on the front door, bringing a stumbling-drunk Nate home from Tony's.

Bad enough to be interrupted. Even worse to face the Oakhaven police. Sarah imagined they were disdainful of her disheveled hair, flushed cheeks, and clutched-closed robe, certain they could sense she was tipsy herself and knew just what they'd caught her doing.

Nate had been too far gone to notice and had puked for half the night.

The worst of it, though, was juvenile court. Sarah had refused to plead for leniency, as Tony's father had. She liked to think she and Roy would have done the same thing if Roy had been alive, but especially with him gone, she wanted a punishment that would be a genuine deterrent to this stupidity. But that day in court, Nate had whispered to her, and seared into her brain, "Why couldn't you be the one who died?"

She'd wanted to die; that's what he didn't understand. She would have gladly died instead of Roy if she could have. She would have done anything in her power to save him. And to hear Nate whisper those words made her wish she *was* dead. She forgave Nate, though. She remembered telling her own mother "I hate you" and meaning it with all her heart in the second she said it—but not after. Those memories of her thoughtless cruelty pained her, and she hoped the day would come when Nate was pained as well. But all the same, it hurt to hear, and remembering it made her blink back tears.

She cleared the kitchen, while Danny continued poring over his vocabulary list. She scraped the uneaten portions into the sink but couldn't bring herself to grind the chick in the garbage disposal, too. She wrapped the chick in the empty tortilla bag before she set it in the trash can.

When Nate came back downstairs to leave for school, Sarah asked, "Do you want me to drive you? Since it's raining so hard?" The high school was only a block away, but she wanted to offer something, she didn't want the argument to be the last words spoken before he left. He didn't answer, though. He didn't acknowledge her in any way; he just went out the front door. Sarah's intention to drive him turned into wanting to run him over.

"How about you, Danny?"

"No, that's okay," he said. "I like the rain. But thanks." Her eyes teared again when he hugged her before he went out the door. He at least wore a raincoat and carried an umbrella. Nate had left with just his sweatshirt hood up. He'd be wet and cold all day. Sarah felt a pang. She should have stopped him. She was a horrible mother.

She stood on the porch and watched Danny walk away up the boulevard. His elementary school was two blocks in the opposite direction from the high school. Oakhaven was so small there were no buses. When Danny waved before turning at the end of the street, she went inside.

Sarah snapped into action in the kitchen. Chopping and slicing were usually meditative tasks for her—time that her mind filled with new ideas and inspiration—but this morning, as she chopped onion, pressed garlic, and grated ginger for the Thai curry, she found her rhythm off. She kept thinking about the dead chick. What was wrong with her? Why had it unsettled her so? Was it just the argument with Nate?

She heated oil in a deep skillet and added her chopped ingredients. This curry was for a book club she catered every month, one of the jobs that was the "bread and butter" of her business, the Laden Table. The Laden Table had first started here in the house when Nate was a baby. Before that, Sarah had been one of the chefs at L'Auberge, a four-star restaurant in town. Once Danny entered kindergarten, she had moved the Laden Table downtown, opening a catering and carryout shop. Every day hundreds of people had wandered in and chosen lunch from her daily-changing menu. She had closed when Roy got sick and sold when he died. Now the Laden Table operated out of her home again. Sarah missed the excitement of the interactions with her regulars—from the Dayton Ballet dancers to the Sheraton Hotel's shoeshine man to the lawyers from the firm that had been next door.

Gwinn Whitacre, one of Sarah's former employees she'd been able to keep part-time, had been urging her to reopen the carryout shop. As much as Sarah missed it, she thought it was insane to even consider, as overwhelmed as she felt at the moment. "Simplify," she said aloud, as she added mushrooms, sweet pepper, and lemongrass to the skillet, tossing and stirring. Her father had always said that to her. She feared she'd forgotten how.

And actually, while the vegetables cooked, she needed to check the amount of sugar-dough flowers already made, as it was time to get serious about Debbie Nielson's daughter's wedding cake. Sarah stirred the skillet contents, then dashed down to the basement. In one corner of the basement sat her son's rabbit hutch, the black-and-white rabbit, Klezmer, blinking at her in the light. On the other side, beyond the storage freezer, were shelves and shelves full of sealed plastic storage containers of sugar-dough flowers. Debbie had ordered a three-tiered spice cake filled with apricot praline cream. It was to be decorated in antique white buttercream icing to match the bride's dress. Debbie had wanted real flowers on the cake—the same used in her daughter's bouquet—but Sarah had talked her out of this. There was always someone who ate the flowers, after all, especially at a reception so large, and the chemicals from the flowers tainted the flavor of the cake. So Sarah and Gwinn would cover the cake with cascades and swags of sugar-dough roses, lilacs, orange blossoms, and hydrangea. Sarah could hear herself telling the students in the class she'd taught just months ago, "Don't wait until the week of your cake project to start making flowers. Flowers can be made and stored for up to six months in advance. If you're organized and give yourself plenty of time to complete a cake, it can be a work of art."

Yeah, right. If you're organized. Sarah skimmed over the labeled boxes. They had plenty of Gwinn's lovely roses and rosebuds. Plenty of lilacs. She'd need to get started on the hydrangea, though. As behind as she was, she looked forward to it. She'd stop at the florist and pick up real hydrangea to review. She'd study it, take it apart petal by petal to note the configuration and shape. She prided herself on making the flowers botanically correct, with petals as thin as the real thing.

If she was going to the florist, she might as well check her stock of florist wire and tape. Moving one storage container, she bumped a roll of florist tape off the shelf and it rolled over near the rabbit hutch, behind a bale of straw used for bedding. Sarah cursed and followed it. As she bent to retrieve it, she spied a magazine jutting from under the bale of straw. A magazine that had obviously been hidden. With heavy arms she pulled it out and turned it over. A *Hustler.*

Sarah tried to swallow the rage that boiled up her throat. *Breathe.* She opened the magazine to an image of a woman bent over, legs spread, presenting herself to Sarah.

Breathe. Breathe. What the hell was she supposed to say about this?

She stared at the woman, and as she did, she heard the sizzling in the kitchen. "Shit!" She ran up the stairs, dropping the magazine on the kitchen island, and stirred the smoking skillet. Some of the peppers had stuck to the bottom, but she was able to salvage the rest.

Salvage. Hmm. A vocabulary word. Now she had a sentence for Danny.

She stirred in the coconut milk, the fish sauce, and the Thai red chili paste. Her chest ached.

She'd found a *Playboy* two months ago in Nate's room, just weeks after finding condoms in his jeans pocket in the laundry. She expected the *Playboy.* He was sixteen, after all, soon to be seventeen. She hadn't been surprised, or angry—mostly sad at having to navigate this territory without Roy. But *Hustler?* She didn't care so much that he had it, but for God's sake, did he have to leave it in the most likely place for Danny to find? It exhausted her to think how she'd ask about this magazine. She was tempted to ignore it, seeing as how they had a platterful of problems already.

She removed the skillet from the heat and covered it. Now all she needed was the seafood. The market that supplied all of the area's restaurants had just opened.

She couldn't stop thinking about Nate as she drove over and hunted for what was best in the market that morning. The mussels would look dramatic with their black shells against the creamy pink sauce, but she settled for halibut and shrimp for the book club. Completing the meal would simply require poaching the seafood in the base while the rice cooked.

Nate still hung heavy in her thoughts on her way home when she drove along the Oakhaven golf course and passed the sunny, welcoming house of her friend Courtney Kendrick. This yellow house, with its periwinkle trim and shutters, had been one of her favorites long before the Kendricks had moved into it four years ago.

Sarah slowed the van.

It struck her that she'd come up with only two blessings that morning, so she added Courtney as the third. Courtney had been doggedly devoted to Sarah's survival in the months following Roy's death.

Sarah looked at the big house, remembering those daily phone calls.

"Hi. So what did you decide to wear today?" Courtney would ask.

"I'm not dressed."

"You should put on that pretty green sweater," her tiny blond friend would declare. "And those black pants you wore to open house. Put those on and come meet me at the Starbucks on Brown Street."

"No . . . I can't." Everything was so impossible then.

"Yes you can. I'll come get you. I have a break in an hour. Get dressed."

And Sarah learned that if she didn't dress, Courtney would come in and *make* her. And drag her by the hand to the car and force her to go drink coffee like a normal person.

Those phone calls: "What have you eaten today?" "How about we get your hair cut?" "Today we're getting your van an oil change." "What's Danny wearing for school pictures tomorrow?"

Sarah blinked away the tears.

Then she blinked again and squinted through the rain.

Courtney's son, Jordan, walked alone down his long driveway toward the road. Jordan was in Danny's fifth-grade class. He used to be Danny's best friend, but in the past couple of weeks, they'd seemed to have had a disagreement that neither Sarah nor Courtney could figure out. It pained both women. Jordan was an odd child, shy and aloof, but Sarah liked him. She was more than a little aware that Danny was odd and shy as well, and that without each other the two boys seemed destined to be outcast loners. Before she'd gotten pregnant, she used to wonder aloud, "What happens if we have the kid no one likes?"

Roy used to kiss her and say, "Then we'll just love him more, because he'll need it."

Courtney worried seriously about Jordan and had told Sarah yesterday that she and Mark were having Jordan tested for Asperger's syndrome, known to cause the sort of social-interaction handicaps that Jordan seemed to have.

The rain poured as heavy as a waterfall, and Sarah knew that Jordan was more than an hour late to school. She pulled her van into the driveway beside him, and Jordan stopped walking and stared at her. He carried his green backpack in front of him, his arms crossed over it against his chest, as if he expected someone might snatch it from him. The rain matted his blond hair to his forehead. Sarah rolled down her window. "What are you doing out here?"

Jordan looked at her and said, "Walking to school," as if she were an idiot.

"Where's your mom?"

"At work." An ob-gyn, Courtney worked in a private practice as well as at Miami Valley Hospital, the same hospital where Roy had worked.

Sarah frowned. She knew that Courtney drove Jordan to school every morning. "Well, is this good timing or what, then? Get in. I'll take you."

But he stood there, as if uncertain. Water ran over Jordan's face, beading in his lashes. It ran off his earlobes and fingertips and the bottom hem of his blue parka, but he didn't move. Sarah remembered herself standing in the rain earlier that morning, how good the shocking cold had felt. She looked into Jordan's face, and he, too, seemed to radiate a sense of new purpose. The wind shifted, and rain poured in the van window, soaking her sleeve. "Come on. Get in," she said, as gently as she could.

Jordan walked around to the passenger side. He put his book bag on the van floor and climbed in.

"Is your dad at work, too?" Sarah asked.

Jordan nodded. Mark was president of Kendrick, Kirker & Co., a huge PR firm.

"Why are you so late for school?"

Jordan shrugged and looked out the window. "I fell back asleep."

"Your mom left you alone?"

"She was on call. She had an emergency."

"Well, we'll get you there." Reaching behind her, Sarah pulled a white cotton tablecloth out of the pile she'd packed for the lunch. "Here. Dry off." He took it from her, and she backed out of the drive. For a moment he just held the tablecloth; then he wiped his face.

Keeping an eye on the road—she'd twice nearly hit deer down here along the golf course—Sarah attempted to elicit some kind of friendliness from this boy. She was never sure if he was just unbearably shy or simply hated talking to her, but she always wanted to try; it seemed too cruel to pretend he wasn't there and drive along in silence.

"I'm cooking for you guys again Friday night," she said. Tomorrow she'd cater curried chicken on rice noodles, with lime-and-pepper sauce, for three couples at the Kendricks'. Mark was entertaining some clients.

Jordan didn't answer.

"Those parties are probably boring, huh?" She wanted desperately to fill this quiet, to be nice to him. "Are there ever any kids your age, or is it just grown-ups?"

Jordan looked straight ahead but whispered, "There's kids."

"Oh, good. Do you like them?"

He shrugged, then pulled the tablecloth around him, as if cold. Looking at him draped in white like that, Sarah remembered that kids at school mockingly called Jordan "the angel," partly because he was so obviously the teacher's pet but mainly because of an incident she'd witnessed at the choir concert rehearsal. The concert was very much a *Christmas* concert, even though the school called it a "holiday" concert, apparently in concession to the non-Christian families like her own. She'd been standing with Danny's class lined up in the gym waiting their turn to go onstage and practice. They watched the fourth-graders sing "Silent Night," and the lights changed to reveal a tableau of little girls dressed as angels. Jordan, standing at her elbow, had said, "I wish I were an angel." He had a way of blurting out the most bizarre statements to no one in particular, and half the time Sarah thought he didn't *mean* to speak aloud. She was certain he hadn't meant to that time, as he startled and blushed at the derisive laughter from the kids in earshot.

"Ooh," Billy Porter had taunted. "Jordan wants to wear a dress and wings."

"Shut up," Danny had said.

Sarah had quieted the kids and scolded Billy—and later praised Danny for sticking up for his friend—but five months later the nickname stuck.

Jordan, here in the van, sighed. She looked over at him. He closed his eyes and leaned his head back. "Are you okay?" she asked. "Are you sick?"

She reached over and touched his forehead. In the second before he rolled his head away from her reach, ovenlike heat met her fingertips. "You're burning up. You *are* sick."

Jordan thrust the tablecloth from him and sat up straight. "Pull in here," he said with urgency, nodding to a gas station at the intersection ahead. "I need to go to the bathroom."

"Sure." Sarah glanced at him. Was he going to throw up? The van bucked across the uneven gravel lot of the tiny station. Jordan grasped the dashboard, his face white.

"Oh, no. They're closed. But we can—"

"There's a port-o-john," Jordan said, pointing.

"Oh, no, hon, you don't want to go in there—" But he was already opening his door. "Jordan, they're so dirty. Can you hang a few more minutes? I'll get you to a cleaner bathroom." He slid out the door, knees buckling as his feet hit the ground. He picked up his backpack, then hesitated. He looked at the port-o-john, then at Sarah, and carefully put the bag back on the floor.

"You need any help?" she asked, but he shook his head. He bit his lip, looked at his pack, then slammed the door. He weaved his way to the port-o-john and disappeared inside it. Sarah pulled up the hood of her rain jacket and followed him. "I'm right outside," she called, feeling helpless. She wanted to go inside with him, but God knows what she'd be able to do to help him, and there'd hardly be room for two. Poor kid. How hideous to be sick inside one of those gross places. She wondered if diarrhea, not vomiting, threatened, because if it were vomiting, she knew she'd rather just do it out here in the parking lot.

When the wind blew the rain sideways against her, she walked under the shelter of the gas station's overhang. A wiry brown-and-white terrier emerged from under a bench near the front door and wagged its stump of a tail at her. She scratched it behind the ears, keeping an anxious eye on the port-o-john.

Jordan was too sick to go to school. Sarah would take him to her house and call Courtney, glad to do this favor for her friend. What had happened that Courtney had rushed off and left him alone, so obviously ill? That wasn't like Courtney at all; she usually seemed an almost overprotective mother. When the Kendricks first moved here four years ago, most of the teachers and parents had worried that Courtney was going to be high-maintenance because she asked so many questions at the back-to-school orientation. Was there much bullying? Did someone monitor the kids in the PE locker room? Could kids take an extra period of art instead of PE if they were involved in extracurricular sports? Everyone understood her worries when they met Jordan—so small, so shy, a loner who shunned the other kids' prompted efforts to include him. Most of the adults found him likable in his oddball way. He was smart and a voracious reader, often lost, it seemed, in his own internal world. He'd won the school spelling bee every year that he'd been here.

It pained Sarah that the kids didn't like him. Danny had at first befriended Jordan, without she or Roy even urging it, but even sweet, kind Danny had begun to speak disparagingly of Jordan lately. Sarah had tried to talk to Danny about it—what had happened? had they argued?—but Danny would only say that Jordan was "mean" to him. Courtney couldn't get anything out of Jordan, other than Danny "didn't like" him.

Sarah had seen Courtney just last night. They'd treated themselves and had made arrangements to go, child free, to El Meson, their favorite restaurant. The owner and the chef stopped at their table, recommended dishes, and offered them complimentary portions of new appetizers they were still toying with, asking Sarah's opinion.

"It's fun coming here with you," Courtney said when they were alone at the table again. "You're famous."

"Only to people involved with food," Sarah said. "And when it comes to food, these people are *geniuses*."

After some sangria and the best paella Sarah had ever eaten, Courtney confided that Jordan's teachers said he'd grown more withdrawn, even less social, since the winter break, even though his grades remained excellent. That's when she'd told Sarah about the Asperger's tests. Courtney's blue eyes filled with tears as she told Sarah that Asperger's was more common in males and its onset was recognized later than autism. She showed Sarah a brochure that said "clumsiness, social-interaction problems, and idiosyncratic behaviors" were reported.

Sarah knew that Asperger's syndrome could not be completely cured, but Courtney said she didn't care. "It would just be a relief," she said, "to have a reason, something to tell people to explain why he is how he is."

They'd talked for about two hours, but Courtney hadn't mentioned anything about Jordan's being sick.

Now Sarah looked across the gas-station parking lot and tried to will Jordan out of the port-o-john. What was taking the poor kid so long? As if it read her mind, the little terrier trotted through the rain to the blue plastic hut. The dog sniffed at the bottom of the door.

Sarah stepped back into the rain. "You doing okay?" she yelled, banging on the john door. "Jordan? Are you all right?" She hesitated but decided she was a mom after all; if she saw private parts of him exposed, it was no big deal. She pulled open the door and stood staring, not comprehending for a moment what she saw.

Jordan sat on the floor, his body facing her, with his knees up sharp by his shoulders. His head lolled to one side, hair touching that filthy seat. Sarah filed away every detail in slow motion—his eyes rolled back white in his head, the puff of gray foam on his chin dripping into his lap, the crotch of his jeans dark, a pool of urine under him. She looked up at his face again, finally seeing it: the needle in his neck.

A thin line of blood dripped from the hypodermic jutting out of his throat.

The terrier barked and jolted her into action.

"Oh, my God! Jordan!" She shook his shoulders, and a small glass vial rolled from the crook of his hip to the floor. She snatched it up—a trace of clear liquid rolled in the vial. "Jordan? What is this? What did you do?" She shook him again, and the needle bobbed. Without thinking she jerked it out, but her stomach somersaulted when she saw the drops of blood that blossomed and dripped down his neck in rhythm with his pulse.

She shoved the vial into her coat pocket before reaching under his arms and hauling him out of the john. Her adrenaline was too much and Jordan much slighter than she expected, so she barreled out of the port-o-john and fell. Jordan ended up on his back, looking up at the rain, mouth open, hands unnaturally bent, fingers fluttering. Sarah scooped him up and carried him to the van, the terrier yapping at her heels. She opened the side door and shoveled Jordan in among the plastic bags of wrapped fish and shrimp, then grabbed her cell phone and dialed 911. She realized she couldn't describe where she was. She had no idea what side street she was on, and no name identified the gas station. "Never mind." She slammed shut the van door and ran around to the driver's side. "I'll bring him to Miami Valley Hospital. Can you tell the ER?"

Sarah tossed the phone into the passenger seat before the dispatcher finished speaking. "Jordan! Jordan!" she screamed as she peeled out of the gravel lot and careened through the rainy streets. "Don't die, don't die, please don't die. Jordan! Talk to me!"

As if in answer, more vomit gurgled out of his throat. In the hurried glimpses over her shoulder, she saw he was twitching, convulsing, but as long as she heard his ragged breaths, she could drive instead of performing CPR. She kept repeating his name until she pulled in to the emergency-room lot, ignoring the red sign that said AMBULANCES ONLY, PLEASE, driving onto the sidewalk, almost hitting the entrance doors.

Throwing the van into park, its windshield wipers still flapping, she yanked open the side door and pulled Jordan out by the ankles until she could reach under his arms. She half dragged him through the double set of doors into the registration area, where three people she recognized rushed to meet her, calling her by name. "Is it Danny?" Nancy Rhee asked her as she and an orderly took the child from Sarah's arms and put him on a waiting gurney.

"No. No, he isn't mine. His name is Jordan Kendrick. Courtney Kendrick's son. She's a doctor here. Obstetrics. I think she's here now." The receptionist bolted for the phone.

Nancy was already rushing Jordan away, announcing, "This kid's in cardiac arrest," and that she needed this and this and that, combinations of words and numbers that made up the language Roy used to speak. Sarah reached into her pocket for the vial. "He took drugs! Here! He took this!"

A nurse snatched the vial from her and ran after Nancy.

A male nurse led Sarah to a chair and said, "Give me your keys, Sarah. I'll park your van." She handed over the keys without speaking, wishing that she hadn't needed to see his name tag to remember that his name was Alan. It had been two years since she'd set foot here, where Roy had worked and where she'd had to bring him at the unexpected end. They'd known he was dying, but she hadn't realized the cancer would be so quick and greedy. She wondered if Roy had known that it would be and hadn't told her. Sarah had sat right here, in this very chair, that last night, waiting for her mother to bring the kids, not knowing she should be holding Roy's hand, listening to his last words. She'd thought they would admit him, that they'd have time to move to a hospice.

The receptionist announced, "Dr. Kendrick's on her way down." The police arrived first, though, and pulled Sarah into an empty exam room and asked her to describe what had happened. She told them and then was free to go.

Knowing that she'd missed Courtney's arrival while she talked to the police, she sought out Alan, who told her Jordan had gone into a second cardiac arrest, which they were working on now. He told her Courtney couldn't see her right then.

By the time Sarah reached home, there was a sobbing message on the answering machine. "Please don't tell anyone. Please don't talk about this. Sarah, please." Sarah shuddered at the hysteria in Courtney's voice. There was a pause, then a thump, as if Courtney'd dropped the phone. Hospital paging codes sounded in the background. When she spoke again, her tone had changed. Collected and soothing, as if she thought Sarah were the hysterical one, Courtney said, "I ask for your discretion, Sarah. I'm sure you understand. We'll handle this. Everything will be just fine," and hung up.

Sarah didn't make the book-club lunch. She was hours late. She called and said there'd been an emergency and apologized profusely. Next month would be complimentary. The hostess was gracious and forgiving. Sarah fretfully paced the house, then rolled pale lavender sugar dough and made three bunches of sugar-dough lilacs she didn't need, just to do something with her hands.

Her hands. She massaged the small blue bruise on the back of her hand, where the mother robin had pecked her. She thought about that blood-streaked suggestion of a chick.

It wasn't until much later in the day, removing the ruined seafood from the van, that Sarah noticed Jordan's green book bag still on the floor of her van's front seat.

CHAPTER TWO

Jordan

J ordan? Jordan? Can you hear me? Do you know where you are?"

He thought it was an angel. So he smiled. But moving his mouth made his teeth click against something. He wasn't there. Not yet. Maybe soon.

"Jordan?" the voice asked.

The voice echoed in his head and spun around in his brain. It sounded in one ear, then the other. He ignored the voice. He liked where he was right now. Rocking on the warm water in the dark.

"You're in the hospital, Jordan, and you're safe."

His raft rocked too far. He almost tipped. Water seeped in all around him. He'd sink.

He didn't open his eyes, but his mind woke up. Really woke up. He was cold, and he hurt. The hospital? He wasn't supposed to be in the hospital.

"Jordan? You're waking up. Can you hear us? Can you blink your eyes?"

Don't do it. It's a trick. Figure it out first. Stay in the dark.

Jordan fell off the raft into the freezing water.

He remembered his plan.

If he was in the hospital, he'd screwed up bad.

And he didn't want to, but he couldn't help it—he heard himself make this sound, like a puppy. A whimper. He didn't do it on purpose. It just came out. And it sounded like it came from far away, not from him.

"Jordan?" the girl voice said. "It's okay. You're all right. You're safe."

He'd never be safe. Not *now*. He tried to open his eyes. The light was too bright. His eyes burned like there was soap in them. His head was so heavy. Like a giant watermelon. Like his brain was swollen and pushing against his skull. And his throat. He tried to swallow. Something was in his mouth and throat. It gagged him. He'd choke. He couldn't breathe.

"Jordan! It's okay. Stop—hold him! Hold his arms!"

Someone else's hands grabbed his and pulled them away from his mouth. He didn't even know he had reached for his mouth. Just like that whimper sound, he didn't mean to do it. Those other hands pinned his arms down by his sides. He stopped fighting. He gave in. He always gave in. He hated himself more than he hated those other hands. But he was so tired. Just go ahead. Get it over with.

"Good boy. I know this is scary. You have a tube in your throat, Jordan. We needed it to make you breathe. For a while this morning, you couldn't breathe on your own. You had quite a close call. You almost died."

Almost? That whimper sound came out of him again. Why hadn't she just left him alone and minded her own stupid business? He was in so much trouble.

"Hey, hey, hey . . . it's okay now. You're alive, and you're going to be just fine."

He squinted at the voice through that burning light. The light tilted away, and the voice turned into a face that smiled at him. He'd never seen her before. Asian. Black hair pulled back. Huge brown cat eyes. He'd almost died, and she'd saved him. He hated her. Did she know how much trouble he was in? How much trouble he was in because of her? *Oh, man. Oh, man.* This was so bad. What would they do to him?

His book bag. Where was his book bag? He tried to sit up, but the hands were too quick and held him down.

"Whoa. Whoa. Let's deal with one thing at a time, Jordan. Calm down. Let's get this tube out of your throat, okay? This is going to feel awful, I'm sorry, and it'll hurt when it's gone. I'm going to count to three, and on three I want you to cough. Try to cough, because it will help push the tube. Okay? One, two, three."

He wouldn't do it. Why would he do something that she told him was going to hurt? He already hurt bad enough. But she kept asking him. He couldn't breathe right. It felt like there was some animal running around inside his chest, like that gerbil in his class at school. Jordan hated all of the people hanging over him like that. So he did what they said. Like usual, he did it.

He coughed. Fire. The tube was so long. Like some giant worm thing. When the last of the tube slithered from his lips, he tried to take a deep breath. Worse. They might as well have pulled a razor out of his throat. There was a creepy, metallic scraping sound.

"Shh, Jordan. It's okay."

Oh. That was him. That scraping sound came out of his own mouth. He closed his lips. The sound stopped. He shook all over, and that gerbil in his chest was going faster and faster on its wheel. What was he going to do? He had to get out of there.

He swallowed. He thought he was swallowing broken glass. The light went dim. He was falling back to the warm water and the rocking. It was better there. He could escape. Paddle. Paddle away on the water, and when they woke him up, he'd be gone. He tried to paddle. But his arms and legs felt wrong. . . . He didn't have his jeans on. Or his parka. Someone had undressed him.

Bright light again. The water was gone. He was in the hospital with no clothes. *Oh, no. Oh, man.* He was in trouble. This was so bad.

"Jordan? You with us?"

He made another sound, like a moan. He didn't mean to. He was being such a baby.

"I know you're hurting, Jordan. But we're doing everything we can to make that stop. My name is Dr. Rhee, but you can call me Nancy, okay? I've been your doctor through most of this. You've had quite a few procedures today. You . . . you had . . . um . . ." she looked over his head and stopped.

He wanted to ask her questions. But he didn't. Even if it didn't hurt so much, he needed to review the situation here. Review. R-e-v-i-e-w. That was a vocabulary word. How much did she know? What could he salvage? Salvage was a vocab word, too. He caught himself going away into his Other Self. The one who got lost spelling words when things got too rough on the one Here Now. He pulled himself back. *Stay here. Find your backpack. Make sure no one sees it before your mom gets here. Figure out a new plan.*

He whimpered again. If he was in the hospital, his mom could come in any second. Did she know already? Maybe he could convince them not to tell her. As long as the backpack was safe. He turned his head to look for it. Bad move. The light dimmed again, but he fought to keep his eyes open. He fought to keep seeing what was Here Now. Black dots danced in front of his eyes. His brain slogged back and forth inside his skull. He blinked hard. When the dots were gone, he saw five people at the foot of his bed. They were on the other side, across from the doctor. Not his mom. Not his dad. But one was a cop.

Something kicked Jordan. From inside himself. Not the gerbil. Something lots bigger kicked against his ribs.

There were a lot of them. And he couldn't even move.

"There are some people here who want to help you," Dr. Rhee said. "They'd like to talk to you, but you don't have to talk to anyone right now, okay? Not until you feel better."

Jordan stayed still. Or tried to. He couldn't stop shivering. No way was he talking to anyone. He'd already messed this up so bad. If he didn't hurt so much, he'd run for it. That's what he should do. There was no fixing this. He should run.

The girl doctor kept talking. Jordan wanted to hate her. But he loved her voice. A girl version of his grandma's voice reading to him, back before she died. No wonder he'd thought the voice was an angel. This was bad. This was so bad.

"You overdosed. You took too much of a drug called Dilaudid, Jordan. *Way* too much."

But not enough. There'd been more than one vial in his mom's drawer. He should've have taken all of it. Stupid. Stupid stupid stupid. What was he going to *do*?

"You also had antibiotics in your pocket. Have you been sick lately?"

He didn't answer. Stupid chicken baby.

"Now, at first we thought it was an accident. But"—she swallowed and looked at the others—"but, Jordan . . . we wonder if maybe you were trying to end your life?"

Another kick in the ribs. Then nothing. Like he'd been paralyzed. Where was the darkness? Where was the raft? *Please* could it just be dark again?

"When we were trying to help you, we found . . . we found a lot of evidence that . . . you've been . . . that someone has treated you very badly. . . ."

He couldn't breathe. Then another kick. A bunch of fast kicks in a row. He sucked in a deep breath, but that made the broken-glass feeling come back. A machine over his head started to whine. Like those emergency broadcast tests that came on TV late at night. *Please?*

"Hey, don't panic. You're safe here, Jordan. We won't let anyone hurt you."

They'd been looking at him *there*. His skin crawled. He wished it really could crawl. Drop off his bones and slip under the bed. Why hadn't he tried harder? Stupid stupid.

"We just want to ask you one question right now, Jordan. That's all until you rest some more, okay? We just want to know if you can tell us who hurt you?"

Stupid stupid stupid. Where was his raft? Where was the water? He had to get out of there. He had to get out fast.

Someone whispered something on the other side of the bed. He turned his head toward the whisper. When he moved, the black dots came back. Swarmed into his eyes. He held his breath. Tried to stop the sloshing in his brain and belly. He tried to blink away the dots again, but the lights dimmed. Good. Darkness crowded in. Lapping water filled his ears. He tried to find his raft.

"It's too soon," he heard Dr. Rhee's voice say from far away.

Too soon for what? What were they going to do to him?

A man's voice, a voice like on the chicken-soup commercials, said, "I told you the cop would scare him. He shouldn't be in here."

The voices blended with the water. Jordan found his raft. Between the sloshing of the waves, he heard "not a regular drug user," "Children's Services," and "suicide attempt."

Suicide was against the law. Would he go to jail? But having the drugs was against the law, too. You had to have a prescription. He was in so much trouble. Please let him stay here in the dark. Please.

A cool hand touched his forehead. For a second he wasn't on his raft but on his bed at home. His eyes popped open. It was the doctor touching him, not his mom. He jerked away. More dots. And a tidal wave in his stomach. He ground his teeth together. He breathed out through his nose, trying not to puke.

"Shh. You're safe here, and we're going to make sure no one hurts you ever again."

Liar. She couldn't promise that. He was in so much trouble. He hadn't asked to come to the hospital. He hadn't told anybody anything. They'd looked at him when he was in the dark and had found out. That wasn't his fault. But it wouldn't matter.

"You think you can sleep?" Dr. Rhee asked.

He closed his eyes, testing it, and knew he could. He didn't think he could open them again now if he tried. His eyelids weighed too much, his brain was soup, his throat full of glass. The rest of his body had this pulse to it, this throb, like a drumbeat. Jordan pictured his body swelling and shrinking, swelling and shrinking, like an injury in a cartoon.

What if he had to pee? With his eyes shut, he couldn't feel anything except that pulsing ache below his waist.

Maybe he'd never feel those parts again.

Please let him never feel those parts again.

CHAPTER THREE

Nate

Nate knew something was up. He knew that something was serious-weird at home, but he had no idea what. All he knew was that Mom was freaking out about something and it was probably his fault.

Nate sat in the dark outside the hockey rink. He checked his watch. Shit. She was almost twenty minutes late. He pulled his collar up higher on the back of his neck. He had his skates hung over his right shoulder, his stick slung over his left. A wicked-cold gust of wind pierced his bones. He knew he could go back inside the Rec Center and wait in the heated lobby, but to get up and walk suddenly seemed like a monumental task. The coach had kicked their asses tonight, and Nate was glad. Hockey was one of the only things that filled his mind enough that he could forget for a while about Dad being dead . . . about how much life in general sucked these days.

Tony and Mowaza had just left. They'd offered Nate a ride home, but he knew that Mom would freak if he rode with Tony. But, shit, he would've been home by now. Nate had been glad when they left, though, because Tony had lit up a cigarette as they stood there talking to him. The last thing he needed was Mom pulling up and seeing that.

What was up with Mom? She'd been in bed when he'd come home from school today. She *never* took naps—well, at least not since that zombie period she went through when Dad died—so he figured she must be sick. Nate had made Danny a grilled cheese sandwich and told him to be quiet so they didn't wake her up, but then Mom had some nightmare and had wigged them both out. Nate had actually had to go into her room and almost slug her to get her to wake up, and when she had, she'd gone off on this rant about drugs. And she was all weird and hyper and made this big meal even though Nate told her he'd already made dinner for Danny.

A horn tooted. He looked up. About damn time.

He walked to the passenger door really slow, limping more than he needed to. He saw his mom's worried, ready-to-apologize face, gearing up for some excuse. He opened the door.

Mom sighed and said, "I'm sorry I'm late, hon. Debbie Nielson called about her daughter's cake. I went over there to take pictures of the wedding dress. We're going to copy the lace pattern in the icing of the cake."

Nate snorted like that was one of the dumbest things he'd ever heard. Actually, the cakes Mom made were amazing, but she'd been late, after all. He climbed into the passenger seat and wondered if he'd ever be allowed to drive again—Mom had yanked that "privilege" since juvenile court. He didn't even ask about it tonight. The van's heat blasted, and he was just glad to be warm.

They hadn't even made it out of the Rec Center parking lot when Mom said, "Nate, I meant what I said this afternoon, about drugs. You can always talk to me. I won't be angry."

He leaned sideways and rapped his head against the window. "What is up with you? Why are you obsessing about this? Do you think I'm on drugs?"

"No, but . . ." She looked at him so long he feared she'd veer off the road. "I know they're out there. I know it's a temptation."

He was sure this was leading up to Tony being a druggie.

"I mean it," Mom said. "I know kids use them. Kids younger than you. Lots younger than you. Think about that: kids who are only ten and eleven using drugs—*real* drugs, narcotics, for God's sake." Her voice rose in that shrill, the-house-is-on-fire voice he hated. "It makes me sick! I don't know what to feel, for someone like that—"

"Who?" Nate asked.

"What?"

"Who are you yelling about? Because I'd wish you'd yell at them, not me."

"I'm sorry." She slumped her shoulders at the wheel. She looked so tired. She always looked tired. "I just love you, is all. I get scared for you."

Nate was really glad she said that but didn't know what to say back to her, and it was suddenly hard to swallow, so he just looked out the window at the houses flying by in the dark. Sometimes he thought she hated him. He knew *he* would, if he were her. He still couldn't believe he'd told her he wished she'd died instead of Dad. His face burned, and he was relieved it was dark. Why had he said that to her? What an asshole.

"So." Mom brightened her tone. "How was it to be back at school? Tell me about it."

She always did that—tell me about school, tell me about the dance with Mackenzie, tell me about practice. Why did *he* have to do all the work? It was like saying to someone, "You give a speech now, and I'll sit back and listen."

"I went to class. The bell rang. I went to another class. That's pretty much it."

She shot him a look but then laughed and said, "You did this seven times, right? You promise?"

He snorted again, happy she took it as a joke.

Before he could think of anything else to say, though, Mom said, "I mean, where would a kid even *get* drugs like that?"

"You're asking the wrong person." Nate looked out the window, wondering if there were freak moms in all the houses they passed.

They pulled into the driveway, and Nate escaped into the house. He was starving, and now he was glad Mom made a dinner after all. Without taking off his coat, he went straight to the fridge and started to eat some of the quiche she'd made, but Mom followed him and cornered him again, that there's-something-we-need-to-talk-about cloud hanging over her. *Shit, what now?*

She almost whispered, "Nate, do you know anything about a *Hustler* magazine I found downstairs by the rabbit hutch?"

Nate choked, sputtering piecrust crumbs. He thought all that crap was over and done with. When she went on and on about how natural it was to be curious but could he please show a little more responsibility about where he left his reading material, his face burned guilty-as-hell hot. He couldn't control it, but goddamn it, it wasn't his.

The *Playboy* she found two months ago was the one Tony stuck in Nate's folder right before he went up to give his speech in English class; it wasn't like Nate went out and bought it himself. And the condoms she'd freaked over, he'd picked up after a demonstration in health class just because everyone else was taking them, too. He tried to tell Mom that. He even told her to call the school, but she just pursed her mouth in that "yeah, right" expression.

He'd wanted to ask her, "Look, you think if I was really going to use them, I'd let them go in the washing machine? Don't you think I'd hide them better than that?" but he didn't want her getting any ideas and making a habit of searching his room. She might find the box of condoms he actually *had* bought and hidden under his bed, in the plastic crate with his swim trunks and beach towel, a place he knew she wouldn't be nosing into when she did laundry. The box was open, instructions read, but he'd never convince her he hadn't used them yet. Well . . . not with Mackenzie anyway. He'd opened one and tried it out, here at home, alone, just to make sure he wouldn't fumble around like some loser when the time came. But try telling that to his mom; she never believed a damn word he said.

He ate another piece of quiche and watched Mom's mouth move, talking on and on. He wondered if his dad had ever looked at dirty magazines. He couldn't picture that, even though he'd once found a book of really dirty stories up in their room. What would it be like to be married to his mom? She was okay. Not a knockout or anything, but what did G.G.—his Grandma Glass—say about Nate's homecoming picture of Mackenzie? "A quiet beauty."

Dad always said he fell in love with Mom's hair. He would come up behind her and hug her and nuzzle her hair with his face while she was trying to cook. She'd pretend to be annoyed, but Nate knew she loved it.

"Nathaniel Laden! Are you even listening to me?" Mom asked.

"It's not mine. Talk to Danny." Her face darkened. Danny never did anything wrong. Danny's the sweet one, he'd heard her tell people.

Nate expected her to yell at him, but she lifted her hands and then left the kitchen. Somehow that stung even worse.

He pitched the last bite of piecrust into the sink. Shit. He couldn't do anything right; why did he bother? He walked down the basement steps and reached for the chain that pulled on the bare lightbulb.

"Hey, Klezmer." Klezmer, their black-and-white Dutch rabbit, blinked and sniffed at him from the hutch next to the utility sink. Nate convinced Mom to let him bring Danny's pet in from the backyard for the winter. Danny's pet. What a laugh. Danny had begged for a rabbit when Billy Porter got one for Easter last year. Nate had wanted to give Danny a rabbit for his tenth birthday, and he'd promised Mom he'd take care of the rabbit if Danny didn't— and Nate had been taking care of the rabbit pretty much since a week after Danny's birthday. Nate dumped his skates at the bottom of the steps and went to the hutch. "C'mere, dude." He lifted the lid. The rabbit stood on its back legs, reaching up for him. Nate scooped him up and carried him back to the steps, where he sat and let Klezmer hop into his lap.

He thought Mom really let him get the rabbit because they all missed having a pet. They used to have this great dog named Potter. She was black and white, a mix between a boxer and a ridgeback, and she had this white zigzag on her neck like a lightning bolt. That's why Dad named her Potter—since she was a girl, they couldn't call her Harry. Dad loved Harry Potter. It cracked Nate up. When the first book came out, Dad bought it for Nate but then kept taking it to read himself. They were always fighting over it and accusing each other of losing the other's bookmark. Dad took it to work once and left it at the hospital. Nate tried to hide it from him after that. Mom bought two copies of the second one—one for Nate and Danny and one for Dad, as a joke.

Dad loved that dog. They all did, but she was really Dad's. Dad used to sing to her, and he was a really bad singer. They'd beg him to stop, but he'd say he was singing for Potter and she liked it, didn't she? And she'd look up at him and wag her tail. She loved him. Every time Dad came in the house, he'd pick her up—and she was a big dog—and say, "Oh, I missed you so much!" Even if he'd only been gone for ten minutes. And she was always overjoyed to see him.

Shit. Sometimes when Dad came home after working almost forty-eight hours and called, "Hey guys, I'm home," Nate wouldn't even go downstairs. Nate hated that. Nate hadn't been mad or anything, just . . . busy. He'd be on the phone or doing something else. He remembered that, and it actually hurt him, like a bruised bone somewhere.

Potter died about two months after Dad did. They had no idea why. Mom said Potter's heart was broken. That hurt, too. Didn't that mean they *all* should have died? Did none of the rest of them love Dad enough?

Anyway, that's why Mom let him get the rabbit, Nate thought. It would've felt wrong to get another dog. And since Danny asked for a rabbit like Billy's, it just seemed like the perfect excuse. And Klezmer was cool, actually. Nate hadn't known anything about rabbits when he got him. He hadn't known the rabbit would have a personality. Klezmer flopped over onto his back in Nate's lap and closed his eyes when Nate rubbed his nose.

The door at the top of the steps rattled. That meant someone had come in the back door. And Nate knew who it was, which made goose bumps race up his spine.

But then he heard Mrs. Ripley call, "Sarah? It's me." Oh. He thought it might be Mrs. Kendrick. He couldn't tell if he was relieved or disappointed that it wasn't.

Just old Mrs. Ripley. Their neighbor was as nosy and weird as they got. She kept this concrete rabbit on her porch and dressed him up in all these different outfits she made herself. Like today, the rabbit—whose name was Sir Nottagoose—had been wearing a big pink bow and holding a giant Easter basket filled with eggs. She dressed him in a Cincinnati Reds uniform for opening day, a leprechaun suit for St. Patrick's, and a turkey costume for Thanksgiving. Sir Nottagoose had about ten different Halloween costumes. It was hysterical, the time and effort she put into these outfits. Mrs. Ripley needed a life. They used to call her the Widow Ripley—but nobody made that joke anymore. Ever since Dad died, Mom had become friends with Mrs. Ripley. Mom wasn't just being nice; she honestly seemed to *like* the old lady. Nate didn't get it.

Nate sat really still when he heard his mom say, "Hey, Lila. Want some coffee?" He didn't want Mom forcing him to make conversation like she sometimes did. Mrs. Ripley acted like Nate was a serial killer or something ever since he got brought home in that police car. That . . . and she knew that Nate was behind Sir Nottagoose's "kidnapping" last fall. She came out one morning and the concrete rabbit was missing from her porch. There was a ransom note where it usually sat. The statue was tied to a telephone pole down the street and gagged with duct tape. It was hysterical—and it wasn't broken or "harmed" or anything; it was concrete, for Christ's sake—but the old lady had no sense of humor about it. She'd freaked, and now Nate couldn't even walk past her house without getting a nasty look.

Nate listened to Mom and Mrs. Ripley's voices above him until he lost them when they moved into the living room.

He kept rubbing Klezmer's nose. Klezmer wrapped his front paws around Nate's arm and acted like he was going to kick Nate with his back feet, but he didn't really. Klezmer never scratched Nate. If Nate put a sock on his hand or pulled his sleeve down, then Klezmer would really kick. The rabbit knew the difference.

Danny wanted to name Klezmer some boring name like Peter or Cottontail, but Nate managed to convince him to go with the name Nate wanted. Nate chose the name because of the cool music his Grandpa Laden had turned him on to. Not that cheesy wedding–and–bar mitzvah crap. Nate liked the old, clarinet-howling, fiddles-wailing music. His friends made fun of him for it, but he didn't care.

Klezmer stopped kicking Nate and rolled over so he could sit upright. "Wanna play ball?" Nate asked him. Nate stretched out his legs, making a bridge for the rabbit to the concrete floor. Klezmer walked down them and tiptoed around the washer and dryer, checking out the piles of laundry on the floor. Nate found the toy ball and rolled it toward him.

He heard footsteps over his head. And his mom's voice saying, "I can't even imagine what was going through his mind."

Damn, were they talking about him again? Mom probably told Mrs. Ripley about the magazine, so now the old lady would have another reason to hate Nate. He didn't know why Mom always told her everything, like Mrs. Ripley was her shrink or something. Mom *had* a shrink. She used to make Nate and Danny go to one, too, after Dad died.

Mrs. Ripley said something Nate didn't catch, and then his mom said, "I'm still trying to . . . process it, I guess. It was so upsetting. I'll never forget it, and there's no one else I can share it with."

Klezmer pushed the ball to Nate with his nose. What the hell were they talking about? He rolled the ball back to Klezmer.

Mom ran some water in the kitchen, so he missed part of what they said next, but when the water stopped, Mrs. Ripley said, "Still, it can't be easy to discover your son might be a heroin addict."

For Christ's sake, Mom thought he was a *heroin* addict? What was the deal? Klezmer pushed the ball back to Nate's feet. He would play this game for hours.

Mom made a moaning noise, and said, "I don't know what to do, if I should call again—"

"Leave her be."

"But maybe she doesn't *want* to be left alone. She didn't leave me alone, thank God, when Roy died. She saved me. She saved this family."

When Roy died. It still made him get cold to hear those words out loud. And now he was clueless. Mom must be talking about Mrs. Kendrick. The goose bumps prickled all over him again. But, what did *she* have to do with this?

"Maybe I should just go back to the hospital," Mom said. "I could sit with her, bring her something to eat or changes of clothes. Whatever. As long as Jordan is there."

Jordan Kendrick? Danny's friend? He was in the hospital?

Nate kept rolling the ball back and forth with Klezmer.

"Just wait," Mrs. Ripley said. "If they don't call today, try again tomorrow. But don't pester them."

Ha. Mrs. Ripley giving advice on not pestering people.

"Sarah, they might be upset that you know, maybe embarrassed, but for heaven's sake you saved the boy's life. She'll call you when she's ready."

Wait a minute. Were they talking about *Jordan* being a heroin addict? The ball stopped at Nate's feet.

"Thanks for letting me unload," Mom said. "That helped."

"Of course, doll." The back door opened. Nate pictured Mrs. Ripley patting Mom's arm, like she always did. "It won't leave this kitchen."

When the door clunked shut, Nate sat there a minute, trying to figure out what he'd just heard. Klezmer got impatient with Nate's distraction and was now playing by himself, pushing the ball with his nose, catching up to it, pushing it again, around and around the laundry piles. That spooky little kid was a junkie? How'd they find that out? And how had Mom saved his life? Damn. Jordan was only in Danny's grade, this wispy ghost of a kid who played on Danny's soccer team. Nate kind of admired the way the kid played as if his life depended on it; he never just went through the motions, like some kids. Yeah, he liked Jordan well enough. Never thought he was as bad as the other kids made out.

And he liked Jordan's mom, too.

Chills snuck up the back of his neck just thinking about her.

It started last September . . . no, actually it started two years ago just after Dad died—that was the first time. But that kiss was all hazy in Nate's memory . . . like he'd been drunk or something. Mom had been so out of it, and Mrs. Kendrick stopped by to check on her. Nate had been sitting in the kitchen. Just sitting there. Staring. And sort of crying because it was all so messed up—his dad *couldn't* be gone, you know? And Mrs. Kendrick had hugged him, which was nice, even though he was too old. Nate didn't care. And she made these little noises, and she kissed his forehead and cheeks. And then his mouth. She kissed his mouth in this way that felt like . . . she was drinking him. For a long time, too. But then she whispered, "No, Nate, you're just sad, that's all," and went upstairs to see his mom. Nate freaked out. *She* kissed *him,* he thought, but then the way she said "no," he wasn't sure. He was mortified. He'd kissed his mom's best friend! What a loser. But . . . that whole month was murky in his mind. He avoided her after that. He hid in his room whenever she came over, and after a while everything felt normal again. Like it had all just been one of those dreams that felt really real.

But last September it all started again. Mom had guilt-tripped Nate into going to one of Danny's soccer games. "Do you know how many of your hockey games he's gone to? This is something he does well, and we need to support him in it." So Nate went and got stuck sitting with Mom and all these dumb moms of fifth-graders. He couldn't find anybody he knew to sit with. He was just trying to watch the game, and Mrs. Kendrick showed up.

All these moms called her up to sit with them. She was carrying this little video camera like she always did and still had on white surgical scrubs and a doctor's jacket on top of a pink sweater. She wore pink a lot. It looked good on her. But, really, anything would. For a mom she was pretty hot. Really small and fit, in a lean-cat scrappy sort of way. You could tell she worked out. She looked like she just *had* worked out. Her face was all flushed, and her blond hair was pinned up, but all these strands of it had fallen out and were floating around her face. Nate couldn't help but think that's what her just-got-laid face would look like.

"We didn't think you'd make it," Nate's mom said to her.

"Me neither," she said. "Ten minutes before I was supposed to get off, the ER sent up a woman in labor. I just helped deliver a healthy, eight-pound baby girl."

For Christ's sake. All the moms oohed and aahed. Mrs. Kendrick ended up sitting between Nate and his mom. She took off her jacket. That pink sweater was sleeveless, and her arms and shoulders were really ripped and muscled, like she lifted weights. She turned to look at Nate and held contact with her weird, glittery eyes. Heat zoomed across Nate's face.

"How've you been, Nate?"

That was an innocent question, right? But the *way* she asked it made Nate think his face was going to burst into flames. All he could think of was her kissing him. "Okay," he said, but his voice came out all geeky. He cleared his throat and managed to say, "Jordan's playing great," sounding more like himself.

"Oh, good."

The other women all started telling stupid stories about labor and babies being born. Mrs. Kendrick at least paid attention to the game, filming it with her camera. She complimented Danny's playing, but Nate knew she was only being nice to his mom.

Sitting next to her jolt-wired him with adrenaline. He tried to watch the game, but he couldn't focus. When he saw Mowaza come into the stands and sit below them, Nate fled.

"Hey, Nate, my man," Mowaza said. "Thought I was stuck here alone."

"Don't complain. I was stuck with a bunch of women talking about labor pains and episiotomies."

"Epizza-whats?"

"Don't ask."

Mowaza laughed and scooted his paper tub of fries toward Nate. They sat there, leaning their elbows on the bleachers behind them and eating the fries.

Nate felt Mrs. Kendrick behind him. Was he just freaking out? She was someone's *mom*. He waited until Jordan made a decent play, then turned to see what she was doing.

She ducked her head and looked away, lowering her camera. She'd been watching him, filming him. Then she looked back and smiled. A shy, "you caught me" kind of smile. Nate couldn't see her eyes behind her shades. He whipped back around to face the field.

"You got any smokes?" he asked Mowaza. "I'm needing one in a big, bad way."

"Is the pope Catholic? Let's take a field trip."

In the bathroom, under the stands, Nate shared a quick cigarette with Mowaza and thought about telling him but didn't. It couldn't really be what he thought, right?

When they left the restroom, Mowaza got in line for a hot dog, and Nate saw Mrs. Kendrick at the end of the rampway that led to the bleachers. She had put her white jacket back on and was watching him. Had she *followed* him?

She lifted her chin and mouthed, "C'mere." Nate couldn't read her expression. Shit, was he in trouble? Did she know they'd been smoking?

She walked out of the stadium and out onto the street. She never looked back at him but walked about a hundred yards and sat down on a curb between two parked cars.

What the hell? He caught up and stood behind her. "Mrs. Kendrick?"

She sat with her knees to her chest. She patted the space beside her. "Sit down. I need to talk to you."

So he sat. They were in this really small space between the cars, and it meant Nate had to touch her. Their legs were pressed side to side. His heart pounded, and he knew that his face was red. "W-what's up?"

She smiled at him, and her eyes had something playful, almost mocking in them. Nate had no idea what was going on, but he was aware he had become unbelievably sweaty.

"How's your mom doing?"

Nate blinked. "What?"

"How is she holding up? Does she seem all right to you?"

You are an idiot! his brain screamed. Here he thought the woman had been coming on to him. Yeah, right. Fat chance, bozo. "What do you mean? Like . . ."

Mrs. Kendrick's face changed, and she said, really soft and gentle, "Since your dad died, Nate." She lifted up her hand and moved his hair out of his eyes. She left her hand there on his head. *She is touching me,* was all Nate's brain could hold. Her fingers were in his hair, just above his left ear. Their heads were so close he smelled her mint chewing gum. "Nate?"

Shit. He'd forgotten she'd asked him a question. "I . . . I, um, I think she's okay now. You know, she's doing . . . all right." He sounded like a moron. And his face still burned.

"Does she have any friends?"

She kind of stroked his hair, and his head filled with her perfume. Somebody walked by, and he wanted to glance up, but he didn't want to move her hand. They were hidden there, down between the cars. That is, if his own damn heartbeat didn't give them away—in his ears it sounded like an amplified drum.

"Um . . . well, yeah . . . sure. . . ."

"Besides me?"

Was she dissing his mom? But her eyes looked soft and full of concern. "I worry," she said, "that she's gotten isolated. That she doesn't have anyone as support."

Nate was dying to wipe the sweat off his upper lip but couldn't move. Even if Mrs. Kendrick was right, why was she telling *him*? What was he supposed to do about it?

He cleared his throat. "She's friends with Mrs. Ripley."

Mrs. Kendrick laughed and kind of thumped him on the head like he'd made a joke.

"No, really. I know she's a little weird, but my mom really likes her. They talk a lot."

Mrs. Kendrick smirked and said, "Anyone else?" She started stroking his hair again. Nate felt a little pissed off, like she thought his mom was a loser or something. But not pissed off enough to want her to stop touching him.

"Sure. She goes running with Ethan Whitacre's mom."

Mrs. Kendrick's hand stopped moving. "Gwinn Whitacre? That cop's wife?"

"Yeah." Ethan's dad was an Oakhaven officer.

"But Gwinn works for your mom. That's different."

"Yeah, but they go to movies and stuff."

She drew her hand away. "Really? A lot?"

"Yeah, they went out just last Thursday. I had to stay home with Danny."

Something new shone in Mrs. Kendrick's eyes. Nate felt like he was talking to the girls at school and thought of the way they'd sulk if their friends didn't save seats for them in the cafeteria. Hadn't she *wanted* his mom to have friends?

"Remember last summer when my grandma came to visit? Grandma stayed with us while Mom went to Cincinnati with Mrs. Whitacre for a day. They stayed in some hotel and did all that spa stuff—massages and nail stuff and all that." G.G. had to really push Mom to go, but Nate decided not to say that.

Mrs. Kendrick stared straight ahead. He felt like he'd answered wrong on a test.

"I think you're her closest friend, though," he said, embarrassed at how eager to please he sounded.

She looked into his eyes. Their mouths were inches apart. "Nate?"

The way her mouth moved saying his name hypnotized him. He loved the way her teeth came together, parted, then came together again. He nodded at her, his eyes on her mouth, wanting her to say his name again. He thought she was going to ask him something, but she didn't. She just kept looking at him. His brain had melted, and he wanted to ask her, ask her about that time in his kitchen two years ago. "Do . . . do you remember . . . ?"

Mrs. Kendrick touched his mouth with a finger, then moved her lips to his. Even as his brain screamed, *What the hell are you doing?* Nate opened his lips for this kiss. His ears were on hyperalert for someone walking by, but only for a few seconds before she kissed him too drunk to care. Damn. Mackenzie didn't kiss like that. When Mrs. Kendrick stopped, she smiled and touched his mouth again.

She stood up, but Nate couldn't make his legs work.

She reached into her pocket and brought out a pinwheel mint. "Your mother would be devastated to know you were smoking. Here." She pressed the mint into his sweaty hand, then took out the video camera from her jacket pocket and looked down at him through it. What the hell? He blinked at the red recording light. "You're sweet," she said, and walked back into the stadium. Nate thought he might melt into the curb. She *kissed* him.

He'd tried to tell Mowaza, but Mo had laughed and said, "You wish! You're so full of shit." And it did seem like that. That kiss, like the first one, eventually seemed like something Nate had imagined so vividly he'd convinced himself it was real. But every time he decided that it was all in his head, Mrs. Kendrick would do something to freak him out again.

Like she brought Jordan to the high-school hockey games and always hung around afterward to talk to him. One night she'd pressed her hand on Nate's chest when she said, "Good game," and let it stay there awhile, but no one else seemed to notice a thing. Not even Jordan, who conveniently watched the Zamboni clean up the ice.

Once, right upstairs, in their own kitchen, while Mom talked to someone on the phone about a wedding cake, Mrs. Kendrick had said to him, "You should come over sometime."

And Nate had looked at his mom, standing two yards away on the phone. He'd looked at Mrs. Kendrick and that way her eyes laughed. He asked, with a challenge in his voice, "What for?"

Mrs. Kendrick had smiled and said, "We have a pool. A trampoline. Tennis court. Lots to do. Come over anytime."

It made him crazy. He even dreamed about her. The sort of dreams he normally loved, but when they featured her, he woke up feeling lucky to still have all his parts.

Nate stood and picked up Klezmer's toy ball, just as the rabbit caught up to it. Klezmer wheezed this funny sigh and flopped down on his side. He made Nate laugh. "Sorry, buddy." Nate hefted him up and held his velvet-pillow fur against his cheek for a second before he lowered the rabbit back into his hutch.

Poor Jordan Kendrick. Nate figured he'd need drugs, too, if Mrs. Kendrick were his mom. He felt sorry for that weird, skinny kid. Nate wouldn't want to piss that woman off. She seemed dangerous enough when she liked you.

CHAPTER FOUR

Sarah

Sarah stood in her kitchen and stared at the phone. She'd just called the hospital, but they said that Jordan Kendrick was no longer a patient there. What should she do? Why didn't Courtney call her? Every time the phone rang last night, Sarah had prayed for it to be word from Courtney, but it was always Mackenzie for Nate.

Jordan's green backpack sat waiting by the back door. The backpack gave her a reason to go over to the house. She could return the backpack and leave quickly if she sensed she was intruding. Plus, she honestly needed to find out about the party tonight. Did they still want her to cook? She couldn't imagine they'd be in an entertaining mood.

Sarah remembered her own reaction when Roy had told her he had cancer. Anything outside the family in those few short months between his diagnosis and his death had shimmered surreal and absurd. Janet Porter's pressuring her to join the PTA had felt obscene. Receiving wedding and party invitations had enraged her, and she certainly couldn't imagine wanting to *host* a party. Sarah knew that Mark and Courtney would probably be in a similar raw state. But the way Courtney had said "don't tell anyone" made Sarah wonder if they'd go ahead with the dinner party. Mark had always struck her as being overly concerned with appearances, much too obsessed with showing off his latest purchases to her in tiresome detail—his new digital camera, the new DVD player, the new camera phone. Sarah always smiled and nodded and mentally willed him to shut up. He was shallow and a bit of a jerk. Dazzlingly good-looking and charming, but a jerk. Sarah and Gwinn jokingly called him Ken because of his beautiful jawline, high cheekbones, and blond hair. He really might decide to entertain clients even if his only child had just gotten out of the hospital.

So yes, Sarah needed to find out about this dinner. She wouldn't risk not showing up and complicating Mark and Courtney's lives even further. She didn't want to inflict that on her friend.

Her friend. Courtney was her friend, damn it. Had Courtney had "reasons" to come over and check on her back in that awful period? Had Courtney waited for Sarah to return *her* phone calls?

Sarah snatched up her purse and left.

Halfway to the Kendricks', she realized she'd forgotten the damn backpack, left it sitting by the kitchen door. Oh, well. It didn't matter. She could run home and get it for them, but first she wanted to see Courtney face-to-face.

She pulled into the Kendricks' driveway, drove past the front of the house onto the side drive that led to the kitchen door—and braked hard.

Three police cars sat by the side door. Two regular cars she didn't recognize blocked the open garage, where Courtney's SUV was visible. Mark's Mercedes was not in sight.

Sarah turned off the van right where she sat, in the middle of the driveway. She walked to the door on leaden legs. Oh, God, what had happened?

She reached the door and opened it to an empty kitchen. Where was everyone? What was going on? "Courtney?" she called. The house was so huge they had to communicate with an intercom; if they weren't nearby, they'd never hear her call. She rang the bell and stepped inside. "Courtney? It's me. Sarah."

Before the chime of the bell had stopped resonating, Sarah was surrounded. Several men and one woman—some in suits, some in police uniforms, most of them wearing latex gloves—came from every direction. Sarah recognized one of the officers—he'd given her a speeding ticket once. She looked for Rodney Whitacre, her friend Gwinn's husband, but didn't see him. Her scalp and rib cage contracted. She couldn't catch her breath.

The tallest man stepped forward. "I'm Detective Robert Kramble." His voice was surprisingly gentle, in contrast to his broad-shouldered, imposing presence. He wore a dark blue suit that would've looked classy if it weren't so rumpled. "How can we help you?"

"I . . . I . . . Is Courtney here?" Sarah felt like a seven-year-old asking for her friend to come out to play. Oh, God. Please let everything be all right.

"She is, but she's on her way out. I'm sorry." Kramble looked at her and waited.

"I just wanted to see her, to see how Jordan was doing. I . . . What's going on?"

"What's your name, please, ma'am?"

"I . . . I'm Sarah Laden. What's wrong? Is everything okay?" What a stupid question. Clearly things were not.

Kramble frowned and cocked his head, as if thinking. With black hair and long-lashed dark eyes, he was good-looking enough to be a detective from a TV show, except for his one slightly crooked front tooth. Kramble snapped his fingers once and said, "Sarah Laden," as if he'd belatedly understood a punch line. "You brought Jordan to the emergency room yesterday morning."

Sarah nodded. So this had something to do with yesterday? "Is Mark here? Can I talk to him?" She just wanted to *see* one of them, to know they were okay.

"No," Kramble said. Sarah wondered which of her questions he was answering. Kramble peeled the latex gloves from his hands, folded them neatly, and tucked them inside his suit jacket the way someone might pocket a handkerchief. "You may be able to help us, Mrs. Laden. I'd like to ask you some questions."

"Why?" She heard voices in the living room and looked, hoping to see Courtney.

A woman officer with short black hair and a serious, almost pouting face, held a stack of papers in her latex-gloved hands and announced, "There are a number of checks written to a Sarah Laden by Courtney Kendrick." Sarah didn't like the way the woman looked at her, with hard, accusing eyes. She certainly didn't like the fact that the woman appeared to be rifling through Courtney and Mark's financial records. What was happening?

Kramble asked, "And why would Dr. Kendrick write you a series of checks?"

"Some for five hundred dollars," the pouting woman said, as if this were a felony.

Sarah scowled at the woman. How dare she act as if Sarah were guilty of something for making a living? "I cater for the Kendricks. I'm supposed to prepare dinner for their party tonight. Only I don't think they're having it. I just came by to check on Jordan and to see how they were all holding up after yesterday."

A male officer, thick and stocky like a wrestler, said, "There's a party on for tonight? That's great!" as if he'd been invited. Sarah stared at him.

"Why don't you have a seat in here?" Kramble gestured for her to come into the living room.

She followed, eager to see if Courtney were in the living room, but she wasn't. Rodney Whitacre was, though. He lifted his head from where he knelt on the white carpet, and said, "Hey, Sarah." His expression was so bleak it chilled Sarah with the certainty that something tragic had happened. Sarah opened her mouth to say hello but then shut it, feeling as stupid as one of the tropical fish in the aquariums lining the walls. God help her. Panic kept its grip on her rib cage. All the furniture in this normally immaculate room was moved from its usual position. The glass coffee table and the replica of Donatello's *David* that stood on it were shoved into a corner. A cupboard she'd never noticed, behind a wall panel, stood open. The shelves of the cupboard were empty—their contents apparently boxed into three white plastic storage bins Rodney was labeling. She couldn't read the labels from where she stood.

Courtney's video camera—the one she brought to all the soccer games—lay on the floor in a plastic bag. A fancier camera, on a tripod, was draped in plastic, too.

"You can sit down if you like," Kramble said. Sarah hesitated before the giant white couch, covered now in plastic sheeting. "It's okay," Kramble assured her. She sat, too stunned to remain standing.

"Oh, my God. Is . . . are . . ." She had no clue where to begin. "Look, I'm not comfortable answering questions until I talk to Courtney. Does she know you're—"

"Yes. Dr. Kendrick gave us permission to search," Kramble said. "How long have you been catering for the Kendricks?"

"Um . . . for nearly three years now."

"And how did you first begin to work for them?" The stocky wrestler scribbled notes. The pouting woman leaned against the wall. Rodney kept stacking what looked like videotapes and DVDs into a fourth storage bin. Sarah heard the sounds of rummaging and drawer opening from rooms down the hall.

"We're friends. Our kids go to school together. She worked with my husband. She knew I catered, and she called me for a party. She liked my work. I've been working for them ever since."

"About how often would she use you?"

"It varies. Two, sometimes three times a month."

The woman officer made a small sound, like disgust. Rodney shook his head as if Sarah's answer were a shame. "Look," Sarah said, her patience wearing thin now that her pulse had returned to normal, "you need to tell me what's going on."

"Yes, I will. But first, Mrs. Laden, can you tell us what your husband does?"

She felt as if this man had just walked in on her naked. She looked at Rodney for support, but he kept stacking and labeling videotapes. "My husband is dead." She enjoyed the wince that wrinkled Kramble's face. "Why am *I* being questioned this way?"

"I'm very sorry for your loss. Could you tell me when your husband died?"

She glared at him and considered storming out of the room and up the stairs in search of Courtney. They couldn't force her to sit here and answer these questions.

"Mrs. Laden?" Kramble's face looked gentle, but Sarah didn't buy it for a minute.

"Two years ago, in February. Two years and two months." Her eyes burned. Damn it, she would *not* cry in front of these people. She pointed at Rodney. "He was at the funeral." Rodney nodded. Then he stood and carried a box out of the room.

"I'm sorry," Kramble said again, and paused, looking up at the ceiling, as if offering a moment of silence. Sarah listened to the bubbling of the aquariums. Finally he cleared his throat and resumed. "You sound as though you were friendly with Dr. Kendrick."

Sarah noticed and was troubled by his persistent use of the past tense. Was this investigation related to what happened yesterday, or was Courtney having to deal with an additional crisis on top of her son's overdose? "Yes, we're friends. She's probably my best friend."

Kramble looked genuinely sad for a moment, sadder even than when she'd told him Roy was dead. "What sort of parties did you believe you were catering?"

Believe? "What are you suggesting? Mark entertained clients. For his PR firm."

"And what was your impression of his clients?"

"They were nice people."

He frowned. "So you were here, at the parties?"

"Yes. Look, what are you getting at?"

"For the duration of the parties? Did you see the guests leave?"

"Yes. I'd serve and clean up. I have two part-time staffers who help me with bigger events like that, and the occasional wedding and bar mitzvah. They were here, too." *What the hell did that have to do with anything?*

He chewed his lower lip.

The pouting woman said, "Some of the checks were for much smaller amounts. What would be the difference in your work for a hundred-fifty-dollar check and one for five hundred dollars?"

"Sometimes they'd just have small dinner parties. Not clients. Associates. Still business, just smaller, more informal. Like the party scheduled for tonight." Was this about money? Some kind of corporate scandal involving Mark? Sarah couldn't get a grasp on the questions.

Kramble leaned forward. "Did you stay for those parties?"

"No, I'd just drop off the food, or cook it here, and then leave. That's what most of my jobs are."

Kramble looked at the other cops, and Sarah sensed an excitement. "We're very interested in these smaller parties. You said these parties were for Mark's associates?"

Sarah shrugged. What did this matter? "Sometimes. Once Courtney was sort of 'wooing' another physician they were trying to get to come to the hospital. They both have to schmooze a lot." Courtney had complained about it. She got tired of being "on," but it was the reality of their livelihoods.

"Did you know any of the guests at the smaller parties?"

"I never really met any of them. Usually I was gone before the guests arrived. Once or twice I crossed paths with people arriving, but I didn't know them."

"Were there ever any children with those guests you saw?"

Sarah blinked. What the hell was going on? She couldn't follow where this questioning was going, didn't like the expression that had been on Rodney's face, didn't like the red blush she felt crawling up her neck. "I . . ." She saw a skinny little blond girl on the periphery of her memory. Mark had been standing outside the kitchen door smoking a cigar with another guy when Sarah pulled up. The other guy went inside, but Mark smiled his Ken-doll smile and helped Sarah unload. When they went inside the kitchen, hadn't there been a girl? A girl talking to the man? The girl had left the room when Sarah entered. But other than how embarrassingly schoolgirl-giddy Sarah became in Mark's presence, she mostly remembered the cigars—how the man had taken his cigar inside and had stunk up the kitchen.

"I do remember a little girl." She saw the officers exchange a glance. "I saw her in the kitchen, and later she was upstairs with Jordan in Jordan's room."

"Why were you in Jordan's room, Mrs. Laden?"

The tone of the question caused goose bumps to tiptoe up her spine, followed by prickling heat. "Courtney took me upstairs to see this new Jacuzzi; they'd had Jordan's bathroom remodeled. But . . . mostly she took me upstairs, I think, to complain about this guy, this guest, who was smoking a cigar."

"What did the little girl look like?"

"She had blond hair—almost white-blond—in two pigtails with ribbons. She was skinny, leggy. I'd guess she was nine or ten, maybe."

"Could you identify her in a photo if asked?"

The question caused real fear to fill her mouth with the tang of metal. "*Why?* What does this girl have to do with you searching this house?" Was someone dead? Had they found the girl's body here?

"Did you see anything unusual in Jordan's room? Or in his bathroom? Any signs of illness or injury?"

Sarah sensed that they were all holding their breath, that they were finally to the point. "Is . . . is this about Jordan?"

Kramble leaned toward her. "What do you mean?"

"Jordan and his drug use?"

"Did you think he used drugs?"

"Well, no, not before yesterday I didn't, but"—Sarah lowered her voice, not knowing if Jordan might be able to hear her—"looking back now, there were signs I guess we all missed. He's always in a trance, it seems. Lost in his head. It makes him seem almost . . . slow."

"He was considered gifted at school," the woman officer snapped, as if Sarah had insulted the woman's own child.

"Yes, I know," Sarah said. "He's gifted *academically,* but socially he has problems. He doesn't get along with other kids. They say he's stuck up. I think he's just painfully shy, but it can come across as sullen or aloof. He's always alone and never looks happy." She wondered if he had somehow brought down this nightmare on his parents. "Is he in serious trouble? Was he selling drugs or something?"

Kramble coughed. Just then a red-haired woman officer escorted Courtney into the living room. She was dressed normally—in a pink cardigan over a yellow floral-print dress—but her face was red and splotchy with tears. She clasped her hands in front of her as if in prayer.

"Courtney?" Sarah stood.

Courtney turned to her, and a wave of relief rolled over Courtney's face. She stepped toward Sarah as if to hug her, but the woman officer pulled Courtney back by the elbow. That's when Sarah saw the handcuffs on Courtney's wrists.

"Oh, my God. Courtney, what's going on? What happened?"

"I . . . I'm under arrest," Courtney said with a girlish inflection of disbelief.

"*What?* For what?"

The woman officer steered Courtney toward the kitchen.

"Wait! For God's sake, you don't have to cuff her! There must be some mistake. You have the wrong—"

"Please. Let me talk to her," Courtney said to the officer. Courtney turned to Sarah, her face anguished. "They're charging me with child endangerment and"—she paused, turning her wide eyes to Kramble as if trying to remember the words, get it right—"c-complicity with abuse?"

Sarah's mouth fell open. All the other noise in the house went mute, as if someone had pressed a remote.

"There's a warrant out for Mark's arrest." Courtney's voice climbed higher with her tears. "For abuse and molestation of children and . . . and . . ." Courtney hiccupped a sob.

Abuse and molestation? Time seemed to slow, as Sarah struggled to translate the words she'd just heard into something she could grab on to or comprehend. They were so absurd her brain dismissed them—this was a case of mistaken identity, they had the wrong people. She felt a sensation of vertigo and feared she might have to sit down, right there on the floor, or she would fall. She took a deep breath and said the only words she knew, the words she believed with all her heart: "Oh, my God. That . . . that isn't true. You've made some kind of mistake. These are nice people, good people."

The officers stared back at Sarah, their faces expressionless. *Everyone says that,* she realized. They expected her to say that. But it was true; she had to convince them.

Chills prickled across Sarah's flesh. "Is . . . is this what Jordan says? Is he accusing you?"

"No." Courtney sobbed. She tried to put her hands up to her face, but they were cuffed together and awkward. "He hasn't accused anyone of anything. But they won't let me talk to him! I haven't been able to see him since they called me from the ER."

"You never got to see him? *At all?*" That poor boy was in the hospital and hadn't even been able to see his mother? "Is Mark with him?"

"Come on, Dr. Kendrick." The woman officer began guiding Courtney toward the kitchen again.

"Wait," Sarah begged, grabbing Courtney's other elbow. "But where *is* Jordan? The hospital said he was released. Is he okay?"

"Mrs. Laden," Kramble said, "you really shouldn't—"

"They transferred him to Children's Medical Center last night," Courtney said. "I'm not allowed to talk to him. He's there all alone.

Please go see him, Sarah. Make sure he's okay. Tell him I'd be there if I could, but they won't let me!"

"Of course. But what happened to him? They think you abused him? I don't understand!"

"Oh, my God," Courtney said. Her lips trembled. "The things that were done to him. Sarah, it's——" And she burst into sobs again. Jordan flashed into Sarah's brain, staring up at her from the gravel parking lot, the rain rinsing the vomit off his pale face and diluting the red pulse into a pink wash over his neck. He'd been hurt when Sarah picked him up? She tried to remember what he'd looked like when she first saw him in his driveway.

"Take her to the car," Kramble said.

The woman officer tried to pull Courtney from Sarah's grasp. Sarah hung on for a moment, engaging Courtney in a bizarre tug-of-war. Afraid of hurting her friend, Sarah let go. "Wait! Courtney, don't worry! I'm coming with you!" Sarah followed after them.

But Courtney called over her shoulder as they moved through the kitchen, "No, Sarah, go to Children's! Please! Check on Jordan!" The woman officer opened the side door.

"Where's Mark?" Sarah asked. "Does he even know this is happening?"

"I don't know!" Courtney wailed as she was led outside. She practically walked backward as she twisted around to talk to Sarah. "He left!"

"What do you mean he *left*?" Every word spoken worsened the scenario.

"He's gone!" Courtney said. Courtney stopped, and the woman officer pulled on her. "Sarah—there's pornography. Child pornography. Jordan *is in* some child pornography. I saw him. Mark was——" The woman officer managed to get Courtney to move in the right direction.

Sarah stared, struck mute and stupid by the sudden iciness that numbed her.

The officer opened the back door of an Oakhaven cruiser.

"His secretary says Mark took the call from the ER and he left! The bastard left! I haven't seen him. He left because he's fucking guilty." The woman tried to maneuver Courtney into the car. "He knew he was caught. He knew I'd find—" The woman officer put her hand on Courtney's head and ducked her into the backseat, then slammed the door, cutting off her voice.

What had Courtney just said?

The woman officer headed to the driver's seat.

Sarah saw herself yesterday, speeding through the rain on the slick streets. The collision of rage and confusion nauseated her, and she quickly shut it off with, *It couldn't be true, it couldn't be true.*

She blinked at the blue sky, the glittering grass.

The woman got inside the cruiser and started the engine.

The enormity of what had happened expanded in Sarah's chest. The pressure made her ribs ache. *They just took Courtney away in handcuffs,* she had to say to herself. *They won't let her see her own son. Her son is in some child pornography. Her husband is missing.* Sarah stared at the cruiser as it drove around her van and disappeared up the driveway.

"Come inside," Detective Kramble said behind her. She hadn't realized he'd followed them. Kramble stepped to the side and gestured like a gentleman for her to reenter the kitchen first. Sarah did, on tingling legs.

"Child pornography?" she whispered. She had to reach out a hand to steady herself. For some reason she remembered how light Jordan had been in her arms. *It couldn't be true.*

"There is *no way* Courtney and Mark were involved in such a thing. I—" How could she make it clear to them? "These are nice people. They like kids, kids like them, they volunteer at school, they . . . they . . . This just isn't possible."

Kramble walked back to the living room. "Rodney? Are those stills back yet?"

Rodney came from down the hall and handed Kramble a manila

envelope. Kramble took it and gestured for Sarah to sit back down on the plastic-covered couch. She did. Rodney paused in the door frame. He said to her, "I didn't believe it either. But it's true." Kramble cleared his throat, and Rodney left.

"Mrs. Laden, Dr. Kendrick just gave you more information than I would have myself. But since she did, perhaps you can help us further." He took an eight-by-ten photo out of the envelope and laid it on the glass table. The wrestler and the pouting woman drew close. "Can you identify this man?" Kramble asked.

Sarah looked at the close-up of Mark's face. His mouth twisted in a strange grimace, as if he were working out.

"That's Mark Kendrick," she said.

Kramble watched an angelfish in an aquarium for a moment, then said, "This man is positively identified in *many* of the pornographic movies. Most of them, actually."

Sarah's nails bit into her palms. How could he say these outrageous things with such a calm, serene face? He could have said, "Mark wore black shoes," for the tone of voice he used. This could not be happening. This could not be true. Mark Kendrick who'd coached soccer? Who'd bought the teachers boxes of candy for Valentine's Day? Who'd "adopted" Danny for the father-son cookout and basketball game, taking him along with Jordan? *Oh, dear God.* "He . . . he couldn't." She could not bear for this to be true. It would destroy her.

"There are five adults who appear consistently in the tapes." Kramble lined up four more eight-by-tens. Sarah buried her face in her hands. She wanted to beg him to stop speaking. She needed time to let this horrifying information absorb. It was too much.

She didn't want to look at the other photos. She didn't want to know.

But she did. All close-ups of faces. Two women and two men. All with those strange, exhilarated expressions. All with hard, cold eyes. Sarah understood that these were stills taken from the videos. That these were the faces of people involved in sex acts. Sex acts with children. Sex acts that had been cut away so she could see only their faces. Sarah shook her head. "I don't know any of these people. I've never seen them."

The pouting woman and the wrestler sighed.

"Why did you arrest Courtney?" Sarah asked. "She's not in these pictures."

Kramble said nothing, but Sarah followed his gaze to the video camera on the floor.

She pictured Courtney at the soccer games with her video camera but quickly forced that image away. *It couldn't be true.*

"She would never do this. She didn't know this was going on. If she knew, she would have called you herself. I *know* this woman." Sarah had thought she'd known Mark, too, but didn't say this aloud. "I mean, Mark's disappearance speaks for itself. Courtney's here, she gave you permission to search. She couldn't have known." They had to believe her.

"What can you tell me about Dr. Kendrick's family?" Kramble asked her. "What do you know about her parents, her background?"

Sarah wanted desperately to help her friend, to convince these people that Courtney could not possibly be connected to something as obscene as they described. "They've only lived here four years. Her parents are dead. Her mother got really sick right around the time they moved here. She died that first year they were here, I think. She had . . . c-cancer." Sarah stumbled over the word.

The stocky wrestler scribbled and turned a page in his notebook with a crisp *snap.*

"And her father?" Kramble asked.

"He died a long time ago, when she was a teenager, I think."

"Any brothers or sisters?"

"No." Courtney was an only child, just like Sarah. Just like Jordan. Oh, God. Poor Jordan. Where had he been going when Sarah picked him up?

"Do you know where they lived before they moved here?"

"Yes. In Indianapolis. Her mother lived in Bloomington."

Snap—the wrestler flipped another page. *They are going to investigate her childhood,* Sarah realized. This was going to be on the news and in the papers. Parents would have to explain to their children. People would talk. And ask questions. And judge.

Sarah heard her own voice repeating, "Courtney didn't know this was happening." But even as she said it, a bright ringing sound made her turn to the doorway. Rodney stood there with a girl's purple ten-speed bike. "Oh, my God. That . . . that's Hadley Winter's bike."

Kramble stood and approached the bike with her. "Hadley Winter?"

"Yes." Sarah blinked at the bike, its presence here confounding her. "It got stolen." That was the last time she'd dealt with the police about something regarding the Kendricks. She wanted this to be that simple, that solvable. Something not so foul and horrifying.

"Can you explain it to us? The bike? Are you sure you know who it belongs to?"

"Yes, I helped her mother buy it. I kept it hidden at our house until Hadley's birthday. And once, when Hadley was over here, her bike got stolen out of the yard."

"Over here?" Kramble asked. "Hadley was here at the Kendricks' house?"

Sarah nodded. "Kids were always over here."

The pouting officer piped up and challenged her. "But I thought you said the other kids didn't like Jordan."

Sarah paused. Everything she said seemed to damn them. "They didn't," she admitted. "But the Kendricks had a pool. And a trampoline." Heat rose to her face again. Even Danny had been aware that the other kids used Jordan, that they came over to play with his parents' expensive toys and didn't really care if Jordan were here or not. But never until this moment had that seemed any more suspect than typical kid cliquishness and cruelty.

"Tell me more about the bike," Kramble said.

"It was missing when she went to go home. And she'd only had it for about a day and a half. She was crying, saying her mom would be so mad."

"Let me guess," the pouting officer said. "The Kendricks helped her look for it."

"We all did," Sarah said to Kramble.

Sarah didn't understand the connection. In Courtney's defense she said, "Mark and Courtney even offered, later, to buy Hadley a new one. They felt so bad it had been taken from their yard. Maybe this is the replacement one, actually. Carol—Hadley's mom—wouldn't let her accept it."

Rodney said in a dull voice, "It still has a 'Happy Birthday' tag on the handlebar."

"Oh." Did a stolen bike even matter in light of child-pornography charges?

"You refer to Hadley's mom," Kramble said. "What about her dad?"

"Well, that's why we all felt so bad about it. Her parents had just gone through this hideous divorce. Really nasty."

Kramble nodded, as if affirming something. He picked up a box and handed it to Rodney, who took it, as if he understood.

Another officer entered the room and set a stack of Wright Elementary yearbooks on the glass coffee table.

Iciness numbed Sarah again, made it difficult to draw breath. Did this mean Hadley was abused, too? Did it mean there were other children besides Jordan? Sarah forced her numb lips to move and spoke carefully, as if reading assembly instructions aloud. "There are five adults in the films." She took a deep breath. "How many children?"

"I can't give you that information at the moment," Kramble said.

"Why?" But Sarah knew why. That was a stupid question. Kramble didn't even attempt to answer it. "How do I find out if—I mean, what if . . . what if . . ." She was afraid to say the words out loud, as if it might make her fear manifest. "I have a son in Jordan's class. He was friends with Jordan. He was over here all the time. I—

Danny liked Mark. I thought his company was good for Danny, with Roy—my husband—gone."

Kramble knew what she was asking. The lines seemed to deepen on his face, and he asked, "Do you have a picture of your son I could see?"

Of course she did, but Sarah froze. She wanted to know and she didn't want to know. She couldn't bear to know and she had to know. She dug through her purse with clumsy, fear-addled fingers and found Danny's school picture from this year. She looked at his open, sunny grin, the light freckles peppering his nose. Oh, dear God. What if . . . what if the boys' falling-out had something to do with . . . with *this*?

"Mrs. Laden?" Kramble's face was open, gentle. Sarah handed him the photo. He glanced at it only briefly, then exhaled and rubbed one hand over his face. He seemed genuinely relieved to say, "No. Your son is not in the films."

Relief coursed through her, making her light-headed. Then the relief turned to shame, as she realized how quickly she'd thrown away her "it couldn't be true" at the possibility that one of her own was involved.

But *someone's* child was in the films. Or was it just Jordan? But . . . if it was just Jordan, why did they have the yearbooks? How *many* kids?

Sarah wanted to return to that morning, when she thought the crisis involved drug abuse. These things Kramble described, adults having sex with children, did not happen in Oakhaven. Elementary-school kids walked to and from school alone. This was the sort of place where traffic stopped to let the parks' geese stroll their fuzzy goslings across the street. Where the theft of a little girl's bike was talked about for days. Sure, every home had an expensive security system, but there was no real expectation of danger.

"Mrs. Laden?" Kramble waited until Sarah nodded. "You said the Kendricks volunteered at school. Can you tell me exactly what they did?"

"Th-they hosted the end-of-the-year party last year." She couldn't make her voice stop shaking. "They both drove to away games. They both chaperoned field trips. Mark used to help coach the soccer team. He didn't do it this year, but he did it last year, and I think the year before that. And Courtney helped with costumes for the winter play."

"She sewed costumes?" the woman officer asked, as if skeptical.

"No, she—" Sarah didn't want to say it. She stared at a fish tank and whispered, "She . . . she helped the kids get into costume."

Only the bubbling of the aquarium filters filled the room.

After a long silence, Sarah asked, "Is . . . is Jordan okay?"

Kramble paused, then said, "He probably will be."

She wasn't sure how to ask the question, or if an answer even existed. "Why . . . I mean, how could this be happening and no one know it? Why didn't he tell someone?"

The plastic squeaked as Kramble scooted to the edge of the sofa. He leaned toward her, his elbows on his knees. "*Most* sexually abused kids never tell. Victims of incest usually work very hard to protect their families."

Sarah had never heard anyone use the word "incest" in an actual conversation about actual people. This was not a movie plot; this was a family she'd known for four years.

She massaged the bruise the robin's beak had left. Yesterday morning rewound in its entirety in her head. She'd seen it all wrong, misinterpreted everything. "*I wish I were an angel,*" Jordan had said. He'd been trying to make that wish come true. "Oh, God," Sarah said.

"Hey," the pouting officer said. "Ask her about the book bag."

"Oh, God," Sarah said again.

CHAPTER FIVE

Nate

N ate sat in his junior English class and wanted nothing more than to be stoned. No one but professional actors should ever say Shakespeare out loud. Didn't this stupid student teacher get that this was supposed to be an advanced-placement class? What the hell were they doing reading out loud like a bunch of first-graders? He'd stayed up all night to finish *Hamlet*. He couldn't sleep with Mom ghost-walking around the house. He'd wanted to get up and go talk to her at two, but then he'd have to tell her that he'd overheard her and Mrs. Ripley talking about Jordan.

He yawned. He'd expected *Hamlet* to send him to sleep, but it was actually pretty cool. He wanted to talk about theme and the ghost and Hamlet's flimsy-ass plan to act insane, but instead he sat there dying of boredom while the class beat the lines to death, pounding out that iambic pentameter like a goddamn nursery rhyme while Miss Sniffen smiled and nodded. They were still only in act I. Tony was reading Hamlet, and he sucked. Mowaza glanced back at Nate with a glazed look in his eyes, then held up his index finger and mimed shooting himself in the head.

Nate slouched down low in his seat and hid himself behind

Mowaza. He pulled his portable CD player out of his bag and put on the earphones. If he kept the volume low and one ear uncovered, he could keep track of class's slow-motion progress. He pushed "play" on his newest klezmer CD, a great band called Brave Old World. If Mowaza heard it, he'd make fun of Nate. Mowaza and Tony called it Nate's "freaky old-people music." He usually listened to more regular tunes when he hung out with them.

Thank God only a few weeks were left before this clueless student teacher went on her way and they got their real teacher back. Miss Sniffen was nice enough, but she'd be better at teaching preschool. Her high-pitched, sugar-cheery voice was painful.

Nate settled into the Old World music. Broken-wineglass-and-curled-sidelocks music. The heavy accordion made him think of his dad. Steady, easygoing. No matter how frenzied the rest of the song got, Nate could listen and always find that accordion, faithfully squeezing out the rhythm. That's how Dad used to be.

But thinking of Dad made him think about Mom. He felt bad for her. And he felt bad for that poor Kendrick kid. If Jordan was out of the hospital, he was probably in deeper shit at home. What would Mom have done if Nate had been hauled home strung out on heroin instead of just drunk?

Mowaza turned around and tapped the desk. When Nate looked up, Mowaza tipped his head across the room toward Tony. Tony's head was bent over his script.

Nate pulled off his earphones. "What?" He listened to the class and recognized the scene. The king and queen were trying to make Hamlet stay in Denmark and celebrate with them. Oh, man. Tony hadn't read the play like he was supposed to. Tony didn't know about Hamlet's mom. Tony's mom was living with the dad of some other kid at school, even though neither of them was divorced yet. Tony got in a fight last week when some kid called his mom a whore. Miss Sniffen probably didn't know about it, even if the rest of the school did.

The whole class squirmed as Tony plodded through Hamlet's soliloquy: " '. . . and yet within a month/Let me not think on't—Frailty, thy name is woman!' " Someone snickered, and Tony lifted his head and glared with bloodshot eyes. Miss Sniffen seemed enthralled.

Nate expected Tony to stop reading, but he went on, his voice daring anyone else to laugh: " 'O, most wicked speed, to post/With such dexterity to incestuous sheets!' "

Jesus, just don't let him cry, Nate thought. When he'd arrived late to Tony's party last month, Tony was already plastered and crying. Everyone else had been too drunk to even pretend to be polite and had fled the room, leaving Nate trapped with the weeping Tony. Tony had dumped all this shit about his mother on Nate, telling him details he'd never wanted to know. There was nothing Nate could do but listen and get plastered himself.

The bell rang, and the class breathed a sigh of relief. "Tony, that was wonderful!" Miss Sniffen gushed. "We'll have you continue with Hamlet on Monday! You should all read with such emotion. See how exciting it can be?"

For Christ's sake.

Nate went to Tony's desk, where Tony stared at the page in front of him. "You okay?"

Tony looked up. "Let's get out of here. I've got some great weed at my place."

Dread settled in Nate's bones. "I can't skip third, man. I've gotta go to chemistry."

"Come on, guy. Don't be a wuss." Tony rubbed his face and stood. "Come with me."

"Can't. Sorry." Nate walked into the crowded hall, lockers clanging, people shouting, and that freshman-girl squealing that made him shudder. Tony stuck to him like a leech.

"Whoa. Hey. What's up, guy? What's this hoity-toity attitude all of a sudden?"

Nate stopped. "I don't have an 'attitude.' Look, I'd love to get stoned. And I'm sorry that was so fucked up back there, but I can't skip. I just got back from suspension."

Tony's face hardened. "What was fucked up?"

"What you had to read."

"What was fucked up about that?"

"Nothing. Forget it." Nate reached his locker, worked the combination, and began unloading books. Tony leaned sideways on the locker next to his.

"You're not turning into a pansy-ass, are you?" Tony asked.

A buzzing sparked to life under Nate's skin. "Would you get the hell off my back? I said no. Not today."

"Your mom's the one that needs to get off your back. She acts like you're in second grade or something. The bitch is crazy."

The buzzing felt like wasps in his veins. It was one thing for *Nate* to say his mother was whacked, but a whole different story for Tony to say it. "Back off. This has nothing to do with my mom."

"Are you saying it has something to do with mine?"

"No. Jesus, would you chill?"

Someone behind Nate squeezed his butt. An image of Mrs. Kendrick flashed through his mind, but he forgot her when he turned and saw Mackenzie smiling on the other side of him. She wore a white ribbed turtleneck and a long straight skirt, her auburn hair pulled back in some complicated braid. As usual, Nate was filled with awe that someone so beautiful, so . . . classy liked him. It made him dizzy.

"Hey." He kissed her on the lips.

"Awww. Isn't that sweet?" Tony crooned, a sneer twisting his mouth.

"Three's a crowd, Tony-o. See you later, man."

"Meet me after third, and we'll go to my place during lunch," Tony said.

"No." The buzzing returned, pulsing in Nate's ears.

"What's he talking about?" Mackenzie asked.

"Tony, I told you—"

"Don't skip again," Mackenzie said.

"I'm not—"

"Oh, I get it. She's got you pussy-whipped."

Mackenzie squinted at Tony, pinching up her face with an I-smell-garbage expression.

Tony grinned. "I mean, he said you gave great head, but I never dreamed—"

The buzz caught and ignited, like an engine starting. Nate grabbed the front of Tony's shirt, yanked him inches from his face, and yelled, "What the fuck is your problem?" He shoved Tony hard, knocking him into another girl at her locker. Both Tony and the girl tumbled to the floor, paper and books flying everywhere. Before Nate could move, a hand gripped his shoulder. Hard. It hurt.

"Nate Laden! You need to come with me."

Nate turned. Mr. Rubio. Oh, man. He was screwed. To his left, Tony brushed himself off and skittered away. To his right, Mackenzie looked at him with huge, wounded eyes.

"Mackenzie, I never said—"

She shook her head, then turned and walked away.

"Mackenzie! He's lying. He's an asshole."

"Excuse me?" Mr. Rubio asked. "Nate, I think you better quit while you're ahead. You don't need to dig yourself in any deeper." Mackenzie disappeared around the corner of the hallway. "Are you all right?" Rubio asked the girl who'd fallen. The girl stood up and clutched a hand to her bloody nose. Red drops sprinkled down the front of her previously white sweater.

"Oh, no, I'm sorry," Nate said. "I didn't mean to—"

The girl glared at him, then examined the blood on her fingers.

"Nate, I'm taking this young lady to the nurse. You need to have a seat outside my office. Do some thinking while you wait for me."

"I'm really sorry," Nate repeated to the girl as Rubio guided her away.

Shit. The hallway traffic already thinned. He slammed his locker, then kicked it. The tardy bell rang. A hush descended, except for the sound of one lone pair of running feet fading down the hallway.

Nate didn't run. He walked down the stairs to the office, where a girl already sat waiting outside Rubio's door.

The secretary sighed and peered at him over her bifocals. "Nathaniel Laden. You just can't seem to stay out of trouble, can you?"

No, he couldn't. He sat on the bench, leaned his head back against the wall, and looked at the clock: 10:45, and his day was already screwed. He considered banging his head into the wall but didn't figure that would do him any good. Better to bash Tony's head for insulting Mackenzie. Shit. Mackenzie walking away like that. Why the hell would she believe Tony?

Nate looked at the girl waiting. She was chubby, her face soft-doughy pale. She looked harmless and sad, the kind who always sat alone at lunch, and Nate wondered what the hell she'd done to get in trouble. She stared back at him. Nate leaned over, elbows on his knees, and rubbed his temples with his hands. The pulsing buzz in his ears hadn't stopped.

What would happen to him? Was this because he'd shoved Tony? Not likely, if Rubio hadn't hauled Tony down here, too. Because he said "fuck" in the hallway? Man. He was gonna get expelled because he'd said "fuck" to Tony Harrigan.

And that girl. He hadn't meant to hurt anyone. He'd offer to pay for her sweater. Face wounds always bled so much—he knew that from hockey—that it was hard to tell how serious it was.

Fifteen minutes passed, and Rubio didn't return. The chubby girl cracked her gum. The secretary tapped away at her computer. Nate's blood buzzed under his skin. He couldn't sit still. He wanted to scream and kick in lockers.

After twenty minutes Nate stood up and walked out the front door. Just up and walked out, even though the secretary called his name and told him he'd better get his butt back. He had to move. Couldn't just sit there. He started walking home.

How did this happen? How could he get in trouble trying to stay *out* of trouble? His mom would kill him. He wished he could keep walking forever and never have to face her. He wished, for the five-hundredth time that day alone, that his dad were alive; if he were, Nate would call him at the hospital. Dad would figure out what to do, how they would tell Mom together. Nate never used to get in trouble when Dad was alive. What the hell was wrong with him? The worst thing that ever happened when Dad was alive was that some of Nate's middle-school teachers said he was "too social" and needed to "channel his energy properly." Nate remembered Dad telling him he'd better straighten up, or he and Mom would volunteer to chaperone the dance and purposely act like dorks to embarrass him.

Nate snorted. They did actually chaperone the eighth-grade dance, but they left Nate alone. He'd been worried that his parents would try to talk to him or hang out with him, but they were cool. They kind of avoided Nate—or let Nate avoid them, he guessed. Mom and Dad danced on a couple of slow dances. Nate's friends thought that was cool—that they looked all in love. Nate really thought they were. And that's what sucked so bad. Bad things happened to the people who didn't deserve it. Not that anyone deserved it, but why couldn't someone die who hated his wife? Or who was mean and beat his kids or something? Why did it have to be *his* dad?

And before Nate knew it, he was crying. Walking down the damn street crying. Jesus, he was such a baby.

He was relieved that the van was gone when he got to the house. He unlocked the door and slumped onto a stool at one of the kitchen islands. Where was Mom? With Mrs. Kendrick? Hell, maybe she'd realize that Nate's problems were nothing compared to heroin addiction. Maybe this Jordan situation could help him.

Not likely. He was in big trouble now. Nate leaned across the kitchen island and rested his cheek on the marble, wondering what he could do to stop the dentist-drill sound in his head. He was just kind of staring, and he realized he was looking at a green backpack he didn't recognize by the kitchen door. He stared at it until the initials penned into the beige hem of the outer pocket troubled him. J.K.

J.K.? He rolled himself off the island and picked up the bag. He undid the drawstring and reached inside. The first thing his hand touched was a thin paperback workbook for school. He recognized Danny's vocabulary book. No, it wasn't Danny's—this workbook was full of red-penciled "100%"s and gold stars. In the back was a pretty detailed doodle of a cat. Nate looked inside the front cover. There, in neat block letters, as small and uniform as typing, was the name Jordan Kendrick.

Whoa. Why did his mom have Jordan's backpack? This whole thing was getting so weird. Were there drugs inside? He reached in again, to the bottom, under the books. His hand touched something soft. He pulled out a Maxi pad. What the hell?

Nate squeezed along the pad's length, wondering if Jordan hid his drugs in them. He sniffed it—not that he'd recognize the odor of heroin—and a bedsheet-right-out-of-the-dryer scent met his nose. He set the pad on the kitchen island.

He picked up the backpack and heard the unmistakable rattle of pills. Sure enough, his fingers wrapped around a bottle, but it just said "Tylenol Extra Strength." Nate opened it and was disappointed to see that that's really all it was. Only seven pills rolled in the bottle.

There were three pencils and a calculator. There was a black notebook with nothing but the kid's name written in it. Hardly seemed like the stash of a hard-core heroin junkie.

All that remained was a five-by-seven unmarked manila envelope. Not fat enough to contain drugs. He pulled it out anyway and felt something shift in the envelope. He undid the metal clasp, and a pile of CDs clattered onto the counter.

Four of them. Labeled with marker—"Feb. 22," "March 13," "March 28," and "April 4." What was on the disks? Music? Photos? Homework? April 4 was only two days ago.

Nate carried the disks into the living room and inserted the one marked "April 4" into their computer. He didn't know what he expected, but he didn't figure it would hurt anything to check it out.

"April 4" opened into a long list of icons—JPEGs for forty photos. He selected the first picture and clicked on it.

The computer whirred and hummed, and then a clear color photo popped onto the screen. Nate blinked. Naked people. Having sex. Whoa. A man and a woman . . . and shit. Nate blinked again and stared, his mind beginning to grasp the image before him. The buzzing behind his ears returned with force.

There was a kid in this picture. The face was obscured by the man's legs, but Nate could tell it was a kid. A kid way too young to be doing this. Some poor boy and two sick, twisted adults.

Nate swallowed, choking on the sour taste rising in his throat. He closed the photo.

He looked at the list. There were forty of these? He clicked on the next photo. The kid's face hidden again. He closed it almost as soon as the photo materialized. Why the hell would Jordan have these?

Nate thought about that.

His stomach turned over, and a sinking sensation spread through his limbs.

He clicked on the third picture. He could see the boy's head and face this time. A boy with curly red hair. He looked angry. The corner of his mouth was bleeding.

Nate clicked through a fourth picture, a fifth, a sixth . . . not really looking, but searching for what he knew he was going to find. On the tenth he found a girl. Her blond hair in two ponytails. She looked scared. Her eyes were pink, and she was crying.

Nate clicked on and on until he found him. At first there was still no face, but Nate looked at a boy's thin body and tried to remember the soccer games and the determined sweeper defending the goal. He tried to remember that fierce player's height, the length of his arms and legs, but he couldn't even make the two images mesh; his brain wouldn't do it.

Nate closed it and clicked on the next picture. This time he could see the face.

The kid was Jordan Kendrick.

The pounding hammered behind Nate's eyes. His hands shook. Shit. That face.

Jordan looked not at the camera, but past it, not really focused. His eyes were seeing something far away from that room, making his face register something similar to boredom.

The man behind Jordan was Mr. Kendrick. Jesus. His own father. Nate had talked to that guy. He'd seen that guy ruffle Jordan's hair. He'd seen that guy stand with his hand on Jordan's shoulder, like any dad, like *Nate's* dad used to do.

Nate thought he might puke.

Even though he hadn't seen her in any of the pictures, Nate remembered Mrs. Kendrick kissing him, touching him, the way she looked at him. He couldn't breathe right; his breaths dropped shallow and quick. He clenched his fists to stop his hands from shaking.

He heard a noise on the front porch and braced himself to tell Mom. But when she came through the front door, she was followed by a troop of guys in suits.

Who were these guys? Why were they here?

His mom stared at him. "This . . . these are the . . . police," she said.

Holy shit. Had the school secretary called the police?

"What are you doing home in . . ." Her voice trailed off as she looked past him at the computer, and he watched her face cloud, her eyes widen.

"No, Mom," Nate said, realizing what she must think. He picked up the disks. "These were in Jordan's bag. It's Jordan, Mom. Look what they did to him."

A police officer took the disks from Nate's hand and sat at the computer.

"Where's the bag, son?" this really tall, black-haired man asked him.

Nate led him to the kitchen island and pointed.

"Did you touch anything?"

Nate nodded. "All of it."

"We'll need to get prints off him." A woman officer went out the front door. Nate looked at his hands as if they were already tainted.

And they were. He knew they were. So much so that when Mom's hands closed on his and she looked up at him, he had to pull free and walk away from her. He wanted to crawl into her lap and press his face against her neck, but instead he went into his room and shut the door.

CHAPTER SIX

Sarah

When the police and Lila Ripley left Sarah's home that day, Sarah closed the door, then slumped against it. She ached all over as if she'd been beaten. And, truly, she would have been less shocked if Courtney had attacked her with a baseball bat than by . . . *this*. She still couldn't grasp it, this awful discovery. Her brain kept rejecting it.

Lila had scurried over after Sarah had come home, curious about Nate's arrival in the middle of the day and the group of people with Sarah. Sarah believed that Lila's nosiness might have finally gotten her more than she bargained for. The photo, still visible on the computer, had given the old woman quite a shock. Sarah had never seen Lila speechless since she'd known her. Lila bounced back, as she always did, and brought tea and cookies over to the officers.

Sarah adored Lila, but when the police were leaving, she had gently asked her to go home. Sarah wanted to talk to Nate and knew he wouldn't talk to her for real as long as Lila was here. Sarah had followed him immediately to his room, of course. She hadn't given a damn how long she kept Kramble or the others waiting. She knew she needed to follow her son. Even though Nate said he didn't want to talk, he'd seemed grateful that she'd tried.

Sarah wanted to talk and share this hideous news with someone—but it kept slamming into her over and over again that the person she wanted to call was Courtney. This had to be a mistake. Courtney could not be involved. She could not have known.

Courtney was in jail.

Oh, God. What would Sarah have done if she'd discovered that Roy had been sexually abusing their children? Sarah couldn't even begin to fathom it. She *could* fathom what hell it would be not to be able to see your own child once you discovered he'd been harmed. Her heart ached for Courtney. And for Jordan. That poor boy. All alone.

Kramble had saved Sarah the trip to Children's Medical Center, telling her Jordan couldn't receive visitors yet.

"Is he all right?" she'd asked. "He's conscious, isn't he? He's recovered from the overdose?"

Kramble had nodded. "Check tomorrow. He'll need friendly faces."

Sarah wanted to see Jordan, to try to comfort him, but also dreaded it. What would she say? He'd been difficult to talk to *before* the abuse had come to light. She wanted to tell him that his mother loved him and would be there if she could.

She went upstairs and listened at Nate's closed door. Not a sound came from inside.

She knocked. He didn't answer. She knocked harder, but when he still didn't respond, Sarah pushed open the door. He lay curled on his side, listening to a Walkman. Something about his fetal position dissolved her heart. She wanted to make him fit in her lap again. She wanted to rock him and kiss his sweet-smelling forehead.

He lifted the Walkman free of one ear. "What?"

"You okay, Nate? Do you want to talk?"

He sniffed. "No. I told you. I really . . . I really need to be alone right now."

"Okay," she said, but she thought maybe he didn't know what he needed, like when he was little and said he didn't need a coat to go out in the snow. Maybe she should sit down beside him and not let him turn her away. But he rolled over on his bed, presenting his back to her.

"I want to tell Danny before it's on the news. Will you help me?"

He nodded.

"I love you," Sarah said, but he'd replaced the Walkman on his ear.

She stared at his back until her eyes filled with tears, then shut his door.

She needed a drink. She tiptoed down to the basement. In the storage freezer, she dug under the Ziploc bags of basil leaves and red peppers, the Tupperware containers of gazpacho, salsas, and pasta sauces, and retrieved a half-empty bottle of Grey Goose vodka. She'd kept it hidden since the night Nate had been arrested.

She opened the bottle and took a swig. Like velvet ice, it rolled down her throat and began to thaw in her chest. Nate's rabbit watched her from its hutch, nose quivering.

Sarah took another swig, then sat atop the freezer with the bottle between her legs. Drinking straight from the bottle reminded her of drinking champagne in the bathtub with Roy when Nate was just a baby. After the tub they'd slipped out into the dark backyard, more civilized, with glasses. Sarah had cut long, curling lemon peels into the flutes along with raspberry liqueur, and they slow-danced with no music. What had they been celebrating? Oh—they'd planted Nate's dogwood earlier that day. Sarah wished she'd savored that dance, that day, more. The ache of that lost happiness, that safer time, bruised her.

She wished she could wash off the queasy disgust that had settled like a film of grease over her since she'd seen the photos on the computer. She'd seen enough to make her sick. She'd seen the fish tanks and that white carpet in Courtney's home, the backdrop for such obscene acts.

She'd seen Mark, this time in action. She still experienced that tingling sensation that overcame her when she'd first seen, with her own eyes, that *this was true.*

Mark. Tall, thin, handsome Mark. The man who chatted with the other dads at soccer games. The man who greeted Sarah with a kiss on the cheek whenever she saw him, a kiss that left her flushed and flustered. The man she'd run into just last week at the market early on Sunday, buying things a normal person bought—half-and-half, some bagels, and some doughnuts. He'd been unshaven and his blond hair was attractively rumpled, so obviously fresh from bed. They'd chatted about whether Danny and Jordan might play spring soccer or try baseball, and both of them admitted how nice it might be to have a season free of sports schedules. That Mark. Mark, with Jordan, his own son. How could he—God, Sarah couldn't even go there. Mark with other children whose faces Sarah was not allowed to see.

Jordan, with other adults Sarah didn't recognize.

But she hadn't seen Courtney. "Courtney," Sarah whispered. Where was Courtney in those photos? *What if she wasn't there? What if she didn't know? What if Mark was solely responsible?* Courtney had no part in this. How *could* she? She couldn't, because . . . because Sarah didn't want to believe she could be so wrong about a person.

She'd been unbelievably wrong about a person in Mark. Abysmally, incredibly wrong. But not Courtney. Courtney could *not* do those things.

And yet . . . and yet . . . how could she not *know?* But Sarah couldn't go there either.

She wished there were some way for Nate to unsee those horrors. He'd seen far more images than she had. She'd do anything to erase them from his memory. He'd stopped seeing a counselor only a few months ago, but she wondered if she should schedule a few more sessions now. Sarah wanted some sessions herself.

Sarah had asked Kramble again if he was certain Danny wasn't in any of the images. Her first instinct had been to beg to search the photos for him—to go to school and find him *right then* and ask,

"Did they ever touch you? Did they ever hurt you?" But Kramble had urged her not to be so frightened that she interrogated him.

"Just listen," he said. "Listen to what he says when he hears this news—and *then* ask."

She'd discovered, as the police had temporarily set up office at her computer, that Robert Kramble was something of a sex-abuse expert. The other officers asked him questions, followed his directions, looked to him for guidance. Although Courtney was nowhere in the images, Kramble seemed intent on implicating her. "Someone had to film it," he said simply, no judgment, no zeal revealing itself in his voice. But it was in his eyes, this *need* to find her guilty, balanced only by the fierce commitment—the love, even—that he seemed to have for the children.

Sarah pressed the cold vodka bottle against her cheek. "Who would do that to a child?" she asked the rabbit.

Klezmer studied her, his face solemn.

Sarah knew that people did such things to children. But there was knowing and there was seeing *exactly who* did that. She rolled the bottle to her other cheek. That poor child. That poor, strange little boy.

This community had always seemed the haven it was named. Half scorned, half envied by the surrounding suburbs and the city for its Mayberry-ish sense of security. Its own residents jokingly referred to it as living "under the dome," as if protected by a magical barrier. Streets were plowed within an hour of snowfall, the average police response time was *two minutes*. . . . How could this have happened here?

She took a final swallow of the vodka, capped the bottle, and buried it in the freezer. She watched the rabbit a moment—missing their dog Potter, missing Roy, wanting him here to help her deal with this—before going upstairs to the kitchen.

When Sarah walked into the kitchen, one of the first things she saw was the homemade calendar Courtney had given her as a gift. Each month was a different photo of the boys, or of Sarah. Goose bumps rose on her neck and shoulders—her mother had always called them "truth bumps." Why did Courtney have to be so good with pictures and film? Every year she did a beautifully edited film of the elementary-school play and burned copies for every single cast member. The photos in this calendar were gorgeous. When Sarah had first opened it, at her and Courtney's New Year's Day "brunch"—where they drank Bloody Marys in their pajamas—she had been stunned. How had Courtney taken some of these photos? Some Sarah had never seen before. She walked close to the calendar, on the side of the family's fridge. The current month, April, was of Nate at a hockey game. God, he was growing into a beautiful man. He sat, helmet off, hair dark and rumpled with sweat, turned in profile, looking over his shoulder at the crowd behind him. He didn't look at the camera but had a searching expression, as if scanning for someone. With the white ice framing him, his air hopeful and wary at the same time. . . . Courtney had really captured something. Sarah loved the photo.

She took the calendar off its magnetic hook and flipped back to March, of Danny in mid-dive at swimming lessons.

February was of Danny and Jordan on the trampoline at Courtney's house. Danny grinned for the camera, hanging in the air, arms and legs spread out in a crazy fling. But Jordan stood on the edge of the trampoline, arms at his sides, looking not at Danny but straight at the photographer. Sarah tried to read his expression. His eyes seemed to glint with something. Anger? Or was she just imposing that now that she knew what had been happening to him?

She flipped to January. One of her favorites. Sledding on a snow day. Nate had actually taken this photo with Courtney's camera before he'd gone off snowboarding with Mackenzie. It was a great shot, of Courtney and Jordan and Sarah and Danny coming to a stop at the bottom of "Suicide Hill" at the golf course. Sarah and Danny, on an inner tube, were still in action, white spray flying up all around them. Both of them had their mouths wide open with laughter. Courtney and Jordan looked right at each other, sprawled how they'd landed, limbs intertwined, separated from their tube, covered in snow dust, pink-cheeked, and laughing. Jordan appeared so genuinely *happy*, so like any kid in the world. How could Courtney be guilty? Look at how he smiled at her.

Sarah moaned. *It couldn't be true, it couldn't be true.* She wanted her hands busy. She needed to cook. Nothing else helped her process and sort. She'd been that way even as a child. Her parents had instilled an appreciation and patience in her for truly good food. Her father kept bees and raised heirloom tomatoes. Her mother rolled homemade pasta and canned. In her childhood home, family meals were the core of their connection to one another. Family crises were always dealt with at the dinner table. So were family joys. All the big events of her life, good and bad, had a menu in her mind. Thanksgivings were Ma's knishes and sweet-potato pie, followed by turkey salad with red grapes and walnuts for the rest of the weekend. Announcing her engagement was pan-seared salmon. Telling Ma and Pop she was expecting Nate was egg salad on toast, then pickled herring for months after. Finding out about Roy's cancer was lamb with pine-nut stuffing on good china. Losing Roy was Lila's baked macaroni on paper plates.

Sarah opened the fridge. A whole chicken sat waiting, like a blank canvas. She could make curried chicken on rice noodles, but that's what she would have been making for Courtney right now if . . . if what? What would be happening to that boy tonight if Sarah hadn't happened to drive by at just the right time? Courtney had always been there when Sarah had catered those parties. *It couldn't be true.* She shut the fridge so hard that condiment jars clinked together and two magnetized photos fell to the floor. She left them there.

She opened a cupboard and looked at the remaining jar of her mother's raspberry preserves. Raspberry-glazed chicken was the last meal she'd made for a party at the Kendricks'. She slammed the cupboard.

Mediterranean chicken salad. Spicy chicken quesadillas with

cranberry-mango salsa. Grilled chicken pieces in pesto sauce. Every damn meal she'd ever made for those parties had chicken in it! She picked up the salt shaker and hurled it into the wall. The sound of it breaking so satisfied her that she hurled the pepper shaker, too, and then the sugar bowl.

She sat at the table with her head in her hands and willed herself to think of a meal, to think of anything besides that horrible image of Jordan and Mark seared onto her brain. Come on. What would she make on a Friday night?

Friday night. Of course. Friday nights had a memory menu as well.

She hadn't observed it since Roy died, and hours remained before sundown, but she craved the comfort of the ritual. She covered the table with a white cloth, then set two candles in the middle. Rummaging in a drawer for matches, she jumped to find Nate standing at the table when she turned around.

She looked down, hiding the matches in her hand.

"Sabbath candles?" he asked.

She lifted her gaze, expecting The Look, or at least disdain, but his face was open, understanding. She nodded.

"Say the blessing," he asked her, like a child asking for a bedtime story.

She started to protest that it wasn't even dark yet, but his face stopped her. She couldn't remember the last time he'd accepted something from her, much less asked something of her outright.

She lit the candles, cleared her throat, then covered her eyes and said the Hebrew words. Her voice sounded high and girlish, like she was giving a speech back in grade school.

When she opened her eyes, she and Nate watched the flames bend and curl a moment, before looking at each other across them.

He tilted his head at the fragments of broken china and the black-and-white grit on the floor. "What happened?"

She hesitated, then admitted, "I threw them."

His eyes widened, and he looked at her with what she thought might be admiration, then began picking up the pieces. She knelt to join him, but he said, "I'll do this. You cook."

So she did. She made challah dough first, knowing it would need time to rise. She covered the dough with a damp dish towel, and while they waited for it, she made chicken soup with floating matzo balls, and potato kugel. After Nate swept up the mess, he joined her. They stood side by side at the sink, rinsing the chicken, peeling potatoes, grating carrots, rolling the matzo balls in their hands, and chopping celery and onions. When the time came, he seemed to take great pleasure in punching down the bread dough, and he leaned, elbows in the flour, on the counter as she braided the two loaves, then covered them to rise again. Other than an occasional "What now?" and Sarah's quiet instructions, they didn't speak a word, but it was their best conversation in a long time.

It fueled her for the task ahead.

When Danny got home from school, he seemed suspicious about settling in to a big family dinner at four in the afternoon. Sarah put the challah in the oven and said, "Something very bad has happened to one of your friends."

"Who?"

"Jordan Kendrick."

"He's not my friend," Danny said, as if that closed the matter.

"Sweetie, what happened to you guys? You told me once he was your best friend."

Danny shrugged. "He's mean to me. He says I'm stupid."

"Well, even if you two have argued, there's still something very bad that has happened. . . ." Sarah stumbled right in. She didn't want to have to say these things to her child. Of course she wanted both of them prepared and warned, but she didn't want them to know, in such a concrete way, that even people they knew weren't always what they seemed. She didn't want to know it herself. But she told Danny that his former soccer coach, a man who called him Danny-boy and sang that song as a joke whenever Danny scored a goal, had raped his own son and three other children.

"But you can't rape a boy." Danny's expression was one of condescending pity for his mother's stupidity. It felt like a fish bone in Sarah's throat to explain to him that yes indeed you could, and how exactly.

Danny's face flushed bright red. Nate looked like he wanted to be sick.

"Why didn't he run away?" Danny asked, in an almost challenging tone. "How come he never told anybody?"

Sarah didn't know.

"He even spent the night once, at Billy Porter's house, during last year's tournament. He could have told Mrs. Porter then." Danny popped a big bite of kugel into his mouth.

As much as his casual, slightly accusatory reaction troubled her, Sarah found herself thinking, *Thank God. Thank God Danny thinks Jordan would have told. So if anything had happened to Danny, he would have told.*

"It couldn't be that bad if he didn't run away," Danny said. "It's probably no big deal."

"Danny, it's a very big deal. I saw him. I told you I took him to the hospital myself! The police were here, today, in this house. I saw pictures of his abuse."

Danny shrugged cavalierly and continued eating. Sarah's pulse quickened, and she itched to shake him.

"What the hell is your problem?" Nate asked him.

Danny looked at Sarah, as if expecting her to scold Nate. When she didn't, he took another bite of kugel and said, "Whatever."

Sarah breathed deep. "'Whatever'? That's all you have to say? This boy used to be your friend. He's in your class. You see him every day, and you can't feel one little morsel of—"

"I don't like him," Danny said.

"It doesn't matter!" Sarah's voice broke. She pushed her chair from the table and stormed into the living room. She paced around the room, furious at Roy for not being here. She snorted. If he were here, he'd take off his glasses, look at her with that maddening condescending expression, that "doctor look," and tell her to calm down. God, sometimes she'd wanted to kill him. *Breathe. Breathe.* Roy would say this was just Danny's way of holding it off. Maybe it was too much to grasp right now. Danny didn't even know a boy could be raped—for God's sake, what was wrong with her? She wanted this day over.

The yeasty aroma of bread reminded her to remove the challah from the oven. She returned to the kitchen and placed the loaves on cooling racks. "All right, guys. It's time for the news, and I want you to watch it with me. I want to see what they say."

The boys followed her to the living room and sat far apart from each other.

Mark Kendrick was the top story, with a stunning photo of him, tan, blond, and smiling. Sarah had seen the photo before; it was on Courtney's refrigerator. Courtney and Jordan had been cropped from the shot. The solemn black anchorwoman narrated the story of Mark's secret pornography "club" while footage ran of the Kendrick's sunny yellow house. The anchorwoman reported that five adults had used children in pornographic material. Mark was charged with gross abuse and molestation of children and creating and possessing pornographic material involving minors. An all-points bulletin was out for his arrest. Another couple had been arrested in Indianapolis and charged with the same. Photos of this husband and wife filled the screen—normal, smiling, professional-looking people, also identified in the videotapes. There were no photos or mention of Courtney or Jordan or the other children. The anchorwoman did report that four children appeared in the photos and videotapes and that all were believed to be related to the perpetrators.

Sarah watched Danny closely, but he showed no emotion as he watched the news and excused himself as soon as the story was over. She followed him and tried to talk, but he insisted he was fine. Her questions—"Did Mark ever touch you?" and "Do you know what to do if someone touches you in a way you're not comfortable with?"—were met with "Mom, *please*," as if she were irrational. As if her concern were insulting.

The evening crawled by. Gwinn Whitacre called to see how Sarah was holding up; Rodney had told her what Sarah saw this afternoon. No one ate the challah. Sarah sent Danny over to give a whole loaf to Lila.

Sarah called the Montgomery County Jail and was told by a dispatcher that inmates could make outgoing calls but could not receive incoming ones because of the volume of people. There were afternoon visiting hours every weekday after court had been in session, and morning and afternoon hours on the weekend.

Carol Winter—Hadley of the lost bicycle's mom—called at eleven, in tears. Sarah's blood ran cold at first, but Carol immediately said, "They didn't hurt Hadley." Carol apologized for calling so late. "I . . . I wanted to call you, but I didn't know. . . . But I knew I was never going to sleep. . . . I just . . . I—I'm so thrown by this. And . . . and I saw the police car at your house this afternoon, and then after the police came to *my* house I just figured that . . . Oh, God, Sarah, is Danny okay?"

"Yes. I don't think he really understands what's happened."

There was an awkward pause. "No, Sarah. I mean, they didn't hurt Danny, did they? He's not one of the children?"

The hair rose all over Sarah's body. "No. No, he's not. I showed a photo of him to the detective, and he said Danny wasn't in any of the pictures. Why? Why would you say that?"

"Oh, thank God, thank God," Carol said. "I just know how close you were with Courtney, and when the detective explained to me why Mark and Courtney were probably grooming Hadley—"

"*What?* What do you mean, 'grooming'?"

Carol's tears started anew. "They didn't hurt her, they didn't do anything to her, Sarah, but I think they were planning to. That detective gave me a box—a whole box of pictures of Hadley that was in their house! They're all perfectly innocent pictures—playing on the trampoline, in the pool, whatever—but they had almost a *hun-*

dred pictures just of my daughter! A whole box just of pictures of Hadley!"

Sarah couldn't breathe. "Why . . . ?"

"That detective said it was because of the divorce. He said pedophiles search for kids who have crises going on in their families."

Sarah winced at the word "pedophile." Just as with incest, she'd never heard that word used in reference to any person she knew.

Carol went on, "I talked to Martha McKenna today, and the police came to *her* house, too. Mark and Courtney had a box of pictures of Katie. Katie's safe, Katie's fine, they didn't abuse her in any way either, but I think Hadley and Katie were on their 'list.' That detective said that pedophiles look for kids who have parents who are never around or families where there's illness—like Katie's brother getting all the attention because of his leukemia—or where a parent lost a job, or a divorce, or a death in the family. Kids in those circumstances are easy victims, because they're hungry for attention they're not getting at home."

A death in the family. Ice hardened in Sarah's lungs. The truth bumps rose on her arms again.

"The police think," Carol said, "that Mark and Courtney took that bicycle themselves, *just so* they could offer to help Hadley and win her trust. Can you believe that? Here I was yelling at her for not locking it up, and they're setting themselves up as the nice people offering to buy her a new one. It's so . . . God, it's so manipulative."

Sarah hated that Carol kept saying "they" and "Mark and Courtney." "Carol, Courtney's not in any of the photos. We know Mark is guilty, but Courtney's not been found guilty of anything yet."

Another awkward pause. "Sarah. Sarah, I know you were friends, but don't delude yourself. How could that woman not know what was going on?"

Defensiveness rose up in Sarah's chest. "But we don't *know* that yet. *You* didn't know your daughter was targeted, right? And you're a good mom."

Carol didn't answer for a moment, and when she did, her voice was gentle and kind. Too kind. Sarah knew that Carol was patronizing her.

"The important thing is that Danny's fine," Carol said. "Hadley's fine. Katie's fine. They weren't abused. Thank God. But I just . . . I just keep thinking about those other children. They said there were four children in the pornography."

"But the news said those kids were all believed to be related to the adults in the pictures."

Carol made a noise. "I'm so thankful they didn't harm my child, but I just can't imagine someone doing that to their *own* child. What makes people do that? What kind of person would do that?"

Sarah didn't know. But when she got off the phone, she went to the computer and looked up "pedophile." *An adult who is sexually attracted to a child or children.* Well, that was no help. Site after site presented itself, including a registry where Sarah discovered that three registered sex offenders lived in her zip code alone. Over an hour crept by as she read "characteristics" and "profiles" of pedophiles. She wanted to find a site that would let her shake off, once and for all, the question of Courtney. But none offered that comfort.

"Popular with both children and adults."

"Singles out children who seem troubled and in need of affection or attention."

"Derives gratification in a number of ways. For some, looking is enough. For others, taking pictures or watching children undress is enough. Still others require more contact."

"A female pedophile usually abuses a child when partnered with an adult male pedophile and is often herself a victim of chronic sexual abuse."

"Women who sexually abuse children are usually 'caretakers' for them, most often mothers or stepmothers, someone involved in a continuing relationship or incest. They are usually possessive and overprotective of their victims."

"Incestuous parents may know soon after the child is born, perhaps even before, that they are going to have sex with the child. Such parents do not act impulsively."

"A pedophile can act independently or be involved in an organized ring."

"Pedophiles are often 'groupers' who actively seek one another out, to swap pictures of their victims and, often, the victims themselves."

"They are usually well-educated family men and have no criminal record. The marriage is often troubled by sexual dysfunction and serves as a smoke screen for the pedophile's true preferences and practices."

Sarah remembered a comment Courtney once made about sex. They'd been out to dinner, and Sarah confided to Courtney that she was surprised by how much she missed sex. Courtney had laughed bitterly and said, "Sex? What's that?"

Sarah had raised her eyebrows and asked, "Do I sense a little trouble?"

Courtney had sighed and said, "Don't you have to be in the same room to have sex?"

So . . . that could be a sign that the marriage was a smoke screen—and evidence that Courtney and Mark were rarely together, which made it more likely that Courtney didn't know what Mark was doing. But . . . Courtney *was* with Jordan all the time, and Sarah found it hard to believe that a mother would not pick up on her own child's distress.

She moaned. She looked at the clock: 2:00 A.M. She felt relieved that this horrible day was finally over.

Sarah crawled into bed, for once grateful to be alone. She didn't think she could tolerate another body next to her right now. Lately she'd been lulling herself to sleep with thoughts of Roy curled against her, his knees behind her own, his lips on her neck. She'd remember how he'd run his warm hand down her side, across the curve of her hip, and over her belly. They'd sometimes fall asleep with his fingers twined in the downy black hair where her legs met.

Not tonight. She didn't want to see those horrendous images of Jordan when she thought of Roy.

She spent most of the night awake, staring at the ceiling, counting questions instead of sheep: Even though Courtney and Jordan were not mentioned on the news, wouldn't everyone know? How would they react? Where was Mark right now? God, what must he think of Sarah? That she was an idiot? Gullible? Naive? And Courtney. In jail. Sarah wondered if Courtney had a pillow. Tears welled in her eyes. *Courtney wasn't in the photos.*

Yet Sarah couldn't help but think that nearly every good picture of her own children taken in the last two years had been taken by Courtney.

CHAPTER SEVEN

Nate

Mom woke Nate up early on Saturday morning as she always did, to tell him she was leaving. She went running every Saturday with Mrs. Kendrick. But wait . . . Nate woke up for real. Mrs. Kendrick was in jail. "Where are you going?" he asked.

"I need to go visit Jordan," she said. "He's been all by himself since I took him to the emergency room."

Nate nodded. When he'd been in the hospital to get his tonsils taken out, either Mom or Dad stayed with him the whole entire time.

When she left, Nate wandered down to the kitchen. Even though there was no school, he'd started to hate Saturdays. He missed Dad the most on Saturdays. Dad had never worked on Saturdays. He always worked on Sundays but never Saturdays. Saturday nights were a really busy time for Mom's work, so it had always been up to Dad to get dinner. They'd started this tradition of having cereal for dinner. Just because it was easy. And they liked it. Dad would joke how they weren't supposed to do any work on Saturday anyway. It wasn't always cereal—sometimes it was pancakes or omelettes—it didn't matter, but it was always breakfast food for supper. Right down to the orange juice.

It was a bummer hanging out in the kitchen thinking of that, so Nate took a box of cereal back up to his room. He sat on his bed eating the cereal dry out of the box and looked up at the corner of his room where he'd seen the bat that one time.

Ever since he'd seen those photos of Jordan, he couldn't get the bat out of his head.

Once, when he was in eighth grade, they'd had a bat in their house. When they told people the story, everyone said, "Oh, yeah, the house is old," like every old house was full of bats—but they only had one once. Never before and never since. Everyone said, "There's never just one bat. They're like mice. They live in colonies." And Mom would purse her lips and say, "Well, this one must've been a scout, then. He went back and said, 'Don't bother.' "

The bat had shown up in *Nate's* room. He woke up and had this hair-stand-up-on-the-back-of-his-neck feeling that he was not alone. He lay really still, wondering if it was a bad dream, or had some sound woken him up? And he heard it: this *swish, swish* sound, almost like a girl in a prom dress—that rustling sound that shiny material makes, only fainter, softer. He was *really* awake then, hyper-alert, hearing everything, smelling everything.

And he saw it. Even in the darkness, he saw that black spot against his white wall in the moonlight. And seeing it made him cold. He didn't know what it was, didn't register it as a bat, but it was *not supposed to be there*. It looked wrong. It made him feel wrong. And he didn't really want to turn on the light to see what it was. He closed his eyes, hoping when he opened them, the spot would be gone. But then he panicked—if it was gone, then where the hell *was* it? So he opened his eyes, and it was still there. But it moved. Shit. Nate reached out to turn on the lamp, and his arms felt like they weighed a ton, like they weren't really even his arms. He turned on the light.

It was a bat.

And it freaked Nate out. He didn't want to move. He didn't know what to do. He'd studied bats. Mom had even read him some bedtime story about a bat when he was little. He knew bats were good, bats were cool—but that didn't mean he wanted one in his fucking room! His mouth and throat went totally dry. Stripped dry. Like in nightmares where you want to yell, but you can't make any sound.

Finally he slid out of his bed and ran out of the room. He shut his door, because he didn't want it to follow him. And he went to get his mom and dad. He felt like a damn baby. He was in eighth grade, for Christ's sake, and hadn't run to Mom and Dad's room for a long time.

He woke them up. It was funny, because Mom was the one who was fine. Dad acted all "I'll take care of it, son, don't you worry about a thing," but when they opened the bedroom door and the bat was flying, Dad turned into a sissy. He ducked and he cussed and made little noises. Mom laughed. She just started giggling at him, and so did Nate. Dad got kind of mad, but not really; he was laughing, too. Dad thought he would toss a towel on the bat while it was flying, but every time the bat flew toward them, he would duck. Then he opened all the windows in Nate's room and tried to chase it out with the towel. This was in January. It was freezing outside. Actually snowing.

They made so much noise that Danny woke up. Danny wouldn't come into Nate's room but kept shouting "Did you catch it yet?" from the hall. Potter started barking.

Nate remembered thinking their family would have to move. He couldn't sleep in this room, and they couldn't live in this house with this *thing* in it. If they couldn't get rid of the bat, it was all over. They'd have to leave.

But Mom finally caught it. While Nate and Dad were ducking and throwing towels at the poor bat, she left the room. They didn't notice, or if they did, Nate guessed they probably thought she was scared and was leaving it to them. But she came back with a cookie sheet and a soup pot. Dad looked at her like she was crazy.

"Don't tell me," Dad said. "You're going to cook something with it."

She laughed. "Just leave it alone for a second. Let it land."

But they'd pissed it off by now, and it kept flying. Mom turned on the overhead light, and it landed. She frowned, looking at it up so high, just inches from the ceiling. Then she glanced around Nate's room, and said, "Nate. Put your desk chair right under where it is." Nate did, and Mom climbed up on the chair and, without even a second of hesitation, put the pot right over the bat, trapping it.

"Oooh," she said, "I can feel its sonar vibes." She wrinkled her nose and curled up her bare toes. "That feels so weird." But then, holding the pot against the wall with one hand, she slid the cookie sheet between the wall and the pot. Then she stepped off the chair and flipped the pot right side up, the cookie sheet on top like a lid. And she nodded at the door. Nate opened it. And then she walked calmly down the stairs, Potter prancing around trying to see what was in the pot. Nate and Dad and Danny followed Mom and opened the kitchen door for her and turned on the porch light so she could see.

She walked down the steps, barefooted in the snow, then set the pot on the ground. She stood up, and only then did she look uncertain. She reached out a toe and nudged the cookie sheet off the pot.

They waited. Nothing. A whole minute passed, and Mom whispered, "Shit." It was one of the first times Nate had heard his mother cuss. She kept shifting from one foot to the other, holding a foot out of the snow. Dad and Danny still stood up on the porch, barefooted, too, but not in the snow.

"Sarah," Dad said, "you need to come in."

She took her foot again and tipped the pot over. The bat slid out into the snow and simply lay there, not moving. The sun was just coming up. It was probably six or something. Nate walked out into the snow with Mom, and they both looked real close at it. Now that it was out of Nate's room, it looked really cool—it had little-old-man hands. And a weird human face. Its wings looked like leather.

They all went inside, and Mom pulled out hand towels for their feet, but they kept looking out the back window, and that bat just lay there in the snow. "It's going to freeze to death," she said. "I feel sorry for it."

Finally Mom couldn't stand it, and she went out there with a broom and was going to nudge it. But Nate didn't think the broom ever actually touched the bat. It was like the bat sensed the broom, snapped to life, and fluttered off. In the whole incident, that was the only time Mom looked startled and acted like a girl. She jumped back with a little shriek. The bat fluttered all feeble across the yard, touching the snow, the way a duck will take off from water, then finally took flight. It looked like it was flying out of their yard, but then it circled back and flew into a little nook in the eaves right above Nate's bedroom window.

"Oh, you little shit," Mom said. And she looked furious.

"You said you felt sorry for it," Dad teased her.

"That was when it wasn't in my house." She stormed up to Nate's room and examined every nook and cranny. No bat. She even took a flashlight and peered into the corners of his closet and down into the floor moldings, looking for how the bat might have come in. She was obsessed for days, snooping around the attic, calling an exterminator. Nothing. They never found another bat.

That was the year before Dad died. They didn't even know Dad was sick yet—but it struck Nate that a year and a month from the bat visiting their house, Dad had died.

Nate would never forget that feeling when he saw the bat against the wall, looking so out of place. So dark. So wrong. And how he didn't want to look at it closely. He just somehow knew that if he saw it clearly, it would be worse.

He'd felt that same sensation when Mom and Dad told him Dad had cancer. The word "inoperable" was like the bat.

And he felt it when he saw the pictures of Jordan. And when he thought about Mrs. Kendrick. Another dark spot Nate didn't want to see. But there it was. And both of those times since the actual bat, Nate wanted someone to be able to fix it like Mom had, so calmly, so certainly. But she couldn't. And Nate couldn't. He didn't know if anyone could.

CHAPTER EIGHT

Sarah

On her way to The Children's Medical Center, Sarah made two stops. First she went to the post office and mailed a note of encouragement to Courtney, in care of the Montgomery County Jail. She hoped Courtney would be out by the time Monday's mail arrived. Then she pulled in to the neighborhood market. She suddenly felt she must bring *something* with her to see Jordan. Or was she just stalling?

Before she'd left the house, Sarah had called Ali Darlen at Children's. Ali used to be Roy's resident at Miami Valley Hospital. Sarah and Ali still got together once or twice a year for lunch or drinks somewhere. Ali knew Courtney; they'd worked together. About a year ago, Ali had taken a job at Children's. This morning Sarah had called her and asked to talk with her about Courtney. Ali had agreed to meet with Sarah. Sarah had woken feeling newly devoted to Courtney. The more she thought about it, the more she was certain Courtney simply couldn't be involved in the pornography. She could not have known what was going on. Ali had worked with Courtney; she'd seen what a fabulous doctor Courtney was. No one with that amount of compassion or skill could be so hideously cruel.

Sarah had even dressed in an emerald green, cabled cashmere sweater Courtney had bought for her last birthday. When they shopped together, Courtney convinced Sarah to buy clothing she'd never select for herself. Most of the clothes Sarah received compliments for were items Courtney had encouraged her to buy. Courtney's choices were more fun, more colorful. Courtney got Sarah to buy V-necks, surplice tops, and necklines that didn't exactly plunge but dropped lower than Sarah normally wore—which was not low at all.

"You've got great cleavage, Sarah," Courtney had chided, when Sarah hesitated.

"But I'm a mom."

"And where's the law that says a mom can't be sexy?"

Sarah had put it back on the rack, but Courtney had later presented it to Sarah on her birthday. The sweater was now one of Sarah's favorites.

Inside, the store buzzed with clusters of conversation, horrified voices, and the names "Mark," "Courtney," and "Kendrick"—the *k*'s clicking like insects, as if a horde of locusts had descended. "Absurd," "not possible," "witch-hunt," were words that lifted themselves above the whir.

Sarah thought of the times she'd gossiped in this very market about horrible news, sometimes even with Courtney. Expressing outrage over moms who drowned their toddlers in bathtubs or locked them in cars and pushed them into lakes. Moms who burned their kids with scalding water or set entire houses on fire with their sleeping children inside. Moms who discarded the babies altogether—in toilets, in Dumpsters, in shallow garage-floor graves.

Only headlines. Not an actual person in her world. Not a neighbor, not her friend.

But all those headlines were about *someone's* neighbor, *someone's* friend.

And it *wasn't* her friend. It was her friend's *husband*.

Sarah looked at every child, imagining what horrible secrets might be under each one's clothes, wondering what visible clue she might discern that she'd missed with Jordan. How could she have been in that home so much and never picked up a single vibe?

Sarah headed for the florist shop at the back of the store. Purple irises, dark and perfect as van Gogh's, stood in water buckets, but flowers didn't seem right for an eleven-year-old boy. There were balloons, but they seemed celebratory, and the one that said "Get Well" seemed a flippant sentiment for repeated sexual abuse.

She did select one plain red balloon, and in the small office-supply section she picked up a sketch pad, some colored pencils, and stickers of soccer balls and African animals. The cards all seemed inappropriate, but she found one with no message—just a photo of a black-and-white cat looking out a window. That would do.

She selected a card for Nate's seventeenth birthday tomorrow as well. The week's events had made her almost forget. She hoped she could think of a way to convey to him how much their time cooking together had meant to her.

On her way out of the store, the combined aromas of rich coffee, cinnamon, and fresh bread stopped her at the bakery counter. She admired the lattice-topped cherry pies, the fluffy pastries, and the chocolate-dipped cherries atop the Black Forest cakes. The display reminded her of the year she'd studied at La Varenne Cooking School in Paris, where several weeks had been devoted solely to pastries, cakes, and meringues. She'd just paid for a caramel latte when she heard her name called.

Janet Porter and Carlotta Imparato approached her with somber faces but bright, almost gleeful eyes. "Did you hear?" Janet asked.

Sarah nodded. Janet held the morning paper, which Sarah had already snatched up the second the delivery boy flung it onto her porch. The paper ran the same photo as the news last night. And offered no new details.

"I'm sick. Utterly sick. We just came from the baseball breakfast, and it's all anyone is talking about."

Sarah nodded again, grateful that Danny didn't play baseball.

"Whoever would've thought?" Carlotta said. "They always seemed so nice. They were so normal-looking." Carlotta seemed almost delighted to have been wrong. She giggled and commented, "Isn't that what they always say about people who turn out to be serial killers and child molesters?"

Sarah smiled a tight smile and took her caramel latte.

"You and Courtney were so close," Carlotta said. "Did you ever in your wildest dreams suspect?"

The question stabbed Sarah. She had already battered herself with, *Are you a moron? It was happening right under your nose.* Sarah stared at Carlotta a moment before asking, "Do you think I suspected and didn't tell anyone?"

"Of course not. How did the police find out, do you know? How did they get caught?"

"*They* didn't get caught. *Mark* got caught."

Carlotta waved her hand dismissively, as if this were a minor detail. "Do you know how *Mark* got caught?" Her question was edged in a patronizing tone.

Sarah shook her head. Carlotta had a smear of bright red lipstick on her teeth, the effect of which seemed ghoulish.

"I'm floored about Jordan," Janet said, pressing a chubby hand to her bosom, each one of her sausage fingers decorated with a ring and scarlet fingernail polish. "He's been in our house a hundred times. He had every opportunity to talk to us, to ask for our help. Surely he knew we were approachable."

"I always thought he was a little odd," Carlotta said. Sarah couldn't take her eyes from those lipsticked teeth. They looked blood-smeared. Carlotta shuddered, exaggerated, fake. "God only knows what they did to him."

No, Sarah thought, taking the first sip of her drink, *she* knew what they did to him, too. She'd seen it.

"Do you know any details?" Janet asked, the red fingernails dancing around her neckline. She leaned in close to Sarah and whispered, "The papers say sexual abuse and pornography, but they don't really tell you anything specific."

"For God's sake, Janet," Sarah said. "These are *kids*." Their strange hunger for scraps of Jordan's suffering made her queasy.

Janet blushed but said, "I just want to know exactly what happened."

"Why on earth didn't he tell someone?" Carlotta asked, staring at the cakes.

"You make it sound like it was all his fault." Sarah's words rolled out harsher than she expected, but she wasn't really sorry.

"I'm just trying to understand him," Carlotta said.

"I'm trying to understand how this child could have walked among us and not one of us sensed what was happening," Sarah said. "I'm not blaming him. I blame myself."

Carlotta's jaw set, and she pursed her lips. She leaned in closer to the glass, pretending to examine the price on a raspberry torte. She wouldn't meet Sarah's eyes.

Janet looked up at Sarah's red balloon. "What's the occasion?"

"Oh . . . tomorrow's Nate's birthday. Just something festive to put with his gifts." She had no idea why she lied, but she didn't want to reveal she was going to see Jordan. "I should get going. I'll see you." She left, knowing they would talk about her the second she was out of earshot.

Sarah drove down the main boulevard, the medians landscaped— spring pansies scattered bright as confetti, the tulips almost mockingly cheerful. She drove through downtown Dayton and crossed the river. When Sarah reached The Children's Medical Center, she sat in the car a moment. She'd been here many times for her own boys—Danny's broken wrist when he fell from the garage roof pretending to be Spider-Man, Nate's numerous hockey injuries. Both boys had had their tonsils removed. She couldn't fathom leaving one of her sons here alone. Jordan had to be lonely and scared. She got out of the car and went inside, carrying her balloon and bag of gifts.

She had almost fifteen minutes before her meeting with Ali, but she headed up to the third floor anyway. When Sarah stepped off the elevator, however, she walked into a group of solemn, cross-armed people standing in a huddle, blocking her way. A tall, red-headed woman stepped aside, making room for Sarah, but as the woman turned, she did a double take. "Sarah! You're early!"

Ali stretched out her arms to Sarah, and the two women embraced. The sensation of being held brought tears to Sarah's eyes.

"We were just talking about you," Ali said, pulling Sarah into the circle and introducing her to what looked like mostly doctors, nurses, and hospital staff. Sarah recognized Detective Kramble, who nodded at her. "We just had a meeting about"—and Ali gestured, as if words failed her—"about Jordan," she said.

"I brought him some things," Sarah said. She tugged the balloon ribbon.

Ali made a face. "He's not seeing visitors."

Sarah turned to Kramble. "Is something wrong? You said—"

"I'm sorry," Kramble said. "That decision was just made."

The rest of the circle began to disperse, with promised reports to one another.

Ali sighed. "We want him to see visitors, but Jordan doesn't want to. Dr. McConnel, his therapist, was talking to us, just now, at the meeting. It's really vital, in order for her to build some rapport with him, for us to respect his wishes. So many things have been done to him without his permission. We want him to feel some control here. We *do* want him to have visitors, eventually. The last thing we want is for him to isolate himself, but right now that goal is overridden by our wanting to get him to trust us."

"Oh. Of course."

"But I'll give these to him," Ali said. "Let's give them to the nurses now, and then come walk with me." Ali took the balloon and bag from Sarah and began to walk down the hall.

Sarah hesitated. Kramble still stood there, and it seemed rude to just walk away. Ali stopped and looked back.

"Thank you for your time this morning," Kramble said to Ali.

"Of course."

"Mrs. Laden." He touched the side of his head, as if he were tipping a hat. It struck Sarah that he'd look at home in a hat, that he seemed somehow not of this era. He stepped onto the elevator, and the doors closed on him.

"Sarah?" Ali asked.

Sarah shook herself and followed Ali. Ali dropped off Sarah's gifts at the nurses' station, then led her downstairs to the courtyard. They sat on benches in a green-and-purple gazebo shaped like a house. The April sun shone down through the "chimney" of this playhouse. Two children laughed and giggled on the nearby swing set. Their mother sat reading a book under a tree.

Ali rubbed her hands over her face. "Courtney," she said, shaking her head and staring up through the chimney. Her face was tortured as she turned to Sarah and said, "You know Roy and I worked with her at the Valley. I *liked* her."

Sarah nodded. "Me, too. I feel so . . ."

"So fucking betrayed?" Ali asked. "That bitch wore a button with that kid's face on it. She had these lovely pictures of him all over her locker. She talked about him all the goddamn time. I thought she was a good mom. And I know she was a good doctor."

Sarah closed her eyes. She listened to the birdsong and the laughter of the children.

"Kramble had us look at some photos and movies this morning," Ali said. "I ID'd Mark. But I didn't see Courtney."

Sarah whispered, "So there's a chance she wasn't involved."

Ali slumped her shoulders. "Sarah, come on. The camera *moves,* sometimes when all five of the other adults are on the screen."

The hair stood on Sarah's arms. *All five of the adults?* The images and configurations that crowded Sarah's mind sickened her.

"She had to know," Ali said. "She let it happen, which is just as bad, if not worse. Where was she during these parties? She pays for you to cater, and then she leaves? She just disappears with a houseful of company?"

"What if she got a page?" Sarah asked, recognizing that her voice rose with too much hope. "She had to go deliver babies at all kinds of bizarre hours."

Ali looked sad instead of skeptical, which made the tears press harder behind Sarah's eyes. "Every single time? That's a big coincidence, don't you think?"

The tears let loose. Sarah wiped them away. "I know, I know, I know. I sound like an idiot, Ali. . . . I . . . She *can't* be involved in this, do you understand? I can't . . . I don't . . . I don't know what I'll do if . . ."

Ali put an arm around Sarah. "I'm sorry. I know this has to be hard." She let Sarah cry for a moment.

When Sarah dug in her purse for a Kleenex and blew her nose, Ali said, "Sarah, even *if* she wasn't there, even *if* she didn't witness it a single time, she knew. How can you not know that your husband is raping your son? And what about the drugs? Jordan had Dilaudid. The Valley had been missing some. They'd had meetings about it. Apparently Courtney was already under suspicion for stealing drugs. The police found a small stash of it at their house, but there's no evidence that Courtney was using it herself. We think she stole it for Jordan as pain medication. Dilaudid would keep him out of physical pain and way out of touch with his psychic pain. We also found azithromycin in his parka pocket, and I think she was trying to treat him herself, you know, so he didn't have to go to a doctor, who might suspect."

"Treat him?"

Ali's huge green eyes welled with tears. "He has gonorrhea, Sarah." Ali stared across the courtyard at the children swinging high on the swing set. She fidgeted with her earrings. "He's had gonorrhea long enough to spread through his bloodstream. He'll have to stay here at least a week on IV antibiotics. It's spread to some of his joints, which is treatable, too, but, God, this kid must have been in pain. We have to test him for endocarditis—the interior of his heart may be infected. So . . . Courtney is giving him painkillers and antibiotics but *not* taking him to a pediatrician? What does that tell you?"

Sarah sensed something give way inside her. She felt woozy, her head too heavy to hold up, just as she had when she'd first seen the pictures. "How . . . why . . . what made you test him for gonorrhea?"

"The ER did that. And for every other STD we have tests for."

"But why? How did they know?"

Ali paused. "I'm telling *you* this, okay? I trust you, Sarah. I wouldn't give this information to anyone who came in and asked. Nancy—Nancy Rhee, remember her? She was the attending when you brought Jordan in. She told us that at first she thought he was your run-of-the-mill OD, which, by the way, has left him with an irregular heartbeat and unstable blood pressure." She coughed and looked across the courtyard. "But when they cleared his chest, he had this bruise that circled his right nipple. It was . . . just too bizarre, something she'd never seen before. And once they got him stabilized, they saw he had scratches behind both ears, odd bruises, and a bite mark. They checked him, and sure enough, he'd been raped."

"Was he . . . injured?"

Ali nodded. "Some fissures, some trauma. Three stitches. Nothing major." She shuddered. "Listen to me: 'nothing major.' You know what I mean. He had no serious physical injury to his colon, but he was *raped,* and not for the first time either. Kramble says this has been going on for years."

Oh, God. Sarah saw Jordan again, huddled in her front seat, clutching a tablecloth for warmth. "Years?"

"Yup. About four years that are documented on videos and images. They found some old Polaroids, much tamer stuff— inappropriate nudity and touching. Probably gradual grooming for the films. Kramble already had school records this morning, and there's teacher descriptions in Jordan's end-of-the-year report cards that should have set off warning bells for someone. A bunch of comments say that he played alone most of the time and that he was too passive—his third-grade teacher said if some other kid wanted a toy he was playing with, he gave it up immediately every time. Third grade was the same year that he refused to let a nurse take off his sweatshirt when he fell off a slide and hurt his arm. We have similar reports in every grade, this passive, loner of a kid who refuses to let anyone touch him." Ali's voice grew louder, with a hard, angry edge. "Just last fall at the start of fifth grade, he refused to take part in the scoliosis exam—you know, where the kids have to strip to the waist, wear those little paper shirts, and bend over so someone can examine their spines? Well, he would *not* do it. He actually kicked the gym teacher and ran from her. This shy, passive kid threw a *fit,* was suddenly not so passive, and no one put it together. I mean, there was a parent-teacher conference about that one, but that was the end of it. I think because Mark and Courtney are charming, well-respected, seemingly *nice* people, no one ever looked at the overall behavior of this kid and said, 'Now, wait a minute.' "

Sarah's eyes stung again, picturing how hideous the scoliosis exam must have seemed to Jordan. She remembered Courtney's exasperation about that teacher conference. Courtney had told Sarah, "Sometimes he's so strange. I don't know what gets into him."

Sarah suddenly remembered, "Courtney told me she worried Jordan had Asperger's syndrome."

Ali laughed a bitter, one-note laugh. "Bullshit. This kid does *not* have Asperger's."

"But she said—"

"Sarah, don't you get it? These people were very good at what they did. Putting out the suggestion of Asperger's just gave a blanket excuse for the perfectly legitimate reasons this boy may have been demonstrating antisocial behavior!"

Sarah blinked. Could Courtney have been *that* manipulative? She remembered the tears in Courtney's eyes as she'd told Sarah her concern.

The two children ran into the gazebo, the girl chasing the boy. They stopped, panting and laughing, staring at Sarah and Ali. "Hey!" called their mother. "Stay over here, okay?" And with a shriek, the boy took off running again, the girl in pursuit.

Sarah smiled at their silliness, then asked, "What will happen to him?"

Ali lifted her shoulders and shook her head. "I don't know. He hasn't even asked about his parents, which is pretty telling. That whole first day, he never asked anyone where his mom or dad was, didn't ask to talk to them or anything. The police haven't found any family on Mark's side, and Courtney's brother doesn't want to be involved. He didn't even know she had a child, apparently, and the kid is . . . what? Ten or eleven?"

The floor fell out from under Sarah's feet. "Whoa, *what*? Courtney doesn't have a brother."

Ali nodded. "In Seattle. Kramble interviewed him on the phone last night."

Sarah felt the gazebo shift. "She told me she didn't have any brothers or sisters."

"Yeah, I know, she never mentioned any to me either."

"No," Sarah said too loudly for the enclosed space, the denial echoing back to her. "I *asked* her outright, and she said no."

Ali looked at Sarah and shrugged. "She lied about a lot of things, apparently."

"Why would you lie about having a brother?"

"Kramble said the brother—whose name is Jordan, too, by the way; how creepy is that?—said that he and Courtney were both sexually abused by their father. Kramble could tell you more, but I guess they haven't seen or spoken to each other in almost twenty years."

Sarah fought the urge to crawl under the bench. Yesterday she'd felt so sure of what she knew; she'd expected the truth to fall down like rain, washing everything clear and clean, but this truth was hurtling down like hailstones.

Sarah remembered Courtney's mom dying. It had happened before she knew Courtney well, before Roy's cancer. She was aware that Courtney had been deeply affected by her mother's death, and Sarah had always figured that was the reason Courtney had such insight into Sarah's own grief. Now she wondered if Courtney's mother had known what her husband had done to her children. What did she think of her children not speaking to each other for twenty years? Sarah's throat closed.

"So . . . this child. Where is he going to *go*?"

Ali shook her head, her earrings jingling like faint wind chimes. "Children's Services is trying for temporary custody. If they get it—which should be no problem with the evidence we have— they'll have to look for a foster placement."

"I'm so glad you're his doctor, Ali."

Ali grinned, but it was rueful. "He's got a kick-ass team assigned to him, and it's a good thing. He's not exactly a cooperative patient. Those early exams, once he was here, were nightmares. It took four of us to hold him down. We felt like monsters. He kicked me right in the jaw." She turned to face Sarah on the bench, twisting her neck so Sarah could see Ali's other cheek. Ali gingerly touched the greenish gray bruise along her jawbone. "These cases break our hearts."

"You don't see abuse like *this* that often, do you?"

Ali tilted her head at Sarah. "Yes. Unfortunately, we do." A beep sounded in Ali's pocket, and she said, "I've got to go. Take care, Sarah. It's great to see you; I just wish it wasn't under such grim circumstances. It's been way too long."

It had been. And rather than just meeting for a quick lunch, Sarah felt a yearning to have Ali and her girlfriend coming over for dinner at the Laden house again, talking around the table late into the night the way they had when Roy was alive.

Sarah stood alone a moment, after Ali left. She watched the children playing. The boy pretended to be a monster and ambushed the girl, leaping from under the slide. The girl ran, laughing and screaming, but tripped and skidded into the playground mulch. Sarah cringed at how hard she landed. The girl sat up, crying, and the mother and brother ran to her. Sarah watched the mother set her on the bridge and kiss the heels of her hands and her knees. "All better?" she heard the mom ask.

The girl nodded, still sniffling, and the mom pulled her into a hug and kissed the top of her head.

Sarah's chest ached, and her nose stung with tears.

When she reached home and found herself standing in her kitchen, she had no real recollection of getting there. She'd been thinking about what she knew about Courtney. She'd found herself *listing* the things she knew for certain about this woman. Sarah knew that Courtney loved to get pedicures and that her favorite flowers were gerbera daisies and that she let the obscenities fly when she was cut off in traffic. Sarah knew that Courtney had met Mark in a college class—Courtney always said "college sweethearts" and rolled her eyes. She loved scary movies and Leonardo DiCaprio. Sarah knew that Courtney had become a doctor because her father was one, too, and Sarah had been to Courtney's office, where her walls were decorated with Georgia O'Keeffe prints and those Anne Geddes photos of the babies in flowers. Sarah had heard Courtney describe her father as "not an easy man." When Sarah had pressed her, Courtney said, "It was hard to live up to him. I felt I lived a lot of my life trying to win his approval. How clichéd is that?" Once Sarah had asked Courtney why she'd chosen her medical specialty. And Courtney said, "I want women to know their own bodies. To have power over their own bodies. I was afraid and ashamed seeing a doctor when I was a young teenager. I hated the doctor I had. I wanted to be better than that. Make the young women feel comfortable and safe."

Courtney had seemed raw and uncomfortable talking about it. Sarah had wanted to ask more, but Courtney immediately changed the subject, saying, "As for obstetrics, I love delivering babies. It's *happy*. I'm dealing with healthy people who have a short-term 'condition' and are going to get well. I love the whole flowering process, the way the body takes control of *us*. Isn't it a trip to think of that? This . . . this *person* came from us? Is a part of us. *Is* us. You know?"

She knew that Courtney liked her lattes with soy milk, that she always bought Junior Mints at the movies, and that she preferred her gin martinis with a cocktail onion instead of an olive. She knew that when Courtney was premenstrual, she craved Sarah's Thai peanut dressing and would eat it with a spoon out of the jar. She knew Courtney's shoe size and that she wore petite smalls in most clothing.

She knew that Courtney was obsessive about her workouts and that she loved to run. Courtney was a great running partner. Their pace was the same. They'd run every Saturday morning. Sometimes Courtney met her straight from a delivery; she'd only had to cancel three times in the nearly four years they'd held the tradition. Sarah knew that Courtney didn't like to talk when she ran, which Sarah loved. Sarah had tried going to an aerobics class with Gwinn once, but Gwinn had blabbed through the whole thing, and that had annoyed the hell out of Sarah. Sarah liked the time to be in her head. She didn't even like headphones. She liked the private time to fill her head with Roy, a luxury she could allow herself because she was doing something else, something productive.

Sarah picked the homemade photo calendar off its magnetic hook again and flipped forward to December, a photo of Sarah and Courtney together. Mark had taken the photo on a night that the Kendricks had invited Sarah's family over for supper. Sarah had felt awkwardly aware of being without Roy, and Nate had been sullen, but it was in the days that Jordan and Danny were friends, and their silliness and laughter had made the dinner fun. The photo was of Sarah and Courtney at the end of the table, empty dessert plates and coffee cups in front of them, in the foreground the pie plate with the one remaining piece of the peach-and-blueberry pie Sarah had brought. Sarah and Courtney had their arms around each other's shoulders, leaning their heads together, Sarah's dark curls mingling with Courtney's wispy blond hair. They looked like college roomies. Best friends.

And now Sarah could add the following to the list of things she knew about Courtney:

Courtney's father had abused her. Courtney had a brother she had lied about. Courtney had stolen drugs from the hospital. Courtney had been treating her son for a sexually transmitted disease. Courtney's son had been sexually abused for at least four years.

And then Sarah thought of things she *didn't* know. It struck her that she had no idea what Courtney filled *her* head with as they ran on Saturday mornings. What was it a luxury for her to dwell on?

CHAPTER NINE

Jordan

Jordan swallowed a fourth bite of his hospital-breakfast oatmeal. It crawled down his throat, thick and dry as art-class clay. He shoved his tray to the side and flung himself back on the bed. The tiny room was bright with sunshine. Cartoon penguins bordered the ceiling. They were supposed to make him feel better, he guessed. But he was in such deep trouble. He'd messed up so bad it made him feel sick. And he had no idea how he was going to fix it.

He'd been here for five whole days, and every night he dreamed about his backpack. In his dreams he always raced to get to the backpack before anyone else opened it. He couldn't even remember what was in it that was so important.

His brain felt full of fog. The days all blurred together here, and he kept making stupid mistakes and saying the wrong things. He pictured his teacher telling the class, "Now, focus. Really concentrate." Oh, man. If only he could be back in class. If only nobody knew, if he could just turn back time like in a movie. But turning back time meant he still had to . . . *concentrate*. C-o-n-c-e-n-t-r-a-t-e. Jordan sat up. If he was going to focus, it meant he had to *stay here* and stop spelling. But trying to remember in his aching head just made everything even foggier. He reached for the sketch pad that Sarah had brought. He selected the green colored pencil, flipped past some pages he'd drawn on, and began to make a list. He would test himself. He would write down what he did remember.

He wrote, "*Day #1. The Plan,*" then paused. The morning that he'd come to the hospital was lost. He didn't know how to get it back. He remembered his plan, but he honestly didn't remember doing it. Dr. Ali had told him this amnesia was a usual thing in an overdose. She said he'd given himself the mental equivalent of a mild stroke. He could see himself in his house—sitting on the staircase—cold and tired. He could see the moment like a flash that made him know this was the day to quit. There was an epiphany— that was a vocabulary word, and he even remembered thinking that he was actually using a vocabulary word at the exact moment of the epiphany—but the hours before and after it were lost to him.

He wrote "*epiphany,*" then a big question mark. He left a blank space, then wrote, "*Woke up in emergency room. Came in ambulance to Children's Medical. Met Dr. Ali. Met Dr. Bryn.*"

Dr. Bryn McConnel was one of the first people who came to his room. She was as short as he was, and she had more freckles than he'd ever seen. Her hair was brown and curly. Really curly, like a bunch of miniature Slinkies growing out of her head. As soon as she told him she was a psychologist, he hated her. That first day all she said was, "Hi, Jordan. I know you're here because something bad happened to you." He hadn't said anything to her. He hadn't even looked at her. He wanted her to go away. She paused for a while but then just kept talking. "I bet you wish I'd just go away and leave you alone. But this is my job. I want to help you get better. I care about you feeling better. You probably don't want to talk about why you're here right now, do you?"

She waited. He stared at the penguin border. She'd wait every time, like she really thought any minute he'd answer her. "That's okay. I know it's going to be hard to talk about. You probably don't even want to think about it. I'll be visiting you to help you with

117

that. I'll be back later on tonight." And she was. When she came back, he was watching a big-cat special on Animal Planet. Dr. Bryn let him finish watching it, then talked about some zoo place near Dayton that rescued exotic animals. Animals that should never have been pets, like crocodiles and tigers that people thought would be fun to have, until they grew too big to control. Jordan would like to go there, but he didn't tell Dr. Bryn. He didn't plan to ever say anything to her, but then out of the blue she'd asked him, "Do you miss your parents?"

An alarm went off in his head. And that gerbil starting running on his wheel in Jordan's rib cage.

"Do you want to see them?"

And before he could think, he was out of bed, on his feet, jerking on his IV stand, making the needle come out and the machine start beeping.

Dr. Bryn had reassured him that she didn't mean right then, that his mom and dad were not there. While a nurse had fixed his IV, Bryn told him about his parents in her no-nonsense voice. She didn't talk in that sugary voice people used on pets, the way a lot of people at the emergency room had. She told him how his mom had to talk to the police before she could come see him. And how the police were looking for his dad. How nobody, not even his parents, had the right to do what had been done to Jordan. It was hard to listen to her when the water-rushing sound started in his head.

He waited until Dr. Bryn was gone and then he asked one of the nurses if they locked the doors at night. He'd asked a different nurse if anyone could find his room. He asked Wendy, his favorite, if the hospital security men had guns. He knew that his dad would never let him get away with this. His dad would kill him for screwing everything up so bad.

Jordan wrote, *"Day #2. The nurses tell Dr. Bryn everything."* She had come first thing in the morning and asked, "Are you worried about your dad hurting you? Do you think he's going to come after you?"

Dr. Bryn and Dr. Ali and the nurses all tried to tell him he was safe. His room was right across from the nurses' station. There was a little window so they could see in his room. A big sign was right outside his door that said all visitors must go to the nurses' desk first. Jordan wanted to keep his door shut, but they wouldn't let him. They said it was important for him to talk to people and not stay alone. They told him that security had been given pictures of his dad. Police were looking for his dad everywhere, not just here in Dayton.

Also under "*Day #2*," Jordan wrote, "*CARE House*." That second day Jordan had been given clothes to wear instead of his hospital pajamas. The nurses unhooked him from his cardiac monitor, telling him it was just for a little while. Dr. Ali made him ride in a wheelchair with his IV attached, and he'd been taken across the street to a place called CARE House. Dr. Bryn had explained it all to him, how he'd only have to talk to one lady interviewing him but that the police and Children's Services would be able to see. He sat in a yellow room that was like Billy Porter's living room, with a couch and a beanbag chair.

The lady showed him pictures of the other kids and asked if he knew them. He decided it wasn't really a lie to shake his head no. He only knew the kids' first names. And only once had he ever seen one of those kids outside the parties—Ashley, that blond girl, had been at the mall once when he was buying school clothes with his parents. All four parents had chatted at the food court, eating Chinese. Jordan and Ashley had sat in silence. The whole time, in his head, he heard that creepy gasping sound she made when she cried. He didn't like to think about the other kids. Would they still have to have parties without him?

After his interview the lady thanked him for talking to her, which Jordan thought was stupid, because he hadn't said anything; he'd only nodded or shook his head a couple times.

Back in his hospital room, Dr. Ali had told him about gonorrhea. Now he knew why he felt so sick all the time, why his knees and hips and elbows, even his wrists and fingers, ached. G-o-n—just one *n*, like "gone"—o-r-r—gotta remember two *r*'s—h-e-a. She told him how people got gonorrhea, but he didn't want to talk about that. And knowing how he got it made him not want to know what it was called. He didn't put the word on his list.

But he did write, *"Child Life."* Dr. Ali and the nurses tried to get him to leave his room. They told him he could go to the Cyber Zone, where there were computers, or to the lounge or the court-yard anytime he wanted; he just had to tell the nurses so they could unhook him from his monitor. He said he didn't want any visitors, and they said they wouldn't make him. He waited to see if they would stick to their word, and it didn't take long to find a catch. All the people at the hospital acted like *they* weren't visitors themselves and bugged him all the time. The nurses kept coming in and asking him if he wanted to play checkers or cards. And these people from Child Life came and tried to get him to go down to the playroom. Please. Did they think he was a baby?

Jordan wrote, *"Day #3: Went to playroom."*

On the third day, the Child Life people *made* him go—he knew eventually someone would make him do something—but it was cooler than he thought. He messed around with Play-Doh and made a cat, a really good one, even if it was green.

The Child Life lady must have told Dr. Bryn what he made, be-cause when Dr. Bryn came for therapy that day, she said, "So I hear you're quite an artist."

Jordan added *"Family picture"* to his list.

Dr. Bryn said, "Today I'd like you to do one thing for me, okay? Then we can do something that you want to do. Which one do you want to do first?"

He looked at her warily, the water sound in his ears.

"I'd like you to draw a picture for me," Dr. Bryn said. "That's what I want."

That was all? He didn't believe her.

"I'd like you to draw a picture of your family."

So Jordan had. He knew what to do. Bryn had given him paper and a pencil, and he'd spent a long time on the drawing. He'd drawn his mom and dad with himself in between them. Everyone smiled. He also drew a cat at his feet, rubbing against his shin. The faces really looked like his mom and dad. Jordan showed it to Bryn.

She'd praised it and talked about it for a long time. At first it was cool; Jordan knew he was good at drawing. Mr. Garcia, his art teacher, told Jordan he was talented. But then Bryn said, "I think you've done a very good job of drawing me what you think your family *should* be, but not what it really is. And I think you've worked very, very hard to do that in your life, not just this drawing. I think I'd be tired if I'd worked that hard for so long."

Jordan stared at her, heart pounding. Then he snatched the drawing from her and wadded it up.

"Why did you do that?"

"You didn't like it."

"I didn't say that. I do like it. I think you're a very good artist." Bryn took the wadded-up paper and smoothed it out with her hands. "May I keep it?"

Jordan shrugged.

She thanked him for doing the picture as she'd asked and said, "Okay. A deal's a deal. Now we'll do something that you want to do. What would you like?"

But Jordan couldn't think of anything. And hanging out with her made him claustrophobic.

Later that day was the first time Dr. Ali told him Sarah Laden wanted to visit him. Mr. Garcia had come, too, and his principal, Ms. Zimmerman, but Jordan wouldn't talk to any of them. That was the day the mail and the packages started to come. He wrote, "*Mail started.*" He asked Wendy how people knew he was here, and Wendy brought Dr. Bryn back to his room. Dr. Bryn showed him an article in the paper about his dad. Dr. Bryn said they had to put it in the news, because Jordan's dad was a fugitive. Fugitive. Like in a movie. Only this wasn't a movie. This was his life. Even though they never said Jordan's name in the article, everyone figured it out and started sending him sweatshirts and crossword puzzles and Silly Putty and a yo-yo. A bunch of cards. The nurses seemed to think the mail would make him happy. Didn't they get it? The mail ruined everything. He thought about what Dr. Bryn had said about his picture. But that made him mad, and he wished he hadn't let her keep it.

There were some cards from his classmates and their parents, saying things like, *"We hope you get well fast"* and *"We hope you're back soon."* He could never go back. Not now.

The letters from his teachers bothered him the most. *"I wish I had known and could have helped you,"* Mr. Garcia's card said. Miss Holt, his own classroom teacher, wrote, *"I'm sorry that I wasn't aware . . ."* blah blah blah. How many times had he asked to go see the nurse? Or to go to the bathroom? Or to sit out in gym? He'd wanted someone to ask him and had been terrified someone would ask.

When he'd freaked out about the scoliosis test, the teachers had called his mom and dad in for a meeting. His parents had shown up looking worried and sad and had spoken to the teachers in quiet voices. Jordan's grades hadn't suffered; it was only his tantrum the teachers worried about. His parents thanked the teachers for bringing it to their attention.

His mom and dad didn't say a word the whole way back to the house, but he didn't like to think about what happened once inside. They'd made it really clear that he was never to draw attention to himself or them ever again. He pushed those memories out of his head. One memory in particular made his eyes sting. What would his mom and dad do *now*? This was way worse than a teacher's meeting. If Jordan was lucky, they'd just kill him.

Jordan looked up at the ceiling. A red helium balloon was starting to shrink and sag in one corner. Sarah Laden had brought that balloon. It was all Sarah's stupid fault that he was here. Dr. Ali said Sarah had taken him to the ER. If it wasn't for her, he'd be dead.

Jordan looked down at his list. What else happened that third day? The days seemed to stretch out forever, and the nights were worse. He couldn't keep track of all the people. He'd forgotten which day he'd met his social worker from the hospital. He also had a case manager from Children's Services, Reece Carmichael. Reece had come a couple of days. And that detective. Kramble. He came almost every day, just to see how Jordan was doing. Jordan should go back and put those visits on his list. But his head ached.

He decided he could go back and add all the visits from people later. For now he would just list the main things that he remembered from each day. He was almost done. He wrote, "*Day #4,*" and wrote, "*New plan.*" He'd started leaving the room a lot, which he knew everyone wanted him to do. He didn't tell them he was exploring all the ways in and out and good places to hide.

The IV stand came along with him no problem, but it was impossible to go outside the room with the cardiac monitor unless a nurse unhooked him. He was chained to the heavy metal box by five wire leads that attached to five different patches on his chest. Each patch had a metal knob, and the leads clamped onto those knobs like tiny metal chip clips. If he wanted to go for a walk, he had to call a nurse. They never seemed to mind unhooking him, but Jordan hated having to ask. He felt like a dog in someone's yard.

He added to the list, "*Dr. Bryn's office. Saw dragon. Broke the angel.*"

That fourth day Dr. Bryn had asked a nurse to unhook Jordan and told him that they were going to her office for their talk, instead of just sitting in Jordan's room. "I have some very cool stuff that I think you'd like. Plus, you need a road trip. Some new scenery."

"A road trip?" Jordan didn't want to leave the hospital. He knew he had to learn to get *out* of the hospital if he needed to, but he panicked at the thought of people seeing him. He never wanted people to look at him again.

"Just a figure of speech," Bryn said, laughing. "It's actually on the same floor, just on the other side of the hospital."

So Jordan wheeled his IV stand along with Bryn. Her Slinky curls bounced when she walked. He couldn't believe how shaky his legs were. Her office wasn't very far away, but Jordan panted and had to wipe sweat from his lip by the time they got there.

Bryn's office walls and ceiling were painted blue with clouds, and there was a painting of a bright yellow-and-orange sun around the light in the middle of the ceiling. Two beanbag chairs and a couch. A table in the middle of the room. Her desk and computer. But what Jordan was most interested in was a shelf along one wall, full of art supplies. He saw Legos, clay, models, beads, all kinds of paper and brushes, pencils, chalk, charcoal, watercolors, oil paint. Along another wall was a shelf holding two dollhouses and a small blue tray full of sand.

"Look around. You can use anything you want."

"What's this?" he asked, pointing to the box of sand. It reminded him of a litter box.

"That's a sand tray." Bryn took it off the shelf and brought it to the table in the middle of the room. She held up a tiny wooden rake. "You can arrange designs in the sand and make scenes using rocks and figures and things. You want to try it?"

He frowned at it. "What's it for?"

"Whatever you want. Just playing."

Yeah, right. Everything he did was supposed to "mean something."

He sat down and dipped the rake in the sand. The sand was thicker than he expected. He pressed down and liked the slight crunching sensation under the rake. He dug a hole, then filled it in. He made a diagonal line from one corner to the other, pushing hard to see how deep he could go before the sand fell in on itself. Then he did another line right beside it, trying to see how lightly he could touch the sand and still leave some kind of visible mark. He looked up, startled at how quickly he'd lost himself. It was kind of hypnotizing.

"Keep going, if you want."

He shook his head. He put the rake down and crossed his arms.

Bryn stood up. "Here, look at all this stuff. Pick some things to use in the sand tray." She opened a cupboard full of shelf after shelf

of miniature figures. On the top shelf were figures of Jesus and angels and Buddhas and saints.

Jordan looked at the saints. "That's St. Francis," he said. "He
protects animals."

"You're right. You know the saints?"

He nodded.

"Are you Catholic?"

He shook his head, then shrugged. "I don't know. We never go
to church or anything." Was that bad? Should he have said that? He
didn't want to make things worse.

"So how'd you learn about the saints?"

"My grandma."

"Tell me about her."

Jordan shook his head.

"Okay. Maybe not today." Bryn always said that, like Jordan was
going to keep coming here forever.

He looked at the figures. The next shelf had all kinds of people.
Lots of different colors and shapes and sizes. Old people. Little kids.
Babies. There was a shelf with every kind of animal. There were
cats. Even one that was black and white like Raja. There were
houses and buildings and rocks and trees and flowers and shells and
colored marbles, and down on the last shelf there were monsters.
Skeletons and vampires and devils.

And a dragon. There were about four dragons, but one was really scary-looking, with fire coming out of its mouth. The fire
looked real. Jordan reached out to touch it. It was smooth and cold
and painted so that he couldn't really tell if it was plastic or ceramic
or what.

"You can use whatever you want to make some kind of picture
or scene in your tray."

"That's all I have to do today?"

Bryn laughed. "Sure. But don't rush it just so you can get away
from me, okay?"

Jordan looked up at the angels. His grandma had told him he had a guardian angel, but it wasn't true. He didn't think his grandma lied to him on purpose. She really thought someone would protect him. She'd be sad if she knew she was wrong. There was one angel in a purple robe that was pretty cool. Its sparkly wings reminded him of a dragonfly, and they rose up out of the angel's shoulders like it was about to take off and fly.

Holding on to his IV stand for balance, he reached and took down the angel.

"You want me to put that on the table?" Bryn asked. He handed it to her. While she did that, he took the black-and-white cat and four red glass marbles. He looked at the dragon but decided not to take it.

He turned around, but he pushed his IV stand too hard and it bashed into the table, jarring the angel that stood waiting for him and knocking it to the floor. One of its wings cracked off right at the angel's back and lay beside it.

Jordan stared at the severed wing lying on the bright blue carpet.

"It's okay. They sometimes break. Don't worry about it."

But looking at the wing made him feel as if someone had reached inside his chest to squeeze his heart. He froze, feeling on the verge of a clue to that day of his plan, balancing on a precipice. One of the hardest vocab words. P-r-e-c-i- . . . *no, stop it. Stay here.* There was something he'd almost remembered. . . . But nothing came to him. Just that weird ringing—like an alarm going off way down the hall. He breathed out slowly.

"Jordan?"

He raised his gaze to Dr. Bryn and blinked.

"You okay? Do you know where you are?"

He frowned at her. Did she think he was stupid?

"You looked like you went somewhere else for a minute. Were you thinking of something? Remembering something?"

He shook his head. Bryn picked up the angel and the wing and asked, "Do you still want this one? Or a different one?"

He didn't answer. He sat at the table in the front of the tray and put the cat and the marbles down beside him. Bryn put the angel and the wing with his other choices and sat across from him.

He took the rake and dipped it in the sand. What should he do? He tried different things—he put a red marble in all four corners and drew a rake line from marble to marble like a frame. He could put the angel in the middle. No, that was boring. He took the marbles out of the tray. He tried different patterns, then finally smoothed all the sand and made straight rake lines from top to bottom on the whole tray. Then he perched the cat in the top right corner of the frame, not really in the sand at all. He looked at Bryn and nodded.

"Could you try to use all the objects you selected?"

He glared. She was making up new rules. He shook his head. Bryn just nodded. "Okay. So this is it. What's the cat's name?"

His heart stuttered over its new extra beat. He shrugged.

"Make one up."

He lifted a shoulder. "Spot."

"Okay, Spot the cat. What's Spot doing?"

"Sitting there."

Bryn laughed. "And what's Spot feeling?"

Jordan paused.

"Is he happy? Sad? Scared?"

"Happy."

"Why?"

"Because . . . everything is smooth and perfect."

Bryn nodded. She cupped her chin in her hands and looked at the tray. "Yes it is. I have a question for you: True or false, you like things to seem smooth and perfect."

Jordan froze again. "You said this was all I had to do."

She nodded. "Just one last question. True or false, that's all."

"I don't know."

"Okay, for a true-or-false question, you have to say 'true' or 'false,'" Bryn teased him. "Saying you don't know is copping out, and you know it."

Jordan rolled the marbles in his palm. "True. Everyone thinks that's true."

"I don't," Bryn said. "But it's okay that you think that. I think it takes a lot of energy and hard work to pretend things are perfect. I think I'd get really exhausted trying to pretend that. Sometimes it takes a lot of guts and bravery to admit that things aren't perfect, that they're not even okay. How would anyone know I needed help if I was always pretending everything was fine?"

Jordan squinted at her. Why would *she* need help? He remembered Mr. Garcia encouraging him to experiment with asymmetry. Mr. Garcia had told Jordan his art would be more interesting if it wasn't so "tidy."

Jordan looked at the sand tray. He shook the marbles like dice and let them fall into the sand. They bounced and left jagged marks on his neat, straight lines. One marble hit the cat and knocked it off the tray.

"Wow," Bryn said. "What's Spot feeling now?"

"I'm tired."

"Tired of what?"

"I don't want to play anymore."

"Okay," Bryn said.

Jordan was surprised she let him off that easy. He liked that she stuck to her word, but it also made him sad, because he didn't really want to go back to his room yet. Bryn took a picture of his sand tray, so he could keep it even after the tray got changed.

Jordan looked at the figures on the table. "What'll you do with that broken angel?"

Bryn tilted her head. "I don't know. Do you want it?"

"No," Jordan said, but he did.

And here it was, his fifth day in the hospital, and he wished he had that wing. He didn't know why, but he remembered that feeling of being on the verge when he looked at it. Maybe today, when he went to Bryn's office, he would ask her for it.

He didn't write "*Day #5*" yet. He closed his sketch pad and walked to his window, pulling his IV stand. They'd unhooked him from his cardiac monitor this morning, so he could wash—finally they let him do it himself—but no one had bothered to hook him back up. He liked feeling that free and hoped maybe he was done with the cardiac monitor for good. He'd dressed in jeans and a school sweatshirt after he washed. He had this weird collection of clothes that people like Dr. Ali and Reece and Kramble had brought him. For some reason they weren't allowed to get any of his clothes from his house yet.

"Hey, sweetie." A voice behind him made his heart jump, and he had to grab the bed rail to stay on his feet. He sucked in breath, wheezing.

It was Wendy. "Sorry. I didn't mean to scare you." She smiled. "More mail for you." She handed him a big cardboard box and a stack of envelopes. "I opened the box for you." Jordan knew they wouldn't let him have scissors or knives. They were all afraid he'd slash his wrists. And maybe he would—he had to do *something* to get out of the mess he'd made.

When she left, he sat on the edge of the bed and peeked into the box. More clothes and a Tupperware container of cookies. It was another package from Sarah Laden. He opened the Tupperware. There were big, puffy sugar cookies iced in bright colors like the kind Danny brought to school for his birthday. Jordan ate one, remembering how Danny had saved two extra ones for them at recess, when everyone else in the class only got one. He opened Sarah's card. It was another picture of a black-and-white cat. This was a cat wearing sunglasses. His skin prickled in goose bumps. Why did they keep sending pictures of his cat? Warning bells went off in his head, like they did whenever he thought of Raja.

Inside the card Sarah had written, *"I hope you're doing better and growing stronger. Please tell Ali if you'd like me to get anything for you. Books? Movies? Any stuff from school? I'm thinking about you. Love, Sarah. P.S. Ali said you needed clothes. I sent you some of Danny's and Nate's old things. I hope you can use them."*

Jordan looked at the box with new interest. He pulled out a few shirts. Sarah had pinned notes to each one, identifying them as Danny's. Danny used to get all red-faced and stuttery when the other boys made fun of Jordan, but now he pretended he didn't see if somebody pushed Jordan in gym. The other boys called Jordan pussy. Wimp. Sissy-boy. The words echoed in the locker room. Even now Danny never said the names out loud. But he didn't go and get the teacher anymore. And he sure didn't cry. Danny may not get good grades, but he was smart enough to know that if he cried, they'd call him a pussy, too. It wouldn't have been too long before Danny started with the names and the shoves himself.

But Jordan wouldn't be there. Because he'd wrecked everything. Oh, man. What was he going to do?

Again Jordan teetered at the edge of a memory. He breathed deep and waited, but the feeling passed. He lifted a faded red-and-blue New York Rangers jersey from the box. Sarah said it had been sent by her older son, Nate.

Jordan knew all about Nate Laden. His mother had gone on and on about Nate's beauty, his body, his look. Jordan had been shocked, because Nate was so old. But before Jordan's dad had said that Nate was *too* old, Jordan had felt a strange mix of hope and surprising jealousy. Then he felt sick to his stomach. Especially since Nate had told Jordan once after a soccer game that Jordan was a "fierce little shit on the field." Nate played hockey, and Jordan's mom had taken Jordan to a bunch of high-school hockey games. Jordan liked that they got to be alone together out of the house, where he didn't have to be on guard. She always made sure Nate saw her there. Jordan got used to seeing Nate search the stands for her, then smile and blush.

Jordan wondered what Nate had thought when he saw the news. And what had Danny thought?

Jordan unpinned Sarah's note, took off his sweatshirt, and pulled on Nate's jersey. It was way too big and hung on him like a dress. He tried to picture himself having a body that filled this shirt, being big and strong, years away from right now.

He gathered up the mail to put in his drawer, but the intercom blurted out some garbled, urgent command, and he dropped it all. He left the cards on the floor. He hated the stupid things that reminded him and triggered the jumping in his chest. They had an intercom at home, because the house was so big.

Thinking of his house made him yank on his IV stand. Time to check out new exit routes. Wendy, at the nurses' station, looked up and said, "Good to see you out and about. Where are you headed?"

"Down to that lounge, with the Xbox." He'd seen it on his walk to Bryn's office.

"Sure. Have fun." He saw Wendy check her watch and write that down. Jordan knew they could see him on cameras, but they wouldn't know what he was up to if he was just looking around the lounge. He walked down the hall on his weak, achy legs, all the nurses greeting him, happy to see him out of his room. Every nerve in his body jangled when he was out of sight of the nurses' station. Jordan was so on alert he figured he could smell his dad coming if he was anywhere in the building. As he walked toward the lounge, he noticed a stairwell and two elevators here at this curve of the hallway. He had just stepped onto the green- and purple-tiled floor of the lounge when a sound paralyzed him.

The sound of water. Bubbling water. He balanced again, right on the edge, and as much as he wanted to be able to remember, he was afraid to fall. He knew that sound.

He took a tentative step past the bookshelf into the lounge. No one sat on any of the purple and green couches. The TV flickered a cartoon with the sound off. He took another step, and there it was.

An aquarium. A huge one with a filter bubbling. Angelfish swam along while smaller, neon yellow fish darted around them. The sound filled Jordan's whole body. He wobbled and caught himself on the arm of a couch. He backed away from the aquarium. He couldn't stay in here. He hated that sound. His heart jumped in some jagged way that made it hard to breathe. He turned around, wanting to run from the sound, but his IV stand caught on some games and videos on the floor. He tried to tip the stand, to lift the wheel over what caught it, and a DVD case popped open, the disk rolling and clattering on the tile.

The disk. Jordan didn't feel his heart jump that time. He felt it stop. The silver disk shone up at him from the tile.

And he remembered.

All sound stopped, except for the bubbling amplified in his ears. The bubbling hurtled him backward in time. Pictures came to him, in mixed-up bits and pieces, but each one led him farther back to what he'd forgotten. His own fingertips on his throat. The stench of the port-o-john. The drumming of the rain on the plastic roof. The green van pulling up in his driveway. Sarah saying, "Get in."

More bubbling. Farther back. The intercom. It was Wednesday night. Wednesday. He was safe on Wednesdays. He could relax and pretend they were a normal family. He was in his room, studying math. The intercom clicked on, and his mom said, "There's somebody here for you." Who? He knew it wasn't Danny. Not anymore. Billy Porter? Billy sucked at math and asked Jordan to help him all the time, even though he wouldn't even sit with Jordan at lunch. Would Billy actually come to Jordan's house just for the math homework? Jordan didn't think anything of it because *it was Wednesday.* Bad things never happened on Wednesdays, so he'd walked downstairs right into it. When he saw the new people, a man and a woman, and the lights set up, he'd even stuttered, "B-but it's W-Wednesday." The couple laughed. His mom and dad laughed. And their laughter broke something in him. Or maybe fixed something in him, because he'd decided not to be "a good, good boy," and he'd fought it, which he hadn't done since those first times. It took all of them to hold him down.

But he didn't fight for long. It never kept the bad things from happening, so there wasn't much point in getting beat up. And so he went away, spelling words, pulling the toughest words from all the vocab tests of the year, sorting them into alphabetical order: A-d-v-e-r-s-e. A-f-f-e-c-t. A-f-f-i-n-i-t-y. A-f-f-i-r-m-a-t-i-o-n. A-l-i-b-i. A-l-l-a-y. A-l-l-e-v-i-a-t-e.

When he returned, vocab words still floating through his dreams, he was in his bed. The house was quiet except for the gurgling of the aquariums downstairs, which he could hear above the hum of heavy rain. He opened his eyes. His mom sat at the edge of his bed. "Hey. How ya doing, cookie?" she whispered.

He lay still. His throat throbbed. His jaw ached. His head felt hollow from the medicine Mom had given him partway through last night. The bee sting of the needle was the only thing that interrupted his vocabulary list—he'd started over at the beginning after that. Mom said the medicine made it "easier," but it actually made it harder for him to concentrate. It made everything slower and thicker and made the room tilt funny if he kept his eyes open. He straightened his bent knees and winced.

Mom touched his forehead and brushed back his hair. Her hand was cool and felt good, but he froze, stomach tightening. She only touched his cheeks and hair, though. "You've got a fever, cookie. Do you feel sick?" He curled up on his side, and she stroked his hair and rubbed his back. "You shouldn't go to school today. I'll call them before I leave." But he wanted to go to school. There was a vocabulary test today.

She got up, and he thought she was going to make the call, but he heard her opening bottles and running water in his bathroom. She came back to his bed with a glass of water and a handful of pills. "Here, c'mon, babe, sit up."

He did, his elbows and hips feeling thick and slow to bend, like old, rusted machine parts. The room went green and wavy for a few seconds. Mom handed him two Tylenol. He moved his heavy tongue and gagged on the familiar, plasticky taste in his mouth. He took the glass and swallowed the pills. "That's for your fever. Now, take this medicine, too." He swallowed four more pills. He wanted to drink more water—every part of his body felt thirsty—but his throat hurt, so he set the glass down.

Mom sat on the bed and hugged him, pulling him against her. He wanted to hug her, with the same longing he wanted more water, but his chest and stomach clenched. "You're one tough cookie, you know that? I'm so proud of you. I love you."

He wriggled free of her embrace and lay back down.

She combed his hair with her fingers.

His skin prickled, and his chest tightened even more. She was sitting here too long.

She kept running her fingers in his hair and said, "Maybe when you feel better, next week, it would be fun for you to invite Danny over after school."

Jordan wasn't sure he'd ever breathe again. He thought he'd solved that. He thought the Danny thing was over and done with.

Mom twirled some of his hair around one finger. "Maybe to swim. Like you used to, after practice. How's that sound?"

Jordan panicked for a second, then remembered how to inhale. "Danny doesn't like me," he whispered. *Danny would never come over by himself anymore.*

Mom rolled her eyes. "Well, then, you need to make him like you. Be nicer to him. God knows he could use some kindness. He's had a rough go of it."

Jordan felt a rush of hatred for Danny Laden. What about *his* life was so rough?

But Mom moved her fingers from his hair to his cheek, and the hatred raced away in shivers. "I need to get you better medicine." She leaned over and held his face in her hands. Her cool hands felt so good on his hot skin, but he clamped his lips shut and turned his head to the side. She let him go. And she stood up. "What sounds good for dinner?" she asked. "Any special requests?"

He shrugged.

She cleared the water glass and rattled more bottles in his bathroom. "How 'bout a milk shake, at least? I'll bring you a strawberry milk shake, and then I'll go get anything else you want. I promise."

Jordan stared at the bathroom door and listened to her voice. Did she go Somewhere Else, too, during the bad things? Just like he did? She must. How else could she be so happy? She brought him a cool washcloth and placed it on his forehead. Then she went downstairs, and as he drifted in and out, he heard her call the school, heard the beep of the microwave, heard her footsteps coming back up the stairs.

Under the covers he pressed his hands against his ribs, trying to stop that awful feeling, like someone forcing him to button up a too-small coat.

"Here, sweetie," she whispered, setting a tray on his nightstand. "Here's some chicken broth and some juice. You need to drink, okay? Drink as much as you can."

He nodded a small, careful nod to keep the washcloth on his forehead.

"Feel better." She leaned over and kissed him on the nose, then left the room.

When he heard her car drive away, he sucked in deep breaths, as if a pillow held over his face had been lifted off. But then, right away, he felt bad and wished she would come back. He should've talked to her. He should've been nice to her. He thought he might cry.

The steaming mug of chicken broth prodded him to sit up and try some; it made him feel better to hold its warmth in his hands. And it soothed his sore throat.

He listened to the aquariums bubble. And the rain. The rain sounded too much like those stupid fish tanks. He wanted to go to school. What would he do if he lay here all day except hear that awful bubbling? At least at school he could think about other things.

He got out of bed, shivering with cold. Stabs of pain shot through his hips with each step he took. He limped into the bathroom and took off his underwear. He wrinkled his nose. He'd bled some. More than usual.

He showered—watching the hot water swirl into the drain. He was too shaky and tired to scrape himself pink the way he usually did. He pulled on clean underwear, jeans, a turtleneck, a sweatshirt, trying to hang on to the heat of the shower. Grabbing his backpack, he shuffled his way downstairs, his joints warming up at last. Yes, he would get to school. He would take the test. Today was gym day. He could skip gym, he bet, since his mom had called to say he was sick. Tomorrow was Friday, so that was art day, and he—

Tomorrow was Friday.

There was a party Friday. He sat down on the bottom step, hugging his backpack. Tomorrow he'd have to do those things all over again.

And that's when he'd had the epiphany. It had been *Wednesday.* He could live with the weekends. He'd even gotten used to them, had figured out how to get through them and move on to the school weeks. But if every car on the drive, every knock on the door, was someone here for him . . . he couldn't do that. He couldn't stay on emergency alert all the time. The alarm had to stop ringing at some point. It had to.

He put his head on his backpack as if it were a pillow. He couldn't do this anymore. Doing what they wanted didn't get him anywhere. Fighting it didn't get him anywhere either. And now it was going to happen *more?* There weren't enough vocabulary words in the world. Not even if he started reading the dictionary.

And he wouldn't be nice to Danny Laden. It was one thing for the other kids to just appear at the parties, but Jordan wasn't going to recruit them himself. R-e-c-r-u-i-t.

He was through. He felt it in the heavy ache of his bones: He would never do those things again. To make him, they would have to kill him first.

He closed his eyes. They wouldn't kill him, though. And they *could* make him; they had before. So . . .

His breath stopped for a moment when the thought popped into his head. He opened his eyes. As much as it made his heart race, he knew it was the answer. They wouldn't kill him. But *he* could.

He lifted his head. When he fought back, it was usually stupid; they laughed at him. They wouldn't laugh at *this,* though.

He walked into his parents' bedroom, trying not to look at the king-size bed. He opened the middle drawer of the dresser as he'd watched his mother do once. He lifted the false bottom beneath the stack of sweaters, and there was everything he needed. He hadn't really paid attention to what she was doing at the time, mostly because he'd been spelling words, but his brain had stored it. He selected a vial of Dilaudid along with a needle and syringe. She usually gave him only a little bit from the vial. What if he used the whole vial? There were also more packets of pills like the ones up in his bathroom. He took those out, too. He would swallow them all, just in case. His heart beat too fast for his breath to keep up.

He started to unwrap the needle from its plastic, then stopped. Maybe he was just being stupid, but it didn't feel like it would be enough just to die.

He wanted someone, somewhere, to know why.

But that meant he couldn't die here, in this house.

He pocketed the vial and the needle and the pills. He walked into the living room, past all those stupid fish he hated, and opened the closet. He reached behind a shelf of Disney movies, bringing out a handful of CDs.

Kneeling there, he shuffled the disks in his hands. He knew in detail what had happened on each of the penned dates. Each party was as separate and distinct to him as a birthday or Christmas. No matter how many words he spelled, he could never get them to fade or blur together.

One was worse than all the others, though. He wasn't sure he wanted to take it with him. He'd tried hard to pretend it had never happened, that day or any other, with or without the cameras. He thought about what it would mean if anyone saw it, and he almost chickened out. But he'd be dead, right? She's the one who'd be ashamed, not him. He slid the disks into an envelope lying on the closet floor and put it in his backpack. He put on his parka and vowed he was never coming back when he limped out that door.

Rain pelted him. The driveway looked endless. He didn't know how far he'd try to go or where might be safe to carry out his plan, when Sarah pulled up beside him. Of all the people, it had to be Danny's mom. Jordan wanted to scream at her, to warn her, but he was too tired. When he was dead and gone, what happened to Danny would not be his problem.

And Sarah had insisted, "Get in."

Jordan?"

Jordan gasped. He was on one of the couches of the hospital lounge, curled on his side. Wendy crouched beside him. "What's going on, sweetheart? Are you all right?"

He jerked himself upright. "I fell asleep."

Wendy raised her eyebrows, and Jordan knew she didn't believe him. "I think we need to call a doctor."

He shrugged off her help and wheeled his IV stand back to his room. He shut his door, even though he knew he wasn't supposed to. He jerked his IV bag free from the stand. He crawled under the bed and balled himself up, which hurt, but the pain felt good and familiar. Dr. Ali'd said he had no business being on an unsterile floor, warning about staph infections that could kill him. Good. He wanted one. Maybe this time they'd let him die.

His mail littered the floor where he'd dropped it. He reached out and scooped it under the bed, sorting through his cards until he found Sarah Laden's latest one. He pictured her pale skin and serious, dark eyes. The way she'd touched his forehead. The scent of shampoo from her rain-drenched black hair as she carried him into the hospital. And he remembered the backpack on the floor of her van. She must be the one who gave it to the police. So his plan had worked, in a way. Except that he was still here. He'd never made a backup plan. He'd never considered that he might not die.

CHAPTER TEN

Sarah

Sarah stood in the kitchen making dinner for her kids and wishing she could go anywhere but where she had to go in a few minutes. All parents with a child in the community schools had received a letter inviting them to attend an emergency meeting in the high-school gym.

Half of Sarah felt that the meeting would only fan the fire of hysteria that had taken hold of Oakhaven. What good would come of gathering all the panicked, outraged people into one place to feed off one another's anxiety and guilt? Sarah would rather mop the entire gym on her hands and knees than listen to more of the inane talk she'd endured all weekend. But the other half of her feared not being a part of that. She needed to hear what was said. She hated that she cared what might be said of her if she didn't go. Everyone knew she'd been Courtney's closest friend.

Been. Sarah still had the stunned feeling of betrayal. She'd been lied to. It felt humiliating and awful, as if Courtney had had an affair with Roy behind Sarah's back. Sarah felt raw and exposed when she went out.

Debbie Nielson had called today and told Sarah that she'd decided to go with a different caterer for her daughter's wedding. Sarah had been gracious and professional, but a cold knot formed in her stomach. The timing seemed so obvious that Sarah had almost blurted to Debbie, "I didn't know! I had no idea what was happening!" Was Debbie thinking what Sarah herself continuously wondered: *How could you know her for four years and never pick up a clue?*

Nothing Debbie said had actually indicated that, but it was hard to shake the feeling of being accused. Sarah tried to clear her mind and focus on slicing scallions and tomatoes.

The *Dayton Daily News* had run a profile of both Mark and Courtney today, which began on the front page and continued in a full-page spread inside. The feature wasn't *just* about them but also about the other two couples, and three individuals, involved in the pornography "club." The *Columbus Dispatch* and the *Cincinnati Enquirer* ran their own versions, too, and all three, as well as *People* magazine and several other bigger city papers, had called to invite Sarah to comment. After politely declining the first two requests, Sarah had let the answering machine get all the calls. She'd even instructed Nate not to answer the phone. She came home from catering a corporate lunch today and deleted six more requests.

Sarah hadn't been prepared for the fact that this was a *national* story—a pornography ring of parents abusing and sharing their own children.

While she was out today, she'd bought all the newspapers and had pored over every word that dealt with the Kendricks, trying to patch together this new information into any semblance of recognition of the people she'd known.

Sarah learned that Courtney's father had had sex with both Courtney and her brother, Jordan. He also made them have sex with each other.

Sarah exhaled when she read that. There was nothing to do with that information but mourn.

Courtney's brother, Jordan Mayhew, had disclosed the abuse to a guidance counselor in high school, but Courtney and the mother denied it all. The community rallied around the dad; he was a respected and beloved pediatrician in a small town. The brother ended up looking like a liar and an idiot. He was only seventeen, but he left as soon as he graduated. The brother said that their mother knew about the abuse and did nothing to stop it. Jordan Mayhew tried to stay in touch with Courtney, but they did not see each other for years. Courtney contacted him when their mother died three years ago, of cancer—that much was true after all—but Jordan Mayhew would not attend his mother's funeral.

So although her mother really did die as Courtney told Sarah, the circumstances surrounding her father's death were quite different. He didn't die when she was a teenager but when she was in her late twenties—already married, already with a baby. Two girls who were patients of Courtney's father accused him of molesting them. He was under investigation for "sexual misconduct" when he hung himself.

Sarah felt as if someone had filled her limbs with ice water.

Mark appeared to be clean on paper—nothing in any records, no previous charges. He'd been fingerprinted for his job, and he was not a registered sex offender. When the story broke in his hometown, though, sure enough, some kids—in college now—that Mark used to baby-sit came forward and said that he raped them. Mark baby-sat frequently when he was in high school. He had been a polite, straight-A student in student government, tennis, and debate. Nobody had recognized, until this recent discovery, that he never hung around other kids his age outside of school activities, that he was a little too eager to be with children. One of Mark's victims—a Robert Winston, who boldly gave his name and allowed himself to be photographed, "Because I didn't do anything wrong and have nothing to be ashamed of"—told the reporter that he *did* tell the truth about Mark when it happened, but his mother didn't believe him. A classmate, who wouldn't give his own name, said of Winston, "He was always in trouble. His dad was never around, and his mom worked two jobs. Everybody just thought he made up the

KATRINA KITTLE

story to get attention. He lied all the time." Winston replied, "I did lie. But I lied to get myself *out* of trouble, not to get myself in it. Why the hell would a kid make up something like that? Everyone hated me for it."

Mark and Courtney did meet in college, during Courtney's undergraduate years. For a service project, their respective fraternity and sorority had volunteered time with a local Head Start program. Mark and Courtney spearheaded a Big Brother/Big Sister–type program.

Sarah's skin tingled.

Reporters had found a former neighbor of Courtney's mother who said that Courtney's son—they didn't use Jordan's name, although what difference that made at this point was lost on Sarah—used to stay with his grandmother for long periods of time. According to the neighbor, Jordan had told his grandmother he was being abused, and even though the grandmother hadn't protected her own kids, for some reason she tried to protect her grandson. At one point she tried to get custody of Jordan, but Mark and Courtney fought it. Shortly into the investigation, the grandmother was diagnosed with advanced breast cancer that turned out to be terminal. During her illness the investigation was dropped.

There were high-school graduation pictures of Mark and Courtney. There was their wedding photo, where they looked so . . . wholesome and naive and genuinely happy. There was a photo of Courtney, in scrubs, beaming with a newborn in her arms, a photo voluntarily given to the paper by the newborn's grateful mother. The article was also full of quotes from people supporting both Mark and Courtney, people who still clung to the belief that *this couldn't be true.*

But they didn't know. They didn't know what Sarah knew about the gonorrhea and the hospital's missing antibiotics and Dilaudid. And that's why Sarah had refused to talk to reporters. She wasn't ready to condemn Courtney yet, at least not publicly. After all she and Courtney had been through, she felt she owed it to her to speak

142

to her in private first. But the very thought paralyzed Sarah. What on earth would she *say* to Courtney? Where would one begin? Sarah's eyes stung with tears for the third time that day, but she blinked them back. She feared she might never stop if she allowed herself to give in to them.

Courtney had been quoted in the article. She'd also refused to speak to reporters, on the advice of her attorney, except to say that she was innocent and she desperately missed her son and wished she could be there to support him at this horrible time.

Sarah searched the articles for Kramble's name but found no mention of him.

God, she didn't want to go to this meeting at the high school. What would she do if she started to cry again? She felt fragile and barely held together, and the thought of going out in public in that state made her wary.

She scraped the scallions and tomatoes into the salad.

Nate walked into the kitchen. "What are we having?"

"Salad with grilled salmon."

"Sweet." He peered into the oven. Sarah felt grateful beyond words for this small compliment. Not even a compliment. Just not a condemnation for once.

"Isn't the meeting at seven?" Nate asked.

"Yeah."

"You're gonna be late."

Sarah glanced at the clock. It was 6:50. She was in no hurry to get there, and she certainly didn't want to be early and have to make small talk with anyone. Gwinn had called and offered to pick Sarah up, but Sarah had declined, needing to keep the option of not going at all, and if she did go, of leaving whenever she liked.

Nate opened the oven. "The salmon's almost done." He poked a fillet with a fork. "You want me to finish? Just crumble it on top of these salads, right?"

"That would be a huge help. You sure you don't mind?"

"I offered didn't I?"

"Right. Well, thank you." Was this because she'd told him he could drive again? That was one of her birthday gifts yesterday. She grabbed her purse and called up the stairs, "Danny! I'm leaving. Nate's finishing dinner for you. It's almost ready."

Danny appeared at the top of the stairs. "Nate's making dinner?" He looked skeptical.

"He's just doing the finishing touches. I shouldn't be gone too long, okay? I've got my cell phone, so call if you need anything."

Once in the van, Sarah peeked at herself in the rearview mirror and tried to hand-comb her hair into something halfway respectable. She applied a fresh coat of lipstick before she backed out of the drive and headed to the school.

The high-school parking lot overflowed with cars, and Sarah circled twice before she gave up and parked on a residential street a block away. It was 7:10 as she jogged into the school's front yard, and she was not alone; a steady stream still came from every direction. At the steps Sarah ran into Libby Carlisle, a funny, talented veterinarian, the mother of a girl in the grade below Danny's. Sarah used to take Potter to Libby's clinic. Libby was now heavily pregnant, and Sarah knew that she was a patient of Courtney's.

"Need a hand?" Sarah asked, offering her arm.

"Oh, my God. Don't mind if I do," Libby said, laughing. She held Sarah's elbow, and together they began to climb the front steps of the school. "Where are the banisters and handrails? It's not that I can't do it; I just have no damn balance. I feel like Humpty Dumpty! And don't say it—I know I look like him, too."

"Not at all," Sarah said.

"That's bullshit, and you know it."

Sarah laughed. "When are you due? It's getting close, right?"

"In three days."

"Oh."

Libby stopped, panting. "No kidding: 'Oh.' 'Oh, shit,' is more like it. What am I going to do without her?"

Sarah knew that Libby meant Courtney. Before Sarah could

think of something encouraging to say, Libby went on, "She called to check on me."

"Courtney?"

Libby nodded. Sarah was shocked. Courtney hadn't called *her*.

"She was great. She gave me advice, a pep talk, and some referrals until she's out. I'm so damn furious. Even if she's out, she won't be allowed at the hospital. Can you believe that? I'm willing to go to the damn *jail* for her to deliver this baby. Help me think of a crime I can commit."

Before stepping into the gym, Sarah asked, "Even . . . even with the accusations, you still want her as your doctor?"

Libby looked at Sarah as if she were insane. "Of course I do. Why wouldn't I? There's no way she was involved in this. She's going to get crucified, though, because even if her name is cleared, she'll be branded forever as a bad mother for not knowing it was going on. It's the curse of all us working moms, Sarah. You know that."

Libby spoke with such certainty that Sarah envied her. And although she wanted to hear people defend Courtney, she found herself wanting to protect Libby. But Libby thanked her for the help and waddled through the door.

A wall of heat smacked Sarah in the face as she followed Libby into the gym, the air heavy with human humidity and tension. She looked for a seat but saw no empty chairs. She made eye contact with Carlotta Imparato, who looked quickly away. Goose bumps rippled over Sarah's scalp. She'd made a mistake by being rude to Carlotta at the market Saturday.

Feedback whined as someone turned on a mike.

Sarah headed for the back of the gym. She passed Gwinn, who waved and pointed to the empty seat beside her that she'd saved. Sarah saw Libby still searching for a seat, though, so she directed Libby to the chair instead. Libby mouthed a thank-you.

Sarah found a spot against the back wall, standing shoulder to shoulder with other parents. The wall was cool but clammy behind her. She pressed her palms to it and tried to calm her racing heart.

The superintendent started the meeting with hollow phrases of comfort for this "difficult, challenging" crisis in which they found themselves. The audience fell quiet, but they didn't really listen yet. They leaned together, whispering, and Sarah appreciated her vantage point. She couldn't see faces, but she could watch body language. Husbands and wives sat close, postures stiff and coiled. Fury seethed from the rigid spines and crossed arms. Sarah was angry, too, but guarded her anger. It felt too frightening, too out of control, to show it to anyone else. It felt like an admission, and it was terrifying to admit she'd been so wrong. No one else seemed to have the same hesitation, though. But because Mark and Courtney weren't there to bear the brunt of that wrath, the crowd seemed poised to unleash it on those who were. Sarah's heart went out to the scheduled speakers. She scanned the row of seated people on the small stage, and something shifted in her chest when she recognized Detective Kramble.

Seeing him there made her feel not so alone. The superintendent's voice became background noise as Sarah studied Kramble. He sat, too large for his folding chair, with his elbows on his knees, leaning forward as if enthralled by the superintendent's comments. Kramble had taken off his jacket, draped it on the back of his chair, but even so, Sarah saw the sweat stains darkening his light blue shirt. She felt bad for him.

She jumped when a man in the audience stood and shouted, "What are you going to do about this?" interrupting the superintendent. Sarah looked to Kramble, expecting him to be angry, but Kramble nodded at the man, his expression one of sympathy.

The superintendent stammered, then turned the microphone over to the Oakhaven chief of police, who read a statement that outlined the case thus far—information the parents already knew. Mark Kendrick was still at large, but Courtney was being held. A bail hearing would take place soon. They were not able to discuss details of the case but wanted to reassure everyone that all of the children in the pornography *had* been identified.

A school counselor spoke next, a gentle woman with a hypnotizing, lullaby voice. She also stressed that all of the abused children in this case had been identified. The Oakhaven schools had been swamped with hundreds of calls from parents wanting to know if their children could have been abused. The counselor wanted to educate parents about symptoms that were common in abused children. She read a list to the gathered crowd: nightmares, eating problems, fear of going to school or to any specific extracurricular activity, fear of separating from a parent, crying, broad changes in personality, excessive masturbation, or an increased desire to talk or ask questions about sex or sexuality. By the time she'd finished rattling off the list, the audience was agitated to the edge of hysteria.

Kramble watched the counselor, his expression a combination of sorrow and disappointment. When he finally stood to take the podium, Sarah found herself rooting for him. Those sweat stains embarrassed her on his behalf, but his composure impressed her. He set his notes on the podium and slowly and deliberately rolled up his sleeves before he spoke. His tall, imposing presence and his assured movement made the crowd shut up and listen.

He hunched over to talk into the mike. "First of all," he said, without introducing himself, "there are many *other* reasons any of those symptoms might occur in our children, *including*"—he paused a moment to stress his point—"including the attention being devoted to this case." Sarah willed him to adjust the mike and stand up straight, but instead he draped himself over the podium and said, "People are talking about what happened. They're talking about sex acts that even consenting adults don't normally discuss in public. Kids hear those conversations, they read the papers, they see the news, and they're being exposed to confusing and stimulating sexual information." He opened his arms. "Come on. The daily paper lately has been reading like soft-core porn!"

A few people laughed, and a communal exhalation flowed through the room. Sarah released a breath she hadn't realized she'd been holding.

"The purpose of this meeting," Kramble said, "was not to alarm you and send you home full of fear but to educate you. To reassure you."

And here, finally, he introduced himself. Sarah learned he'd worked in child abuse for fifteen years, specifically in child sexual abuse for the last ten.

"I know, nobody likes to think that sexual abuse of children happens in a 'nice' neighborhood like this."

Sarah actually saw some people nod.

"No one likes to think about child sexual abuse at all. It's frightening. It's disgusting. It's not discussed in polite society."

A murmur rippled through the gym.

"But one in four girls and one in six boys are sexually abused before their eighteenth birthdays. That's a lot of children. A *lot*."

Sarah processed these statistics with horror.

Kramble went on, "Sixty-seven percent of the victims of *all* reported sexual assaults are children. You can check those statistics through the Department of Justice or the National Center for Missing and Exploited Children or any number of other organizations. The point I'm trying to make is that child sexual abuse is *not* unusual. It's a common problem, kept common by silence. It's not pretty, it makes us uncomfortable, so we don't talk about it, therefore allowing it to happen." He paused. "Now, I imagine, the hardest thing for you to accept is not that these crimes happened here but that none of us suspected them."

People nodded again. Sarah thought Kramble was smart to use "we" and "us." He made everyone in the room breathe again.

"We want to keep our children safe, so we tell them to look out for bad touches from strangers," Kramble said. "In our worst fears, we picture that 'dirty old man' or 'crazed monster,' but most child victims are sexually abused by someone they know and trust. Most successful child molesters are attractive, white, upper-class, educated people who violate every common preconception about the nature of a sex offender. Sexual predators only rarely sneak into our houses in the middle of the night. Those cases make the national headlines *because of* their rarity. Most of the time we invite them in through our front doors. We give them permission to coach, to teach, to befriend our kids, because we don't recognize them as predators. We think sex offenders are monsters, and surely *we* would recognize a monster, right? Except for the fact that they enjoy having sex with children, child abusers look and act pretty much the same as everybody else. They have jobs and families, they're liked by their coworkers and neighbors, the sort of people whose friends will say, 'It can't be true. I know those people. They're nice people.'"

A collective moan rose from the gym.

"Researchers have spent lifetimes, and I've spent years, searching for the profile of a typical child molester, but we've concluded that there simply isn't any such thing."

Sarah felt the dissatisfaction. No one wanted this to be true.

A woman in the back row, only a yard away from Sarah, stood up and asked, "But isn't it true that abusers were all abused as kids? That it's a cycle? Isn't that a profile?"

Kramble did his patient nod, the nod that Sarah realized told people, *I'm listening to you. Your concern has been heard.* "You're absolutely right, that *some,* not all, sex offenders were abused themselves as children. But you need to know that the high number of molesters reported to be former victims comes mostly from the *self-reports* of arrested molesters. These people are masters at manipulation. The offender who claims he was a victim himself gets more empathy. This has become strangely comforting to some people—it gives some kind of motivation to the offenders and lets us feel bad for them. If offenders are just victims, too, then we don't have to face the reality of the cruelty, the fact that there are people out there who prey on others for reasons we simply don't understand—because they *like* to, because they can."

The woman who had asked the question still stood. An awkward silence fell.

Kramble cleared his throat. "*But* even in the cases where there is evidence that the offenders were abused themselves, the offenders' methods and modes of operation vary widely. And it is important to note that not all people who were abused as children grow up to perpetuate abuse."

Goose bumps prickled across Sarah's spine. Had anyone else noticed that he touched his own chest as he said "not all people who were abused as children"? Is *that* why he was so passionate about this work?

"It is *not* a cycle that has to continue," he said. "Not at all."

And with that he moved into what these concerned parents could do now, outlining helpful ways to discuss the situation with their kids without alarming them or asking suggestive, leading questions, and how to arm and educate their children to prevent abuse.

He took questions from the crowd, and Sarah leaned against the wall and wished she could sit down; her legs quivered. It was so damn hot. The man to her right wore too much cologne, and in the heat the thick scent made her nauseous.

No one mentioned Jordan, and Sarah knew that people wanted to "protect his privacy," but it felt wrong not to speak of him, as if they were denying what had happened to a child they knew. Looking back, there were clues that seemed to have neon arrows pointing to them, but as each clue had presented itself, Sarah had simply noted its strangeness and then dismissed it. Like the way Jordan seemed to live inside his own head, muttering those odd statements: *"I wish I were an angel."* Was it just the setting, the little girls in their angel costumes, that made Sarah not take that statement for the obvious suicide wish it now seemed? And once at school, while Sarah stood with some kids waiting for their rides, Jordan had said, "I don't want to go home." When Sarah had asked, "How come?" he had at first looked startled, then shrugged. Sarah had never pursued it.

She wiped the sweat off her neck and swallowed. The cologne clogged her head. She angled her body to the left, but the woman on that side had had a few cocktails, and the alcohol fumes reminded Sarah that she hadn't eaten. White sparkles danced at the edges of her vision.

Kramble took more questions, still huddled over the podium like some giant, with his sweat stains spreading. Sweat trickled down Sarah's own sides, between her breasts. She pulled her shirt away from her skin and blinked hard against the white sparkles.

"Damn, it's hot," Cologne Man said.

Sarah nodded. The movement made her dizzy. She sagged against the wall.

Carlotta Imparato stood and asked, "Why didn't Jordan ever tell anyone?"

There. Someone had said his name. Just like at the market, Carlotta sounded so accusing. This abuse had been going on for years. Did Carlotta think a kid in elementary school was supposed to be brave and together enough to go make a police report against his own mom and dad?

Kramble said the same thing, but with much more tact. "I can't discuss details of this case in particular, but I can tell you that it is common for a child not to tell. The National Center for Missing and Exploited Children actually has an ad slogan that goes, 'The sound a child makes when sexually assaulted is often silence.' Kids freeze when they're faced with something they can't understand. A young child is not going to know how to understand or explain a sex act. He'll think an adult he loves wouldn't do anything wrong. And imagine the additional confusion when a child is abused by his own parents. It's a rare kid who will tell his mother and father no. Would *your* kids say no to you? Haven't you raised them to respect your authority even if they have doubts or complaints about what you ask? It's hard for us to understand, but in most cases of incest, the kids don't *want* their parents to be punished or put in jail. All they want is for the sex to stop."

People shook their heads, as if in disbelief. Sarah didn't understand how the crowd could seem as angry at Jordan as they did at

Mark and Courtney. She leaned her spinning head against the wall and prayed for the meeting to end.

But the questions went on and on.

Janet Porter stood up. "The paper this morning said that Courtney might get off scot-free if she pleads insanity."

Kramble sighed, his exhalation amplified through the crowded room. "I can't discuss details of this case. It's an ongoing investigation."

Another man in the auditorium stood up to say, "It wasn't insanity. The paper said that since Courtney was the victim of sexual abuse, she may not have the capacity to know that her own behavior was bad for kids."

A woman in the back row stood and shouted, "How can you not know it's bad to have sex with a fourth-grader?"

Libby Carlisle hauled her giant-bellied self up from her chair and called out, "Courtney's not in the movies, though."

The man said, "She probably filmed it. She had that video camera everywhere she went!"

Too much outrage boiled in the room, and it needed a target. Instead of questions, people began standing simply to spout off. One man claimed that if he saw Mark Kendrick anywhere, he planned to shoot him. Another woman said she hoped they both got the electric chair, only to have ten other people leap up with "better" ideas: one of which was that they should be gang-raped and the video distributed for all to see.

The white sparkles crowded into Sarah's vision. She left her spot on the wall and weaved toward the exit, the room going wavy, the white sparkles leaving only a small tunnel through which she could see. She fumbled through the crowd, terrified she'd faint before she made it outside. Her legs seemed to dissolve with each step, and the voices blurred into one roar. She flung open the same doors she'd entered through with too much force, and the bang rang out like a gunshot. She stumbled outside and gulped in the fresh air as if it were cold water. She half sat, half fell onto a step and put her head between her knees.

Gang-raped. Educated people, people with children, had suggested that. How would that help Jordan or those other kids?

Sarah breathed in shallow pants. Sweat soaked her clothes; she was as drenched as the day she'd hauled Jordan out of the port-o-john. The breeze raised truth bumps on her wet skin. She remembered Jordan being seriously injured at a soccer game, knocked down in a tumble of arms and legs. Someone's cleats had raked his thigh open badly enough to require eight stitches. He didn't cry or show any signs of pain. Sarah even remembered the odd way he'd said, "There's blood on my leg," instead of, "I'm bleeding," as if he were totally removed from the injury and the leg in question. How much training did that take?

Sarah kept her head down, concentrated on her breathing. The white sparkles dimmed, and she looked at the moss in the cracks of the cement steps between her feet. If only she'd known. Every part of her ached to go back in time to rescue that strange little boy.

The doors clunked open once behind her, then twice, and voices spilled down the stairs. The meeting must have ended. She knew she should stand up and go home—God knows she didn't want to have to speak to anyone—but she felt incapable of moving just yet.

Someone patted her back. "Are you okay, sweetie?" She looked up to see Gwinn Whitacre and Libby Carlisle standing there.

Sarah tried to smile. "I got too hot. I'll be fine. Thanks."

It took several more rounds of "Are you sure?" and "Yes, thanks, really," before Libby and Gwinn finally went on their way, Gwinn looking reluctant and concerned. Sarah made a mental note to send a thank-you note, or a pie, or something. She felt desperate to hang on to the few loyal friends she had. Sarah waved as Gwinn looked back once more.

"Sarah Laden?" That steady voice made her look up again. Robert Kramble stood beside her. "Are you okay? I saw you run out."

He saw her? In the back of the gym? "I . . . I think I almost fainted."

"Wait here," he said, and turned to fight his way upstream through the exiting throng. His authoritative tone made Sarah want to get up and leave. He couldn't just boss her around. But she put her head back down between her knees. She imagined herself invisible, floating above the crowd and its savage, ugly words.

"Here, Sarah." Kramble's voice returned. She lifted her head, and he offered her a cold Sprite. Sarah rubbed the can over her face and neck before popping it open and taking a swallow.

He handed her a wet paper towel. She set the Sprite down and pressed the towel to her cheek. The swarm of people parted around them on both sides.

Kramble sat beside her, his jacket over one arm. His sweat—which she had expected to stink—was almost pleasant, with a cilantro-like edge. The hair at his temples curled with dampness. Sarah lifted her own hair off her neck and placed the paper towel there. "Thank you," she said. She rubbed her face.

"What happened to your hand?" Kramble asked.

Sarah pulled her hands from her face and stared at her palms, confused. He took her left hand and turned it over, pointing to the tiny scab and the blue bruise, now spread to the size of a quarter.

"Oh. A bird," she said. "Defending its nest."

He nodded and, to her relief, asked no more questions about it.

Sarah spread the fingers of her left hand wide and stared at it. Her hand went wavy, as the gym had moments ago. The white sparkles threatened to return as she remembered. "Oh, my God," she whispered.

"What?"

"I just remembered. . . ." And she told him how two years ago, when Danny and Jordan were in the third grade, she volunteered in class during an art project. The kids were writing "I am" poems, describing themselves using similes and metaphors, and were to illustrate their poems with their own actual-size silhouettes, which

Sarah and another mom traced onto big sheets of paper. They had the kids lie down and traced their outlines from head to toe. Jordan had refused. He'd said to Sarah, "I don't want to draw my body," and later had said in that spooky way he had of talking to no one in particular, "I hate bodies."

Carlotta and her husband walked past Sarah and Kramble, down the stairs. Carlotta stared over her shoulder at Sarah talking to the cop.

Kramble followed Sarah's gaze, then asked, "So did he ever do the drawing?"

Sarah nodded and wiped her eyes with the back of her hand. Kramble fumbled in his jacket and handed her a white cotton handkerchief. She stared a moment. Who used those anymore? She took it and patted her face. "Oh, God." She sighed. "I was so exasperated with him. All the other kids were so into it. Some of the poems were great. Hadley—you know, the girl with the bike?—her poem started with 'I am a rainy day with a smile,' and she drew herself with raindrops dripping down out of her braids."

Kramble grinned.

"And my son Danny, he wrote 'I am black, a storm cloud,' and he filled his body in with lightning streaks. See, this was just after . . . I mean, this was . . ."

"Your husband had just died," Kramble said. "Danny was angry."

Sarah nodded, new tears spilling down her face. Damn it, why was she being such a baby? She touched Roy's wedding ring on its chain around her neck and pressed it against her breastbone. "The poem and the picture actually helped us talk about how angry we were that we lost him." Kramble waited while she dabbed her eyes again and finally gave in and blew her nose on the handkerchief. "But Jordan . . . he finally let me trace him when he saw me trace a girl standing up. This girl had on a short skirt and didn't want to lie down, so I taped the paper to the wall and traced her that way. And I saw him watching and asked if that would be okay, and he let me. But then"—her voice rose too high; she couldn't control it—"once he had his outline, he filled in the entire body with handprints of red paint. No face, no clothes, just a body filled with handprints."

She stared at her left hand again. "He *did* tell us. He told us over and over again. And we were too stupid to see it. I let this happen. I—"

"Shh," Kramble said. He shifted to face her and reached, as if to take her hand, but pulled back. "You'd just lost a husband. You had two children of your own to look after. This is not your fault."

She had wanted him to say that, but the words were not the comfort she expected. "Why do you do this?" she asked.

He cocked his head. "Do what?"

"This work. Sex abuse. How can you stand it?"

He faced forward again, looking out at the schoolyard. "I *can't* stand it," he said, as if that were the answer.

They sat in silence a moment. Most of the crowd had gone, and the clatter of folding chairs being stacked echoed from the gym behind them.

"I was around Jordan so often," she said. "And if I'd only . . . I don't know, if I'd only—"

"Only what? Name one thing you could have done, should have done."

"Had a fucking clue," Sarah snapped.

To her surprise, Kramble laughed, revealing that crooked front tooth.

"No, I mean it. All these signs."

"They only seem like signs after the fact."

"How do you think they found each other?"

"You mean the Kendricks?" Sarah's abrupt changes of subject did not seem to ruffle him; it made her wonder if she could be bold enough to ask him what had happened to *him*.

Sarah nodded.

"I'm sure you read the papers."

Sarah stared across the schoolyard, remembering that photo of Mark and Courtney in college, arms around that beaming little girl.

The breeze chilled the sweat on Sarah's neck. She shivered. Kramble picked up his jacket, and for a split second Sarah thought he was going to offer it to her, but he took a pack of cigarettes from the pocket instead.

She used to smoke in college, until she learned that smoking numbed one's taste buds, which seemed detrimental to a chef. Not to mention she'd married a doctor who fanatically practiced what he preached. But she recalled how lovely a cigarette could be as one lingered after a fine meal and dessert. She watched Kramble light up and enjoyed the casual, familiar gestures. She almost asked for one but didn't. The nicotine would make her dizzy.

Sarah pulled the paper towel—still damp but now warm—from under her hair. A teenager rode by on a bike and glanced at them. Sarah realized she and Kramble looked like a couple, idling here on the steps after everyone was gone.

She folded the paper towel into a square as she asked, "But . . . how on earth did they discover that they have this . . . this *thing* in common?"

He exhaled smoke in an angry rush. "We've seen that happen over and over again. It could take *us* weeks, even months, to diagnose a man as an incestuous father, but a female child molester can go out and find herself a child-molester husband like *that*"—he flicked his ash. "It's as if they have letters painted on their foreheads that are invisible to everyone else."

Sarah shook her head, trying to imagine it. "I mean, how does it first come up? What kind of offhand comment or . . . I don't know what . . . could offer a hint? It boggles my mind."

Kramble shrugged. "It happens. Think about it. There's always a connection, some common interest. I mean, how did you meet *your* husband?"

Sarah blinked. "In . . . in college."

"But how did you *meet* him, really, start a *relationship* with him?"

She thought a moment. "We lived across the hall from each other, in this dingy apartment building. This was when I was at the CIA."

She saw his startled look and laughed. "That's the Culinary Institute of America."

He chuckled.

"Anyway, we said hi and stuff, and I thought he was cute; we'd talk if we ran into each other on the stairs or doing laundry in the basement, stuff like that." As the words left her mouth, it was as if each one weighed a ton, leaving her lighter and lighter the more she talked. "But . . . oh, my God, you're right. There was a connection, a . . . a recognition of something in common: in December he noticed my menorah. My parents had sent it to me, and I was feeling homesick, and I put it in my front window and lit the first candle. And he told me later he'd been wanting to ask me out, and when he saw that, he bought some challah and some wine and knocked on my door. And it was funny, because I happened to be baking my *own* challah right then, and I invited him in, and we tasted them both. And the stuff he'd bought was horrible, practically inedible . . . and mine, well, mine was *really* good. And it started snowing, this really pretty snowfall, and we went for a walk in the snow with the bottle of wine he'd brought. We kept passing it back and forth, hiding it under our coats, and we tried to feed the store-bought challah to some ducks, but they wouldn't eat it either. . . ." She trailed off and didn't tell Kramble how she made Roy dinner that very night, and they became lovers before they ever ate the meal. How Sarah's butt and the backs of her thighs had been coated in flour from the kitchen counter. How so often their lovemaking revolved around food.

"That's a great story," Kramble said.

Sarah blushed. "What about you? Are you married?" He wore no ring.

He shook his head but, after another exhalation of smoke, said, "Divorced."

"Because of this job?"

He seemed to consider that. "No. Not really. But that's a convenient excuse."

"Do you have any kids?"

His long-lashed eyes darkened, and he suddenly looked tired. "No."

Sarah yearned to ask him. To find out if he'd been abused, if that's what drew him to this work. But she felt awkward, sitting here so close to this cilantro-scented stranger in the deepening dusk. Or maybe she felt awkward because she realized she *liked* sitting with him. "I . . . I should get home. Thank you, so much, for this." She gathered the Sprite, the wadded lump of paper towel, and the hand-kerchief and stood.

Kramble stood, too, took the Sprite can from her, and dropped his cigarette into it. "Feeling better?"

"Yeah." But she weaved a little on the first steps. He caught her elbow, and as she glanced down at his arm, she saw it: a Y-shaped scar, snaking vertically up the inside of his wrist. Her face burned, and she looked away, as if she'd seen him naked.

Here was her chance, to ask as casually as he had of her hand, "What happened to your wrist?" But the answer was too obvious, too painful.

"Why?" she asked, looking away from him, down the street, now full of empty parking spaces. "Why do people do this? Is it . . . is it an illness? Like a mental disorder?"

"Maybe." He released her arm. "Maybe not. But illness or no ill-ness, it *is* a crime."

Sarah looked him in the face again. "Yes, it is." People she'd known, people she'd *liked,* were criminals.

She squeezed Kramble's hand. "Thank you." And as she walked to her car on unsteady legs, she wasn't sure what she had thanked him for: his kindness? his work for Jordan? his own survival? Or for being the first man to touch her in two years.

CHAPTER ELEVEN

Nate

Nate searched for the paper when he got home from school. He found it on the kitchen island, his mother's breakfast left uneaten beside it. The day's headline made his stomach smolder. Mrs. Kendrick was going to have a bail hearing. It might turn out she'd be released until her trial. Christ. She could be out as soon as tomorrow, but the article predicted she'd be considered a flight risk, since Mr. Kendrick had bolted like the big chickenshit asshole that he was, and the bail would be set sky high.

Nate hated how everyone acted like they knew all along, remembering this weird thing or that: The way the Kendricks had loved having kids over at their house. The way Mrs. Kendrick always volunteered to carpool but hardly ever let anyone reciprocate. No one could remember ever being alone with Jordan. The way Mr. Kendrick always told the other parent soccer coaches, "It's okay, you can go home," when they were waiting for kids to get picked up after practice. The way Mrs. Kendrick always had that damn video camera everywhere she went. Apparently two fifth-grade girls now claimed that Mr. Kendrick had kissed them a year ago. They'd even told their parents, but they'd said *Mark*—because both the Kendricks always insisted that kids call them by their first names, which all the parents now claimed they'd always felt was "inappropriate." So these girls said *Mark* had kissed them, but their parents assumed they meant a little boy named Mark, and those parents had talked to the boy Mark's parents, who had appropriately scolded him.

Nate hated hearing those stories, told in that jaded, cynical, I'm-not-surprised tone. Bullshit. If they *knew*, Nate wanted to yell, why didn't they *do* anything?

But that made him feel cold all over.

The back door rattled, and his mom came in, wearing her white double-breasted chef's jacket, balancing two metal pans and several Tupperware containers in her arms. "Hey," she said. She saw the newspaper and set her load down on top of Mrs. Kendrick's picture.

Nate felt bad for Mom; Mrs. Kendrick was her best friend. Shit. It would be like finding out Mowaza was having sex with his own little sister or something.

"There's some leftover Cajun salmon spread. Want some?"

Nate stood. "Maybe later. When I get back. You said I could take the van, remember?" He reached to take the keys from her hand, but she held on to them.

"Do I remember?" she teased him. Nate grinned. "Now, *you* remember: If you go anywhere besides Books & Company and CD Connection, you won't be allowed to drive at all."

"Jesus, Mom, all right. You told me this a million times."

She made a face and tossed the keys to him. "Don't say 'Jesus.' It's crass."

He rolled his eyes.

"Watch your speed," she said as he opened the back door.

"Okay."

"And make sure you lock it. I left my warmer pans in there, and my copper roaster."

"Okay."

As he walked out to the garage, she called, "Be careful."

He slapped his forehead. "Thank God you said that! If you hadn't reminded me, I was probably going to drive like a maniac."

"Smart-ass."

"Mom," he teased her. "Don't say 'smart-ass.' It's crass."

"Get out of here," she said, laughing.

When he backed out of the garage, she stood on the porch, waving to him, looking about-to-cry pathetic. "Don't go anywhere else!" she yelled after him.

But that's the first thing he did. He hadn't been behind the wheel for five minutes before he was jeopardizing his driving future again. He hadn't been to Children's Medical Center since he had to have his jaw x-rayed a year ago, and then he'd been too damn miserable to pay attention to how to get there. He'd looked up directions on the CMC Web site in the computer lab at school. But driving downtown made him sweat. Traffic was crazy, and a huge bus changed lanes right in front of him, and he had to slam on the brakes. He didn't relax until he'd found the hospital, but then he was sorry he was already there.

His tight throat and parched mouth made him feel like a baby. Part of him wanted to flee right then, but hell, he'd already lied to Mom; he might as well stay and accomplish his mission. He wanted to be able to tell Mackenzie he'd done this.

When he'd shown up at her house that day after he'd found the disks, she'd answered the door, arms crossed and scowling but had softened when she saw his face. She'd pulled him inside, whispering, "Oh, my God—what's wrong? What happened?" She wrapped her arms around him and stood on tiptoe to kiss his eyelids. He adored her for acting like that Tony fiasco had never happened, but later Nate had brought up Tony's comments himself.

Mackenzie'd listened to his apology, her porcelain, unmade-up face impassive. "You never told him I gave good head?" she asked, eyes narrowed.

"No, I swear."

"Well . . . don't I?" she asked, her lips pursed in a mock scold.

"Well, yeah, I . . . I mean, you *do* . . . but I never, you know, said—" until Mackenzie'd burst out laughing and kissed him. He pictured the one time she'd done that to him, that Best Day of His Life, a snow day with no school. He and Mackenzie had snowboarded on the hills of the local golf course until their clothes grew stiff-crusty in ice. They peeled them off, back at her empty house, their skin pink beneath the frosted layers. While they waited for the dryer, they burrowed into her bed, naked. They'd done that before, although they hadn't actually done "it" yet. They'd also never done what she did that day, slipping her head under the covers, her warm mouth kissing a path down his thawing chest and stomach, until the path ended but her kisses didn't, and he'd believed he might levitate. She'd hummed and giggled through the whole thing . . . which hadn't lasted very long.

But he couldn't picture that now without the images altering, blending with images from the disks. He'd see Jordan doing what Mackenzie had done, or he'd see Mackenzie, but he'd see himself yanking her by the hair. Both images freaked him out—he didn't even know which one repulsed him more, but both trashed his favorite memory.

He'd admitted this to Mackenzie. They'd lain on the floor in her living room, and she cried as Nate described the photos to her. He told her everything—except about his run-ins with Mrs. Kendrick. He was afraid to admit that to her, but even without knowing, Mackenzie said, "You have to go see him." Nate knew she was right. And he couldn't sit here in the parking lot forever. If he was going to do this, he needed to do it. He took a deep breath of the warm, spring air and headed for the doors.

The hospital smell hit him at once. This was a clean, cheerful place, but it had the same taint scrubbed-sterile scent that made him think of his dad. He felt raw and exposed.

He'd seen his mom's note by the phone: *"Jordan. CMC. 3 West."* He pondered the directory a moment and found an elevator.

Two doctors, both in green scrubs, got on the elevator after

Nate. He watched one fiddle with his stethoscope, tapping it in his hand as he talked about an FUO, which Nate knew was a "fever of unknown origin." The gesture was so familiar, so like his dad's, that he felt his throat close. He practically fled the elevator on the third floor.

He approached a nurses' station and selected a sweet-looking, chubby nurse, whose name tag said "Wendy." "Excuse me." Nate had to clear his throat to get sound out. Damn, his mouth was so dry. "I'm looking for Jordan Kendrick's room?"

Wendy looked up and examined Nate with a for-the-police-artist's-description squint. Her expression softened, and she said, "I'm sorry, sweetie. He won't see any visitors today."

"Oh." Nate was thrown. He'd never considered that. "Okay." He turned around, embarrassed by the relief flooding through him. What would he have said to the kid anyway?

"If you tell me your name, I'll be sure to tell him you came by," Wendy said.

"Oh. Um . . ." Suddenly Nate didn't want to give his name. Would Jordan even remember him? "That's okay. I'll come back later."

But this made Wendy frown. Shit. Why had Nate come? He walked back toward the elevator, but as he approached it, the doors opened and Dr. Ali Darlen stepped off, looking down at some papers she held in her hand. Nate froze. She'd cut her hair; it was short and spiky now, but he remembered the long red wave of it falling forward the night his father died. It'd brushed his cheek as she bent to shake him awake in the waiting room. She'd led him by the hand to where his mother sat with his father's body. This memory blind-sided him, as if he'd skated onto the ice midgame, with no helmet, no face guard, no pads. She was turning his way. Would she recognize him? He lunged for a water fountain. He drank and drank until he saw her pass him in his peripheral vision. He wanted to keep drinking, but he needed to get out of here. The elevator doors had

closed already, so Nate walked past them, down the hall in the opposite direction.

He shouldn't have come. He could've just gone and bought
some new CDs with his birthday money. But no, he'd lied to his
mom, and he'd probably get caught, as usual, and he hadn't even
seen the kid, the whole damn reason he'd come here.

There had to be another elevator or stairs down here. He passed a
lounge with a TV blaring and saw a vending machine tucked back in
an alcove. He could use something to drink on the way home. He
stepped into the lounge. Nate walked past a table like a restaurant
booth. Some kid sat on one of the seats with his back to Nate. As
Nate stepped around the kid's IV stand, he glanced down and saw the
kid was working on something, head bent over his hands, engrossed.

At the machine Nate put in a dollar and pressed the buttons for
an orange Gatorade. While he waited for the bottle to drop, he
looked at the loud TV. No one was watching it. Damn. That would
drive him crazy. The poor fish in the aquarium next to it must hate
it, too. Nate retrieved his Gatorade, opened it, and drank half the
bottle in one chug before turning to leave.

The kid at the booth looked up.

It was Jordan Kendrick.

They stared at each other, mouths open.

"Hey," Nate said.

Jordan looked panicked. He had a napkin in one hand that he
wrapped around the other. He glanced over his shoulder, then back
at Nate.

Nate capped his Gatorade, then uncapped it again. "How are you
doing?" he asked.

Jordan slouched down until only his head showed above the
table. "What are you doing here?" he whispered.

Nate's face warmed. "I came to see how you were."

Jordan narrowed his eyes.

"Only the nurse said you didn't see visitors. Not that it mattered, since you obviously weren't in your room anyway. But listen, it's okay. I didn't know it was you sitting here. I . . . I don't want to bug you."

Nate walked past the booth, but Jordan twisted around, peering over the back of his seat. He looked past Nate, down the hall, then up at the ceiling.

"Did you come by yourself?" Jordan asked.

Nate nodded.

"Are you leaving now?"

Nate could take a hint. "Yeah, I can leave. I just wanted to say hi and tell you I'm sorry, you know. . . ."

"Can I walk downstairs with you?" Jordan asked. He looked up at the ceiling again. Nate looked up, too. What was the kid looking at? The clock?

"Um, sure, I mean, are you supposed to—"

"They want me to get more exercise," Jordan said. He stood, holding one arm to his chest, still clutching the napkin. He wore Nate's old Rangers jersey, which hung off his shoulders and draped almost to his knees. The jersey made Nate's eyes sting, reminding him that Jordan could've been spared, might be somewhere whole and healthy, or at least not here in the hospital, if Nate hadn't been so conceited that he'd actually believed Mrs. Kendrick's coming on to him was perfectly normal. What had he thought, that he was such a stud the woman couldn't help herself? Before Nate could ask the kid what was wrong with his arm, Jordan snaked around him, and, clinging to the wall, left the lounge with surprising speed. Nate looked back at the IV stand. Oh. So that wasn't Jordan's.

In the hall Jordan looked back at Nate, then up again. "What do you keep looking at?" Nate asked. But this time, over his shoulder, he saw the camera in the ceiling. He frowned. "Hey, are you supposed to—"

"Come on," Jordan whispered, opening an unmarked door. "This way."

"What are you doing?" Nate asked. He followed the boy into a stairwell. Jordan practically ran down the stairs, and he wasn't very steady. He needed to hold the railing, but he kept his left arm held tight to his chest and groped along the wall with his right. Nate heard the kid gasping for breath. "Slow down. What the hell's your hurry?"

Jordan stumbled on a landing, and for a second, Nate was terrified the kid was going to fall down the next flight. Jordan used both hands to catch himself and ended up sitting on the top step. He dropped the napkin, which Nate saw was bloody. "Whoa. Hey, why are you bleeding?"

Jordan clutched the bleeding hand back to his chest. He used his other arm to push as he scooted on his butt down two more steps.

"Hold on." Nate descended the stairs, but Jordan scrambled to his feet to face him, his back to the wall, balancing unsteadily on a step.

"You're bleeding. Let me see." Nate reached for Jordan's arm.

Jordan yelled, "Don't touch me!" and kicked Nate in the shin. Nate dropped his Gatorade, which went plunking down the stairs with a hollow slosh.

Jordan's eyes widened, as if he couldn't believe he'd kicked Nate. Nate might've laughed, if it hadn't felt like he'd been cracked with a ball bat.

Nate backed up several steps, eager to put distance between himself and whatever the kid thought his intentions were. He rubbed his shin as Jordan took two more steps down and reached the landing.

"Jordan, man, I won't hurt you." Nate hated how thick and about-to-cry his voice sounded. "But, shit, you're bleeding. You're breathing like you just finished a damn marathon. Are you sure you're supposed to go downstairs?"

Jordan slid down the wall and sat cross-legged on the landing.

A door opened somewhere above them, and a woman's voice called, "Jordan!?" Nate watched the kid freeze. He didn't answer. The voice said something Nate didn't catch, and the door clunked shut.

Jordan exhaled.

Realization washed over Nate. "That was your IV stand back in the lounge, wasn't it?"

Nate figured the blood was from a botched job of pulling out his own IV. "Are you trying to break out of here?"

Jordan's eyes flicked to Nate's.

"Oh, good plan," Nate said. "Very good plan."

Jordan glared at Nate.

"And where the hell are you gonna go, Einstein?"

The anger drained from Jordan's face. He shrank against the wall and closed his eyes. He whispered, "The social worker's coming again today. They're putting me in a foster home."

Nate didn't know what to say to that. He sat down, three steps above Jordan. The images from the disks superimposed themselves every time he looked at the kid. He cleared his throat. "Nice shirt," he finally joked, just to say something.

Jordan opened his eyes, face changing. As pleasant as could be, as if they were chatting at a bus stop, he said, "Thanks. How're playoffs?"

Nate shrugged. "I got kicked off the team."

"Get out. No way."

"Yeah. I skipped school. It's no big deal—I was supposed to get *expelled,* but the principal cut me a break. There's only one game left anyway."

Jordan nodded, and asked, "How much do you guys practice off-season?"

"Well, we do weights and we—Look, you gonna sit here on the stairs all day? What the hell are you doing?"

"What are *you* doing?" Jordan threw back. "Why are you here?"

A slapped-cheek heat smarted across Nate's face. "I told you. I came to see you."

"Why?"

Nate didn't know how to answer that. "Because. It was a pretty awful thing that happened to you. I just . . . I don't know. . . ." He felt stupid.

Jordan studied him a moment, then coughed. The cough turned into a wheeze.

"You okay?"

"This was probably really stupid," Jordan said, leaning his head back against the wall.

"Tell me what you want me to do. You want me to go get someone?"

Before Jordan could answer, the door swung open on the landing beneath them and a security guard shouted, "Here he is!"

Nate moved between the guard and Jordan. "He's okay. He's on his way back to his room." But the stairs crowded with orderlies and hospital security. Nate shielded Jordan from the crowd, feeling like the enforcer on a hockey team, with Jordan his star player, his Wayne Gretzky. No one was going to touch this kid if he could help it, not that anyone seemed to want to; they all hung back, and with his shin still throbbing, Nate couldn't blame them.

Dr. Darlen charged into the stairwell, taking two stairs at a time to reach them. Nate wanted to hug her when he saw her this time, but she didn't seem to recognize him. She just shot him a nasty-ass look, then asked Jordan, "What do you think you're doing?"

"I went for a walk," he said, raising his chin. Nate admired the bit of attitude the kid threw at her. "Look." Jordan pointed at Nate. "I decided to see visitors."

Dr. Darlen shook her head, her eyes glittering. "You are in so much trouble, you little . . . You scared me." She wiped her eyes and said to the crowd, "Thanks, you guys. Can I get a chair down there?" People moved into action at her command.

"Nate, I need you to help me." She'd recognized him after all.

"You know him?" Jordan asked.

She nodded. "His dad was my boss for a while."

Jordan squinted at Nate. "Your dad's dead."

"Yeah." Damn, did this ever get any easier? "He used to work at Miami Valley."

Dr. Darlen tilted her head and studied Nate a moment before directing him, "Walk beside him in case he falls. I'll spot in front." As bossy as ever.

"I can walk," Jordan said, but he wobbled as he navigated the six or seven steps.

At the next landing, they went through the door to the hall, where an orderly produced the requested wheelchair. No one said a word on the elevator trip back to the third floor and Jordan's room. Nate followed along, wondering when he could politely leave.

He waited in the doorway as Dr. Darlen helped Jordan into bed and tucked his legs under the covers, her long earrings jingling as she worked. The kid sank back against his pillows. He looked like he'd been run over.

Wendy, the chubby nurse from the desk, came in, and Nate backed against the wall, trying to stay out of the way. She crossed her arms and said to Dr. Darlen, "I told this boy Jordan didn't see visitors."

Jordan said, "I want him to stay."

Nate felt a combination of victory and terror at those words.

Dr. Darlen and Wendy both seemed happy. "Good," Wendy said. Nate almost wished they'd tell him to leave.

Wendy cleaned and bandaged Jordan's arm. She ran a new line into the back of his hand and reattached him to what looked like antibiotics. Nate wondered what they were for.

While Wendy messed with the IV, Dr. Darlen lifted the Rangers jersey and began rehooking the cardiac monitor, clamping the leads onto the metal knobs like miniature jumper cables. Nate looked at the kid's bony chest and wondered who the hell was attracted to that. Who looked at that skinny, bird-skeleton body and got turned on?

He looked instead at the cardiac monitor itself and the two orange lines of rhythm that appeared, dipping and peaking across the black screen.

Wendy held Jordan's wrist and said to Dr. Darlen, "He got rid of his ID bracelet."

Dr. Darlen ran both hands through her spiky hair like she wanted to pull it out. "Where were you going to go, Jordan? Don't you understand that you're very sick and you need to be here?"

Jordan smoothed his top blanket and wouldn't look at her.

When Wendy left, Nate sidestepped his way to the chair on the other side of the bed.

Dr. Darlen fiddled with a knob on the monitor. "Jordan, don't ever pull a stunt like that again. And you, Nate, you of all people know better. I can't believe you were a part of this."

Nate's pulse peaked, just as Jordan's did on the monitor, the number jumping from 76 to 98. He looked at Jordan, expecting the kid to speak up and set her straight, but Jordan gazed casually out the window even as Dr. Darlen continued to tear into Nate.

"Did you think for one minute about the ramifications of this, or were you just off on some juvenile adventure? What were you thinking, 'This'll be fun; let's piss off the nurse?'"

Nate'd never expected this from Ali, who'd always been one of the few adults in his life who was fair and asked for his side of the story. Once, when he was a kid, he'd had a crush on her, and she'd been really cool about it and hadn't made him feel too stupid. He'd felt really stupid later, though, when he realized she was a lesbian. By the time his mom and dad had talked to him about it, he'd already figured out that Priah was more than Ali's housemate. Jordan still gazed out the damn window and said nothing, the little shit. "Sorry," Nate said.

"I'll *make* you sorry if you try it again." She gave him a warning glare, then turned her attention back to Jordan. "You could've done serious damage to yourself."

Jordan nodded, studying the new IV in his hand.

She rubbed her forehead, shutting her eyes as if in pain. "It'll be okay, kiddo," she whispered. "Nothing is official on this foster home. We can figure something out. You're safe. We'll make sure you stay safe. Your father is not going to hurt you ever again."

Jordan seemed lost in the examination of his hand.

Dr. Darlen sighed. "All right, you guys. Stay out of trouble. I'll see you this evening, Jordan." She left the room, leaving the door open behind her. Nate felt abandoned, like the goalie waiting for the penalty shot.

"Why did you do that?" Jordan asked, his face ready-to-run wary.

"What?"

"Why did you act like you helped me escape?"

"Well, you weren't exactly jumping to my defense, were you?"

"You could've told her. You didn't even try."

Nate shrugged. "I get blamed for everything. I'm used to it."

Jordan frowned and tapped the IV in the back of his hand.

"Look," Nate said, "I should probably get going. I just wanted—"

"Why do you all keep sending me pictures of black-and-white cats?"

"What?"

"Your mom sent me this card." Jordan shuffled through some mail on his table. "And then Danny drew a picture of Raja, and I wondered if—"

"I think that's supposed to be our rabbit," Nate said, taking Danny's picture from Jordan. He opened Danny's homemade card. It said, *"Dear Jordan. I'm sorry. We all really miss you."* He snorted. Bullshit. He'd heard those little fifth-grade shits torment Jordan. "I thought you and Danny were pissed at each other."

Jordan shrugged. "The teacher made the whole class make cards."

Ouch. "So what's the deal with you guys? What did you fight about?"

But Jordan reached for the card back. He squinted at it. "*That's* supposed to be Klezmer?"

"I know. Danny kind of sucks at art." Nate noticed a sketch pad, open on Jordan's table. An excellent pencil drawing of a cat stretched out on its back stared up at him. He remembered the drawing inside Jordan's vocabulary book, too. Nate imagined a lonely, abandoned cat starving to death in that giant yellow house. "Do you have a cat? Is someone taking care of it?"

"No."

"I could go feed it and—"

"I don't have a cat," Jordan said.

"But you said 'a picture of Raja,' and I thought—"

"I don't have a cat!" Jordan snapped.

"Jesus, all right. I was just asking." Man, this was as bad as dealing with Tony; no way to know what would set him off. "Look. I'm not sure why I came. I just wanted, you know—"

"They might let my mom out of jail." Jordan regarded Nate, as if to gauge what he thought of that. The orange line in the monitor rose, the number jumping to the nineties again.

The smoldering in Nate's belly returned. "Who told you that?" he asked.

"She did."

Nate's scalp shrank.

"She wrote me a letter from jail yesterday. Actually, she's written me letters every day, but they didn't let me see them until yesterday." The kid's voice was calm, but the monitor surged again, the lines climbing like the jagged peak of a mountain. If Nate didn't look at the monitor, he'd never know Jordan wasn't talking about a boring, cookie-baking, soccer mom. "She says they can't hold her because there's no proof she did anything wrong."

"No proof?!" Nate wished he could see what his own pulse was doing.

"She didn't do anything."

"Jordan, how can you say that? She—"

"You *liked* her."

The statement, and the calm, cold way the kid said it, the way he overpronounced "liked," yanked Nate's feet out from under him and slammed him against the glass. He gasped for the breath that had been punched from his lungs. "No I didn't."

Jordan rolled his eyes, and the orange line began to level out.

Nate tried to shrug off the shiver that snuck up between his shoulder blades. He thought of Mrs. Kendrick's hand on his chest, her vampire kisses that leeched him dry, how he'd daydreamed about dropping by her house. . . . He shoved those thoughts from his brain. Shit. They got replaced with images from the disks. "No I didn't," he said again. "I thought she was psychotic. I didn't want anything to do with her."

It shocked him that Jordan laughed. "Yeah, whatever," the kid said with a smirk. "You're so full of shit."

"No, *you're* full of shit if you think there's no 'proof' she did anything wrong. What—just because we couldn't identify her in any of the pictures?"

Nate winced as he realized what he'd just revealed to the kid, but Jordan didn't seem to catch it. The kid looked confused, almost alarmed, as he asked, "She wasn't . . . ?" Then the cardiac monitor yelped once, the number jumping to 121, as Jordan registered what Nate had admitted. He stared at Nate, then looked away, blinking. Shit. Now not only would Nate see the pictures every time he looked at the kid, but the kid would know it.

Nate's face blazed. "I'm the one who found . . . the disks."

Jordan looked down at his blankets and didn't move or respond.

"Look," Nate whispered. "I'm really sorry about what happened to you—"

"They'll probably set the bail really high," Jordan said in a cool, clear voice.

It took Nate a second to catch up to this jump in conversation. "She told you that?"

The kid shook his head, pulling his blanket up around his chest. "No, she just tells me that she can't wait to see me when she gets out." He said it with no emotion. Nate couldn't tell if Jordan was being sarcastic or serious. "She says she's sorry I'm in the hospital and she wants to come stay with me, even though we'll have to be supervised. She knows it'll all get worked out and the people who did this won't be able to hurt me or any other kid again."

Nate pressed his hands to his flaming cheeks, then briefly covered his ears, but that only amplified his pulse. He tried to think of something to say.

Someone stepped into the doorway and made both boys jump. Nate saw the brief slant in the orange lines. A black man, in jeans and a blue polo shirt, said, "Hey, guy," in a rich, deep voice. "I heard you had yourself an adventure today."

Jordan glowered at the man. "I have a visitor." Damn, the kid was actually rude.

The man didn't seem to mind. "That's cool. I'll just be across the hall until you're done with your guest. Then we need to get down to business, all right?" The man smiled at Nate before he crossed to the nurses' station.

Jordan groaned and scooted down low in his bed. "That's the stupid social worker. He's in here bugging me all the time. Him and this psychologist!" He spit out the word "psychologist" like it tasted bad.

"Sorry, man," Nate said, even though he couldn't think of a person who needed a shrink more. He stood and shoved his hands into his pockets. "I gotta go anyway. Um . . . I'll come back sometime." He paused. Why had he said that? "If you want."

Jordan peeled back the tape on his hand and didn't answer.

"Anything you need?"

Those orange lines vaulted again, and, still fiddling with the tape, Jordan whispered, "To get out of here."

CHAPTER TWELVE

Sarah

Sarah hauled the stone gargoyle out to the garden. Ma and Pop had sent it, as some kind of encouragement, she guessed, after she'd told her mother about Courtney and Jordan on the phone.

Sarah had finally broken down in tears telling her mother about the day in Courtney's house with the police, the conversation with Ali, and the meeting at school. Her mother had stayed on the phone while Sarah wept. Once she'd started, it was hard to stop. "I don't know what to do," she'd sobbed. "I feel like I don't know her. Every day I don't go see her in jail makes it that much harder to *ever* go."

When her mother tried to comfort her by saying, "Of course you're grieving for the loss of your friend," Sarah had irrationally argued that Courtney *wasn't* her friend, because Sarah had never really known her.

And before the conversation ended, Sarah heard herself returning to the old, "And maybe she'll be found not guilty. We don't know. We weren't there."

"But what about the pills?" her mother asked. "You told me she gave Jordan antibiotics."

Sarah moaned. "I hate this." She felt schizophrenic. She was an idiot who'd been duped. But her friendship with Courtney—the friendship she'd genuinely believed in and been inspired by—didn't dissolve, it wasn't nullified by the horrible discovery, was it?

And Sarah had cried all over again when the FedEx man delivered the gargoyle today. Sarah look at the statue. It was about two feet high, heavy and gray, streaked with greenish black in the folds of its catlike, crouching legs and the details of its wings.

Ma's note said it was for her garden. Sarah plunked it down. Weren't gargoyles supposed to protect their keepers from bad spirits? So should it face toward the house or away from it? Sarah liked how threatening it looked, claws out, teeth bared, wings unfolded, as if ready to fly at an intruder. She wished its fierceness were contagious; she needed a little herself. She cocked her head and studied it. Somehow its animal quality, its huge eyes, or maybe the little tuft on its tail, made it appealing instead of just scary.

The wind rattled the garden gate, and Sarah whipped around to face it. She felt constantly on guard since Courtney's bond had been set at half a million dollars. Detective Kramble had called Sarah yesterday to let her know. He said the provisions of the bail required that Courtney stay out of Oakhaven except when on official business to her lawyer's office or for a court appearance. If out on bail, Courtney was to stay away from all children under eighteen and could not have contact with Jordan except under Children's Services supervision. Kramble had given Sarah his cell number and told her to use it anytime. He'd also promised to let her know if Courtney left the jail. Rumor had it that Mark had taken all their money when he bolted. He was still a fugitive. Would Courtney try to contact Sarah if she got out? What would Sarah say to her? Maybe she should have visited Courtney.

Kramble had advised Sarah not to go to the jail. "I've been trying to work with this woman," Kramble said. "She's a queen of manipulation. She's going to figure out what you want to see and then show that to you. Do yourself a favor and don't go."

"But she's my—" Sarah had started to protest.

"She *wasn't* your friend," Kramble said. "You only thought she was. She *wanted* you to think she was."

Sarah was still troubled by the fact that Courtney hadn't ever called her. Courtney had asked Sarah to check on Jordan, after all. Didn't she want to know if Sarah had seen him? Courtney was probably getting reports directly from the hospital, though. But still . . . Or was Sarah being presumptuous to think that she'd be high on Courtney's list, with all her meetings with attorneys and police and Children's Services.

Sarah shivered. She wore tattered overalls and one of Roy's old flannels over a turtleneck. She dug her gloved fingers into the dark soil, the primal smell of earth filling her nostrils. She dropped pea seeds into the furrow she'd dug, then patted dirt over them. Pink blooms peeked from their buds on Nate's dogwood, and Danny's white apple blossoms had just opened. The forsythia bushes blazed yellow bright as neon. From the kitchen window, the weather had looked warm and inviting, as colorful as the basket of eggs that had adorned Lila's concrete rabbit. But out here the wind blew raw and damp.

She tucked pea seeds into another row, imagining the dirt as a womb, the seeds the eggs. Libby Carlisle had had her baby yesterday. Without Courtney. A little girl.

That reminded her—Sarah stood and wandered past the old sandbox to Danny's apple tree. She climbed onto the stone bench beside it and looked down at the four blue eggs in the robin's nest. There they were, still perfect, still whole.

The phone rang inside the house, and her shoulders tightened. With three weddings in the works, she should answer—the high-maintenance mothers-of-the-brides called daily to fret over their menus, and nine times out of ten the phone calls ended with Sarah's price climbing ever higher. She was still nervous over the timing of Debbie Nielson's cancellation. Only one other person had canceled, a first-time customer who claimed to be canceling her event altogether, which Sarah wanted to believe. She hopped off the bench and flung her gloves aside. She bounded onto the porch and through the back door. The machine had already picked up, and her heart plummeted as she heard the voice: "This is Joyce at Wright Elementary School—"

She snatched up the phone. "Hello? Is Danny all right?"

"Oh—" The secretary seemed startled. "Well, yes, he's all right. But there's been an incident of some concern, and the principal and Danny's teacher would like to speak to you."

"An incident? Is he hurt?"

"He's fine. Would it be possible for you to come to the school now? It's important."

"Of course. Where's Danny?"

"He's with the principal. He won't be returning to class until we resolve this."

Sarah hung up, grabbed her keys, and ran for the van. Oh, God. What incident? What could have happened? She sped the whole way, half expecting to get pulled over.

She parked in front of the school and ran up the sidewalk. For a split second, her reflection in the glass doors stopped her. She was in those awful overalls. The wind had pulled sections of her long black hair free from her braid, and they danced around her head. A smear of dirt smudged one cheek. She yanked open the door, breaking her reflection. Who the hell cared what she looked like? Where was Danny?

The secretary led her to the conference room, where the principal and Miss Holt looked up at her from their giant blue swivel chairs around a table. "Mrs. Laden, thank you for coming in." Ms. Zimmerman, the principal, rose and extended a hand to Sarah.

"Oh, I'm all muddy," Sarah said, showing her dirty hand. "I was gardening." Ms. Zimmerman smiled graciously. "Where's Danny?" Sarah asked.

"He's in time-out at the moment," Ms. Zimmerman said. "We wanted to talk to you alone first. Please, have a seat."

Sarah did, her heart hammering.

Miss Holt, Danny's teacher, cleared her throat. "Mrs. Laden, this morning, I caught Danny passing around a pornographic image of Jordan Kendrick."

Sarah's pulse stopped. "*What?*"

"He's said unkind things and made jokes about what happened to Jordan before today," Miss Holt went on. "I reprimanded him, but I didn't do anything more than that. It's not like Danny, and the counselors warned us that a lot of kids might not understand the reality of what happened to Jordan. But this morning, when I found the picture, I sent him down to the principal's office. Not two seconds after he left my room, the fire alarm went off. From my door I saw him running at the end of the hall, away from the broken alarm."

Sarah felt sick, both from what Danny had done and from the horror in the teacher's eyes. "But you've found him since then," she said. She wanted to know where he was. She wanted to get her hands on him.

"Yes," Ms. Zimmerman said with a sigh. "While we evacuated the building, another teacher stopped Danny trying to leave school grounds and brought him to my office, where we sorted out what happened. Danny admitted, just a moment ago, to pulling the alarm."

"I can't believe this. I'm so, so sorry."

Miss Holt nodded. "We just wondered if you were aware of any changes in him, if there was anything going on at home that might help us understand this a little better?"

Sarah shook her head. "No. I mean, we've been thrown by the Kendrick case."

"We all were," Ms. Zimmerman said.

"But . . ." Sarah felt that same ice water in her guts as when she'd first seen the photos. "He . . . he'd argued with Jordan. I think. They used to be friends."

The women nodded.

"Something happened," Sarah said. "Do you know what it was?"

"We were hoping you could tell us. The day before we found out—the last day Jordan was here at school—he even refused to be partners with Danny for a class activity."

That broke Sarah's heart. "I just . . . I don't . . . I haven't noticed anything wrong or any other changes besides that." She hated admitting that, as if it were proof that she was a horrible mother. The last thing she wanted was to offer more evidence of her family's apparent dysfunction, but she heard herself saying, "To be honest, I've been consumed with his older brother, who's been a bit of a discipline problem at the high school."

"I'm sorry to hear that," Miss Holt said, so sincerely that Sarah loved her for it. "I always enjoyed Nate so much."

Sarah's eyes watered. She wiped at them, then realized she was probably streaking mud across her face.

"How are the boys handling the death of their father?" Ms. Zimmerman asked.

Sarah froze. "That . . . that was two years ago." She never dreamed she'd hear herself say that. She was the one always being told those very words.

"Sometimes it takes a while for grief to surface," Miss Holt said. Both women leaned toward Sarah now, sweet, sympathetic concern in their eyes. "Especially if Danny might have been too young to truly understand it initially."

Sarah felt her back stiffen. She'd been ambushed. "I . . . I don't think so." She wanted to change the subject. "So what happens now?"

"School policy is a mandatory three-day suspension for the fire alarm."

For God's sake. She might as well home-school, as much as her kids were out.

Ms. Zimmerman smiled apologetically and went on. "And we're required to notify the police and fire departments. We don't press charges, but they do a good job of impressing the seriousness of the offense on the student. We'll contact them now, if that's all right with you."

Sarah agreed. Ms. Zimmerman excused herself to make the call, and Miss Holt went back to class. Sarah went to the bathroom and scrubbed her hands at the miniature sink. She washed her face with wet paper towels and patted her hair down with damp hands. Why would Danny do such a thing? This was the same sweet boy who used to *cry* telling Sarah that no one had chosen Jordan for a team in gym class.

She stood outside the room where Danny sat waiting. They said she could talk to him while they waited for the police to arrive, but she found she didn't want to right away. For a split second, she felt fury at him—he had no right to do this; she depended on him to be the good child—but she knew that was unfair, so she finally went in.

Danny lifted his head from the table, his eyes red and weepy. Something melted within her, but she clenched her stomach muscles and said, "You are in so much trouble."

He nodded, and tears ran down his cheeks.

Sarah began to cry, too, which infuriated her. "I love you, Danny. You know that. But . . . I can't even speak to you right now." She sat at the opposite end of the table in a small, child's chair. Papier-mâché birds hung from the ceiling. Sitting under this enormous flock of outstretched, swaying wings unnerved her. From below they took on a sinister quality, as if they might swoop down and attack. "Why did you do this?"

He lowered his head to the table and hid his face in his arms. The door opened, and Ms. Zimmerman ushered in the police.

Sarah's stomach rolled over when Detective Kramble stepped into the room with another officer. The sense of relief almost startled her, made her feel foolish. Heat flushed her cheeks. Why did she only ever see this man when she was at her absolute worst? She still had his handkerchief, clean and ready to return, but this wasn't the appropriate time to mention it. The men ducked their heads under the colorful hanging birds, but Kramble bumped a blue-and-pink eagle, which pecked him in the temple with a dull thunk. He frowned at it, then made eye contact with Sarah and nodded.

The other man, who introduced himself as Officer Woolridge, did most of the talking. He asked if Danny knew the handicapped students in the school who had to struggle down the stairs during the alarm because the elevators couldn't be used during a fire. He talked about the massive expense involved in answering a false alarm, the criminal charge that could be brought if the school didn't choose to protect Danny. "What do you think would have been the right thing for you to do when your teacher sent you down to the office?" Woolridge asked.

"To just go," Danny whispered. "To do what they told me. I'm really sorry."

"And I'd like to talk to you about why you got sent to the office in the first place," Detective Kramble said. Color rushed back into Danny's face. "Where did you get this picture of Jordan Kendrick?"

Kramble laid the picture on the table. From Sarah's seat the picture was upside down, but she could see it clearly enough. It showed Jordan with just one other person, a woman, mostly in shadow, her face turned away from the camera. This photo was much tamer than the ones from the first disk Nate had opened. An almost artful, gentle pose, it was really erotica, not porn, nothing shocking if it weren't for the fact that one of the participants was obviously a child. She thought of the *Hustler.* Maybe Nate was right; maybe it was Danny's.

"From my computer," Danny mumbled, looking at the table.

"How do you mean, from your computer?"

Danny paused and looked confused. "I . . . I got it on the Internet."

"Are you sure?" Kramble's voice was urgent. "What search words did you use?"

Danny breathed in that odd, gaspy way that usually preceded his throwing up. "I don't know. I . . . I don't remember. It was just a joke. I'm sorry. It's not funny."

"No it's not," Sarah said. "It's not funny at all. Why would you do this? And are you telling me you know your way around porn sites?"

Danny shrank down in his seat. His mouth puckered as if he'd tasted sour milk.

"Danny," Kramble said, and Sarah was grateful for the softness in his voice, his broad shoulders caving in on each other as he leaned toward her son, "how did you find this picture of him? We need to know. It can help us help Jordan."

"It was on TV," Danny said defensively, as if they were accusing him of lying. "On the news. They said Jordan was on the Internet."

Kramble shook his head. "No. We've *tried* to find him on the Internet. This picture is really important. We need your help. Now, try to remember: how did you find it?"

Sarah thought they were missing the point. It wasn't *how* she cared about but *why*. She didn't give a damn about any clue in the Kendrick case; she only cared about what this picture revealed about her son.

"It was on my computer in the computer lab. It was just there. I didn't look for it."

Ms. Zimmerman frowned. "Here at school? I thought you said you got it at home."

Danny's face scrunched up, and he gulped in ragged breaths. "No. Here. When I logged on, that's what came up."

Kramble chewed his lip and rapped a drumbeat on the table with his knuckles. He turned to Ms. Zimmerman. "May I have access to your computer lab?"

"Absolutely. I'll introduce you to the webmaster. She can help you with anything you need."

"Thank you."

While they discussed these details, Sarah felt invisible. She looked at the photo on the table. That was an image they hadn't seen?

Sarah coughed, and Ms. Zimmerman and Kramble turned back to her and Danny.

"Danny," Ms. Zimmerman said, "since this happened so early in the day, we'll consider this the first day of your suspension. You can return to school on Tuesday. I hope you'll spend a lot of time thinking during your three days off."

"Believe me, he won't have three days *off*," Sarah said. "But he'll have time to think."

"Thank you, Mrs. Laden, for coming in and supporting us in this." Ms. Zimmerman rose, signaling that the meeting was over.

Danny tearfully apologized again. Kramble seemed to hover in the doorway, as if waiting for Sarah, but Ms. Zimmerman spoke to her, telling her to take what they needed out of Danny's locker, since he wouldn't be permitted back on school grounds until Tuesday. Sarah asked Danny what books he needed, and when they stood up from the table, the principal had led Kramble away.

They gathered Danny's things, then got in the van and drove. Neither said a word until Sarah pulled in to the parking lot at the hardware store. "What are you doing?" Danny asked.

"You'll see. Come on."

Inside, she bought a hasp and a padlock. Danny looked confused but didn't ask questions. Back in the van, he said, "Mom, I'm sorry."

"Good. You should be," Sarah said. "I can't control what you do in the lab at school, but I can control it at home. I'm putting this lock on the computer cabinet. You're not using it again unless I'm in the room with you."

"But I told you! The picture was there! I didn't do it!"

"Even if that's true, you printed it, Danny. You passed it around. And you pulled the fire alarm."

He dropped his chin to his chest.

"And you're going to work your little butt off until next Tuesday. You're going to dream about going back to school."

"It's not fair. Nate gets in trouble all the time, and you don't make *him* stay off the computer. You don't punish *him* like this."

She pulled in to their driveway, cut the ignition, and turned to face him. "Nate doesn't hurt anyone but himself. He gets punished—"

"But you never make him—"

"But he has never, *never* hurt anyone else. He's never ridiculed someone's pain or disrupted the entire school. Don't you understand what you've done? How serious it is?"

Danny stared at the van floor.

"Do you understand?" Sarah repeated. "If you don't, we'll talk about it until you do."

"I understand."

"Good. Then you need to go inside and clean both bathrooms while I do this. And I mean clean them. There's all kinds of hardwater buildup on the tiles in the upstairs shower. I want it all scrubbed off. You know where the cleaning stuff is."

He hesitated as if he didn't quite believe what he'd heard.

"I meant what I said. You're going to wish you were back in school."

He sulked into the house, and Sarah followed on shaky legs. She hated to ruin the computer cabinet, but she drilled on the hasp, padlocked the cabinet shut, and added the key to the chain around her neck that held Roy's wedding band. She felt he would approve. She also felt that this never would've happened if he'd been here. "Damn you," she whispered. "Leaving me alone with all this shit."

After checking on Danny in the upstairs bathroom, she went outside and slowly trudged down the back steps to finish the abandoned peas.

Some of her tomato plants in their little plastic containers had tipped over in the wind. She carried them out to the sun every day in aluminum casserole pans and took them back down to the warm basement at night. She righted the plants that had fallen, repacked the dirt over their roots, then checked her watch. Soon Nate would be home. She'd grown used to these conferences with Nate's teachers; she'd developed a thick skin and a sense of separateness. But Danny in trouble felt new, raw, and wrong. Why would he do something so cruel? What had happened between him and Jordan? She planted rows of mint and lettuce. She worked blindly, rotely, trying to lose herself in it.

She looked at the gargoyle and pictured how her own parents would handle a situation like this. There'd been only Sarah, the one child, but there'd been a slew of cousins and friends always around the table at night. If anyone was in trouble, everyone knew it.

She stopped with her hands in the earth and saw, as if on video-tape, her own bat mitzvah. Her mother, dressed in a lilac suit, smelling of roses, had turned her by the shoulders to look at all the gathered faces—all the people in her life who genuinely cared about her piano recitals and her scarlet fever, about her double back flip off the lake dock and her C-plus in penmanship. "Remember these faces," her mother had told her. "Remember this love. It is your greatest treasure."

Sarah stood up and brushed herself off, thinking maybe she should've moved back to Michigan to be near Ma and Pop after Roy died.

She went up the steps to the back door and called, "Danny? Can you stop what you're doing and come down here?"

It took a while, but he appeared in the kitchen, frowning and wary. "What?"

Sarah gestured to the kitchen table. "Do you want to talk about this?"

A look of outright panic crossed his face. "No. I said I was sorry."

His fear puzzled her. "What are you afraid of, Danny?"

"I'm not afraid."

"Sit down a minute. Please?" She sat, but he didn't. "Tell me— try to tell me what went through your mind, hon?" She recognized a pleading, desperate tone in her voice.

He scowled. "Nothing. I thought it would be funny. I already told you—"

"Why would it be funny? Just because it was Jordan?" Sarah

could almost feel his panic, like the pulsations when standing near an electric fence. "Why aren't you two friends anymore? What happened? Did he . . . did he or his parents ever try to . . . touch you or—"

"*Mom!*"

"Danny, it's important—"

"*No.*" He didn't look afraid anymore. He looked irritated, which relieved her. He rolled his eyes, reminding her of Nate. "He made fun of me first. He said I was a 'brainless moron.' "

"But, Danny, now that you know what he was going through at home—"

"But I *didn't* know!"

"We'd already talked about it when you printed the picture. It was on the news."

"No, that was—" He stopped.

"Danny? What, hon?"

He made an odd sound, a groan and a sigh combined, a sound he frequently made when he labored over math problems in his homework. "I don't know, okay? I'm sorry! How many times do you want me to say I'm sorry? Can I please finish the bathroom?"

She sighed. Maybe it was too soon. "Yes, but first can you carry my flats of seedlings down to the basement?"

Danny pouted past her to the yard. She followed him and watched him take one flat and go in the back door. She'd call the therapist tonight and beg for the earliest appointment she could get for him.

"Hey." An unexpected voice startled her. Nate stood on the driveway, probably wondering what she was doing, frozen there, arms crossed, staring at the door where Danny had disappeared. "Mom? Could I talk to you—about something important?"

Something about his expression made her legs go weak. The first thought that entered her mind was that Mackenzie was pregnant. He never talked to Sarah about anything important; he seemed to actively avoid talking to her at all, so she knew it was urgent.

"You wanna go inside or talk out here?" She wanted to sound casual, but her voice quaked.

Nate looked around the yard like a person who'd never been here before. He frowned at the gargoyle statue but didn't comment on it. "We could just stay out here, I guess." He had his hands in his jacket pockets and kept shifting his weight from one foot to the other. He turned abruptly and sat on the back steps. Sarah walked over and took a seat beside him.

"I want to ask you something, and you have to promise not to be mad."

Her pulse quickened. "I can't promise if I don't know what it is. But I'll try."

"I want to ask you a favor."

"I'll do it if I can." He hadn't asked her for anything since Roy's death. Except for the blessing on Friday night. It had felt so good to be able to give him something he wanted—for there to *be* something she could offer that he'd value. His eyes were earnest, his face grim. "Nate, I'd do anything I could for you. I hope you know that. I love you."

He nodded and whispered, "I love you, too, Mom." He drew his legs up and wrapped his arms around his knees. "This is really important to me. Don't think I'm not serious."

Danny came out the back door for another tray of seedlings.

"I know you're serious," Sarah said. "Tell me, what is it? What can I do?"

Nate took a deep breath, and Sarah braced herself for the news. "You know how you and Dad used to tell us that our job was *tikkun olam?*"

Danny turned his head as he stepped down the stairs past them. Sarah remained still, letting her brain absorb the unexpected question. The phrase meant "fixing the world" in Hebrew. It had been at least three years since they'd been to synagogue together, since Roy had gotten sick. Why was Nate bringing up something from when he was fourteen?

"You used to say that helping people who needed it was an obligation of being human. You said that's what being 'religious' was really about for a Jew." She frowned but nodded. "And you told us the rule that"—and here, to her surprise, he began to recite—" 'those who have enough give, and those who don't have enough take.' "

She nodded again. "That's right." He was certainly stockpiling ammunition for something big. She watched Danny take his time picking up another tray and knew he was lingering intentionally, listening to this conversation.

"Well, we have enough to give, don't we?" Nate asked.

She searched his face for a clue as to what this was about. "Give what to who?"

"Come on. We have it pretty good, don't we? I mean, we lost Dad, but we've got a lot. We're actually pretty okay, all things considered."

Without warning, tears blurred the sight of her first child. She reached out to touch his shoulder, and he didn't shrug away. "You're right, Nate. We're pretty okay."

Danny finally picked up a tray and headed toward them.

Nate took a deep breath. "I . . . well, I've been going to visit Jordan."

Her stomach bottomed out. "What?"

Danny dropped the tray. The plastic containers clattered as they hit the stairs. Dirt peppered Nate's and Sarah's legs. She lifted a little green tomato plant from her lap, its white roots looking fragile and vulnerable unwrenched from its soil bed.

"I . . . I . . . I'm sorry. I'm really sorry," Danny said. He knelt at their feet and picked up plants and tried to sweep dirt back into containers.

"It's okay," Sarah said. "Just leave it. I'll replant them later." But he didn't stop. She returned her attention to Nate. "You've gone to Children's to see Jordan?"

"Yeah. I've gone, like, three times now. I even went today at lunch."

Danny looked up, and Sarah felt his panic pulsations again.

"You actually *see* him?" Sarah asked. "He talks to you?"

Nate nodded.

"I . . . I—Why didn't you tell me this?"

"I just . . . I don't know. After I saw those pictures, and . . . I just felt like . . . I don't know. I just wanted to go talk to him."

Sarah decided to ignore the fact that he'd lied about where he took the van. She concentrated on filling her lungs with air and exhaling slowly. "Okay. So what do you want to do for him? You know I've been sending him clothes and books and—"

"I know. But . . ." He scooted on the stairs so that he was directly facing her. "Could we foster him, Mom?"

Sarah stared into his green eyes. She wanted to laugh but, thankfully, didn't. She felt paralyzed. She couldn't breathe, she couldn't hear her heart beat, she couldn't think of a response. She sensed Danny, frozen at her feet.

"See, he's wigging out about this," Nate said. "He can't stay at the hospital much longer. They keep bringing him foster-care prospects, and he's freaking, Mom. Mrs. Kendrick keeps sending him letters from jail. It's pretty screwed—"

"She sends him *letters*?" Danny asked.

Nate nodded.

Sarah's shoulders tensed.

"What does she say to him?" Danny sounded horrified.

"That she's sorry, it's all a mistake, and she can't wait for them to be together again—"

"Are you serious?" Danny's eyes flashed with anger.

A muscle spasmed in Sarah's shoulder. A mistake was forgetting to pick up your kid on time, not allowing your husband to . . . Sarah couldn't believe she and Courtney had sat on these very steps together, laughing as they imagined the sort of women that might be able to put up with their sons someday. Trying to picture their future wives. Courtney had said, "Nate'll catch a looker, that's for sure." Sarah reached up to massage her own shoulder.

"Think about what happened to him, Mom," Nate said. "You saw it. I know she was your friend, but we have to help him." He turned to Danny. "Don't you think this is a good idea? Don't you think we should do it?"

Danny stuttered a moment before saying, "Yeah. Yeah, we *should* help him." He seemed too eager to agree with Nate. Wanting to make up for what he'd done?

Sarah sighed. "Oh, Nate, I . . . Of course I want to help him, but this is pretty complica—"

His earnestness sifted away, settling into something cold and hard. "I knew you wouldn't do it." He stood and jerked open the back door.

"Nate!" She reached out to stop him and grabbed his jeans at shin level. He yanked his leg away. "Nate, don't run away like that. If this is important to you, talk to me about it."

"Why? You won't do it. You're just gonna defend your sicko 'friend.'"

Sarah stood so rapidly that Nate flinched, as if he expected her to strike him. But she only stepped close and said, "That is not fair. You have no idea how hard it was for me to find this out." She wiped her eyes roughly and turned away.

Poor Danny crouched frozen at the bottom of the steps, among the scattered plants.

Sarah expected Nate to storm off, but he stayed. He said, "I'm sorry," in a tone that made her believe it.

Sarah sat back down on the steps and took a deep breath. "Sit here and talk to me about this." He didn't sit, but he stepped closer, to stand beside her. "I'm not saying yes or no. I just want you to think about this with me. I'm on my own here, and it's not like you two are a piece of cake to keep track of. You've been in a lot of trouble lately, and that doesn't help—I can't work when you're suspended. And Danny just got suspended today."

Danny stood up, holding the tray with the haphazardly potted seedlings.

"For what?" Nate asked as Danny hurried past them and down the basement stairs.

Sarah waited until he was gone to tell Nate.

Nate's face darkened. "Jesus."

She let that go and took another deep lungful of air. "Right. So." She rolled her shoulders. "Don't you understand how complicated this is, Nate? This is important to you, you say, and I think it's very noble of you, but this thing that's important to you means a lot more work for me, doesn't it?"

"I'd help you."

"How?" He gave her The Look. "Nate, I'm serious. How will you help?"

"I'll . . . I could deliver stuff for you. I'll help you shop. I don't know. What do you want me to do?"

She wanted him to be a good person in the world, and here he was, trying.

She couldn't believe she heard herself saying, "I don't even know how we go about fostering him."

He seized on it. "There's this class you have to take. They'll pay for his expenses and his doctor bills and everything. They give you money, so you don't have to worry about it being expensive. Jordan's case manager told me all about it. He'd help you."

Sarah looked out across the yard at her flats of seedlings waiting to be put into the earth. Having Jordan in her home brought her family closer to Courtney. Sarah was surprised at the dread this thought burdened her with. She wasn't sure she wanted any contact with Courtney. But . . . helping Jordan didn't mean siding herself with Courtney one way or the other. Maybe her family needed to get outside themselves, to deal with someone whose woes were worse than their own. And there was that look on Nate's face. That look she loved and wanted to keep.

"I'll talk to this case manager. I can't promise anything yet, but I'll see."

"Really?" His voice came out breathy and boyish.

She nodded.

"Thanks, Mom."

"I'm not promising," she warned again.

"I know." He did that nervous shuffle. "I know."

She smiled cautiously, and he smiled back. "Could you fold the laundry for me and put it in our rooms?"

He started to protest but stopped and grinned, realizing he was being tested. "Sure." He disappeared inside the house.

Sarah ran her fingers through her hair, any semblance of a braid long gone. What had she just done? She knew that Jordan wouldn't come live here. How on earth were *they* to help this poor boy? She'd look into it, find the reason it was impossible, and be done. But she had to do that much. Nate had asked her for something.

The phone rang, and Nate called, "Mom? It's for you."

She wearily stood and went inside the house. "Hello?"

"Hello, Sarah, this is Robert Kramble. Um, listen—"

"Oh, God, did someone pay her bail?"

"No, no. Nothing's wrong. I have a question for you, and it's a little awkward. I'm—"

"Is it about Danny? Did you find anything at school? I'm so mortified I don't—"

"No, no, please don't worry. This . . . this is . . . nothing about what happened today."

Sarah waited, distracted by Nate foraging through the fridge, vaguely recalling the scent of Kramble's skin and that crude scar snaking up his wrist.

"I was wondering," Kramble said, "if I could see you sometime."

Sarah moved to look at her catering calendar on the open fridge door. "Sure. Mornings are the best for me. Do you want me to come to the station?"

He laughed. "You're not making this very easy."

Something in Sarah's brain snapped to attention. "I'm sorry. What?"

"I mean, can I see you as in take you to dinner sometime?" Sarah flushed—her face, her whole body went warm. Adrenaline tingled her fingertips. Her free hand went to the wedding band on its chain, resting near her breastbone. "Sarah?"

"Oh, um . . ." she began as Nate closed the fridge and bit into a pear. He grinned at her with sparkling eyes, as if they were partners embarking on some great adventure. She didn't know what words would come, wasn't sure if she'd say yes or no. "I . . . I don't think I'm available," she croaked. Oh. She covered the phone to clear her throat. Nate went down the stairs to the basement, and she spoke in a hush. "Thank you, though. Really. I . . . I . . . Please don't be offended, but things are just too . . . delicate right now."

"Oh," he said. A long pause followed.

"I'm sorry," she whispered. And she was. The tingling had stopped.

"No need to apologize. I understand." She almost believed him. He went on, his voice still warm, if overpolite. "I'll let you go. I'll contact you if Mrs. Kendrick's status changes."

"Thank you," she said, too brightly, feeling ridiculous.

"Well. Okay, then. Good-bye."

"Good-bye." She replaced the phone in its cradle and steadied herself at the kitchen island, unable to take in enough oxygen.

She looked at the clock.

God help her: There were still eight hours left in this day.

CHAPTER THIRTEEN

Jordan

Jordan stared out his hospital window and wondered if he'd die if he jumped from here. He didn't want to meet with Reece Carmichael and Sarah Laden. He wished he could just go home and have everything be normal again.

He plopped backward on the bed and curled up on his side. Everyone kept telling him that his life wasn't normal. That no one should have to live like he had. Well, it was more normal than this. More normal than police and social workers and Dr. Ali and Dr. Bryn bugging him all the time. He didn't want to live in a foster home. How had it all gotten so messed up? He'd ruined everything. He almost wished his life were the way it used to be. At least he knew what to expect.

He sat up and kicked the wall, then stood and paced the room again. If he had to be here, he was glad to be free of all the IVs and monitors. Glad that the ache in his joints had gone away. He felt okay today. Even his old headache had left him, that constant burning behind his eyes. Chronic headache, Ali'd told him. A tricky word, "chronic." He'd pictured it with a *k*, but it was *ch*. Chronic headache from his low-grade fever. "Low-grade" made him picture the fever sitting at a desk in school, getting C's and D's on its homework.

Like Danny Laden. Did he really want to live in a house with Danny? Why couldn't they just let him live with his mom?

Jordan returned to the window and searched for that familiar tall figure he always expected to see: his dad crossing the courtyard, heading for the doors. And just like his father's hands on him, Jordan was so sure it would happen that it almost disappointed him in a sickening way when it didn't. Once it was over, he could relax. Dreading it burned up all his energy.

His heart slipped in that extra beat. He didn't want to have this meeting with Sarah. He had to go somewhere, didn't he? But living with Danny? Would it be safer to be in the same house with him, to hear what Danny said? Or as far away from him as possible?

In some ways it would be great to be friends with Danny again. He'd liked those days when Danny had stayed over and they made up monster stories and new endings to movies they'd seen. Danny wasn't like the other boys at school. Danny never did all that stupid wrestling around or punching for no reason. But . . . Jordan didn't think they'd be friends again. Not after the things Jordan had said to Danny. He'd tried to get Danny to hate him, so it was a *good* thing when Danny stopped defending him—it meant that Jordan had done Danny-boy a favor.

What if Danny had figured it out? Jordan didn't think Danny was smart enough to put it together. That was always Danny's problem—he wasn't smart enough. And he got even stupider when a grown-up looked twice at him. Probably because his dad had died. Why couldn't Jordan's own dad have died, instead of his grandma?

His grandma. Jordan moaned. He never should have tried his plan. He should've learned his lesson and remembered that bad things always happened if he told. If he'd just kept his mouth shut, his grandma would still be alive. "See what you did to her?" his dad had said. "You broke her heart." Jordan missed her. He wanted to go stay at her house now. They'd walk in the woods and look for fossils and bones and neat bugs.

But his grandma had lied to him. His mother had a *brother*, Dr. Bryn had told him. It was bad enough that his mom had never told him this, but somehow even worse that it changed everything about his memories of his grandma—it made the movies of her in his mind all murky and the colors wrong—and she'd always been the safest memory of all.

And he couldn't figure out why this mattered to him—how would it have made his life any different to know he had an uncle in Seattle that he never saw or talked to?—but it *did*. It made him feel like he'd been tricked and laughed at.

The knock at the door made him jump. "Hey, big guy, how's it going?" Reece stood in the doorway with Sarah Laden. The sight of her made Jordan dizzy, and he had to blink hard to keep the room from disappearing in the shadows that crowded in. He heard the rain pouring on that day, smelled the eye-watering stink of the port-o-john.

He blinked again and brought the room back into focus.

Sarah smiled. "Hi, Jordan."

They stared at each other for a moment, then both turned to Reece. Reece directed Sarah to one chair, and he sat in the other. Jordan sat on the bed.

Sarah held a round tin in her hands. When she noticed Jordan looking at it, she seemed surprised to see it there. "Oh! I brought some brownies." She pried off the lid, letting loose the heavy smell of chocolate. Jordan's appetite nudged him for the first time in weeks.

She handed him a thick wedge of brownie in a napkin.

He looked at the knobbly texture of the brownie. "What's in these? Nuts?"

"No, pieces of Heath Bar."

Saliva flooded his mouth. "Wow," he said around the mouthful he bit off. Soft, chewy, and still warm in the center.

Reece scooted his chair closer to Sarah's. "Can I have one, too?"

"Sure." Reece and Jordan dug in to their brownies, but Sarah just held hers, hardly eating from it.

Sarah talked about how Nate would move into Danny's room if Jordan came to live with them, so he'd have a room of his own. Jordan tried to listen, when he wasn't distracted by the jumble of video clips that flashed through his mind: Sarah standing in the port-o-john doorway staring at him as the rain soaked her hair. Sarah yanking him up in her arms and cramming him in with the grocery bags on the van floor. He heard her screaming his name over and over again as she drove. She'd taken one turn so sharply that he'd slid over and thumped his head on the door.

"Jordan?" Reece'd asked him a question and looked worried.

Jordan sat up straighter. He needed to pay attention. He was surprised that his brownie was gone. Just some crumbs were left on the napkin in his hand.

"Do you have any questions for Sarah?"

Jordan thought of a million things, but he didn't know how to put them into words. And he didn't think "Could I have another brownie?" was the sort of question Reece meant. He shook his head.

Sarah handed him another brownie as if she'd read his mind. He tried to make this one last, letting each dark mouthful melt into pudding before he swallowed. "You already know Nate and Danny," Sarah said. "You think you'd have any problems living with them?"

He tried to keep his face blank as he searched hers. Had Danny told her?

"I know you and Danny had a falling-out." Jordan wasn't sure exactly what that meant, but the chocolate turned to thick paste in his mouth. "I know you used to be friends, and maybe you can be again. Danny thinks so. What do you think?"

He reached for his water glass. It took several gulps before he could say, "Sure. Danny's all right."

He saw her shoulders lower. "So would you like to stay at our house for a while?"

Jordan turned his water glass in his hand, tipping it to one side, watching the ice tumble into new shapes.

Sarah waited for his answer. Her eyes were so big and brown they seemed more like dog eyes or deer eyes, not a person's.

Jordan didn't know what to say. What would his mom do if she found out he *agreed* to go live somewhere else? The gerbil wheel started to spin inside his ribs again.

Sarah leaned toward him and took a deep breath. "Your mother was my friend." She looked worried, like she was saying something wrong, but she didn't look at Reece, just at Jordan. "I had no idea what . . . what was happening in your house. But I feel like I got to know you because of all the time you spent with Danny. I care about you, Jordan. And so . . . I want to help you."

Jordan stared. He didn't want to say yes. Why didn't someone just *tell* him what to do? He hated choices. They were impossible. And what would happen to him if he said no? At least he knew the Ladens. He knew he had to go somewhere.

Jordan felt like he was stepping off the high dive. "All right," he said, surprised by the spinning feeling that rushed into his head.

Reece grinned. "Whew. Thank you, guy. I can breathe a little easier."

Sarah smiled, too, but Jordan thought she looked scared. He knew *he* was scared. What would his mom do?

"When do I come over?" he asked.

"I . . . I don't know." Sarah turned to Reece.

"Probably not until next week. Sarah's got to get licensed by the state to be a foster mom. We're going to speed up the paperwork on her, since this is considered an Emergency Foster Care situation. We'll help her get it all done, but there's rules we need to follow. Laws. That sort of stuff." Reece waved his hand as if laws and rules were silly. "And your therapist wants to meet with Sarah. She wants to meet the whole family, with you there, too."

The gerbil wheel picked up speed. Jordan didn't like that idea. He'd gotten used to Dr. Bryn. He didn't mind drawing pictures for her or playing with her houses and figures, but he didn't want to do that in front of anyone else. He didn't want to tell Reece that, though, because Reece would tell Dr. Bryn, and then she'd ask him why, and he'd have to try to explain it. He didn't *want* to understand the things she wanted him to talk about. So instead he asked, "Do I go back to school?"

Reece asked, "Do you want to?"

Yes, Jordan wanted to say. He wished more than anything—well, actually he wished for a lot of things: that he was at home and his mom and dad were normal, that he still had his cat and his grandma, that he'd actually managed to kill himself—but *almost* more than anything he wished to go back to school and learn new lists of words. But now . . . everyone knew. He knew people would look at him and think about the stuff they read in the papers.

Jordan needed to know something. He tried to think of the perfect angle, the right approach to get the information he wanted. "What if people say bad things about my mom?"

"A lot of people probably *will* say bad things about your mom," Reece said.

"She didn't do anything."

"The way most people see it," Reece said, "her job as your mother was to protect you. And she didn't do a very good job. That makes a lot of people angry at her."

Sarah nodded and looked sad.

Jordan didn't think the police had all the facts. He tried to decide if that was good news or very bad. He wasn't sure, but he decided to try for more information.

"It wasn't her fault," he said.

"Help me understand it," Sarah said. "I get angry at your mom, too. If it's really not her fault, tell me why."

They watched him and waited. He tried to think of what to say. "She . . . she wasn't . . . ." he wished he knew how to explain. "She didn't . . ."

Jordan didn't know how to tell them his mom would stay in her bed with a cloth over her eyes in the dark. When she did that, Jordan knew it was his fault. He *tried* to do what they wanted, but maybe if he did better, she would get out of bed and be his mom again. Jordan would bring her party leftovers and beg her to eat. One time she knocked the food out of his hands, splattering her bedroom wall with red pasta sauce. "Stay the fuck away from me!" she screamed. He backed out of the room, hardly able to breathe, but stopped when she whispered, "Why do you feed me? You shouldn't fucking feed me." And she'd turned all mean and ugly, her face changing into someone he didn't know. "You'd still feed me no matter *what* I did, wouldn't you?" It was like he'd lost his body—he couldn't move or defend himself. He just stood there when she slapped him across the mouth and jabbed her finger hard into his chest. "I could burn you. I could cut you. I could do *anything*. And you'd still come sniveling back to me,"—and she'd started mimicking him, in this baby voice that wasn't how he talked at all—" 'Mom, are you okay?' 'Mom, please eat,' 'Mom, don't cry,' " until she was throwing things. When a lamp crashed into the wall, he'd run outside and hidden in the woods behind the house. He stayed outside until dark, shaking and crying, but when he finally came back, she acted all sweet and nice, as if nothing had happened, just like she did after the parties.

"Jordan?" Reece asked. "You okay?"

Jordan shook himself. "What about my dad?"

"That's the thing, guy," Reece said. "We have evidence on your father. But your mom's not in any of the pictures."

There. They'd said it. The gerbil wheel went crazy. Something was screwed up in a big, bad way. But maybe . . . maybe this meant he wasn't in as big of trouble as he thought.

He pressed a hand to his chest, wanting the wheel to stop. "I don't wanna go back to school."

Reece nodded at Jordan. "You can be privately tutored. We already looked into that. I can talk to your teachers and get your assignments."

Nate had told him he'd found the disks. But Nate had also told him there were no pictures of Jordan's mom.

How long before his mom realized that nobody had seen that disk? And where was it?

Jordan didn't know for certain whether or not Danny had nosed into his backpack, but he knew for damn sure that someone had gotten there before Nate.

CHAPTER FOURTEEN

Sarah

Sarah stood in the Children's Services lobby waiting for Reece. He was twenty minutes late, and it felt like an omen: She wouldn't be allowed to foster Jordan. She hated the weak part of herself that wondered if she should wish for that? If she didn't get approved, she'd be saved from her own insanity, saved from having to eventually deal in some fashion with Courtney. *And* she would still be on Nate's side, able to commiserate with him about how unfair it all was.

But the prospect that she might be denied made her chest ache. She clutched a bulging manila envelope containing all the documentation the agency requested, but her hands felt slick on the paper, and she tucked the envelope under her arm and wiped her hands on her tan linen pants. This morning she'd recognized a realization that she *needed* to foster Jordan, to deal with and process in some way what had happened. She didn't want to think too much about that realization; it scared her. She wished Reece would get here.

She ought to be relieved for a moment to rest, to simply stop moving. Her schedule was insane today, and the addition of Jordan threatened to make more days like this one. She mentally checked off what she'd already accomplished:

1. *Made and delivered ten pounds of cilantro-lime crab salad for a corporate lunch.*

2. *Met with Ali over lunch to get her fourth and final personal recommendation for her fostering file.*

Still to do today:

3. *Meet with Reece to deliver her fostering file paperwork.*

4. *Meet with Dr. McConnel, Jordan's therapist. (Sarah prayed Dr. McConnel was on schedule, or the remainder of the list would be thrown off.)*

5. *Pick up Danny and take him to his therapist on the other side of town.*

6. *Get back to the house by six for the home visit. Nate had promised to have dinner ready. Sarah guessed the social workers would be seeing them how they really operated.*

Something Ali'd said at lunch nagged at Sarah. When Sarah had worked up the nerve to announce, "I got asked out on a date," Ali had responded with, "He asked you already?"

Ali had grinned and leaned toward her. "This is sooo cool. What did you say? What did you tell him?"

"How do you know about it?" Sarah felt the sweetness of her secret tainted. "He told you?"

"He just wanted to know your circumstances, if you were available. Tell me, what did you say?" Ali clapped her hands together like a little girl.

"I said I couldn't."

Ali's face fell. "Why?"

"He understood. He'd just been at the school that day with the whole Danny fiasco. I only said not right now."

"Wait a minute. Who are you talking about?"

"Detective Kramble."

"*Kramble* asked you out?"

Sarah blinked. "Who were *you* talking about?"

Ali laughed, and Sarah felt her stomping her feet under the table.

"Who did you think I was talking about?" Sarah insisted.

Ali grinned and looked around the crowded diner. "Oh . . . I just thought you meant someone else. No big deal."

"Who did you mean? Someone from the hospital?" Sarah tried to run through all the doctors and technicians she knew, but they were all way too young or married.

Ali leaned across the table again. "You said *no* to Kramble? What's wrong with you? He's got a good job, he's great with kids, and my God, Sarah, are you *blind*?"

Kramble's long dark lashes and broad shoulders flooded into her memory. But she shook her head. "If you think he's so sexy, *you* go out with him."

Ali made a face. "Very funny. Not my type, remember?"

"Of course. And that's precisely why *your* endorsement of him as datable material doesn't carry much weight."

Ali grinned. "Oh, come on. Can't *you* appreciate an attractive woman and recognize her beauty even if it would never cross your mind to sleep with her?"

Sarah realized how she'd been tricked. She'd allowed the subject to shift. Who had Ali been talking about? Sarah caught her beleaguered reflection in a glass lobby display. Who would be interested in her? Was it the radiologist who x-rayed Nate's jaw after a hockey fight last year? She'd forgotten his name, but he was cute, and he'd been flirtatious.

And now that she thought about it, Kramble *was* sexy even if it was hard to separate his sexiness from the fact that he was a child-sexual-abuse detective, a person possibly abused himself. Even though some dangerous unknowns prowled the edges of the fantasy, her fingers longed for the furry down that his shirt collars hinted at, promising fine softness across his chest, growing coarser, she imagined, beyond his flat stomach.

Roy's belly had been soft. Not fat, but soft. Comfortable. Just like their sex—no talking, no wondering, no figuring it out. She could lose herself. It was joyful.

With Kramble it wouldn't be comforting. It would be new, unfamiliar, slightly terrifying. But . . . the terror made her feel alive. Just the possibility made her feel lighter. Younger. More beautiful. She turned her head to the side, still examining her reflection in the display window, but the new angle caused the reflection to shift, and her face was replaced with an image of Reece approaching the front door, arms laden with file folders.

God help her, was it *Reece*? She fought the urge to run away and hide. She felt naked facing him with this thought in her head.

She turned to see him push the door open with his back. "Thanks for waiting, Sarah. Sorry I'm late." He shook his head. "A little visit this morning turned into a removal. Took the police forever to get there. Follow me."

She did, relieved to be behind him as he led her down a narrow hallway.

"You removed kids from their home?" she asked.

"Yup."

"God . . . why?"

He sighed. "The usual. Inadequate guardianship."

They reached his office, and he unlocked the door and dumped the armload of files on his already cluttered desk. He sat down, his face drawn and weary. Sarah sat in the chair across from his desk in the tiny room. "What's that mean, 'inadequate guardianship'?"

He rubbed his face with his hands. "This morning it meant Mom was too stoned to keep her robe closed while we were there. No food in the cupboards or fridge."

"Why did you need the police?" Sarah pictured a SWAT team busting down doors.

Reece took his hands away from his face and leaned back in his chair. "You think it's easy to take someone's children away from them? It doesn't matter what twisted things they do to their kids themselves, they'd easier let you cut off their hands."

Sarah looked at Reece with newfound respect. She tried to picture someone taking her kids away. She scratched at the hint of a scab remaining on the back of her hand and looked around the tiny office while he dug through some papers on his desk. There was little decoration. Some photos of kids on a bulletin board, yellow and orange Post-it notes all over the walls, most of them with names, addresses, and phone numbers. A few had fallen to the floor, which made Sarah vaguely anxious.

He picked up a pencil and looked across the desk at her. "Okay. Let's check this off."

She reached into her crammed envelope. "I have everything you asked for. Here are medical reports for me and the kids. All healthy."

He chuckled. "I figured."

"Verification of car insurance, verification of income, copy of my driver's license, my substitute-care plan—oh, and did you get the criminal-records check for Lila Ripley, my neighbor? She's the substitute-care provider. She and Gwinn Whitacre."

"Yeah. They both checked out clean. So did you."

"Did you expect otherwise?"

He raised his eyebrows in mock seriousness. "You seem the dangerous type to me, Sarah Laden. I had no idea at all what I might unearth on you."

She liked that thought, and she liked that Reece might think it, but she laughed and said, "Please. Here's the copies of my utility bills and proof of residency. I don't have pet vaccination records because Libby, our vet, says there's no shots a rabbit needs."

He laughed and held up his hands as if in surrender. "I wish everybody was as good at this as you."

The envelope was empty. "Well . . . that's everything. What now?"

"Just the home visit this evening and a final crash-course pep talk." He sorted through the documents, assembling them in a specific order, then set the stack of papers aside. "Have you had lunch?" His tone was hopeful and implied that he was starving.

Sarah smiled an apology. "I just came from lunch with Ali."

"Yeah? Oh. Well." He picked up the stack again and shuffled Sarah's documents around on the desk. Did he suspect Ali'd spilled his secret? Sarah felt certain he was the one Ali had meant.

"But, Reece, if you haven't eaten, I can get a coffee or something. I have more than an hour to kill before I meet Dr. McConnel, and it doesn't make sense to drive home, then drive back to this side of town."

"You sure you don't mind?"

"Not a bit."

She rode in his car, which was clean but full of files, empty water bottles, and a clear plastic bag of lollipops. He had a bumper sticker that read, CHILDREN SHOULD BE SEEN AND HEARD . . . AND BELIEVED. He drove her to a small dive of a place painted teal with pink shutters. Sarah was glad she'd already eaten—until she stepped inside. The aromas sent her back to summertime meals in her Grandma Ruthie's kitchen. She was sorry to order only coffee.

Reece ordered fried chicken livers and Swiss chard. "You grow any greens in that garden of yours?" Reece asked.

"I grow some mustard greens that'll kick your butt."

"I've got a great recipe for greens," he said. "You start with some olive oil in a pan."

She nodded.

"Sauté some onions in there. Throw in some garlic—"

She had to laugh. "You know that's the start of every good recipe in the world, right, Reece? You could throw your shoes in there and they'd taste good!"

He laughed, a rich, resonant sound that bubbled up from his belly.

"You should make this recipe for me," she said, a thrill rippling through her.

He raised his eyebrows, and she froze. She'd let Kramble's offer make her giddy. God, was she *flirting*? Flirting with her possible foster kid's case manager? That was classy.

"Sure," he said. "I'd love to." He smiled.

Sarah turned her coffee cup around in its saucer. "Maybe once Jordan comes to live with us—I mean, if I pass this inspection."

"Sarah, don't you get it? There's still the home visit, but unless we discover that you're running a crack house or keeping seventy-four cats or something, you passed."

"Really?" It seemed anticlimactic and unreal. She didn't feel terror or excitement. She really didn't feel anything except this vague weight of, *What have I done?*

Reece watched her, and Sarah felt as though she were standing before an open oven. She touched her cheeks, but Reece looked down at his plate, spearing up more greens.

Sarah cleared her throat. "So what happens next? How soon will a trial start?"

"Good question. Bobby Kramble's been an amazing advocate for Jordan, and he's committed to getting this trial under way as soon as possible."

A surge of pleasure moved through Sarah at hearing Kramble spoken well of. And she liked that Reece called him "Bobby."

"I like how he's been with Jordan," Reece said. "He's gone slow, invested time in the kid, built a relationship with him." He sipped his iced tea. "Even so, this mess'll probably drag on over a year. At least. You need to start assessing how long you're willing to have Jordan in your home. And how you might feel about adoption."

The room slanted. "Adoption?"

"Don't panic. I just want to be honest with you. My official recommendation is that Courtney's parental rights be terminated. Mark's aren't even in question. In Ohio only two crimes carry possible life sentences: murder and raping a child under thirteen. He's got multiple counts, plus the porn. Even if we don't get life for him, we'll have no problem dumping his custody. And Courtney has filed for divorce."

"She has?" Sarah's stomach flipped. Was she still searching for signs that Courtney was innocent?

"Yeah. So I'm going to urge for Jordan to be legally freed for adoption."

She felt so stupid. It'd never crossed her mind that Jordan would need someplace to live *for the rest of his life.*

"Sarah, don't stress about this." Reece's forehead creased. "You're acting as our emergency foster placement until a permanent placement can be found. You can apply to be the permanent placement or not. I don't want you to think we were going to sneak up on you with this and expect you to keep him forever."

That muscle spasmed in Sarah's shoulder again, the tension creeping up her neck. It was one thing to help care for a friend's child, quite another to *steal* that friend's child. Would Courtney interpret it that way? And besides, she *wasn't* Courtney's friend anymore . . . was she? It now seemed as if they'd never really known each other. That thought exhausted her, made her so heavy and sad that lately she caught herself sometimes crawling back into bed after the boys left for school. She craved the escape of sleep but found her mind relentless at night, affording her no real rest. "But . . . the courts *will* free him for adoption, won't they?" She didn't know which answer she feared more. *This is not my problem,* she forced herself to think as concern and protectiveness added weight to her shoulders.

"I hope so, but it would help if we had Courtney in some of the pornography." He set his silverware down. "But we don't, so unless Jordan tells us something, which isn't likely, chances are she's going to get a second chance. Reunification is a real possibility."

"But wait, you just said you were recommending termination of her custody."

"I am. But I don't get to decide myself. Children's Services will make a report, but there's still a trial. And I've got to warn you, it's a lot tougher to get convictions for a female sex offender than a male. No one wants to believe that a woman, especially a kid's own mother, would do something so horrible."

"But there's the drugs. She was treating him for an STD."

Reece nodded, his eyes sad. "Courtney is attractive, wealthy, articulate. She was well respected at her job and in the community. She's written Jordan daily since she's been in custody. She calls the hospital multiple times a day. She asks to speak to him—we've managed to prevent that so far—and asks for his medical reports and talks to his nurses. She's cooperative with her counselor. She's doing everything right."

Sarah saw Jordan's face again, that look he had on that day in the van. The determination in his eyes when he went into that porto-john. Courtney was doing everything right now that she'd been *caught*. How long would Jordan's former life have continued if he hadn't decided to try to end it?

Reece went on, "Without direct evidence of her involvement in the pornography, it's going to be tough. We don't always win, Sarah. Sometimes, even *with* convictions, the kids return to the parents."

"You're kidding me."

Reece shook his head. He pointed to a little girl at a nearby table. "If I got up and fondled that girl, you'd call the police and I'd be charged with assault, no question. But if her *parents* do it, you call the social workers. It's 'family business,' and no one wants to interfere. And the same organization that is there to help the little girl has to try to rehabilitate the parents, too. Girl goes home. Gets molested again. Happens more than you want to know. I wish people *did* want to know, actually. Might make it happen less."

Sarah pictured Courtney and Jordan living in that huge house as if nothing had ever happened. What would you say to a child after something like that? Would Courtney try to sit with the other moms at soccer games? A bitter taste filled Sarah's mouth, and she gratefully accepted the refill of her coffee.

"But," Reece said, leaning back in his chair, "let's not dwell on what's out of our hands. Helping Jordan is in our hands, so let's concentrate on that."

Sarah nodded. She poured the cream and found herself idly trying to match the exact color of Reece's skin with her coffee. A few more drops and she had it.

"Don't have any Hallmark visions of Jordan fitting in and you all living happily ever after. I want you to see this for the disruption to your family that it's likely to be."

She stirred for a moment. Roy flashed into her mind, dead in the hospital. Her children's faces as she told them their father was gone. One of the worst things she could imagine had happened to her. And she'd survived. She realized it as if for the first time. She felt unafraid in a way that was totally new to her. "All right. I know it won't be easy, and I'm trying not to have unrealistic views of it. If there's trouble, we'll figure it out."

He grinned. She was mesmerized by the flash of his white teeth against his skin and neat black goatee. It struck her that not only had she never kissed a black man, she'd never kissed a man with facial hair before.

"You never know unless you try, right?" he asked, and for a horrified moment she feared she'd said that thought out loud. But no, he was talking about Jordan. She nodded. "Okay, then," he said. "How do you feel about this weekend?"

Sarah's stomach slid under the table. "Th-that's tomorrow. Saturday's tomorrow."

"Let's say Sunday morning?"

Her head spun. She was afraid to move, for fear she'd fall out of her chair, but she managed a slight nod. God help her. What had she done?

Sarah was still somewhat dazed when she arrived at Dr. Bryn McConnel's office. She was surprised to find the woman so young and so *small*. She immediately envied the doctor's amazing curly hair; she had the most perfect curls Sarah had ever seen on someone not in a movie or an ad.

"Call me Bryn. It's great to meet you."

"Reece Carmichael just told me I'm approved," Sarah blurted. "We're really going to do this." She recognized that her voice sounded full of fear. She tried to sound more confident as she added, "He's supposed to move in on Sunday." Move in? That sounded wrong.

Bryn laughed. "And it's terrifying, isn't it?"

Sarah nodded.

"Do you like coffee?"

"Yes," Sarah said, although she'd already drunk about a pot today. The aroma of good hazelnut coffee was too tempting. Plus, she wanted something to do with her hands.

"Your family is taking on one of the most difficult jobs in our society," Bryn said, pouring coffee into a yellow Fiestaware mug. "So you're smart to be terrified. But I want you to know you'll have my help." She handed Sarah the mug and gestured to a turquoise creamer and chartreuse sugar bowl on the table. Sarah stirred in some cream while Bryn told her about some support and discussion groups. Bryn told her how she planned to continue seeing Jordan at least once a week, hopefully twice, when he moved in with the Ladens. How she'd want to touch base with Sarah at least that often.

Sarah found herself looking at Bryn's face, wanting to be comforted but wondering if she could really trust this woman. How could she know that this person was who she seemed to be? How could Sarah know Reece? Or Kramble for that matter? Courtney had seemed as genuine, as competent, as caring as all of these people.

Bryn pulled her legs up under her on her chair. "What would you like to talk about?"

Sarah had so many questions she wished she'd made a list. "I guess, how *is* he? I . . . I don't understand how someone could go on after what's been done to him."

Bryn nodded. "Kids are amazingly resilient. To a point, of course. He's terrified of his father finding him. But he's going on, as you say. He's very bright. He has this sly sense of humor. You're right, though: Jordan has been very damaged. When I first got his history, I dreaded meeting him and expected our sessions to be painful for *me*. I thought I'd be rejected by him for a long time. I did discover, though, that there are two things in Jordan's favor. The first is that it looks likely that the sexual abuse didn't begin until he was seven or eight, the age when Courtney began to be abused herself. That's not uncommon. It appears Courtney managed to provide adequate—not great, mind you, but sufficient—mothering during Jordan's most crucial development. That's good, because it means Jordan can form attachments. If he'd been abused his entire life, I'd expect to be seeing this boy forever."

Sarah hadn't even known what sex was when she was seven.

"He's been traumatized, of course, and his ability to trust is disrupted, but the fact that he can form attachments is critical. He has even formed relationships here. He seems especially willing to accept your son, Nate."

Sarah felt lifted, as if her spine had lengthened. "You've met Nate?"

Bryn smiled and nodded, those curls bouncing. "He's a great kid, Sarah."

"Thanks," she whispered. "What's the second thing? You said there were two things in Jordan's favor?"

Bryn pulled her legs from underneath her and leaned forward, her face bright. "The second thing is that he loves art. This is great, because he's not a talker. Kids will rarely talk about their abuse. They need it understood and shared, but not in language. So many kids come in here and won't do or say anything, but Jordan is always willing to draw or sculpt, and he expresses a lot through his artwork. Actual progress is being made."

The woman's happiness was so sincere that Sarah smiled, too. She pulled her own legs up under her and, clutching her mug, asked, "Can . . . can I ask you about Courtney?"

Bryn nodded. "Of course. I understand you were friends?"

Sarah sighed. "I thought we were." Sarah turned her mug around in her hands and asked, "Have you met her?"

"Oh, yeah. Initially I welcomed her involvement in Jordan's therapy. But it only took one interview to realize she's not workable."

The tiny balloon of hope deflated in Sarah's belly.

"I told her that since her view of what happened was so different from the caseworker's and what the medical evidence suggested, I felt it wasn't in Jordan's best interest to have her be a part of his therapy."

"Did you like her?" Sarah asked. She knew that her voice was too high, too girlish.

Bryn cocked her head. "Actually, I didn't. But I see why others did. She has social skills and a certain charm. But she's very damaged, Sarah. She uses people."

Sarah winced. She told Bryn all about Roy's death, how Courtney had been there for her. "No matter what was going on that I didn't know about," Sarah said, "she really helped me. I can't let go of that."

"You don't need to let go of that. She *did* help you. But it's important for you to also see that helping you was not really her intention. You were an overwhelmed, grieving, single mom. A pedophile's dream."

Sarah winced. She mouthed the word: "Pedophile." She hated when people referred to Courtney as one. Mark was one—no doubt about it. Courtney might be a lot of things: a bad mother, neglectful, abusive . . . but Sarah simply could not make herself imagine Courtney doing the things she'd seen in that photo. Using that word for Courtney shamed Sarah too deeply. Made her feel a bad mother herself. *How could she not have known?*

Sarah looked up at Bryn. "Was she only after my son all along?"

"We don't know that. You do have a child in Jordan's age range. More probable, though, in your preoccupied state, you were less likely to notice the oddities of the Kendricks. You're respected and liked in your community. Your friendship with them made them more acceptable, more trusted, more 'okay.' "

Sarah didn't want to accept this and felt herself draw up her defenses. This woman couldn't *know*. Sarah couldn't have been duped so easily. There had to have been some real connection, some genuine thread. There had to be.

Bryn stood and refilled Sarah's coffee cup, then her own. Gently, she said, "Offenders are misread over and over again because people like you and me expect those who use us to have the decency to feel bad about it." She shook her head, flouncing those spectacular curls. "But they don't. Instead of feeling remorse over hurting or deceiving others, most sexual offenders feel satisfaction, a kind of childlike pride in putting one over on people."

Sarah reached forward for the turquoise creamer. She watched the white cream spiral and blend into the dark coffee. Intellectually she understood what this therapist told her, but emotionally her brain couldn't wrap around it yet.

She pictured all the times she'd drunk coffee with Courtney. Tears pressed against Sarah's throat.

Bryn reached across the space between them and squeezed Sarah's hand. "Hey," she said. "You'll be okay."

And all Sarah could think was that Courtney had performed that very same gesture. Courtney had said those very same words.

CHAPTER FIFTEEN

Nate

At 2:03 A.M. Nate woke up and knew he wasn't going back to sleep. And it wasn't that awake-because-he-drank-too-much-Coke feeling. It wasn't the awake that came when he heard something in the house or had a freaky dream. It was simply awake.

Jordan Kendrick was moving into their house tomorrow morning. *This* morning, really. In about seven hours. And it freaked Nate out. He'd wanted this, but now that it was about to come true, it terrified him.

He turned on his light, popped a klezmer CD into his Walkman, and listened to the mournful tunes. This would be Nate's last night in his own room for a while. Jordan was already changing their lives. Maybe not directly, but some of the new changes wouldn't be happening if Nate hadn't set this in motion. Like that feeling Nate had gotten last night when he'd heard Mom laugh at the home visit. Mom had served her famous monster cookies, hockey-puck thick and lumpy with M&M's. When Reece and Lorraine, the other social worker, tasted them, they moaned like they were having orgasms or something. Reece had said, "Oh, man, I gotta have a glass of milk with these." And Mom had laughed. It was such a rare sound that it actually startled Nate. It was a for-real, laugh-out-loud laugh that wrinkled her nose. He had to smile, watching her. But it made him feel cold. And he got even colder when she actually went to get the glass of milk.

The worst, though, came at the end of the visit. Reece asked Mom, "Are you seeing anyone? Do you have a boyfriend who might be here at the house at any time?"

Nate had almost busted up laughing at the absurdity of the question. Get real. But Mom's face stopped him: A hot, red wash crawled up her face. "No," she said. "But . . . would it be a problem if . . . if I did?"

What? Nate had felt like he'd stepped off a cliff into thin air. While Reece and Lorraine asked Mom a ton of questions and Danny just sat there looking terrified, Nate sat across the room from his mother and tried to look at her like he didn't know her and just saw her in a crowd somewhere. Damn. She was old, but she was pretty. A boyfriend? How the hell could she have a boyfriend? But, shit, it had been two years. Hamlet's mom didn't wait two *weeks.* Two years. What was wrong with that? But it made his jaw tighten, made him tense.

And it was worse because she *blushed.*

Damn. Now he was really awake. He might as well do something. He reached for his paperback copy of *Hamlet.* He was supposed to write a scene in iambic pentameter that provided an answer to one of the questions left hanging in *Hamlet.* There were so many he wondered why the play was famous. Tony claimed he was writing a sex scene between Ophelia and Hamlet. Big surprise. Mowaza planned a scene revealing that Ophelia was pregnant, which at least explained why she flipped out when Hamlet was such an ass to her, but Nate was more interested in Hamlet's mother, Queen Gertrude. Was she guilty, too? Or just clueless? He thumbed through the script, looking over her lines on the pages he'd dog-eared. Maybe he should go downstairs to the computer and start writing this scene. He ditched the Walkman, pulled on some sweats, and tiptoed into the hallway.

About the same time it struck him that he wouldn't be able to use the computer because of that pain-in-the-ass padlock—and no way would he consider waking Mom up at two in the morning—he saw light glowing from downstairs.

The hairs on the back of his neck lifted. It freaked Nate out that Mr. Kendrick was still out there. Jordan had told Nate the police would never catch his dad.

He crept down the stairs, every nerve and muscle charged, wondering if he should go grab his hockey stick, and peeked around the corner into the living room. There sat his mom, in her yoga pants and T-shirt, in front of the computer, braiding and unbraiding her hair over one shoulder as she read the screen. Laughing at his jitters, he stepped into the room.

But Mom jumped up from her chair and let out a little shriek.

"Jesus, Mom. You scared me," he said.

"*I* scared *you*?" She laughed, holding a hand to her heart. "Look at us. We're a little jumpy, aren't we?"

"Do you *ever* sleep anymore? What are you doing?"

"Oh . . ." She glanced at the screen, and Nate saw a photo of a young African-American girl's face, with text beneath it. His mom turned back to him, and he noticed that her eyes were pink and watery, like someone stoned. "This is the Children's Services Web site."

Nate pointed to the photo. "Who's that?"

His mom looked down at her bare feet and fidgeted with the neckline of her T-shirt. "They have this . . . menu, I guess you'd call it, of the kids who need homes."

He looked at the little girl. She beamed a huge, toothy grin at him, eyes sparkling, no hint at all in that happy face as to why she was on this computer screen looking for a home. "What happened to her parents?"

His mom shrugged. "The bios don't tell you that."

Nate sat in the chair she had occupied, to read the text. Mom sat on the arm of the couch, reading over his shoulder.

The screen read, "*Monique is a very affectionate, friendly, and outgoing child. She interacts well with adults and peers. She enjoys reading, drawing, and skating. Monique is in counseling to address posttraumatic stress disorder due to her past experiences. It is important to Monique that she is allowed to maintain contact with her older brother.*"

He clicked the corner of Monique's picture, and it shrank to become one of about forty smaller photos, with names and ages listed beside them. Damn, there were *so many*.

At the home visit, Nate thought the questions Lorraine and Reece asked were such bullshit. Actually checking that the windows opened in case of fire, that their wiring was in good condition, that they had running water and no firearms. Stuff like that. Reece had said, "I know all this seems rather ridiculous, but the bottom line is, we're entrusting you with someone else's child. We have to know that this child is safe."

Someone else's child. Nate kept forgetting that. It seemed stupid that some kid who lived in a house where anyone who wanted could have sex with him might be considered in danger living with this family because one of their windows was painted shut. Or that faulty electrical wiring was a more serious threat than the sick stuff he'd seen in the photos.

And here were forty kids who were all "someone else's child," too. They couldn't all have parents like the Kendricks, could they?

"This is depressing," Nate said of the forty faces. "Why are you looking at these?"

"Oh, I was e-mailing Reece and just started looking around."

Nate clenched his jaw. He didn't know why the idea of his mom e-mailing Reece disturbed him. He looked at her, in her sweats on the couch. She looked haggard with no makeup on. She sat on the couch and drew her legs up under her. "What are you doing up?" she asked.

Nate closed the site and shut down the computer. "Couldn't sleep."

Curled up on the couch, she looked as if she'd sit there forever and listen to whatever he wanted to say. He drilled several phrases in his mind. Something like, *I think it's all my fault Jordan ended up in the hospital.* Something like, *I knew Mrs. Kendrick was sick and twisted a long time ago and I didn't say anything because I thought maybe . . .* maybe what? That he'd get to screw her? That they'd have some kinky, made-for-TV-movie affair? He took a breath and asked, "So . . . how'd Danny's appointment go?" He hadn't asked Mom yet. He'd asked Danny, who just shrugged and said, "Okay, I guess. I don't know why I have to go."

Mom leaned her head back against the couch. "I don't know. He really, truly can't seem to tell me why he printed that picture. All he'll say was that Jordan was 'mean' to him. I'm not in there with him for the appointment, remember." She sighed.

Nate did remember. He'd hated the therapist Mom sent him to at first but then was really glad he had him. It was easier to talk about Dad to someone other than Mom. He was always afraid he'd just make Mom cry.

"So tell me," Mom asked, "do you know how to get to porn sites on the computer?"

"Mom, Kramble said Jordan wasn't *on* any porn sites. The Kendricks were too smart for that." He watched Mom frown. She looked like a person trying to remember something. "Why? Did Detective Kramble find something in the computer lab?"

"Not yet. He wants to talk to Danny again." She chewed her lip, then looked up at Nate. "You never answered my question: Do you know how to get to porn sites?"

"I've never tried."

She pursed her lips and raised her eyebrows.

"I haven't! God, you always act like I'm some sex maniac, Mom."

She said softly, "I owe you an apology, don't I? That *Hustler* magazine really was Danny's, wasn't it?"

"It sure wasn't mine. Down in a dark basement with a rabbit watching me is not exactly my idea of a great place to"—Jesus, what was he saying?—"To . . . you know."

Mom looked at him with the oddest expression. "To what?"

"Nothing. I mean, you know what I mean." His face burned. His knee bounced. He wanted to disappear even thinking about that in the same room as his mother. He turned back to the dark computer and played with some keys.

Mom laughed. He glanced at her, but she'd covered her face with her hands. "Ohh . . ." She looked up at the ceiling. "There are times I really, *really* wish your dad was here."

Nate laughed, too, feeling a little less stupid. This was one of the first times they'd mentioned Dad without being sad or serious. He cleared his throat. "Everything's fine."

"You sure? I'm not supposed to have some talk about . . . that?"

"Mom! What do you think I need? Instructions?" His ears were so hot they actually hurt.

She laughed again and pulled her hair across her face for a second. "I don't know. I never had a brother. I have no idea what I'm supposed to tell you."

"You don't have to *tell* me anything. I figured it out. Like, years ago."

Her face was as red as his felt, but they both laughed. She suddenly grew somber and asked, "So you think Danny's just . . . masturbating with this porn?"

His face managed to burn even hotter. He shrugged.

"Well, *Hustler*'s pretty disgusting. And then the Jordan picture! That's too disturbing, that he'd use an image like that to—"

"I bet showing the Jordan picture was something different," Nate said, not wanting to picture Danny getting turned on by those images. This conversation was whacked-out. "He was trying to . . . I dunno, get attention or something."

"But . . ." she shook her head, pale worry replacing the fading red in her face.

Nate studied his own bare feet, gnarled and callused from his skates.

After a silence Mom said, "I hope Danny and Jordan are going to be okay together."

"Mom! He's coming *today*."

"I know. I know. I'm not saying I'm changing my mind. . . . But I sure wish I knew what made them so unfriendly to each other. What if Jordan finds out what Danny did at school? And Danny needs help. Doesn't it seem unfair to bring the focal point of his problem—whatever the problem is—into our house? I don't want Danny to think I care about Jordan more than I care about him."

Something weird had just passed between them. Nate sensed it, and from his mother's expression, he knew she did, too. It felt unfamiliar, almost scary for her to confide in him. They hadn't argued for weeks. This new way of being felt like speaking a foreign language.

Nate'd worried about Danny and Jordan, too, but he didn't want to agree with her. He owed Jordan, and there was no way to tell his mom that. "We can help them both, can't we?"

She smiled. "We're going to have to."

She ran a hand through her thick black hair, scratching her scalp and yawning. Watching her made Nate yawn, too. He looked at his *Hamlet* script and thought, *Yeah, right*. His eyelids felt sticky when he blinked, like they might glue shut. "Night, Mom." He stood, and he almost leaned over her to kiss her on the forehead. He saw the movement in his mind, felt it in his muscles, but he stopped himself.

He left the room and went back to bed.

CHAPTER SIXTEEN

Sarah

arah felt light-headed when Jordan arrived at the Laden house on nine o'clock Sunday morning.

"They're here!" she called up the stairs when she saw the city car. "Just act natural. We don't all have to greet him at once. Where's Danny? Now, remember, we need to give him space and not hover—"

"Mom, chill, okay." Nate rolled his eyes in the way that drove her crazy, that suggested her every request was neurotic. "Jesus, just relax."

"Nate, I've asked you not to say that."

Sarah let Reece and Jordan into the house. Everything she did felt surreal and dreamlike. She had to keep telling herself this was really happening.

Jordan sat on the couch, his posture and expression expectant.

"Hey, man," Nate said. "You're finally here."

"Yup." Jordan nodded, then looked at Danny. "Hey, Danny," he said.

Danny's face turned red, and he muttered, "Hi," then looked away.

Poor Danny, Sarah thought, watching Jordan frown. If Danny didn't telegraph his embarrassment so obviously, maybe Jordan would never know what Danny'd done at school.

It touched her that Nate tried so hard to make small talk. Danny tried, too, but he fidgeted and always looked at Nate or Reece, not Jordan. In spite of their efforts, conversation quickly deteriorated to a series of questions and answers. Jordan submitted to this interview, but with a forced courtesy that hung heavy in the room.

Sarah found it hard to look at Jordan without picturing what had been done to him. It amazed her that he seemed so together, that he looked as he always had—like any eleven-year-old boy. She couldn't imagine herself able to function if she'd been through what he had.

"We have Popsicles," Danny said out of the blue. "Do you want one?"

Sarah saw Jordan's eyes light up, but he said, "No, that's okay. Thanks."

Danny headed into the kitchen. Another tortured silence fell in the room.

"I'm gonna have one, too," Nate said. He unfolded his lanky frame from his chair and followed Danny.

Jordan stared after Danny for a moment. *Oh, God,* Sarah thought. *Please let this work.* When Jordan returned his gaze to hers, he seemed to shrink. He stood and stuck close to the couch, barely meeting anyone's eyes when he said, "Um . . . I guess maybe I will have one."

When he was gone, Sarah turned to Reece and whispered, "What have I done?"

He smiled at her. His eyes twinkled. "It's gonna be okay. Today will be strange. There's no way around it." He glanced toward the kitchen and said quietly, "He's really nervous. Ali told me he didn't eat any of his breakfast."

"Maybe I should start lunch now." She'd welcome something to keep her hands busy.

Reece chuckled and squeezed her shoulder. "Sarah, it's only ten. Relax. You're doing fine. Look, this is the perfect time for me to slip away."

It seemed so abrupt; she felt unequipped. Sarah hated the abandon-ment she felt when Reece left, but she fiercely shook it from her. She'd gotten through worse than this on her own. She understood why Bryn had had them do a project together when the whole fam-ily met with Jordan for a therapy session. Bryn had showed them a dollhouse on the table and a cupboard full of figures and objects. "I want you all to make a world together. Using any of these things you want, work together to create a world inside this house." Sarah had felt awkward and sheepish, like when she was asked to participate in games at Danny's school, but now she missed having something active to do.

She wandered into the kitchen, where the boys sat around one of the kitchen islands with their Popsicles. Danny sat between Jordan and Nate, his big brother's shadow today, like the old days. Sarah got herself a raspberry Popsicle and sat on a stool.

The conversation was strained, mostly led by Nate asking Jordan about soccer, until Jordan winced and pressed a hand to his fore-head. "Ow."

"Brain freeze?" Nate asked.

Jordan nodded, eyes shut tight.

"It's from your teeth," Danny said. "Your brain freezes when your teeth get cold. Don't bite it. You have to *suck* it."

A horrible silence froze the room. Oh, dear God, this was torture.

Sarah thought of those images from the disks. She risked a glance at Jordan, whose face—the color of his cherry Popsicle—told her he was thinking of those images, too.

Danny looked mortified as well, and Sarah wondered how many other photos he'd seen wherever he found that picture of Jordan.

Jordan ignored Danny's comment and turned to Sarah. "Can I go to the bathroom?"

"Sure. You don't have to ask," Sarah said.

She exhaled when he left the room. She was so tense her neck ached. She sat with her sons, fidgeting in awful silence, as if they were *all* strangers brought together to live in this house today. She fought the urge to to chase after Reece's car, waving her arms and yelling, "Never mind!" She realized now that their "world-building" exercise was being reenacted here: Danny had plunged in, grabbing handfuls of deer and rabbits, filling the dollhouse with all kinds of animals. Nate had been the rational, patient leader, negotiating space for the others. And Jordan had gone so long without responding that Sarah feared he was refusing to participate.

She cleared her throat. "Reece said we should all do what we'd regularly be doing. We need to give him some space to watch us and get used to the house." The boys looked at her and nodded, but no one moved. "What do we normally do on Sundays?" Sarah felt desperate.

"Can I go work on my science project?" Danny asked.

"Absolutely," Sarah said. "Good idea."

Nate snorted. "Danny volunteering to do homework?"

"Shut up."

"Nate," Sarah said, "maybe today would be a good day to move Klezmer back outside."

"You still have Klezmer?" Jordan said from the doorway.

He didn't have the Popsicle anymore.

"Yep," Danny and Nate said in unison. For a split second, Jordan's face registered utter delight, but then it vanished beneath his passive, neutral mask of disinterest. Sarah wondered how long it took for a child his age to perfect that mask.

"You wanna see him?" Danny asked.

"No." It was too quick, too defensive.

"Come on," Danny said. "Last time you saw him, he was just a baby."

"No," Jordan said again, too insistently for Danny's friendly offer.

Danny's mouth dropped open, and he blinked. Another pause fell. Sarah felt sad for Danny. He was trying so hard.

"So," Sarah said brightly. She turned to Nate. "You think you'll put the hutch under Danny's tree again?"

Nate narrowed his eyes and said, "Yes," slowly, as if Sarah were psychotic. *Come on,* she willed him. *Give me a break. Work with me here.*

"Why is it Danny's tree?" Jordan asked.

"Me and Danny both have trees," Nate said, pointing toward the backyard. "They were planted when we were born, so our trees are as old as we are."

"We could plant one for you," Danny said. "And *you'd* be lucky—you'd get to pick what kind you want."

Sarah stared at Danny, amazed. It was sweet—a great idea, actually—but Jordan looked alarmed now.

"But . . . but I'm not . . . I'm not really in your family."

"But you are *now*," Danny said.

"But . . . but just for a while. Not really."

Sarah saw Danny's face change. "Okay," he said, giving up. "Whatever. I'm gonna work on my science." He left the kitchen.

Sarah chewed on her Popsicle stick. Any discomfort she experienced was nothing compared to what this child had been through.

"You wanna see your room?" Nate asked. "You could unpack your stuff."

Sarah felt something akin to terror as they disappeared up the stairs. It was the same feeling she'd had when she first brought newborn Nate home and left any room he was in. It was all she could do not to follow them.

She waited a few minutes to go check on Danny, so it wouldn't appear she was following the boys.

"Hey," she said, slipping inside Danny's room, now crowded with Nate's belongings as well. He jumped up from his bed, then exhaled and dropped his shoulders when he saw it was her. She noticed he wasn't working on his science project. "Jordan doesn't know about what happened at school. You don't have to be so nervous about that."

"I'm not nervous." He pushed his black curls out of his eyes.

"Okay." Sarah tousled his hair and left him alone.

In the hall Jordan hovered in the door frame of Nate's old room. "Uh . . . I think I'm done unpacking. Is this okay?" He stepped back, as if inviting her to inspect his room.

"If it's okay by you, it's okay by me. It's your room."

"For now," he stressed, his face serious.

"Right. For now." She gazed into that somber face. He looked so much like his mother—the same wispy blond hair, the same high cheekbones, the same blue eyes. It made Sarah miss Courtney. The old Courtney, that is. The one Sarah thought she'd known. Sarah remembered telling Courtney that her eyes were the color of Lake Superior in July. She'd even shown her a photograph of Ma and Pop standing on their deck, the lake sparkling like a jewel behind them.

"So I can go downstairs?" Jordan asked.

She felt a melting sensation in her chest. "Yes, of course. You don't have to ask permission. We want you to make yourself at home here."

He nodded and followed her to the kitchen. He stood at the back door and watched Nate play with the rabbit in the yard while Sarah puttered around making lunch. Nate moved the rabbit hutch out of the basement and situated it under Danny's apple tree. He put in fresh straw and hooked up the water bottle.

Jordan just watched. Sarah didn't try to make conversation, and neither did he, and after a while the silence was comfortable.

"Here, taste this." Sarah gave him a chicken salad sandwich. "Does it need more mayo?"

He shook his head. He ate it all. She gave him another. She opened up a bag of chips, and he ate half of them while she made sandwiches and sliced up a watermelon. Sarah never bought chips—or Popsicles, for that matter—but she and Danny had tried to select things they remembered from Jordan's house for him.

When she called the boys for lunch, Jordan said he wasn't hungry anymore. He wandered around the backyard and garden while they gathered at the table.

Nate started to pick up his sandwich and head for the living room, but Sarah said, "I'd really like us all to sit down at the table."

Danny and Nate paused, and she braced herself for resistance, but none came. They sat down. They ate together, but in silence. After lunch they all went their separate ways.

Sarah joined Jordan in the backyard. "Wanna see something cool? There's a nest of robin eggs in that tree." She stood on the bench and gestured for him to join her. He hesitated but then climbed up beside her. Sarah peered down into the nest. "Oh, my gosh! They hatched." Tiny pink heads—all mouth, it seemed— wobbled on pipe-cleaner necks from the depths of the nest.

Jordan stood on tiptoe to see the baby birds, and Sarah's heart lifted at his smile. The mother robin shrieked her staccato warnings, and Sarah said, "Watch out for her. You go after her kids and she'll get you. See?" She held out her hand to show Jordan her scar, but his face changed. Something dark moved behind his pale blue eyes, and he jumped down.

Sarah felt bad that in their effort to give him space, Jordan ended up spending the rest of the day alone. He went inside the house to his room and closed the door. When she knocked later, to remind him to take his medicine, she heard the unmistakable sound of furniture dragging across carpet before he opened the door. From the marks on the carpet, she guessed he'd had the desk chair against the door. She said nothing about it, but her throat tightened.

He said he was tired at dinnertime and didn't join them then either. Around seven o'clock he came downstairs, and she showed him where the leftovers were and told him to help himself. He cleaned up after himself impeccably.

When everyone headed to bed, he came downstairs to watch TV. Sarah never went to bed unless her kids were in their rooms. But for this one time, she let it go. She didn't sleep, though. She crept downstairs once at twelve-thirty, and sure enough, he was awake on the couch, the only light from the TV itself, watching some old Hitchcock film. She thought she was quiet, but he jumped to his feet and asked, "Is it too loud? Do you want me to turn it off?"

"No, no, it's not too loud at all. I'm amazed you can even hear it. I didn't mean to startle you; I was just . . . checking on you. You need anything?"

He shook his head, and Sarah looked at the TV. A man was being strangled. He grabbed at the rope around his neck, but the attacker kept hold, his face ablaze with power.

"Won't this give you bad dreams?" she asked.

He looked at her as if he weren't sure she was serious. "I don't dream about things on TV."

Sarah's eyes stung. *Of course he didn't.* She wanted to scoop him to her and hug him, but she knew that would be little comfort to this child. They stuttered through some more small talk, and she went away.

She crept back down again at three. The TV was still on, but muted, and Jordan sat with his back in the corner of the room, his head leaning against the front door, asleep sitting up, knees drawn into his chest, arms wrapped around them.

For either of her own children, she would have turned off the TV, kissed his tousled hair, and escorted him up to bed, but she didn't. She tiptoed away.

She thought again of that dollhouse therapy exercise. When Jordan finally did participate, he'd plunked down a fire-breathing dragon in front of the only door, blocking any exit from the dollhouse.

"Jordan!" Danny had said. "Come on. Take it out. The dragon will eat the rabbits."

Jordan had shrugged.

"How about this?" Bryn asked. "I asked you all to work together. Is there a way we can make room for the dragon so that the rabbits can be safe?"

"How?" Danny asked.

"Exactly," Bryn said. "How? Is there a way you can find?"

"Hey, look," Nate said. He stood by the cupboard and held up a little segment of fence. "There's fences and cages here. We could build a fence."

"No, put him in a cage," Danny said.

"There's not a cage big enough," Jordan said.

"Sure there is," Nate said. He held one up. "This will work. Look." He set the golden cage down over the dragon.

"It's not a real cage," Jordan protested. "It doesn't have a bottom or a lock. He'll just knock it over."

Nate laughed. "Dude, relax. It's a plastic dragon, okay? It's our world. If we say he can't get out, he can't get out."

Jordan opened his mouth, eyes blazing, but then seemed to change his mind. His eyes glazed over, and his face slipped on a neutral expression.

Sarah fell asleep dreaming of that dragon rattling its cage. She woke at six. Jordan's bed hadn't been slept in. Downstairs the TV was off, but he wasn't sleeping in the corner. Had he run away? She'd never entertained this possibility. A series of chastisements raced through her brain—you *knew* this was a bad idea, this was a disaster waiting to happen, what on earth made you think you could do this?

But then she saw him. The back door was open, and through the screen in the early-morning light, she saw him sitting with Klezmer in his lap, stroking the rabbit's nose just where he liked it, up between his eyes.

The rush of relief made her feel shaky, and it struck her that she'd been very naive when she'd agreed to do this.

CHAPTER SEVENTEEN

Jordan

Jordan stood in the Ladens' dark kitchen, drinking a glass of milk before he went to bed. He came down here every night to check the doors and peek out the windows at the backyard and driveway. Lots of places his dad could hide. Maybe behind Nate's dogwood or in the corner by Danny's apple tree. Those stupid trees Danny kept talking about. Sarah had told him that he could pick out a tree to plant if he wanted. But they didn't get it. He wasn't staying here. His dad wouldn't let him. They were all such morons, acting like everything was going to be okay. And even if the police caught his dad, Jordan wanted to go to his own home. With his own mom.

Jordan peered through the window at the bushes by Mrs. Ripley's back porch. That would be a hiding place, too. His dad was watching everything he did. Waiting. This was so bad. He almost wished his dad would just show up and do it—whatever he was going to do to Jordan. Dreading it made him sick.

Jordan could see Mrs. Ripley moving around her kitchen, talking to herself. Or was she singing? He didn't like watching her without her knowing. It made him think of other things he didn't like, so he turned his back to the window, leaning against the sink.

He heard Sarah call, "Hey, Danny? Can you run down to the basement and bring up some more toilet paper? It's on the shelf beside the washer."

Jordan set his glass in the sink and waited for Danny's protest. "Why do I have to do it?" came the whine. This might be the moment Jordan had been waiting for.

He heard Sarah say, "Because I asked you to. Now, do it, please."

Jordan figured he had two or three more rounds of this before Danny came down here and got the stupid toilet paper.

"I didn't use the last of it," Danny said. "Whoever used it up should have to go get it. It wasn't me." But his voice moved closer, growing louder, in the upstairs hallway.

Jordan crept down the basement stairs in the dark. He felt for the washer and then the shelf. He grabbed the plastic-wrapped twelve-roll pack of toilet paper and hugged it to his chest. Finally. It had taken a whole week to get Danny alone.

Footsteps thudded over his head as Danny tromped through the kitchen. The light clicked on at the top of the stairs, and Danny thunked down the wooden steps. It wasn't until he reached the bottom that he saw Jordan standing there waiting.

Danny grabbed the railing, and his body jerked like he'd been shocked.

"Do you have it?" Jordan asked.

Danny's mouth hung open, but he didn't speak.

"Something's missing, out of my backpack, Danny. What did you do with it?"

Danny glared at Jordan and turned to go back upstairs.

"Hey, wait. Your mom wants the toilet paper, right?"

Danny looked to the shelf, saw it was empty, then frowned at Jordan, seeming to finally recognize what Jordan held.

"I'm not mad," Jordan said. "I know why you took it. I just need to know where it is."

"I don't know what you're talking about. Give me the toilet paper."

Jordan clutched it tighter and shook his head.

Danny clenched his fists, acting like he was going to beat Jordan up for the toilet paper, and Jordan almost wished he'd try. Dannyboy might be surprised to discover that Jordan fought back these days. But Jordan knew that Danny would never hit him. He'd never hit anyone.

Danny looked over his shoulder, up the stairs.

"No one can hear us," Jordan said. "That's why I came down here."

Danny's mouth began to tremble. "I didn't know."

"Nobody knew." A fist of anger clenched in Jordan's belly. He'd worked so hard for no one to know. And it was all ruined. This was his only hope.

"No, I didn't know what the disk *was*," Danny said. "I thought it was homework. I just . . . I just thought it might be your paragraph for Miss Holt or something. I didn't know."

"Now you do. So what did you do with it?" Jordan *had* to get it.

"I just—I didn't . . ." Danny's gaze wandered around the basement, and a tear shone on his cheek. Jordan didn't have time for him to cry. "When you, you know, were mean to me that day, at your pool, and told me not to come back . . . you said your parents thought I was stupid and they were just being nice to me because my dad was dead—"

"Yeah, yeah, yeah, but what did you *do* with it?"

"You were really . . . saving me, weren't you?"

Jordan stared at his friend. He remembered how it made him hurt inside to say the things he'd had to say to Danny. How he'd tried to think of the worst things, to make sure Danny never came back. "How long did that take you, Sherlock?"

Danny's face clouded. Jordan didn't know why he'd said that. He didn't have to be mean anymore, did he? What was wrong with him?

"Not long when I saw the pictures," Danny said. "Why didn't you just tell me? Tell Billy? Tell *somebody*?"

"Where's the disk?"

"You were such an asshole. You said your parents couldn't believe you'd be friends with me. They . . . they didn't really say that, did they?"

"Danny, who cares? Where is it?" He heard footsteps overhead.

"It's gone."

Before Jordan could question him, Sarah's voice came from the top of the stairs. "Danny? You down there?"

All color drained from Danny's face. *No.* Jordan needed to ask Danny more. "Y-yeah."

"You seen Jordan?"

"H-he's down here, too."

She quickly descended a couple steps, low enough to peer at them. She knew that something was up, Jordan could tell. All week she'd seemed terrified of leaving Danny and Jordan alone together, not that there was much chance of that happening, with Danny practically holding Nate's hand every single second. "Everything okay?" Sarah asked.

"Yeah," Jordan said. "We were just talking about school."

Sarah smiled, relief softening her face. "Do you miss it?"

"Kinda," he said. "But Danny says I'm lucky now that they're doing fractions. My tutor hasn't given me any yet."

Danny stared at him, eyes wide. It felt almost good, familiar and comfortable, to make up a lie. Jordan handed him the toilet paper.

"Well, hurry up, you two. It's almost ten. You need to get to bed."

"Okay," they said, both heading for the stairs. But she walked away, ahead of them.

Jordan grabbed Danny's T-shirt. He whispered, "What do you mean, 'It's gone'?"

"Jordan—I was . . . There were pictures of me. I . . . I couldn't let—"

"You were in a swimming suit!"

"But still . . . is . . . is that what they would've done to me? Those other pictures?"

Jordan didn't say anything for a minute. He suddenly felt like he hadn't slept for three months. He heard his mother's voice: *Well, make him like you.* He shrugged. "I don't know." And he felt his own eyes sting with tears. "No, Danny. No. I wouldn't let them. That's why I said that stuff. That's the only reason." He wrinkled his nose against the burning feeling in his face. The look in Danny's eyes made Jordan feel . . . happy. Jordan was glad Danny knew he didn't mean those things.

"Don't tell anyone, okay?" Danny asked.

Maybe Danny's dumbness could help Jordan. "I won't if you won't."

Danny frowned. "But everyone already knows about you."

"But that's the only disk with . . ." Jordan looked at the floor. He didn't want to say the words out loud. His throat got thick. His voice went raspy, like when he talked to Dr. Bryn. He looked into Danny's blank face, waiting for Jordan to finish his sentence. And Jordan realized: Danny didn't have a clue. He had no idea what Jordan had been about to say. Jordan's heart did that funny jump, kicking in its extra beat. Danny thought people really cared about pictures of him swimming. Please. "I just wanted to know what happened," Jordan said. "I knew I put five disks in the backpack, but the police only had four." He took a deep breath. "So what did you do? Did you, like, smash it?"

Danny paused a second too long before nodding. "Yeah," he said, in this fake-cheerful voice. Another extra beat hit his ribs. Jordan knew that the disk still existed somewhere in this house. He'd have to look for it. But Danny shared a room with Nate now that Jordan had moved in. It wouldn't be easy.

Danny continued up the stairs, but at the top he stopped. Without turning around, leaving Jordan staring at his back, he said, "I'm sorry, Jordan, about the things we said. Billy and those guys. We didn't know."

"You never said anything, Danny. It's okay."

"But I . . . I just—you know. I didn't try to make them stop."

The feeling inside Jordan was new and very strange. He didn't know what to do with it.

"It's okay," he said again. He reached up and patted Danny's back.

Jordan couldn't sleep. He was wide awake. What did that mean, he wondered, wide awake? Could you be narrowly awake? He sighed. That's the sort of thing not being able to sleep would leave him wondering about for the rest of the night. He looked at the clock. "The wee hours," his grandma had called them. What did *that* mean? They weren't shorter. They actually felt longer when you were awake during them.

He liked this bed better than his own old one. Only room for one, that's all, just like the hospital. He could lie in almost any position and feel both sides of the bed.

He smiled in the darkness, remembering what a chicken Danny had been the first time he'd spent the night at Jordan's house. He'd made Jordan close his closet door and his bathroom door before they turned out the lights, and Danny had to turn the lights back on to get up to pee. Danny *loved* ghost stories and stories about monsters and vampires and stuff, but he'd get himself all hyper and scared every time. Back in third grade, Danny thought there were monsters under the bed. He told Jordan they had to keep their hands and feet in the bed. If they let their arms drop over while they slept, the monsters could grab them and pull them under.

Jordan let his leg drop over the side and tapped his toes on the floor. He wasn't afraid of the monsters under the bed. Had he ever been afraid of such make-believe monsters? He couldn't remember any. He'd never even been afraid of the dark. He kind of liked the dark.

No, the only things under this bed were Jordan's shoes. His running shoes from Kramble, the gym shoes he'd had on when Sarah took him to the ER, and a pair of sandals and some brown leather shoes Reece had brought from Jordan's house when they were finally allowed to get some of his stuff. Deep inside one leather shoe was the broken wing he'd stolen from Dr. Bryn's office. He thought he was busted the day all the Ladens came to therapy and they had to make a "world" together in a dollhouse. Sarah had picked out that purple angel. Danny and Nate had complained because it was broken, but Sarah said she wanted it anyway. Jordan kept waiting for Dr. Bryn to ask him, "What happened to the other wing?" but she didn't.

Deep inside the other shoe were the letters from Jordan's mother—he folded each one as small as he could and crammed them into the toes of those shoes so none of the Ladens would look at them.

He knew that Reece and Dr. Bryn had read all the letters. Who knew who else? At least they didn't try to pretend they hadn't read them—the envelopes were always opened when they gave him the letters, and Dr. Bryn asked a lot of questions about each one. How did it make him feel when his mother said this? What did he want to do when his mother said that? Dr. Bryn made him show her his letters back to his mom, too.

Jordan closed his eyes and tried to fall asleep again, but in his head he saw his mom's big, loopy handwriting, with the fat circles dotting all the *i*'s. Their letters were full of code phrases. She had realized, along with Jordan, that one disk was missing. Jordan's face burned in the dark—because the police hadn't found it at the house, now she knew that Jordan had taken it. He hated that she knew. And since the police hadn't reported it when they found Jordan's backpack, she knew that something was up.

Jordan had written back to her, wanting to make her believe that the disk with her pictures on it was gone. He wanted her to know that they had a chance to be together again. He'd written something like, "*Everyone believes all the stuff about you in the news. I tell people that none of it is true, but I think we're the only ones who know the real story.*"

Dr. Bryn had asked, "You tell people that none of *what* was true?"

"The stuff on the news."

"What stuff?"

Sometimes he hated Dr. Bryn. She knew what he was talking about it. Why did she want him to say it? The words stuck in his throat. The one time she got him to whisper words for what his father had done to him, he waited for something to hurt him. He knew it would happen. And sure enough, he woke up later in the night because he felt his hair being yanked, pulling his head back and back until he couldn't swallow. Dr. Bryn said those were "body memories." Well, he didn't want body memories. He didn't even want a body. And if talking about the bad stuff made body memories happen, he didn't see the point. M-e-m-o-r-i-e-s. He pictured the word "memories" in his mom's handwriting, a little heart over the *i*.

In today's letter Mom had written about "*getting rid of this nightmare.*" He knew she was asking about the disk: Had it been destroyed? Broken into pieces and thrown away?

He didn't have to tell her the truth. She hadn't told him the truth, not about her brother. Jordan had asked about his uncle in a letter, but his mom had ignored his question. So Jordan felt like he could ignore certain questions, too. She didn't have to know about Danny. He could tell her the disk was gone and let her think that *he'd* destroyed it that very first day of his plan. To protect her. Then she'd want to be nice to him, and they could live together without his dad.

His dad. Jordan sat up in bed. He knew he was never going to sleep unless he put the chair against the door, tipped so that the back was under the doorknob. This was the first night he hadn't. He knew that the Ladens heard him move it around, even though no one said anything. He hated that they might think he was afraid of *them*—that he might think they wanted to do those things in the pictures. Tonight he had decided it was better without the chair, so if his dad did come, it could happen fast and none of the Ladens would get hurt, too.

Jordan turned on a lamp. He liked this room. It used to be Nate's. Nate had left him a Cincinnati Zoo poster of white Bengal tigers and an autographed poster of Wayne Gretzky.

He didn't feel like reading. And he didn't feel like doing any of his homework either. Every day Reece took him to the Children's Services building, where he met his homeschooling tutor. His teachers weren't giving him very much work, probably because they felt sorry for him, but he *wanted* to do what all the other kids were doing. He'd already worked two units ahead in vocabulary and was reading about ancient Egypt in history while the class was still on Greece. He wanted to get some books from the library on cat mummies. Maybe he and Danny could make a cat-mummy sarcophagus. It would be a way for him to bury Raja after all. And Danny could take the sarcophagus to school for extra credit.

Jordan wiped his damp neck with his hand. He was hot in his sweats and turtleneck. It was humid and muggy for May, and Sarah hadn't turned on the air conditioner yet. He couldn't wait until she did. He wanted the windows shut. Sarah'd given him a fan, but he wouldn't use it. He didn't like the noise it made, covering the other sounds in the house. And hadn't Nate told him yesterday that he smelled? Nate had said it nicer than that. He'd asked if Jordan needed some deodorant. He was glad Nate told him, though. It was true. Just the sort of thing he would've gotten in trouble for before, drawing attention to himself.

He pulled off his turtleneck. Whew, he did stink. He got out of bed. He avoided the creaky spot on the floor and went to the full-length mirror on the closet door. If his chest and back were covered, there was nothing awful on his arms or neck anymore. He narrowed his eyes and looked at his bony chest and all his ribs. Dr. Ali said he needed to gain weight. He'd heard her and Dr. Bryn call his weight "failure to thrive," which bugged him, since he'd always gotten A's in everything. A breeze stirred the curtains and ran across his naked back. Jordan shut his eyes. He would sleep without a shirt on tonight.

A thump vibrated through the quiet house, but it didn't scare him. He knew that sound. Danny always got up to pee around now. Jordan knew everyone's routine. He listened to Danny's footsteps in the hall, the loud echo of his peeing in the quiet house, since he never shut the door at night, the flush. He waited for the *pad pad pad* of Danny's feet going back to his room—but they stopped outside Jordan's door. The doorknob turned, and Danny poked his face in without knocking.

"Hey," Danny whispered, then closed the door behind him. "I saw your light on. I can't sleep either." He wore a pair of shorts and a T-shirt. Danny plunked himself on Jordan's bed. Jordan saw himself picking up his turtleneck and putting it back on. Or putting on another shirt. But he couldn't move. He just stood there like an idiot.

"I'm really glad we're friends again," Danny said.

Danny could say stuff like that. If anyone else said it, it would sound cheesy or dorky, but Danny was just like that. Jordan had missed Danny. Danny was one of those people who never hurt anyone. He picked the ugly girls first as his partners in science. He picked the fat boys first when he got to be captain of a team in gym. There was something nice and good about Danny that made Jordan feel better even if they just sat at the same lunch table together and didn't say anything.

"I really believed you, all that stuff you said," Danny said. He sat cross-legged on Jordan's bed, and Jordan could tell that Danny was going to stay there for a long time.

"I'm sorry," Jordan whispered. He'd *wanted* Danny to believe it, but his nose burned again, thinking of saying that stuff to Danny.

Danny cocked his head. "How come you never told me?"

Jordan froze. He was still standing there in front of the mirror. He didn't know what to do with his hands. A rushing-water sound started in his ears.

"I wish you would have told me," Danny whispered, tracing the pattern on the bedcover with his finger. "I would've helped you."

Jordan stared at Danny. Danny kept looking at the quilt. They couldn't talk about this. Jordan couldn't answer those questions. He couldn't breathe right. "R-remember how we used to make up monster stories?" Jordan asked.

Danny looked up, somehow grinning and frowning at the same time. "You always did that," he whispered.

Jordan didn't know what he meant.

"Every time I asked you a question . . . and the answer had to do with . . . you know, *that,* even though I didn't know it, you'd change the subject or make up a story."

Jordan pictured himself running from the room. Something. Anything. They couldn't have this conversation.

"Like that one time," Danny said, "when you were limping, and you made up that story about how one night the monsters under your bed got a hold of your leg and you had to kick and fight and you just barely managed to keep them from pulling you underneath."

Jordan swallowed. It felt like he had glass in his throat again, like that first day at the hospital.

"And when I found that bloody towel in your bathroom, you said that was from a fight with the monsters, too. But it was really from . . . from that stuff in the pictures, wasn't it?"

Jordan just sat down on the floor where he was. What all had Danny seen? He didn't want to have to wonder what Danny was picturing whenever Danny looked at him. The water sound in his ears hurt him, made his jaw and neck ache.

Danny kept tracing that pattern with his finger. "I just wish you would have told me. But it's okay that you didn't. I bet I wouldn't have told anyone either."

Jordan pulled his knees to his chest and wrapped his arms around them, trying to concentrate over the water sound. The words Danny spoke hovered in the air before him like a bubble in a cartoon. That always happened when they touched him.

"Anyway, I'm really glad you're okay. And I'm glad you're here."

Jordan opened his mouth, but no sound came out, just like when he tried to talk to Bryn.

Danny flopped forward on his belly on Jordan's bed. He draped one arm over the side and idly poked at the carpet with his finger. They didn't talk for a really long time. Jordan wondered if Danny was going to fall asleep in here.

Just as the water sound had almost disappeared, Danny sat back up and picked up Jordan's sketch pad off the nightstand. "This is really good," he said.

Jordan couldn't remember what picture he'd left it open to, but he knew it was a picture of Raja when Danny said, "So what really happened to your cat?"

The gurgling filled his ears again. And a word appeared in the air before him: "grave." G-r-a-v-e. It meant solemn. S-o-l-e-m-n. Don't forget that n. Life-threatening. T-h-r-e a-t-e-n-i-n-g.

"That was a creepy story you made up about him," Danny said. "About that boy who was the slave of the monsters."

Jordan had made up that story just last fall. They'd been doing a play at school about the Underground Railroad.

"You said before the boy was a slave, he used to go stay at his grandma's."

That was because his mother loved him, right? She took him to his grandma's because she didn't want to do the things she did. And she didn't want his dad to hurt him either.

"And the boy and his grandma went to a movie, and when they came back, there was a cat on his grandma's porch. They just found it there, and the cat wouldn't leave. And they took care of it all summer long. And when the grandma died—Hey, how did she die? I don't remember. Did the monsters kill her?"

Jordan shook his head. *I did,* he thought. *I never should have told her. I made her sick.*

"Oh. Well, anyway, after the grandma died, the boy got taken prisoner by the monsters. They made him their slave."

He really shouldn't say "monsters." It felt wrong, and he couldn't help but worry that his mom would somehow know, but she couldn't, could she?

"And the monsters killed the boy's cat because the boy tried to escape."

He shouldn't say that. It had been his fault. Being such a baby at school. Making the teachers call that meeting.

"And the boy never tried to escape again."

Well, until that day in the rain, that day of the epiphany.

"Hey," Danny said softly. "Are you okay?"

Jordan's body shivered with silent sobs, and he wiped his eyes with the back of hand. He tried to make himself stop crying. He buried his face in his knees.

"It wasn't a story," Danny said. He didn't even make it a question. He knew. "Your . . . your mom and dad killed your cat, didn't they?"

Jordan kept his face buried.

"Was it because you tried to tell someone?"

He shut his eyes tight. He heard the floor creak and knew Danny had gotten off the bed. Danny sat down beside Jordan and put his arm around Jordan's shoulders. Jordan hated the feeling. It made him want to elbow Danny in the ribs and slam him against the wall until his bones crunched. He shoved Danny off and stood up. "Don't. Don't touch me, okay?" His whole body shook.

Danny's face looked up at him, pale, eyes wide. "Sorry," he whispered.

Jordan walked to the mirror and pulled on the turtleneck he'd taken off.

"I'm really sorry," Danny said. Jordan could tell that Danny was crying, too.

He wanted to reassure Danny that it was okay. Danny shouldn't cry about it. Danny was only trying to be nice. But Jordan didn't know how to say these things. If Jordan didn't talk about the bad things, they didn't have to be real yet, no matter what anybody else said. He didn't want Danny to cry.

Jordan pulled his turtleneck sleeve down over his hand and wiped his eyes, then his nose.

"Here," Danny said. He handed Jordan the box of tissues that had been on the nightstand. He reached out and patted Jordan's shoulder once but drew his hand back really fast.

Jordan sat down again and clamped his hands over his mouth when he couldn't control his sobs.

Danny put the box of tissues in Jordan's lap. He sat beside Jordan for several minutes. Finally Danny said, "Maybe . . . maybe I should go get my mom."

Jordan shook his head. "No," he rasped out. He took a tissue and blew his nose. He had to show Danny he was all right. He got up and crawled back into bed and pulled the covers up to his chin. "I'm okay."

Danny didn't look convinced. He stood at the door for a minute before he said, "Okay. See ya." He left the room and closed the door without a sound.

Jordan pushed his face into his pillow and cried himself empty and exhausted.

An hour later he positioned the chair under the doorknob and finally fell asleep.

CHAPTER EIGHTEEN

Sarah

Sarah saw the light turn yellow at the intersection before her and sped up at first, then changed her mind. Her tires squealed, and the bag of groceries fell off the passenger seat.

Damn it. Courtney was out of jail.

Out of jail. She might even be out walking, crossing Sarah's path at any moment.

Sarah couldn't believe it. And she couldn't believe the emotional effect the news had had on her.

She'd been at the seafood market when Kramble had called her. She'd flushed when she heard his voice. She had just been thinking about a dream she'd had about him.

She and Roy used to joke about their sex dreams, teasing each other that they rarely had such dreams about each other. "People don't need to dream about what's real," Roy had said. He used to wake her sometimes at 2:00 A.M. when he came home from the hospital, freshly showered, smelling like soap. They'd lie sideways on the bed, sometimes moving to the floor to keep their headboard from bumping against Nate's bedroom wall.

But since Roy had died, he did appear in her dreams. All of her sex dreams were about him. Until last night.

When she first surfaced from that dream, she'd been flushed and purring. But as she truly woke up, a sick misery had settled on her, like she'd been unfaithful to a living Roy. She'd been flustered and distracted all morning.

And she knew that even though Kramble had only invited her to dinner, they would end up in bed if she wanted them to.

Would he be a little rough-and-tumble? She pictured them tearing clothes and panting and knocking over furniture. Or did that image only come to her because he carried a gun?

But there was that scar . . . that history. Maybe he wouldn't be rough at all, but fragile and cautious. Whatever history he'd survived, he'd risen above it, gotten married, even. She pictured Kramble at his wedding—pictured it happening under a chuppah even though she knew he wasn't Jewish. Pictured him smashing the wineglass under his heel, as if it were his past, breaking that other life into shards that could be swept away.

And then there was Reece. Sarah scrunched up her face and groaned as she remembered her dream. She'd dreamed about Reece, *too*. She'd hardly been able to look at him without blushing this morning when he'd picked up Jordan for a session with Bryn and for Jordan's tutoring session at Children's Services. Reece was every bit as sexy as Kramble but in an entirely different way. She imagined him slow and luxurious. She saw candles and massage oils and maybe even blindfolds. No, not blindfolds. She'd want to see her white hands on his dark skin. Her pale legs wrapped around his coffee-colored torso.

A car honked behind Sarah. The light had changed. *Get a grip.* She drove on.

Courtney was out of jail.

Sarah had been thinking of that lovely, sexy dream as she selected shrimp for the eight pounds of spicy shrimp-and-fennel pasta salad she was making for a University of Dayton graduation party tomorrow. When her cell phone rang, she felt a hassled irritation in her chest, but when she heard Kramble's voice, she had an urge to cover the mouthpiece with her hand, as if her recent thoughts about him hovered in the air and might whisper their way through to nibble his ear. "Yes, hi." Her voice was too perky and fake.

"I have some important news," Kramble said. "Courtney Kendrick is being processed out of jail right now."

Sarah nearly dropped her bag of shrimp. Several slipped out of the plastic bag onto the market floor. *"What?"*

"I told you I'd call you if that happened. I just found out. Her brother is here. He posted her bail."

"Oh, shit. . . ." A tremendous wave of adrenaline crashed through Sarah's body. Her legs went rubbery, and she crouched on the floor. *Oh, shit. Oh, shit. Oh, shit.* She clutched the cell phone in the crook between her ear and shoulder and picked up the slippery shrimp to put back in their plastic bag. "But I thought they didn't talk to each other! How did this happen?"

"He apparently contacted her after I interviewed him. She's called him collect many times from the jail."

Why didn't anyone tell me? Sarah wanted to scream. "What do I do? What should I do?" She had collected all her wayward shrimp but remained crouched.

"Sarah, it's okay. Don't do anything differently. She's aware of the very strict regulations regarding her visitation with Jordan until the trial. She knows that any violations of those regulations will land her right back in jail, so even if she does discover where he lives, I think she's too intelligent to come—"

"Oh, my God. Jordan will want to see her. What if he—"

"Sarah, calm down." His tone was not at all insulting but soothing. "We're with you, okay? I told Reece already, because I knew he was with Jordan this morning."

It half comforted her, half unnerved her to know he was so aware of their schedule.

"He's going to tell Jordan. Courtney has already asked for a visitation. We're going to do everything we can to hold off until tomorrow. Reece feels it's important to give Jordan time to process this and get ready for it. And we're, of course, hoping for a change of heart from him. Maybe he'll reveal something new once he's actually faced with seeing her again."

Sarah nodded, although he couldn't see her. She was finding it difficult to breathe.

"Sarah?"

"Yes."

"You okay?"

"I . . . I guess. Listen, thanks for calling, for warning me—"

"Of course. You have my cell number. Use it. For anything. Okay? This is going to be all right."

"Thank you, Bobby." As she snapped her phone shut, she winced as she realized she'd called him Bobby. Oh, dear God.

When she'd stood up, she left her bag of shrimp on the floor. And she'd walked right out of the market without it, had driven all the way home before she realized. Then had to drive all the way back. She couldn't find the bag—some irritated employee had probably found it and emptied it back into the bin. She'd started all over.

All she could think of was that Courtney was out of jail. She was out, free on the streets. What would she do? Would she contact Sarah? Did Sarah *want* her to? What if Courtney didn't—what if Sarah never saw her or spoke to her again. . . . Sarah imagined that Courtney might be "done" with her. Sarah hated that betrayed, raw feeling. She ought to be used to it by now, but she felt it afresh as she pictured Courtney thinking that there was nothing more Sarah could do for her. But the most unnerving thing was that she couldn't really imagine Courtney at all, had not an inkling what the woman was thinking—or what the woman had *ever* thought, really. She could hardly picture her at the moment. Someday Sarah would *have* to see her again. She'd have no closure if she didn't. And she certainly wasn't handing Jordan back to Courtney without seeing her and being convinced . . . convinced of what? She didn't feel she'd ever be convinced that Jordan should live with Courtney again.

Damn. She almost missed her own street. The tires squealed as she whipped the van around the corner.

Back home, inside her kitchen, Sarah poured the shrimp into a colander and began the process of peeling and deveining them. What was she going to say if she ran into Courtney somewhere? Courtney didn't know where Jordan was staying. That, combined with the fact that Sarah had never gone to see Courtney in jail, filled her with heavy dread. Her cheeks still burned when she remembered a conversation with a new client who'd come to look at wedding cakes. The woman had been gossipy and eager to discuss the Kendrick case. Sarah had felt uncomfortable, but she'd faked her evasive way through the appointment. She needed the job. Two more clients had canceled their events, and Sarah suspected that it had to do with people's knowledge of her friendship with Courtney.

This new client, however, seemed to have looked Sarah up *because* of her connection to the Kendricks. "You were friends with Dr. Kendrick, right?" the woman had asked. "Mark's wife?"

Sarah heard herself saying, "Oh, I wouldn't say friends. But I worked for them, you know." Why had she lied?

The woman frowned. "But Mark said you were friends. I used to work for him, at Kendrick, Kirker & Co.? He really recommended you, when I first told him about the wedding, way back before . . . before we knew about any of this. He said such nice things about you. And he made it sound like you and his wife were really close."

"We were friendly," Sarah said. "But I wouldn't say *friends*." She still felt like such a shit for saying that. But why should she?

She kept on peeling shrimp. Her cell phone trilled on the kitchen island behind her. Damn. Of course her hands were all nasty with shrimp goo. She hurriedly rinsed and wiped them and snatched up her phone right before it switched to voice mail.

"Hello?" Just as she said it, she had a flash of panic that it would be Courtney.

"Hey, Sarah, it's Reece." His deep, calm voice grounded her.

"Is Jordan okay?" she asked. "Kramble already told me the news."

"Yeah. Jordan's mad as hell that I won't let him stay with her."

"Oh." Sarah tried not to feel hurt that he'd so quickly want to be rid of them. Naturally he wanted to be with his own mother. And would he want to do that if Courtney had hurt him? Wasn't that a sign in her favor? But Sarah couldn't muster the "it couldn't be true" anymore. It had evolved into a monotonous internal refrain of, *You know it's true, you know it's true.*

"Don't worry. Everything is going to be fine. He's more terrified than ever about his father, though. We're going to spend a little more time with Bryn. Looks like we might have a visitation tomorrow. Earliest would be afternoon, say two. We're cranking out details and trying to prepare him for it. I'll have him back around dinnertime. Is that okay?"

Sarah was surprised at the tug in her chest. "Sure." She'd expected to feel a weight released; it would be a blessing to have an afternoon free, without Jordan's brooding, wounded presence underfoot. But she wasn't as overjoyed as she suspected.

She finished the call with Reece and returned to her shrimp, grateful to have work to do. It kept her from pacing the house or having a breakdown. She bagged up the shrimp shells for the trash, then blended red pepper, olive oil, lemon rind, and garlic in her blender. It took nearly two minutes to get a smooth consistency, and as she shut off the blender, she heard the back door click open.

She wheeled around, heart pounding, as Gwinn Whitacre came into the kitchen. "Hey, Sarah!"

"Oh, my God, you scared me."

"Well, I knocked, but you couldn't hear me with that blender going. I have amazing news! I came running over here to tell you in person."

"I already know," Sarah said. "But thanks."

Gwinn's shoulders slumped, and she pouted her lips. Sarah looked at her friend and smiled; it was as if the room had suddenly brightened. Sarah knew she should feel frumpy in Gwinn's presence—Gwinn always had great hair and impeccable makeup—yet it was hard to feel anything but loved around Gwinn. Sarah usually laughed so much when they were together that she forgot to worry over such details. Gwinn's almost freakish height and a rather large nose kept her from seeming too Barbie-ish. And Sarah liked Gwinn for always wearing heels, for not doing anything to disguise her height.

"How can you know already?"

"Kramble called me."

"Well, shit. I wanted to be the one who told you the good news."

Sarah snorted. "I'd hardly call it good news. Pull up a stool. There's coffee."

But Gwinn stood, French-manicured hands on her hips. "I don't think you know what I'm talking about, because it is very, very good news. *They caught Mark.*"

Sarah set her spatula down so quickly that the red pepper mixture freckled across the kitchen island. "What?"

"Yes! I *am* the first!" Gwinn came around the island and hugged Sarah. "They caught him, the prick. He was in Vegas, can you believe it?"

"That's wonderful."

"That's what I was telling you." Gwinn opened a cupboard and took out a coffee mug. She helped herself to cream and poured coffee. "Rodney was home for lunch, and it came over his radio while we were eating. I'm surprised you didn't hear us cheering from a block away. This is one bit of news I'm sharing with you with Rodney's full blessing. Mark Kendrick will soon be on his way back to Dayton." Gwinn opened a drawer and got herself a spoon.

"Vegas," Sarah said, sitting on a barstool. "I'm not sure what I thought he was doing all this time, but that just astounds me. Vegas."

Gwinn sat across from Sarah, stirring her coffee. She took a sip. "Mmm. You always have the best damn coffee." She gestured with the spoon when she talked. "Mark is totally screwed, right? With all the evidence against him, he doesn't have a prayer. So he's got nothing to lose. He could provide some answers, you know? He can tell us how involved Courtney really was."

"But who would believe what he says? He's not exactly a reliable witness."

"Still . . ."

"Now it's my turn for news," Sarah said. "Courtney is getting out of jail today. I mean, she *is* out by now."

"Shit. Who paid her bail?"

Sarah filled her in on what she knew.

"Oh, Sarah," Gwinn said, putting down her spoon. "Have you seen her since . . . that day at their house?"

Sarah shook her head.

"Have you talked to her?"

She shook her head again. "This has been so hard," she whispered. She feared she might cry.

"Of course it has," Gwinn said. She came around the island and hugged Sarah again.

"Are people talking about me?" Sarah asked. "At school?"

Gwinn put her hands on Sarah's shoulders. "No."

"For real, Gwinn. I need to know."

"People ask me how you're doing," Gwinn said. "I think they all sympathize."

"Would you tell me if they did talk about me?"

"You know I would. And then we'd egg their houses together." Sarah had to laugh.

Gwinn let Sarah go and returned to her stool. "Seriously, Sarah. People think you're wonderful for taking in Jordan."

"Does everyone know he's here?"

Gwinn thought a minute. "No. There's never been an official announcement or anything, but the people who know you can put two and two together. I think most everybody in Danny's class probably knows."

Sarah nodded. The faculty at school knew, of course. Jordan and Danny's class had made cards for Jordan, and the teacher had sent them home with Danny.

"Courtney doesn't know where Jordan is," Sarah said.

"Well, hell, no one is going to be stupid enough to tell her."

"People do a lot of stupid things."

Before Gwinn could answer, Sarah's cell phone rang again. "Oh, for God's sake, this has been nonstop this morning." She answered.

"Sarah, this is Robert Kramble again. This time I have some good news for you."

"You caught Mark Kendrick."

His startled silence made Sarah laugh.

"Gwinn Whitacre just told me."

Kramble laughed, too, and Sarah sensed his true happiness and relief. "This is really great," he said. His enthusiasm made him sound boyish. "The cleaning lady at his hotel recognized him and called the police."

"Jordan is going to be so relieved," Sarah said. She watched Gwinn get a new spoon out of the drawer and dip it in the red pepper sauce.

"Yes, but . . . it's complicated," Kramble said. "I know Bryn will help him with it, but . . . the kid was convinced his dad was stalking his every move just waiting to get revenge. And yeah, sure there's some relief in finding out he wasn't, but there's also something else. It's hard to articulate, but . . . but you have to really care about somebody to seek revenge, right?"

Tears welled in Sarah's eyes. "And he's going to realize his father didn't give a shit?"

"Right."

"Oh, God." She sighed. "This poor boy."

"Hey. This poor boy has proven that he's pretty strong, all things considered. I just wanted to let you know. I didn't want to be the bearer of only bad news."

"Thanks." Sarah wanted to say something else, to let him know how much she appreciated it, but Kramble said good-bye, and Sarah clicked off the phone.

"This is fabulous," Gwinn said, licking her spoon.

"It better be. Now I need to marinate this shrimp in that sauce for four hours." Sarah poured the sauce into a shallow dish.

"Are you okay, Sarah, really?" Gwinn asked. "This whole Courtney thing . . . I'm worried about you."

Sarah stirred the shrimp into the red pepper mixture. She smiled at her friend. "Thanks. I think I'm okay. I'm confused, I'm angry, I'm depressed, I feel guilty, but—"

"Guilty? Why should you feel guilty?" Gwinn picked up the empty blender container and ran her finger down the side, licking off more of the sauce.

"It wasn't as if I was just an acquaintance. How could I genuinely like someone who was . . . who was so . . . God, I don't even know what to call it."

"Evil?"

"No." Sarah put a lid on the dish and set it in the fridge. " 'Evil' seems wrong. Mark seems evil to me, but somehow Courtney doesn't."

"That's only because you know Courtney's story. It's like Kramble said at that awful school meeting, where Carlotta went insane and starting screaming—knowing that Courtney was a victim makes her seem less evil herself. But where does it end? We think her father was evil for abusing her, but what if her father was abused, too? And whoever abused her father? They're still doing evil. Once you find out Mark's story, you'll probably feel sorry for *him*. You're too nice, Sarah."

"Hey," Sarah said. "You asked if I was okay. I'd be a lot more okay if you weren't judging me, okay?"

"I'm sorry." And Sarah could tell Gwinn meant it. "But I worry."

Sarah sighed. She put the fennel bulbs on her cutting board and began to chop. "I think about her all the time, try to replay the times we were together, try to spot clues I missed, and I can't find anything. I hate to think I was so gullible."

"They fooled a lot of people."

"I think if I saw her, and talked to her, I might figure out what I felt. Does that make sense? One day we're chatting over coffee, the next day she's being taken away in handcuffs. I've never spoken to her about it."

"But what would you say to her?"

Sarah paused, the knife angled over a fennel bulb. "I have no idea. But I think I need to see her. I need some answers that only she can give me."

"But she *won't*." Gwinn leaned across the island toward Sarah, her gaze intense. "She'll just lie. She's a psychopath, Sarah."

Sarah resumed chopping. "Well. Maybe she is. Maybe she will lie. But somehow I don't think I'll have any peace unless I talk to her myself. I know it doesn't make sense, but I feel like I'd be able to tell she was lying—not that I could ever tell before—and then I'd know and I'd feel better. I just—There's a part of me that can't accept it yet. It's naive, it's stupid, it's all kinds of things, but that's the truth." Sarah's eyes burned.

"Oh, Sarah," Gwinn said.

Sarah set down her knife, picked up a tissue, and blew her nose. "I guess in answer to your question, I'm not okay. I'm a mess."

"You're no mess. You're one of the strongest people I know."

This statement shocked Sarah. She stared at Gwinn, her rib cage filling with gratitude. Before she could speak, her cell phone rang again.

Gwinn laughed.

Sarah reached for the phone, saying, "This'll be Jordan's case manager telling me they caught Mark." She answered with a chipper, playful, "Hello?"

Silence.

Sarah felt stupid. "Hello?" she asked again.

"Sarah?" the familiar, breathy voice asked.

Sarah heart slid down to her toes. *Oh, shit. Oh, shit.* She looked at Gwinn, but Gwinn was taking another swipe down the blender's side. Sarah turned her back to Gwinn, knowing that her face would give her away.

"Yes? This is Sarah Laden," she said, her tone formal.

"It's . . . it's Courtney."

Sarah couldn't breathe.

"Oh, Sarah." Courtney sounded like she was crying. "I'm . . . sorry. I'm sorry."

Sarah's brain was in a white panic. She didn't want Gwinn to know who it was.

Courtney went on. "I want to thank you, so, so much. . . ." Her voice cracked. "For taking Jordan to the emergency room. You . . . you saved his life, Sarah. I know you did. . . ."

"Could you hang on for just a moment?" Sarah asked.

Courtney said nothing, but Sarah held the phone to her chest and whispered to Gwinn, "I really need to take this. Frantic bride."

Gwinn laughed and stood up. "I gotta go anyway. I just wanted to tell you the news."

"Thanks. You're wonderful."

Gwinn kissed Sarah on the cheek. "Hang in there," she whispered. She pointed to the blender. "And make some of that for me." She let herself out the back door.

Sarah kept holding the phone to her chest, certain Courtney would hear her racing heartbeat. Sarah went to the door and locked it before bringing the phone back to her ear. She heard the faint sound of Courtney's breath. Sarah opened her mouth but felt as if she'd never spoken in her life.

"Are you there?" Courtney asked.

"Yes," she whispered.

"Oh, Sarah." And Courtney was crying again.

"I . . ." Sarah couldn't make her lips work. Hadn't she just received her wish? There was so much she wanted to ask, so much she needed to know, but she only listened to Courtney's quiet crying.

Sarah held the phone in the crook of her ear. She picked up her knife and immediately felt better, more confident. She sliced the fennel bulbs slowly and deliberately, trying to form words in her brain. "You told me you were an only child," she finally managed.

Courtney sighed, a ragged sound. "I didn't know," she whispered.

Sarah froze, knife poised over a new bulb. She didn't want to acknowledge what Courtney said.

"I s-suspected, but I didn't want it to be true. . . . I . . . I didn't do anything to stop it. . . . I didn't want to believe it. I hate myself. . . ."

Sarah kept chopping but felt the ache in her own chest harden. How could that be true? How could she not know? She realized she'd been hoping that somehow Courtney would have an explanation, that there be some reason no one else had considered, that exonerated her beyond a shadow of a doubt. Naive, hopelessly naive, but Sarah recognized this desire at the same moment she recognized that the desire would not be fulfilled.

"How could I believe that about a man I loved? If someone I thought I knew so well could do that . . . God, how could I be so stupid? I . . ."

The hairs lifted on the back of Sarah's neck.

"Jordan," Courtney whispered. "Sarah, I'm horrible." Her voice was muffled. "How could I have turned away? He tried so hard to tell me, and I just wouldn't believe it. It couldn't be true. It couldn't be true."

It couldn't be true. Sarah's own mantra. Until now. Her skin tightened all over her body. *It was true.*

"How?" Courtney wailed. "How can I ever look at him again?

I'm so sorry. How will he believe that? How will he trust me? He must hate me, and I deserve it."

Sarah felt she was observing herself from a great distance. Admiring the excellent performance. Chilled by the fact that Courtney was so convincing. Sarah realized she was chopping the fennel far too finely for this recipe. She scraped it off the cutting board into a bowl.

"I get to see him tomorrow. I want to see him, more than anything, but it terrifies me, too."

Faint dizziness unsettled Sarah as she looked down at a fennel frond on the floor.

"Have you seen him?"

Sarah's breath stopped. *Don't ask me that. Oh, shit, don't ask me that.* Sarah paused so long she knew she had to tell the truth. "Yes."

"Oh, God, how is he?" Courtney's desperation jumped through the phone line.

"I . . . I saw him in the hospital." That wasn't a lie. "I went to visit him like you asked me. He seemed . . . okay. He's going to recover . . . you know, physically."

"Do you know where he is?"

Sarah held her breath. She hadn't wanted to lie outright. But fear pounded through her. "No." Sarah wondered what she was afraid of. What could Courtney do? It wasn't like she'd come busting down doors. Sarah couldn't imagine her trying to harm anyone. But still . . . Sarah was afraid. And the uncertainty over *why* was scarier than the fear itself.

Sarah placed a plum tomato in the middle of her cutting board. She tried to picture what Courtney was doing while she talked. What did she look like after weeks in jail? "Where are you?" Sarah asked.

"I . . . I'm not at the house. I can't be in Oakhaven. We're at a hotel in Tipp City."

Good. Sarah wanted her far away. Sarah heard a noise in the

drive and panicked that Nate was home already, but it was just Lila watering the hostas on the side of her house. Sarah didn't want either of them to know she was talking to Courtney.

"You don't know what this means to me," Courtney whispered. "That you'd talk to me at all. I felt so alone, so . . . abandoned."

Sarah sensed that these words were meant to give her a jolt of guilt. Guilt that she should have visited the jail. But the words "alone" and "abandoned" conjured an image of Jordan walking down that driveway in the pouring rain. Jordan on the floor of that port-o-john. Jordan in those photos.

"I want to help you, Courtney. But you have to help me, too, okay? Help me understand it. They said, at the hospital, that Jordan was sick." The silence swelled on the other end of the line. "You took medication from the hospital, right? You were *treating* him for a venereal disease. So . . . how did you . . . how could you not know what was going on?"

Courtney didn't speak for nearly a minute, and when she did, her voice was muffled. "I know, I know. I was . . . afraid. I'll never forgive myself for that."

Sarah absorbed this. It was true that Courtney may have been afraid, but she should have been *more* afraid for her *son*. That was her job. She was his mother. These words burned on Sarah's lips, wanting to be released.

"I miss him so much. How is he? Is he doing okay?"

"I don't know," Sarah said as neutrally as she could.

"Sarah, please. I need to know. Where is he?"

Sarah diced the tomato. "You'd have to talk to Children's Services. You know that."

"I'm sorry," Courtney said, in a voice almost like a child's. "I'm sorry. I just . . . God, I miss him."

"I'm sorry, too. I am. You'll see him tomorrow, you said. Hang in there, okay?"

"I'm so scared."

Sarah wanted to put down the receiver. This woman's pain and neediness, even over the phone, was nearly unbearable. And that feeling of fear would not shut off. It drained her, depleted her. Is this what Jordan had felt every day of his life?

"What if I lose him?" Courtney wailed.

"Shh," Sarah said, but she didn't know why.

In the background, on Courtney's end, Sarah heard a knocking sound, and then a male voice asked, "Who are you talking to?"

"Sarah Laden," Courtney said, her voice defensive.

"Is that your brother?" Sarah asked.

Courtney didn't answer.

Sarah diced another plum tomato, took a deep breath, and asked, "The things that happened to Jordan . . . they happened to you, too, didn't they?"

"That is *not* true," Courtney snapped.

"It was in the papers. All the magazines. Your brother said—"

"It's not true. It's a bullshit story."

"Why did you tell me you were an only child?"

"It is *not* true," Courtney repeated, her words clipped and overpronounced.

"Okay," Sarah said but didn't mean it. She didn't accept what Courtney said but knew there was no point in arguing with her, knew there was no way to win. "I have to go."

"Oh, okay," Courtney said, childlike and sad again. "Can I see you? Will you meet me somewhere?"

No, no, no. Sarah inhaled with a gasp as she hung up, pretending she hadn't heard this final question.

CHAPTER NINETEEN

Nate

Nate loved the little jolts of electricity her lips passed to him, her mouth warm-minty bold. Their teeth clicked, and Mackenzie drew back, shifting her weight on the hood of her Honda, laughing her breathy trill. The moonlight made her glow.

Nate breathed her honey-musk perfume and tried not to think about Mrs. Kendrick. He discovered the slightest salty flavor as he nibbled Mackenzie's neck. Mackenzie made a satisfied, purring sound.

A car door shut down the block, and Nate tensed. He'd been paranoid ever since Mom told him that Mrs. Kendrick was out of jail. The car started and drove away. He exhaled. He was psyched that they caught Mr. Kendrick, but the thought of Mrs. Kendrick roaming around somewhere gave him the creeps.

Mackenzie lifted her long legs and wrapped them around his own, pulling them crotch to crotch.

Mrs. Ripley's porch light snapped on. Nate backed off, and Mackenzie sat up.

"Is that you, Nate Laden?" Mrs. Ripley called through the dark.

"Yeah," Nate answered, the word a "so what?" challenge.

"You've been out there a long time," she scolded. Nate knew she'd been watching them.

"I'm just talking to my friend," Nate said. But Mrs. Ripley stood there, silhouetted in her doorway, until Nate called, "Good night."

"Good night," she said reluctantly, and closed her door. The porch light stayed on.

Mackenzie scooted off the hood to the sidewalk. "Yikes. Was she watching us?"

"She watches *everything*. She knows every damn thing that happens on this street."

"What's her rabbit dressed as today?" Mackenzie asked, taking a step toward the porch.

"Don't," Nate whispered. "She's still watching us."

Mackenzie turned back around. "It's dressed like a jockey for the Kentucky Derby!"

"Jesus, she needs to get a life."

"Look, she even made it a little stick horse." Mackenzie pointed to the rabbit.

The porch light snapped off.

"Oops. I hope she didn't think I was making fun of it. Well . . . I should get going." She slid into the driver's seat, and Nate leaned in the open window. "Thanks for the movie."

"Movie?" Nate asked. "Did we see a movie?"

She laughed. Man, he loved her laugh. She touched his cheek. "Call me tomorrow?"

"Yeah. I'll call you when I'm back from Jordan's therapist."

"Why do you have to go?"

"It's just a part of his therapy. Sometimes I go. Sometimes Mom goes. Sometimes we all go. His doctor is really cool."

Mackenzie still stroked his cheek, "And he has to see his mom tomorrow?"

"No 'has to' about it. The way he sees it, he 'gets to.' He's practically jumping for joy."

"That's just wrong." She drew her hand away.

Nate leaned in further and kissed her, planning to linger only briefly, aware that Mrs. Ripley still watched them, but damn, he loved her mouth, her taste, her honey smell.

The porch light snapped back on, and Mrs. Ripley came out, slamming the door. They watched as she began to sweep her porch.

Mackenzie cleared her throat and grinned at Nate. "Night." She started the engine and turned on the headlights.

He stood there in the street until her car had rounded the corner. He watched Mrs. Ripley a moment, who acted like he wasn't there. As he walked to his own driveway, she stopped sweeping, went inside, and turned off her porch light again.

Lights were still on all over his house. He headed up the front porch steps and a voice from the darkness said, "Hey."

He almost pissed himself, even though he recognized Jordan's voice right away. "Jesus! You scared me." Nate scanned the dark street. "You shouldn't be out here, man."

"*Why not?*" Jordan's voice was icy.

Nate didn't answer. He knew that Jordan knew why he'd said it. Nate sat on the top step and peered through the shadows at Jordan, knees drawn up to his chin, on the porch swing. Was he watching for his mom? Hoping she'd come by? "What are you doing out here?"

"I *was* just hanging out."

Nate didn't like the emphasis on "was." "What's the matter?"

"Nothing."

They sat in silence awhile, listening to Mrs. Ripley's bug zapper, before Jordan got up and went inside. Nate felt his great mood disappear.

Nate stood and went in, too, locking the front door behind him. He found Mom in the kitchen, surrounded by the cheesecakes she made every weekend for the local grocery store. She still moved with that manic energy she got when she was upset. He knew she'd been cooking all day, probably ever since she found out about Mrs. Kendrick.

"I'm home," he said, stopping in the doorway.

"You're late."

Don't argue. "I've been back awhile. We were talking outside."

She smiled, one hand on her hip, the other holding a spatula. "Talking? Lila sure didn't think you were *talking.*"

"She called you?"

From the living room, Danny starting chanting, "Nate's in lo-ove, Nate's in lo-ove."

"Shut up," Nate called over his shoulder.

He couldn't believe it when his mom laughed. "Just remember: There's a time and a place—and it generally isn't in front of Lila Ripley's."

He smiled back, cheeks hot. Sometimes Mom could be cool. He tried to think of something to say to her, to convey that, but he couldn't think of anything. He stood there in the door frame and watched her arrange chocolate slices into the top of one smooth, yellow cake. The smell made his stomach growl.

She glanced up and noticed he was still there. "Want a slice?" She gestured to the cakes lining every available inch of counter space. "You can have anything, except the orange-and-pine-nut ones." She pointed. "Those are chocolate, a couple chocolate-caramel, and we've got raspberry, blueberry, and turtle."

"Chocolate," Nate said, sitting on a stool at the kitchen island.

"Ah, good choice." She put hefty slices on saucers and stuck chocolate pieces on the top before handing one to Nate.

She poured herself a cup of coffee and sat across from him.

Nate got himself a glass of milk.

The tart-creamy cake dissolved in his mouth. He nodded his approval. Mom grinned.

They ate in silence a few minutes before she cleared her throat. Looking down at her cake, she said, "So you and Markenzie are getting pretty serious."

Nate paused before swallowing and shrugged.

Mom cleared her throat again and glanced toward the living room. Nate knew what was coming when he saw the blush crawl across her cheeks. In a hushed voice, she said, "I hope you're not rushing into a . . . sexual relationship."

Oh, shit. "Mom," he protested.

"Nate, there's nothing wrong with discussing this. Are you . . . sexually active?"

He remembered them talking about Danny that night, that odd feeling of her confiding in him. That memory made him brave. "So what if I am?" he asked, taunting her a little. "It's a mitzvah, you know, to make love on Shabbat. You and Dad always told us that."

Mom seemed to choke on her coffee. She coughed. "If you're telling me you had sex tonight, I doubt very much it had anything to do with honoring God."

Nate was amazed she wasn't freaking. Her pursed lips and stooped shoulders were the only clues to how stressed she was.

They were silent. After a moment Mom took another bite of cheesecake. Nate did, too. Danny came into the kitchen. "Ooh, can I have a piece?"

"Sure," Mom said with fake perkiness.

Nate watched her slice a piece while Danny called up the stairs, "Hey, Jordan! You want a piece of cheesecake?"

"No thanks," came the muffled reply from behind his closed door.

Nate was relieved that Danny took his cake and returned to the living room.

Nate kept his eyes on his cheesecake. He thought about telling Mom he hadn't had sex yet, but he didn't. Besides, maybe he'd successfully changed the subject.

No such luck. He braced himself when Mom cleared her throat again. "You never answered my question, Nate," she said. "Are you sexually active?"

"Mom!"

"What's wrong with talking about it? Do you really think you're ready if you can't even discuss it without squirming?"

He scowled at her. "Oh, so if I talk about it with you, you'd say

I'm ready? Okay. Fine. Let's talk." He crossed his arms, challenging her. She fidgeted with her coffee cup.

"Do . . . do you discuss it with Mackenzie?" Mom asked, looking down at the cup she turned between both hands.

"Hello? What do you think? I'm planning to drug her or something?"

Mom looked up and met his eyes, and he knew he'd answered her question. At least she didn't make a huge deal out of it. She just nodded. "Do you have a plan for contraception?"

"Yup. Sure do." He wouldn't look away, daring her to ask more. "What else you wanna know?" She'd started this, after all.

She held up her hands, as if in surrender. "Believe me, I don't want to push you. And I really wish your father were here to be having this conversation. I just . . ." She folded her arms on the island and leaned on her elbows. "Look, sex is a pretty wonderful thing."

"You're kidding," Nate said. "Really?"

Mom smiled and rolled her eyes but didn't laugh. "Don't be in a hurry, Nate. Sex is very powerful. It engages very powerful emotions. Don't rush into it, because getting there is just as powerful. And once you've made love, it's hard to go back to just holding hands. It'll change things between you two, and you have to be ready for that."

Nate nodded. He couldn't believe she was being so calm and cool about it.

Mom took a long drink of coffee and looked down into the bottom of her cup for a while, turning the cup around and around. Then she leaned on one elbow, her chin in her hand, and watched Nate finish his cheesecake. The silence felt okay again. "You done?" he asked her, pointing to her few remaining bites. She nodded and laughed when he finished hers off, too. Damn, this stuff was so good. Nate could probably eat a whole cake himself. He opened the dishwasher and put the plates inside.

They stood there leaning against the counter, surrounded by cheesecakes. Nate felt that his mom wanted to say more. He wanted to say more, too, but he didn't know what.

He sat back down on his stool at the island and watched her wash her hands and begin to cover each cheesecake with a plastic top and label it.

"You know Reece is coming to dinner next weekend," she said.

Nate's spine stiffened. "Why?"

Mom looked over at him, pen poised over a label as if startled at his tone of voice. "You know—a home visit, just a required check-in. Why? What?"

Nate shrugged. "Nothing." Jesus, what was wrong with him?

Mom looked at him a moment, her cheeks red. She opened her mouth to say something but then shut it and began stacking the cheesecakes in the storage refrigerator, the big one that was only for the Laden Table stuff and not for the home Laden table. "What should we eat when he's here?" Mom asked into the awkward silence.

He got a crowded feeling in his chest. Why did she care what they ate? "Nothing special—you always go over the top. Why can't we just order something in?"

She closed the fridge and looked at him as if he'd suggested they serve ramen noodles. "I will not go 'over the top.' I was thinking something casual, like pizzas."

"Mom, your idea of pizza is something with a rye crust and . . . and some weird green sauce and anchovies. Why don't we just order real pizzas? You know—what everyone else in the world considers 'casual,' a pepperoni pizza delivered to your door." Mom made everything from scratch. Everything. If she made a pumpkin pie, she started with a whole, for-real pumpkin. Even though it tasted great, it took forever. Dad used to buy box cake mixes and premade piecrusts and canned chicken broth and put them in Mom's pantry as a joke. She reacted the way Mackenzie did when *someone* (hello? Mowaza was her lab partner) put a dissected frog leg in her science binder.

Dad. Ever since Mom's reaction to that "do you have a boyfriend?" question, Nate didn't want his mother cooking for this man. Any man.

Mom put her hands on her hips. "All right, Mr. It's-a-Mitzvah, tell me what's wrong with a pepperoni pizza?"

"Please! We've never kept kosher." Mom opened her mouth to protest, but Nate teased her, "Except maybe in a noncommittal, half-assed sort of way."

Mom laughed. "See, when I was growing up, that's what your grandmother worried about—would I eat kosher when I went out on dates. She didn't worry about whether I was having sex in the back of the van."

"Whoa. Hey, I'm *not,* okay?"

Danny appeared in the doorway with his empty plate, eyes wide. "What are you guys talking about?"

Nate and Mom laughed. "Nothing," Mom said, busying herself wiping off the counters.

"Actually," Nate said, fighting to keep a straight face, "we were talking about keeping kosher."

Danny wrinkled his nose. "We're not going to, are we? That's such a pain at G.G.'s house. I thought you were talking about sex."

Nate stared at his brother. So did Mom. Danny blushed. "I heard you say it!" he protested, like he felt the judgment in their stares.

"I was just talking about the differences in what your grandma worried about and what I worry about, with the world changing so fast," Mom said. "That's all." She looked around the kitchen and said, "It's almost midnight. You guys need to head upstairs."

Nate wondered if Mom's weird rule would always apply, even when he came home from college someday. If she went to bed, everybody had to be upstairs in their rooms, or she said she couldn't sleep. He felt a sudden stab of guilt, picturing her when he did go away to college. Would she be able to sleep at all? A lump formed in his throat.

By the time Nate brushed his teeth and washed his face, Danny was asleep in the room they now shared, his breath gravelly. Nate undressed in the dark. Danny seemed better lately. He and Jordan were friends again. But twice now Nate had found his desk and dresser drawers rearranged, like Danny had snooped through his stuff. It wasn't as if Nate was some neat freak and always put his stuff in exactly the same place, but tiny differences made him notice it. When he'd mentioned it to Danny, Danny denied it but looked so panicked that Nate knew it was true.

He pulled down his covers and lay on his back in bed. Shit. Some nights he could just tell he wasn't going to sleep. Before, it was no big deal, but now that he'd moved into Danny's room, Nate couldn't just turn on lights and read or listen to music.

He tried to focus on the distant traffic on the main road one block away. He tried to copy Danny's breathing, but it was too slow and his own mind too awake to focus on that for long. He tried to focus on *anything* besides Mrs. Kendrick. Where was she? Could *she* sleep? What did a person out on bail *do*? Could you walk around, go to the grocery story? He kept catching himself looking for her at the movie tonight.

The movie. He tried to think about Mackenzie, then stopped himself. No point in going there. Another reason sharing a room sucked.

But then he couldn't *not* think about her.

Cursing under his breath, he got out of bed and pulled on a pair of sweats to head to the bathroom.

"Hey," Jordan whispered as Nate stepped into the hall. Jordan's small form was silhouetted in his doorway, a reading lamp on behind him. "I can't sleep either." He opened his door wider, and Nate went in, sort of relieved, sort of disappointed to be interrupted. He was glad that even though Jordan and Danny were friends again, Nate and Jordan still kept having their talks. The kid was cool. Nate knew he wasn't half as strong a person as Jordan.

Nate sat on the end of Jordan's bed, leaning against the wall.

Jordan sat in a chair, facing him, propping his feet up on the bed.

"So are you happy they caught your dad?"

Jordan looked at him like he was an idiot. "What do you think?"

"Well, I don't know. You don't act very happy. You haven't said anything about it."

"What do you want me to say?"

Nate sighed. He hated when Jordan was this way. This was obviously not going to be one of those great talk nights that Nate wrote about in his English journal.

Jordan drew his knees up to his chest and wrapped his arms around them. "How soon do you think he'll be here in Dayton?"

"I don't know. If they fly, he could be here tonight. Maybe he's here already."

Jordan chewed his lip. He looked stressed.

"Jordan, chill. He's in police custody. He can't hurt you."

Jordan shot Nate a look of disdain but didn't comment on what he said. "Was it on the news? Do you think . . . other people know he's coming back?"

"Yeah. It was all over the news. Why?"

Jordan shook his head, then tucked his chin in between his knees. Without looking at Nate, he said, "Sorry about before, on the porch. I wasn't mad at you."

"That's cool." Nate looked around his old room, at all of Jordan's drawings now hanging on the walls. Most of the drawings were of a cat or of Klezmer. A long silence fell, but in the sleepy quiet of the house, it was comfortable. "I figure you're, you know, kind of nervous about seeing your mom tomorrow."

Jordan frowned. "I'm not nervous. I . . . I just . . . I watched you and Mackenzie, but I was already out there when you guys pulled up. I wasn't spying on you."

Nate laughed. "It's okay. We were on the street, for Christ's sake. We weren't really doing anything."

"So . . . so you do more than that sometimes?"

Damn, what was next, *Danny* drilling him on his sex life?

He looked at Jordan, who eyed him warily. Nate thought about what Mom had said about sex bringing up powerful emotions. What emotions had Jordan felt? Nate took a breath. "Yeah. We do more than that sometimes."

"Like what?"

"Jordan, this stuff is kinda personal. It's supposed to be private. It's—" Nate stopped. Words like "private" and "personal" seemed like a joke after what those people had done to Jordan.

Jordan crossed his arms and turned his head to look at the curtain blowing in the breeze. "I just . . . I don't get it."

"Look, man, the stuff that happened to you, that's not anything close to what I do with Mackenzie. It's totally, totally different. It can be really good. It can be a way to show you love someone." He felt stupid. He sounded as cheesy as his mom had a few minutes ago. He saw those photos on the disks and wondered if it would ever be possible for Jordan to understand what he meant.

Jordan made an impatient move with his legs, kicking the bed.

"I'm sorry," Nate whispered.

Jordan got up and stood at the window, his back to Nate. "Why should *you* be sorry?"

Nate didn't know what to say. He leaned against the wall again and waited. He watched the kid's back, between the two blowing curtains. Nate yawned.

Still looking out the window, Jordan said, "I know where my mom is staying. I saw the address on Reece's desk." He turned around and pulled a piece of paper from his back pocket.

Nate felt his insides drop down into the bed.

Jordan stared at him, holding out the piece of paper. "It's not that far. I looked on a map."

Shit. Nate closed his eyes a moment.

"Would you take me?"

Hell, no, Nate wanted to say, but he made himself be kind. "No, Jordan. I'm sorry. I . . . I don't think—"

"You took the van to see me, and you weren't allowed."

"Yeah, but I *wanted* to see you, and a hospital is a pretty safe place . . . and . . . you know . . . you're supposed to be supervised when you talk to her."

Jordan still held out the paper. "Please? You could take me tomorrow after therapy."

Dread settled into Nate's muscles. "No. Mom's dropping us off. And even if she wasn't—"

"I *need* to talk to her."

The kid's desperation made Nate's stomach ache. "You *can* talk to her. At the agency, tomorrow at two."

Jordan dropped his arm and his eyes flashed hatred. "You're afraid of her."

Nate let that slide off of him. "I'm not afraid of her. But I should've told someone about your mom. Maybe then you wouldn't have ended up in the hospital."

Jordan sneered. "Told someone *what* about my mom? That you wanted to do her?"

Blood rushed to Nate's face. "She kissed me, Jordan."

Jordan rolled his eyes.

"That's not normal," Nate insisted. "A grown woman shouldn't be kissing some high-school guy, okay?" He saw those pictures in his head again and thought how laughable that must sound to Jordan. Jesus, the kid must think Nate was flipping over nothing.

Nate felt *sick* when he thought about the jerk he'd been. What if he'd told his mom, way back after that first kiss? That was two years ago. The kid could have been out of that house, away from those psychos. But . . . really, even if he'd told, would it have stopped anything other than Mom being friends with Mrs. Kendrick? Nate had known that Mrs. Kendrick was whack, but he'd had no real clue.

Jordan whispered, "Please? She never hurt you."

"But she hurt *you*."

"No she didn't. You all think you know what happened, and you don't know shit."

"I know this much," Nate said. "I don't think you want me to go to therapy with you at all. I think you only wanted to arrange it so we'd have the van and could go see her."

Jordan stared down at the floor.

"So that was all bullshit? All that crap you told Bryn about trusting me?"

Jordan lifted his head. "No! I meant that. I . . . do. I do trust you."

"Yeah? Good, because I'm trusting you: You better not lead your mom to this house."

Jordan shook his head. "I promise," he said. He sat on the bed. "She doesn't know I'm here."

"She better not," Nate said, giving himself chills with his own icy-sharp voice. "She better not come anywhere near my family."

He felt something give way inside him as he watched the kid's face shift into a look so lonely he seemed to shrink before Nate's eyes.

"But she's *my* family," Jordan whispered.

Jordan's eyes blurred and his nose stung, but he didn't cry. Jordan brought his legs up on the bed and curled into a fetal ball, staring across the room with blank, dry eyes.

"I'm sorry," Nate said. He wanted to reach out and touch Jordan's back, to pat it, the way Mom used to get him to sleep, but he didn't. He was sitting here, shirtless, with another boy. If Nate touched Jordan, would Jordan think Nate was trying something like in those pictures? That thought made Nate afraid to even speak. He couldn't think of anything to say to end the conversation they'd had, and he didn't want to just get up and walk out.

The kid didn't move. He just stared in his freaky silent way, as if Nate wasn't there.

"I'm sorry," Nate said again. That was true. He was sorry the kid was here. Not because he didn't want him around; actually, he felt something like love for this strange, spooky boy. No, he was sorry for all the twisted shit that had brought Jordan to this place.

Nate sat there looking around this room that used to be his own. He looked up in the corner at the spot where that bat had landed all those years ago.

He felt that cold paralysis again, just like when he'd seen the bat for real. Picturing Jordan having to be with Mrs. Kendrick was another wrong, furry, dark spot against that white wall.

CHAPTER TWENTY

Sarah

Sarah rushed up to the Social Work lobby of The Children's Medical Center. She was seventeen minutes late to pick up Nate and Jordan. The boys were not waiting for her in the lobby, and Sarah nearly panicked, but the receptionist told her that they were still inside Bryn's office.

Sarah was grateful for a chance to sit down a moment. She felt sweaty and frazzled. She'd dropped the boys off and then left to deliver the cheesecakes and the shrimp-and-fennel pasta. An accident on 75 had made her late getting back to the hospital. Thank God, Bryn was running late, too. Even though this was going to wreck the rest of the day's schedule, Sarah hoped it was a good thing that she was keeping the boys overtime. As long as Jordan was in that office, Sarah didn't have to take him to see Courtney. She couldn't squelch the feeling of dread, the feeling that this meeting was going to change everything

Sarah caught her breath, wondering what Jordan would even say to his mother today. What on earth could Courtney possibly say to him? Sarah hadn't told anyone that she'd talked with Courtney. It had been stupid, even dangerous. What if Courtney mentioned it?

Would everyone think Sarah was hiding something? Courtney had called *her,* after all. Why didn't Sarah just say so? She hated this ripped-in-half sensation and hypervigilance. How long could she sustain this before she had a nervous breakdown? *Breathe.*

She dialed her home number on her cell phone.

"Hello?" Danny answered.

"Hey, sweetie. Listen, we're running behind here. The guys aren't out of Bryn's office yet, so we're going to pick you up on the way to the Rec Center. Get your stuff packed, and I'll swing by to get you as soon as Nate and Jordan are done. Be ready, okay? I'll honk."

"But I don't have to be at soccer for a whole hour!"

"I don't have time to drive all the way to the Rec Center and then come all the way back to get you. You'd be late. So you're stuck riding along with us."

Danny groaned.

"Today's a little crazy," Sarah reminded him. "I need to get Jordan to the agency by two. Work with me."

"Okay," Danny said. "Oh, Detective Kramble called you."

Her face flushed. "Yeah? Why?"

"To check on us."

"Did he leave a message?"

"He just said to tell you he called."

"Am I supposed to call him back?"

"I dunno."

"Danny . . ." Sarah sighed. "Okay. Go get ready."

She snapped the phone shut. Kramble. She couldn't shake the sense of hypocrisy she felt this morning. Much of that lecture to Nate last night had been a lecture to herself. She didn't know Bobby Kramble. She wasn't even sure she *liked* Kramble. She couldn't imagine the two of them having a conversation about anything but this case—how could she talk about herself, her life, without talking about Roy, who wasn't exactly safe date material?—but, to her own surprise and dismay, she *could* imagine herself and Kramble in bed.

Bryn's door opened, and the boys walked out. Bryn gave Sarah a wave.

"Hey, guys," Sarah said. They nodded at her. Sarah regarded Jordan, hoping to see a sign. Anything—doubt, fear. But he still had that bright look in his eyes. "Everything go okay?"

"Fine," Jordan said, the way he always responded.

"It was cool," Nate offered, then shoved his hands in his pockets.

Sarah decided she didn't need to bend herself out of shape to make conversation. Bryn and the receptionist said good-bye to them, and they rode the elevator in silence.

In the van Sarah turned on the radio, but Nate scowled at the music that burst forth. He fiddled with the switches, then shut it off as if disgusted with the choices.

Fine. They could drive along in silence. That was okay with her. She did worry, though, that Nate would somehow know what she'd been thinking about Kramble. Who was she to tell Nate that he needed to really *know* someone first, when right now she'd like to have just the sex *without* the dinner, the chatting, and all the work that went with it? God help her, what she wouldn't give for a good, sweaty romp with Roy down by the washer and dryer. And later they could sneak upstairs and act as if nothing had happened, grinning at each other occasionally.

"Mom?"

She turned, startled, to Nate.

"Are you okay?" he asked.

"Yeah. Why?"

"You looked . . . I dunno, sad."

She shook her head and turned onto their street. "There's been a change in plans. We've gotta pick Danny up on the way to the Rec Center."

The Look crossed Nate's face, and it struck Sarah that she hadn't seen it in a while. "I'm gonna be late," Nate said.

"I *know*. And I'm sorry. Today is complicated, okay?"

She slowed in front of the house and tapped the horn. She

checked her watch. Damn it, they *were* going to be late to the Rec Center, and Danny would probably be late to soccer, and so went another day of playing relentless catch-up. Jordan would probably be late to meet Courtney. Would everyone think Sarah had done that on purpose? She honked again.

After a moment she pulled in to the driveway. She didn't want to keep honking and annoy the neighbors. She picked up the cell phone and called her home number. The phone rang unanswered, and the machine picked up on the fourth ring. "Danny, we're in the driveway. Get your butt out here!" she said.

When he still didn't materialize, Sarah muttered, "For God's sake, what is he *doing*?" and shut off the engine. She felt her neck and shoulders tighten. She'd need a massage just to get through the damn day at this rate. She slipped out of the van, shutting the door on Nate and Jordan's sulky silence.

The front door was slightly ajar, the air-conditioning she'd finally turned on seeping out into the humidity. The first tremor of concern rippled through her. "Danny?" she called, opening the door. She nearly tripped over his gym bag, packed and ready, inside the front door.

She stopped. Danny stood in the doorway to the kitchen. His face was pale, his posture stiff, unnatural. "What's wrong?" she asked.

The floor swayed beneath Sarah's feet as Courtney Kendrick came into view behind him. Or some version of the Courtney she'd once believed she'd known. The woman who stood there, in jeans and a pink sweater, had dark circles ringing her eyes and skeletal cheeks. That photo from the calendar came into Sarah's mind: Sarah and Courtney leaning their heads together, arms around each other. This was not that woman.

Sarah had imagined many reactions if she ever saw Courtney again. But this . . . this . . . contempt was not one that she'd pictured. Courtney nervously swept a finger behind one ear, tucking back that tousled hair. Sarah felt like she'd cornered some stray, feral creature.

Any little remaining scrap of Sarah's doubt dried up.

"Sarah." Tears spilled out of Courtney's eyes. "I'm sorry. I'm sorry."

"Danny, come here," Sarah said. She reached out her hand, and Danny walked like a zombie across the living room to her. She put an arm around his shoulder, pulled him close. He felt cold. Once she had Danny safely next to her, rage rose up in Sarah's chest and throat.

"What are you doing here?" Sarah hardly recognized her own voice, splintered with disgust and hatred. Sarah's whole body trembled, listening for a van door. Please, please let Courtney not see Jordan.

"I need your help," Courtney whispered.

"You have to leave. You're not supposed to be in Oakhaven."

"I need to see Jordan."

Over my dead body, Sarah wanted to say. An urge to strike Courtney moved through her. How *dare* she? After all the lies, after all she'd done, how dare she come into Sarah's home and ask for help? "You have some nerve," Sarah said.

"Please," Courtney said "I know he's living with you. Just—"

"Talk to Children's Services," Sarah said. "Get out. *Now.*"

Courtney stared at Sarah as if sincerely hurt by her tone. Sarah thought of her cell phone in the van. Time to leave and call Kramble. "Come on, Danny." She pulled Danny outside and slammed the door behind her. If it were possible to lock Courtney inside, she'd do it. Danny moved woodenly, awkwardly. "Hurry, hon," she pleaded.

But they were too slow. Half the yard still stretched before them when Sarah heard the front door open. She moved in slow motion. It was every nightmare she'd ever had.

Jordan opened the side van door, asking tentatively, "Mom?"

"Shit!" she heard Nate say.

Sarah wanted to reach for Courtney's arm, wanted to stop her, but she kept her mind on, *Get to the van, get to the phone, call the police.*

Jordan stepped down from the van and stood, uncertain, on the lawn, as Courtney came to him. The smile on his face was in sharp contrast to his body language. He actually took one step back and flinched when Courtney wrapped her arms around him. She cupped Jordan's face in her hands, kissed his hair and forehead, then hugged him to her, pressing his head into her chest. Jordan's arms hung limp. His body reaction told Sarah all she needed to know.

Sarah was nearly at the van, but Nate almost knocked her down as he rushed from the van at the embracing pair. He yanked Jordan from Courtney's arms and stood between them. "Get out of here!" he yelled at Courtney. Sarah opened the driver's-side door and reached for her phone.

"Nate, I—" she heard Courtney say.

"Get out!"

"Please, you don't—" Courtney grabbed his arm.

"Don't touch me," Nate said. "Don't you *ever* put your fucking hands on me again." Sarah stared in horror as Nate shoved Courtney hard and she fell, sprawling, on her back. Nate stepped toward Courtney, as if to kick her, but Jordan leaped on Nate's back, hurling him to the ground as well. Jordan's fury shocked Sarah; it stole her breath like a blow to her gut. Once Nate was down, Jordan slammed punch after punch into his head. Sarah felt each punch as if it landed on her own skull.

Sarah dropped the phone and ran toward them as Courtney pulled Jordan off Nate.

Sarah breathed again when Nate immediately scrambled to his feet, the back of his hand to his nose.

"Don't hit her!" Jordan screamed at Nate. "She never hurt you!"

Courtney scooped Jordan against her, arms crossed over his torso, as if to keep him from attacking anyone else.

They all stood a moment, panting and staring at one another. A *ding-ding-ding* came from the van's open driver's-side door. Sarah glanced back at the van and saw Danny talking on her phone. Thank God.

"Get out of here," Nate said to Courtney. It physically pained Sarah to see the blood that ran from his nose and mouth, spattering his white T-shirt in dark, thick drops. Nate spit a mouthful of blood into the grass. "You make me *sick.*"

Jordan tried to wrestle from his mother's arms again, but Courtney held tight.

"She never hurt you!" Jordan yelled at Nate.

This was insane, out of control. *Get here, get here,* Sarah willed the cops.

Courtney clamped one hand to Jordan's mouth, the other tightened across his torso. The hand on his mouth dug in, the nails embedding in flesh.

Courtney locked eyes with Sarah, and Sarah hated the glittery blankness there. Like shiny cellophane on an empty box. Had she *ever* known this woman? *You thought I was a fool.* She felt naked, betrayed, and sick with her anger.

Jordan tried to say something, and Courtney dug her claws in harder. Sarah saw blood welling around Courtney's nails. "Courtney, stop it! You're hurting him." Sarah couldn't undo the pain already inflicted upon this child, but she'd be damned if she stood here and let him be hurt again in her own front yard. Sarah reached for Jordan, but Courtney backed away, dragging Jordan with her.

"Thank you, for taking care of him. I knew you would." Courtney kept walking backward, edging her way out of the yard.

Sarah followed her. Nate did, too.

"Let him go!" Nate yelled.

Courtney started to run. *Shit.* Adrenaline surged through Sarah. She would chase them for miles to get that boy back. Her heart sank to see Jordan willingly cooperate and run with Courtney. Nate beat them to Lila's driveway and cut them off.

Shrieking tires ripped through the neighborhood. A line of cruisers came from both directions on the street. Cars pulled in to Lila's driveway and tore up the grass in Sarah's yard, boxing Courtney and Jordan in. Uniformed officers sprang from the cars. Sarah saw Danny, still with the phone at his ear, stare into the mouthpiece with amazement.

Then Lila Ripley stepped onto her porch and shouted, "What took you so long? She nearly got away!" and Sarah understood the speed. Thank God for nosy neighbors.

Police officers surrounded Courtney and Jordan.

"Let the boy go!" someone commanded.

Courtney cupped Jordan's face in her hands again. She pressed her forehead to his and whispered something. Jordan shook his head, as if answering no.

"Release the boy and raise your hands in the air," that voice commanded again.

Courtney kissed Jordan lightly on the top of his head and stepped away from him. Officers rushed in immediately.

Sarah went to Danny, who had sat down in the middle of the driveway. She sat beside him, her arm around him. "Honey, are you okay?" she asked him. "Did she hurt you?"

Danny shook his head—she didn't know to which question—then leaned forward, away from her, and vomited onto the driveway. Relief crashed against the walls of Sarah's own stomach with such dizzying force that she felt for an instant as if she were on a rocking boat. She stroked his back and watched Courtney get handcuffed.

Lila pointed down the block as she talked to an officer taking notes.

Nate came toward Sarah, pulling the bottom of his T-shirt up to his bleeding nose.

Kramble's face dropped into Sarah's view. "Are you all right?" He touched her hair. His face was chalky white, his lips thin and pursed. Sarah thought, *He was scared, too*. She nodded. She felt better that he was here.

"Danny?" Kramble asked. "Did she hurt you?"

Danny shook his head again.

Sarah turned in time to see a handcuffed Courtney being put in a cruiser.

"Her brother called us," Kramble said. "Right before Lila Ripley did. He thought she was sleeping, but then he realized she was gone. She'd climbed out the hotel window. And taken all his credit cards and the rental car."

Sarah saw Jordan standing alone in the yard. He didn't watch his mother; he stared at Danny.

"Danny?" Kramble asked. "What did she say to you? When you answered the door?"

Danny shook his head. "I didn't answer the door! She didn't knock. I was in the kitchen when Mom called, and when I hung up and turned around, she was there."

"Was the door unlocked?" Kramble asked.

"She has a key," Sarah said dully. "Last December she brought in our mail and fed the rabbit when we went to Michigan to see my folks. Lila was in Florida." Sarah had never asked for the key back. She'd forgotten all about it.

Kramble helped them both rise. Nate was at her side, and she hugged him, hugged him tight and for a long time, so relieved and grateful that they were all okay. When she released him, she pulled the T-shirt from his face. "Let me see." His nose and lower lip still oozed blood, and he had a jagged tear in his skin in the bottom corner of his left eye.

Kramble peered close and whistled a low note. "You're gonna need some stitches, buddy. Mrs. Kendrick did that?"

Nate rolled his eyes and looked sheepish. "No. Jordan."

"Too bad. I'd love to slap assault on her on top of everything else."

A wave of missing Roy crashed over Sarah. She needed his calm presence. Needed him to tend to Nate. Like the time Nate had gashed his chin open during a hockey tournament. Roy had gone out to the car, brought in his kit, stitched Nate up, and let him stay and play the next game. Everything used to seem so *mendable*. Sarah felt her face crumple. Hot tears stung her eyes.

"Hey, hey," Kramble said. "It's all okay. Everything's okay now." He held Sarah's elbow and said, "Let's get Nate to the ER and Danny and Jordan to the station."

"The station?" Sarah asked.

"Why?" Danny looked panicked.

"This was all over the police scanners. TV crews are going to be showing up any minute. Let's get somewhere with some peace and quiet, so we can sort out what just happened."

"Oh." Sarah felt dazed. Wasn't this bad enough already?

She looked at the van. The door still stood open, the *ding-ding-ding* patiently alerting them that things were not as they should be.

"My van—" Sarah said.

"We'll drive you," Kramble said.

"No, my keys. I need to get my keys."

She thought Nate was going to get the keys, but he passed the van door and went to Jordan, who stood, still and alone, in the center of the yard. Nate stopped near him. He put a hand on Jordan's shoulder, but Jordan snapped to life and shrugged him off with the speed of a striking snake. He moved in a fury to the van, snatched the keys, and slammed the door. The new silence seemed oppressive. Jordan walked up to Sarah and shoved the keys into her hands.

"Are you okay, Jordan?" she asked, but he walked to a police cruiser without speaking and climbed inside. Sarah's heart hurt. That poor boy. That was the meeting with his mother he'd so looked forward to. Even Roy wouldn't have been able to mend him. Nothing seemed mendable anymore. Now things got broken and just kept falling further apart.

CHAPTER TWENTY-ONE

Jordan

J ordan let Kramble lead him down the hall at the police station. He hated the feeling of Kramble's hand on his shoulder, but he was too tired to shrug it off.

"Here." Kramble pointed to a wooden bench. "Why don't you just hang out here for a minute." Jordan obediently sat. Obedient. O-b-e-d-i-e-n-t. He stared at the red-and-blue tiled floor.

"Sorry there's nothing more comfortable, with a TV or something." Jordan didn't pull his eyes from the floor. This building used to be a school, he could tell. It felt like being in school, sitting out here in the locker-lined hall. People talked behind the cloudy glass doors—that glass with the chicken wire inside it that reminded him of Klezmer's rabbit hutch. He closed his eyes and imagined he'd talked in class and got sent out to the hallway. That's all. Just his name on the board, nothing more. But he opened his eyes again, lifted his head past Kramble still standing there, and saw the Wanted posters across from him. Heard the distant crackle of radio static and fragments of a conversation about a meth lab in someone's basement. This wasn't school. This was a police station, and he was in big trouble.

And talking in class? They'd been trying to get him to talk *more* since they brought him here two hours ago.

Kramble crouched in front of him. "We took your mom to the jail, okay? That's where your dad is, too. That's a different building. They're not here. No one's going to hurt you."

Jordan nodded. They'd already told him this a million times. It didn't matter.

"You want something to eat? Or a Coke or something?"

Jordan shook his head.

Kramble's knees popped as he stood. "Sarah and Nate are back from the emergency room. I need to talk to both of them, so it's gonna be a while. You sure about food? There's chips. Candy bars."

Jordan shook his head again, without looking up. Kramble finally sighed and said, "Okay. Let us know if you need anything. I'm right around the corner," and he walked away.

Jordan exhaled, glad to be left alone. His mouth felt tight and sore from his mother's nails. His head ached, and his torn knuckles stung. He'd never punched anyone before, and it'd felt good, which scared him.

They'd put Danny in a different room. Jordan had known that his only chance to get the truth out of Danny was to talk to him before Sarah and Nate got back from the emergency room, but now it was too late. He had no idea where Danny was right now. And he didn't want to move. He'd seen the wall of TV monitors in the front office when they'd arrived. He knew that someone—probably that chubby lady who didn't smile when she'd buzzed them in—was looking at him sitting here on this bench right now. It made that water sound rush in his ears. He wanted to look around for the camera but was afraid to. It was better to ignore the camera altogether. Put himself somewhere else. He closed his eyes.

His mom had come for him. She hadn't forgotten about him like his dad had. She loved him, and she was going to take him away, far away from his dad, where it would just be the two of them. Without his dad, his mom would be okay, and the bad things would stop. Jordan tried to picture their new house. He'd get another cat and maybe a rabbit like Klezmer. He'd have his own bedroom and—

He opened his eyes, breath sharp. He'd pictured his mother slipping under the covers, too. *Stop it.* Kramble had told Jordan that Jordan's dad told all the police that his mom had molested Jordan all the time and that she'd filmed all the parties. Kramble always said "molested" or "raped" or "had sex with" as if he was talking about anything people did every day, like go to school or eat breakfast. Everyone else always said "abuse" after pausing for a second, like they didn't know what to call it. They weren't supposed to call it *anything.* If you didn't, it was easier to pretend it never happened.

He closed his eyes again, but he couldn't keep his mother out of his dream room, so he stopped trying to picture one.

His dad had told the police that his mother's "abuse" had been filmed once. Now they knew—but why should they believe him? Jordan thought he'd had everything under control, but now his dad was blabbing stuff and his mom's secret brother was *here* in Dayton. He'd paid his mom's bail, was staying with her. Why? What did he want? Kramble told Jordan that his uncle called the police when Jordan's mom disappeared. The uncle had been afraid for Jordan, had come to the police station, to make sure "the boy" was all right. Jordan sort of wanted to at least *see* what his uncle looked like, but mostly he wanted him to go back to Seattle. Thinking about it made Jordan want to crawl under this bench and sleep for weeks.

Kramble came down the hall, with Nate walking behind him. "I brought you some company," Kramble said.

Nate held a blue gel ice pack on his right cheek. A pale green hospital bracelet circled his wrist. Five black stitches outlined his lower lip, and two sat like little bugs next to his eye.

"We're going to talk to Danny again, with Sarah," Kramble said. Then the detective walked away, leaving Jordan and Nate alone in the dim hall. Nate clutched the blue ice pack over half his face and studied Jordan with his other, bloodshot eye. Jordan didn't know what to say. Nate lowered himself stiffly to the wooden bench and stretched his legs out in front of him. Then he leaned back against the wall, tilting his head to one side so that the ice pack stayed balanced on his cheek, and crossed his arms over his chest.

Jordan swallowed a sour taste rising in his throat as he looked at what his punches had caused. He saw his mother skidding onto the grass from Nate's shove and tried to feel the fury that had filled him before, but it felt far away. He pictured a whole ocean between that fury and now. The fury had disappeared when his mom had whispered to him. Just before she got taken away, his mom had held his face and asked, "Do you know where my disk is?" Danny must have said something to her. And her words had caused the thought to sneak into Jordan's head that nothing had changed.

Nothing had changed. If she'd taken him with her, the same bad things would happen over and over again.

He pressed his own fingernails into the cuts around his mouth. *Stupid,* he told himself. Stupid to think it would be different.

Stop it. Stop thinking like that. He dug his nails into the cuts she'd made. He pressed until his eyes stung with tears. All he'd wanted was to be done with this.

Jordan decided that he didn't care if right this minute Danny was spilling the beans. He hoped that maybe Danny *would* spill them, and for a few minutes he saw a picture of Danny hefting a heavy cloth sack and little black beans, like coffee beans, pouring out all over the police station's floor.

Jordan looked up at Nate's face. The Ladens would probably kick him out of their house. Nate hated him now. That made Jordan feel dizzy. He'd do anything for Nate. That dumb tree came into his head. He'd finally decided that if Danny brought it up again, he might say yes. Good thing they hadn't planted one for him already. He pictured Nate yanking it out of the ground and snapping the trunk in half. "Nate?" he whispered.

Nate turned his head and caught the ice pack as it slid off his face. The cheek shone purple beneath it. "Yeah?"

"I never told her where I was staying."

"Okay," Nate said, but in a weird tone like he didn't really believe him.

Jordan hated the wringing feeling in his chest. He opened his mouth, took a deep breath, and felt as if he were stepping off a cliff. "I was afraid she'd just leave." That was true. His dad had been so far away. Jordan had even looked at it on a map. All those days of seeing his dad in every shadow, and the whole time he'd been halfway across the country? Jordan had been afraid his mom would run away, too. It hurt to say it out loud. And he shouldn't even think it, so he deserved to hurt. "I thought I'd never get to see her again."

Nate put the ice pack back on his bruised cheek. "Jordan, man, don't you hear yourself? You say she never hurt you, but why would she run if she's not guilty?"

Jordan hated Nate for asking that. He was glad Nate's nose was swollen, glad his lip was split and that he probably tasted the rusty metal of blood when he moved his tongue.

Nate leaned his head against the wall and said, "It's fucked up, man. I'm sorry." Nate touched his stitches with his teeth. "But we're all okay. We're all safe."

Safe. Jordan thought about that, saw the word in bold type, in all capital letters, on white paper: **S-A-F-E.** Exactly how it sounded, no tricks, but . . . , it felt like a word from some other language.

Maybe he really, finally was safe, with his dad in jail. Maybe no one would believe his dad's stories. Maybe his mother did love him. Maybe with his dad in jail, his mom really would change.

Jordan brought a hand to his face and lined up his own fingertips on the crescent-shaped nicks his mother's nails had left there. He squeezed until his eyes watered again, for the bad things he'd thought about her. *Keep your mouth shut, Danny,* he prayed, picturing the impossible task of picking up all those coffee beans and stuffing them back in the sack.

CHAPTER TWENTY-TWO

Nate

Nate pulled the van into his own driveway and scowled at the car parked in the front of his house. Reece was here. He was picking up Jordan for some art-therapy class, but he was way too early. Nate knew that Reece was early on purpose.

Nate slammed the van door and hefted his gym bag to his shoulder. He'd been skating with Mowaza. He hadn't been on the ice since he got kicked off the team, and he was surprised at how much he'd missed it. Skating was part of his "pre-Jordan" life. Goose bumps tickled his scalp as he recognized that some things about the pre-Jordan life were *better*. Fostering Jordan had been his idea, so he shook the feeling away and went in the back door.

A street-fair aroma hit him—strong enough to reach through his swollen nose—at the same time Mom's laughter reached his ears. Damn. He walked into the kitchen. Mom and Reece sat at one of the kitchen islands and were just laughing their asses off about something.

"Hey," Nate had to say. They didn't even hear him come in.

"Hey there, big guy," Reece said. Damn, the man was such a goof.

Nate squinted at some sunflowers in a vase next to Mom. "Where'd ya get those?" he asked.

Sure enough, Mom blushed. "Reece brought these. Wasn't that nice?"

"You're early, aren't you?" Nate asked Reece.

Mom furrowed her brow with her "What's up your butt?" look, one she frequently used on him in public.

Reece just laughed as if Nate had made some joke.

"Where's Jordan?" Nate asked.

"He's changing clothes," Mom said. "He was helping me in the garden. How was the rink?"

Nate shrugged and wandered over to the stove. He looked into the skillet of simmering chicken pieces and breathed deep. The aroma transported him downtown to the National Folk Festival last summer and the Cajun ribs on those giant trash-can grills. The spicy meat had kicked ass, washed down with the beer he, Tony, and Mowaza had convinced some hippie guy to buy for them. "Wow," Nate said. "What are you making?"

"Jambalaya."

"For what?"

"Actually, for us."

"You're a lucky man," Reece said to Nate. Nate didn't answer him. *Don't be expecting me to invite you to stay.* "And I didn't mean to interrupt you, Sarah," Reece said. "You go back to what you were doing."

"Oh, you didn't interrupt me. I'm always doing something in here. It's my therapy."

Nate reached into a skillet and snagged a piece of chicken, dropping it on the counter when it burned his fingertips. He gingerly touched the chicken piece and gauged it safe to put in his mouth. "That's hot. Spicy hot." His lower lip throbbed where the stitches had been removed yesterday. Most of his bruises had faded to green and yellow, only his nose still a light, puffy blue. Mackenzie liked to kiss his bruises, brushing them with her lips and eyelashes, which made him a little sad they would soon be gone. "I like it." The spices opened his stuffy nose, made him breathe easier. The flavor on his tongue took him back to that sweaty, humid night downtown, where thousands of people danced shoulder to shoulder on Courthouse Square. Mackenzie twirled in her red sundress. That was the first night they'd kissed each other, sitting under the trees.

"Wanna help me?" Mom asked.

Nate was embarrassed that he was acting like such a baby. "Sure." He set down his gym bag, glad to stay here instead of leaving her alone to laugh like that with Reece. "What do I do?"

"You want to chop these scallions?"

"Okay."

"What can I do?" Reece asked, standing.

"You can cut this celery," Mom said. She gave Reece a cutting board, and Nate used the wooden chopping block. Nate cut several bunches of the sharp green onions into tiny slivers, relishing the satisfying feel of the slice. Mom alternated between stirring the crackling, popping chicken pieces in the skillet and tending to a giant pot on another burner.

The doorbell rang.

"I'll get it," Nate said, wiping his hands on his jeans. He was hoping it was Mackenzie. She'd said she might come by after her volleyball practice. But when he opened the door, he stared at Kramble, holding an arm of bright orange-and-yellow tiger lilies. Damn. For a second Nate panicked that he'd forgotten Mom's birthday or something.

"Hi," Kramble said.

Nate wasn't sure what to call Kramble. Mr. Kramble? Detective? Officer? He *wanted* to call him a jerk and tell him to get out and stop coming around so much.

"Is your mom at home?"

"Yeah."

Kramble cocked his head at Nate. When the detective opened

his mouth to say something else, Nate stepped out of the doorway and said, "Come on in. Follow me."

Nate led him into the kitchen and hated how Mom's eyes lit up when she saw him and the flowers. A crowded feeling pressed against Nate's chest. The two men greeted each other and acted like it was perfectly natural for them both to be here, bringing flowers and just kicking it with Nate's mom.

"Nate, could you keep stirring this for me?" Mom asked. He fumed as he stirred, and Mom put Kramble's flowers in another vase. All the fresh flowers reminded Nate of his dad's funeral and how their house had started to stink of dying flowers, rotten water, and pollen in the weeks afterward. He watched Mom smile at Kramble and hoped she remembered that, too.

Nate kept stirring, scraping the bottom of the pot harder than he needed to. Kramble didn't seem to have any *reason* to come over, like at least Reece had. Now he just showed up whenever he felt like it.

Jordan and Danny came into the kitchen. "Oh, man, that smells good," Jordan said. Nate stared at the kid: He smiled. His face was rested and tan from working with Mom in her garden, the scabbed cuts around his mouth faint now, like cookie crumbs he hadn't wiped away. "Did you ever make that for my mom?"

Mom bit her lip. "Um . . . no, I don't think so."

Jordan turned to Reece and said, "In your official home-visit report, could you tell them I'm starving to death here?"

Everyone busted up with laughter again at that. Even Nate had to smile. Jordan had made a *joke*. That was a first.

"I know what you mean," Reece said in a stage whisper. "Her cooking isn't fit to eat, is it?"

Jordan smiled and shook his head. He whispered, "I only eat seconds to be polite."

Mom grinned like some maniac. Shit, now even *Jordan* was flirting with her?

"Here, Danny," Mom said. "Will you chop some tomatoes?" She

scraped the scallions and celery that Nate and Reece had chopped into the pot Nate was stirring, then placed four tomatoes on the cutting board.

"We should have a party," Jordan said. "When my mom gets out. You could make all her favorite food, and all of you could come over to our house."

Mom kept smiling somehow, but it was frozen. Nate hated the hold-your-breath silence in the room.

Nate had expected Jordan to freak after his mom got hauled away by the cops for the second time, but he'd become cheerful, more relaxed. Maybe he was relieved to have his dad locked up. That made sense. What didn't make sense was the way the kid talked all the time about getting to live with his mother. Nate had even talked to Dr. Bryn about it the other day, lingering after a session, asking, "Could I talk to you about something? Alone?" Dr. Bryn had asked a worried-looking Jordan to wait in the lobby and closed the door.

"Why does he do that?" Nate asked. "We all *know* Mrs. Kendrick molested him. Why would he want to live with her?"

Dr. Bryn sighed and coiled one of her curls around her finger. "Sit down." When Nate had, she said kindly. "He wants to live with her because she's his mother."

"Yeah, but—"

Dr. Bryn held up a hand. "The fact that Jordan loves his mother and wants to live with her has nothing to do with whether she's innocent or guilty."

"Yeah, but—"

"Nate." Dr. Bryn smiled, eyebrows raised. "You asked me a question. Do you want to hear my answer?"

Nate shut his mouth and leaned back in his chair. "Sorry."

"Children often love the parents who abuse them. A child usually fears losing that parent if he reports the abuse more than he fears the abuse itself. Kids are willing to tolerate ongoing abuse from parents if it means they'll get *any* sign of love or kindness."

Nate nodded, but her answer still didn't cut it for him.

"For Jordan," Dr. Bryn said, "his continued support of his mother and his constant verbalized wishes to live with her are intentional announcements to us, to everyone, that his mother didn't hurt him. If they get to be together again, it 'proves' her innocence in his eyes. It's part of his denial, Nate. Jordan is mightily skilled in denial. Eventually he needs to confront how his mother used him and betrayed him, but that's *really* hard work. Try to imagine it. Most victims of sexual abuse work on that for their entire lives. It would be unrealistic for us to expect an eleven-year-old to sail through his emotional recovery, right?"

Now Nate felt stupid. When she put it that way, it seemed miraculous that Jordan talked to the Ladens at all.

"For now," Dr. Bryn said, "Jordan finds it lot easier to avoid the hard work and just pretend. He's telling us what he thinks he *should* tell us."

She looked at Nate to see if he followed. "Do you see—just because he *says* it doesn't mean he *believes* it. He's trying to convince himself every bit as much as he's trying to convince everybody else. The truth is something he's avoided for a long time. It's how he survived. And it's helping him survive still."

Now Nate stirred the jambalaya with renewed force. Dr. Bryn had been cool to talk to him. Nate had told Mom about the conversation. It helped a little, but it still felt like a kick in the shin every time Jordan chattered away about "getting" to live with his mom after the trial.

No one spoke after Jordan's party suggestion. Nate suddenly felt he had eaten too much, even though he'd only had one chicken piece, and the room was hot and uncomfortable. He saw Mom look to Kramble. What were people supposed to say?

"You really want to live with your mom again?" Danny asked. Nate looked at his brother, who seemed sincere and bewildered.

Jordan's eyes were fierce as he turned to face Danny. "Yeah, I want to go home. I mean, you guys have been nice and everything, but I miss my mom."

Nate's knuckles were white on the ladle he held.

"But your mom—" Danny started.

"She didn't do anything," Jordan said, staring at Danny.

"But—"

"She didn't do *anything*." Jordan overenunciated each word, and his blue eyes sparkled with a high-fever shine.

Nate didn't like the belligerent look on Danny's face—the look he got those rare times he was sure he was right about something.

"But Jordan's mom did too—"

"*Danny,*" Mom said in a warning voice. He turned to her, and she shook her head.

Danny got that "it's not fair" look on his face. He looked down and chopped his tomatoes like he was killing bugs.

"Hey," Jordan said, "how long do you think the trial will last? Because Danny was telling me about how you go to Michigan every summer." He turned to Reece and Kramble and told them, "Their grandparents' backyard is Lake Superior. There are rafts and inner tubes, and they go kayaking, and once they saw a moose. If Sarah got permission from my mom, I could go, too, right?"

Holy shit. Nate stopped stirring and just stared. Reece opened his mouth, but Mom jumped in first. "Of course we want you to come with us sometime, but we're probably not going to be able to go to Michigan this summer."

"What?" Danny perked up on that. "Why?"

Damn. Nate hadn't even thought of the trial interrupting Michigan.

"I have to be here for the pre*trial* stuff, sweetie." Nate knew that Mom was trying to remind Danny: *Remember what we talked about? Please, let's not talk about the trial.*

But Jordan wouldn't drop it. "But the trial won't last *all* summer, will it?"

Kramble nodded. "There's both their criminal trials and the custody trial for your mom. They might not have even started before the summer's over. It's pretty complicated."

"Not really." Damn, why wouldn't the kid shut up? Jordan addressed the whole kitchen, confident and cheerful. "There won't be any charges against her. You'll see." Nate saw him glance at Danny. "So we could go to Michigan. Is their backyard really Lake Superior?"

Danny nodded, but he frowned.

Mom seemed too dazed to say anything. That tight, crowded feeling in Nate's chest began a slow-motion slide toward his guts, but when Kramble and Reece both reached out to pat Mom's arm closest to them, the feeling clenched again.

"All right," Reece said with fake cheer, "we'd better get going." He stood up and put a hand on Jordan's shoulder. Jordan shrugged the hand off, but there was nothing unfriendly about it; it was just what Jordan did. It struck Nate that he'd never touched Jordan, and Jordan had never touched him— well, except to kick or punch him. Nate thought about the way he and Danny touched each other— wrestling, jostling, leaning on each other. Something like that would be *huge* for this kid.

"See ya later," Jordan said, and headed for the front door.

Reece lingered a moment. He sighed and shook his head before following Jordan. Nate hoped Kramble would get the hell out, too, but he sat down on a stool the second Reece and Jordan were gone. Mom sat, too, with her chin in her hands.

"Is it true?" Danny asked. "That he could go back to living with his mom?"

The muscles in Kramble's jaw bunched tight. "It's way too soon to tell."

That meant he might. No way. This couldn't be happening.

Mom looked about to cry. Kramble slumped forward on the counter. "She and the kid are airtight on this bonding together against the dad. She's actually made well placed statements that she feels safer in jail. She's said that maybe this was the best thing that could've happened to Jordan—getting placed in a safe home, since she wasn't able to provide one as long as the husband was around."

"That is such bullshit," Nate said. No one scolded him.

"But everyone *knows* she's guilty," Danny said.

Kramble looked like he might spit. "We just found out that we're getting the worst judge for the custody trial."

"What do you mean?" Nate asked.

"This judge always rules against Children's Services. She's got this big chip on her shoulder about government interference in families. She's gone against my recommendations every single time she's been a judge on a case of mine. She wants families together."

Mom buried her face in her hands.

"So it *is* true?" Danny asked in disbelief. "Jordan's right?"

Kramble said, "It's a *possibility* we can't rule out. Unless we can dig up someone to testify against her—besides her husband—photos, something like that."

Danny looked genuinely bewildered. "But you've *got* photos."

"Not of Jordan's mom," Nate said. "Mr. Kendrick said they filmed her once, but no one can find it. It makes him look like a liar, which only makes Mrs. Kendrick look less guilty."

Nate had read everything about Mr. Kendrick that he could. The guy seemed more than happy to blab about all he'd done. Bryn had told Nate that was common—that if it wouldn't hurt their cases, most sexual predators bragged about their exploits. Mr. Kendrick's case was so screwed, he had nothing to lose, so it seemed almost like he was proud to talk about how he'd always planned to abuse Jordan, how he'd abused other kids all the way back when he was just a kid, too.

Mark Kendrick had never been abused himself.

"So what happened to him?" Nate had asked Bryn. "What made him that way?"

"Some people just *are* this way. There's not always a reason we can understand."

Nate *hated* that. It wasn't right. It wasn't how things should be.

No one in the kitchen spoke.

Danny stared at his chopped tomatoes a moment, then said, "No way." He pushed the cutting board toward Mom. "These are done," he said, and went out the back door. Nate wondered if Danny was going to pay some attention to "his" rabbit.

Mom picked up the cutting board and slid the tomatoes into the pot Nate was stirring. "You don't have to keep stirring it so much," she said. "It'll be all right."

Was she trying to get rid of him?

"What next?" Nate didn't want to leave. The tomatoes melted into an orange stew.

Mom looked like his question made her happy. "How 'bout that big white onion?"

"This smells fabulous," Kramble said. "Whatever it is."

"It's jambalaya," Mom said, "and I'd love for you to have some. If you can stay."

"I would like that."

Shit. Nate picked up the knife. His shirt itched. He didn't know if it was from Kramble staying for supper or from thinking about Mrs. Kendrick. He remembered recognizing her in the yard and the blurred-panic rush that had washed over him. Not panic that she'd harm them but panic that his mother would realize what had happened between them.

Nate picked up the onion. It was heavy in his hand. He set it in the middle of the cutting board.

"Keep your mouth shut," Mom said.

He looked at her, that panic rush rising in his chest again. What was she saying?

"Keep your mouth shut and you won't cry," she said matter-of-factly. He stared at her, feeling like an idiot.

She pointed to the cutting board. Oh. Shit, she meant the onion. He nodded, clamped his lips shut, and began to cut.

"There's still hope," Kramble said, but he didn't sound like he believed it.

Mom put a green pepper on the chopping block and shook her head. "You hear him talk about her."

Nate kept slicing.

"Sarah," Kramble said, "the kid is in denial big-time."

"That boy has brightened," Mom said, "blossomed, changed personalities at the mere thought of returning to his mother."

"Mom! Jesus, you think that makes her okay?" The onion immediately burned the inside of Nate's nose and mouth, watering his eyes. "Shit."

Mom turned to him, her face set. "*Nothing* makes her okay. But what if the worst happens . . . ?" she faltered. "What if she does get him back? How do we help her then?"

Nate's eyes felt raw. "Help her?" Nate asked. "There is no help for her."

"I don't think anyone can fix what's wrong with Courtney Kendrick," Kramble said.

"But what will you *do*?" Mom insisted. "If she gets him back, what then? Do you just wash your hands of him? What is the *plan* if she regains custody? Because if you don't have one, good goddamn luck getting me to give him up."

Nate had only ever heard Mom talk in this fierce, "don't bullshit me" tone back when Dad first got sick. Some doctor didn't return her call fast enough one day, and she went on a rampage at the hospital to get answers. Nate had been half embarrassed and half in awe, lurking along behind her as she stormed into the private lounge. Mom looked like that now, and Kramble stared back at her, just like that doctor two years ago. Nate realized he hadn't seen this side of Mom since before Dad died.

Nate heard the front door open and Danny came through to the kitchen and stuck his head in the door frame. Why had he gone all the way around the house? "Hey, Nate, c'mere. I wanna show you something."

"We have company, man. Show me later." Nate didn't want to leave Mom here alone with Kramble.

"Is something wrong?" Mom asked.

"No. I just . . ."

"I'll come look," Mom said, standing up.

"No." Danny's face reddened. "Forget it." He disappeared from the door frame.

Mom looked at Nate, and Nate saw the plea in her eyes: *Go.*

Nate shrugged and walked into the the living room, where Danny handed him a CD with a tiny piece of straw stuck to it.

"This, uh, this was in Jordan's backpack. I thought it was his paragraph for Miss Holt. I was going to copy his homework, but then . . ."

That feeling that had crowded into Nate's chest all evening splintered into tiny shards that stuck between his ribs and made it hard to breathe deep. He sat at the computer—which had been left unlocked—and turned on the monitor. "Is this what I think it is?" he whispered. Danny didn't answer but stood near him, glancing over his shoulder toward the kitchen.

Nate slipped in the disk and the familiar list of JPEGs appeared. "I really thought it would be homework," Danny whispered. Nate opened the first photo.

Another photo of Jordan, only this one had just one other person posing with him. A woman, her face turned up and away. But even without the face, Nate knew her. He'd studied that silky blond hair often enough. He'd admired those muscled arms.

Danny made a small moan, but Nate felt triumphant. "Yes," he hissed. They had her.

"I hit 'print' before I knew what it was," Danny said. "Mom called me into the kitchen for something, and when I came back, I saw it. I took it to school, to tear it up and throw it away, so no one would see it here, in the trash or anything." Big, fat tears pooled up in Danny's eyes. He looked again, toward the dining room and the stairs. "Billy Porter got in my backpack to borrow my calculator, but he found this and showed everyone. I just told everyone I found it in the computer lab."

"Don't you get it? This is *great.* This is a gold mine. We gotta show Kr—"

"No!" Danny grabbed Nate's arm. Those tears ran down his

cheeks. "I can't!" he whispered. "I can't because they'll see. . . . I don't want them to see. . . ."

All at once a missing piece locked into place. Those shards felt more like knives. "Danny—did they . . . did they . . . do anything to you?"

"No! Nothing happened, but I . . . I'm on the disk. I don't want people to think I'd do the things that Jordan did." He glanced at the screen. "I don't want them to think . . . to think . . ."

If Courtney Kendrick were in the room right this second, Nate would rip her fucking head off with his bare hands. He clicked through photo after photo. If that bitch had laid one finger on his brother . . .

Nate kept clicking through pictures of Mrs. Kendrick with Jordan. Caressing him, fondling him, and then . . . Jesus Christ. The real deal. With her own son. Nate'd whipped through the photos at high speed, but he stopped, unable to believe what he saw. When he really looked, the picture was even more disturbing. Mrs. Kendrick, holding Jordan on her, in her, was crying. Her face was red, her makeup streaked. Nate stared.

"He . . . he saved me," Danny said, in that gaspy, trying-not-to-cry voice. "He made me leave. He was such a jerk. I hated him. I didn't know . . . that if . . . if I stayed, then maybe . . ." He lifted his eyes to the image and cringed. "But I didn't know this was the only disk with *her,* or I would've told you sooner, I swear, I just didn't want you to think—"

Nate couldn't stand Mrs. Kendrick's face. He clicked on another photo. It was Danny, in the Kendricks' swimming pool. He grinned at the camera, black curls plastered back against his head. The photo was totally innocent. Only in context with the others did it make Nate's head throb. Danny on the diving board. Danny at the side of the pool. Danny doing a back flip. All artfully taken, skillful shots, of a beautiful boy, nearly naked.

And in one, Mrs. Kendrick leaned over Danny, behind him, as he sat in a lounge chair, her hands on his shoulders, her breasts, in her purple bikini, brushing his neck and ear. Danny smiled in the photo, but it was strained, and he had his hands crossed unnaturally over his lap. Nate knew the feeling well. Mrs. Kendrick had that power. And a boy's body betrayed him every time.

"Hey, Mom?" Nate called.

"No, don't—" Danny tried to hush him.

"You guys need to come see this."

"Nate, no—"

"Danny, we *have* to, and you know it, or you wouldn't have showed it to me."

Danny ducked his head as Mom and Kramble came into the room. Nate knew that this was the easy part.

The hard part would be telling Jordan.

CHAPTER TWENTY-THREE

Sarah

Sarah approached Jordan's bedroom door. It had been less than forty-eight hours since Danny had shown them the disk, but it felt like a year that she'd carried the stone of dread and sorrow for Jordan in her chest. This new wound on top of all the other wreckage made it hard to breathe when she looked at him.

Sarah knocked on his door. She didn't expect an answer. He hadn't spoken to any of them since that night they told him they'd found the disk. He'd climbed the stairs to his room and crawled into bed with all his clothes on, even his shoes. Except for occasional trips to the bathroom, he hadn't moved.

Nate had spent Saturday night sleeping on Jordan's floor. Sarah had spent that Saturday and Sunday in the hall. Reece and Ali and Bryn and Kramble had told them the same thing: Give him time. Give him space. *Was* there enough time and space in this boy's life to heal him?

"Jordan? I'm coming in. I have some breakfast for you." She opened the door. He lay on his side, his back to her. She carried the plate of strawberry and banana slices and a blueberry muffin to his nightstand, which she'd moved so that he had to at least sit up to reach his food. She traded the plate for the one she'd left there last night. He'd finally eaten something—a few apples slices and what looked like three bites of the peanut butter sandwich. He'd also removed his shoes. One shoe lay at the foot of the bed, still laced. The other was across the room, a slight scuff on the wall above it suggesting that it had been hurled or kicked.

Danny had finally revealed everything in a rush of relief, babbling nonstop to Kramble—how he'd found the disk, why he lied, how Jordan had made him promise. When Courtney had snuck into the house, Danny'd refused to tell her where Jordan was, even though she kept saying, "I know he lives here. Where is he? When is he coming back?" Danny said Courtney had been nice and friendly, as always, like nothing bad had happened and she hadn't just been in jail. When Danny wouldn't tell her when Jordan would be back, Courtney had sweetly suggested that Danny might want to help her since she had pictures of *him* and he might have to go live in a foster home, too. Danny had blurted—in that thoughtless Danny way—"No you don't! *I* have that disk!" just as Sarah had honked in the driveway. Courtney had begged and pleaded, "Please, please, please give it to me, Danny, please." Danny said Courtney had promised never to tell he'd posed for pictures if he just gave her the disk.

Sarah took a deep breath. Although Courtney hadn't hurt Danny physically, it made her want to break things when she thought of the damage Mark and Courtney *had* done. Danny had cried and asked her, "Why did they pick me, Mom? Out of all the kids that were over there, why did they want it to be *me*? Is there something wrong with me? Could they tell?" Sarah didn't tell Danny she'd feared the same thing: What was it about Sarah that made the Kendricks think her child was easy prey? She'd thought she was a good mother. God knew she *tried*. The Kendricks made her question everything about herself. Bringing her entire family face-to-face with this twisted, repulsive perversion. Making Sarah look at everyone she knew and wonder what secrets they had. The Kendricks had changed them all.

Sarah looked at the defeated little form curled there on the bed. "Hey, Jordan? I'm going outside to work in the garden. You wanna help me?"

No answer.

"It's really beautiful outside today."

Nothing.

"Okay. I'll be in the backyard." She left his room. She couldn't keep watch forever. When Roy had died, she'd longed to cave in the way Jordan had, but she couldn't because of the boys. Having two people dependent on her had forced her to impersonate a functional human being most of the time—buying groceries, having the shingles fixed on the roof, nodding as Nate's teachers reported he'd had some "bad days" but was doing as well as could be expected. She could be that real person for them but not for herself. How many mornings had the sun risen on her still in her clothes, curled on top of the covers just like this boy, convinced she could not get up and walk through the day?

And who was it who convinced her that she could? Who had held her hand and led her along the road back?

But that woman had sexually abused her own son and had apparently planned to abuse Sarah's.

Sarah carried all her tomato plants out into the yard, taking trip after trip up and down the basement steps as if it were a timed event, making herself breathe hard, making her hamstrings ache. She snatched up the plants with a satisfying ferocity.

As she brought the last tray of plants into the yard, frantic bird-calls grabbed her attention and a flash of yellow caught her eye. A big yellow cat was halfway up the apple tree, headed for the nest. "Hey!" Sarah dropped the flat of tomatoes and ran at the cat. The cat froze, clinging to the trunk, and hissed at her.

"Get out of here!" The cat fixed its golden, unblinking eyes on her. Sarah stepped into the garden and snatched up a large, round rock, one of the row markers for the corn. The cat began to scramble down the tree. "Get *out*!" Sarah screamed. She hurled the rock at the cat, only barely missing it. The tree shuddered as the rock hit the trunk with a solid thump, leaving a dent in the bark. The cat bolted away.

Sarah stood, panting, fists clenched. The taste of blood made her aware that she'd bitten her lip. She looked at the rock now lying at the foot of the tree. It was bigger than the cat's head. She might have killed it.

She sucked on her cut lower lip and knew that she'd *wanted* to kill it.

The robins still flew panicked circles around the yard, darting and fluttering at Sarah's head. Sarah ignored them and climbed onto the stone bench to peer into the nest. Empty. Were these the babies or adults flying? Sarah couldn't tell anymore. When she stepped down, the robins returned to the tree.

Sarah closed her eyes and inhaled and exhaled with slow deliberation until her pulse returned to normal. Then she knelt in the garden and used a trowel to dig holes for the tomato plants she was finally putting into the earth. The aroma of soil and basil baking in the heat perfumed the garden and soothed her. Her skin drank in the sun.

The clack of the back door made Sarah lift her head. Jordan stood on the porch. Warmth moved through her chest, as if her heart soaked up the sun's rays as well. "Hey."

He didn't answer. That was okay. It was enough that he'd come outside, that he could stand to be in the same yard with her. To her surprise he let himself in the garden gate and wandered barefoot among the rows he'd helped her plant. Already corn was visible, along with radishes, mint, all kinds of lettuce and greens. The peas were nearly ready to produce.

He stopped at a tall structure of wooden stakes and chicken wire. He frowned.

"That's my bean tepee," Sarah explained. "Eventually beans will grow up those poles, all over that wire, and cover the tepee completely. I keep one little door clear, and it makes a great hideout."

Jordan touched one of the poles with his toe, then wandered up and down the garden rows. Sarah continued planting tomatoes, sneaking glances at him now and then.

He knelt beside the gargoyle her mother had sent. He touched the stone figure's wing. "Do you believe in God?" he asked her, not taking his eyes from the gargoyle.

Sarah stopped digging, her heart racing as it had when she'd seen the cat. After three days of silence, conversation felt fragile. She felt an obligation to say yes, but somehow it was impossible to lie to this boy. "I used to," she said. "I'm not sure I do anymore."

Jordan visibly relaxed, as if he'd been holding his breath. "My grandma did. She said everything happens for a reason." He stood and shoved his hands into his pockets. "If that's true, I think I might hate God." He said it calmly, but Sarah felt her throat tighten.

She knew that some people might argue it was God's plan for this boy to find her family, but she wanted to know why it was God's plan that he needed to.

Jordan walked to her, stepping between the rows.

He crouched low and sniffed the shiny green basil plants. He kept looking at the basil as he asked, "What will you say about her? At her trial?"

Sarah's hands froze on the trowel. She found herself holding still, as if he were a bird that had landed here beside her. She whispered, "I'll tell the truth."

His forehead wrinkled. "What do you mean?"

She shifted to sit cross-legged. Jordan stayed crouched, his arms hugging his knees. She traced designs in the earth with her trowel and wondered how he'd react if she said the wrong thing. "The truth is, I never suspected that anything bad was happening to you. That's what I'll say. If I had, I would have tried to help you sooner."

He squinted at her, and she wasn't sure if it was just from the sun.

She sensed that he wasn't going to fly off. "Why did your mom use a caterer for . . . those other parties? Was it just to explain the people who came over? The cars in the drive?"

Jordan opened his mouth, the answer readily available and about to be shared. But then he shut it and dug his finger in the dirt. He seemed to *want* to talk. Should she keep going? Or let him initiate it? She had no idea what she was doing.

"I have a feeling that I was just a person used to keep up their façade."

Jordan looked up sharply, the movement frightening her. "Their what?"

"Façade? It means . . . um, like a front, a fake appearance."

He tilted his head. "How do you spell it?"

She smiled at this odd request. "F-a-c-a-d-e."

He looked suspicious. "*C?* Really?"

She nodded. "It has a little accent on it, like this"—she drew it in the dirt—"only I don't remember what it's called. That's how you know it's pronounced like an *s*."

"F-a-c-a-d-e," he repeated. He spelled it in the dirt. "So that's what it's called."

Sarah nodded. He'd been good at the façade. Far too good at it.

He buried one hand, packing the dirt around it with his other. "So that's all you'll say about her?" She marveled at his casual tone, the playfulness of his actions, but all the while he was assessing and gathering information.

"I'll just answer the questions." She watched the breeze lift his hair, now dull and greasy from three days without washing. The sudden constriction in her throat surprised her.

Jordan pulled his hand out of the earth and studied his dirt-caked fingernails. "You met my uncle, didn't you?"

Sarah blinked. "Yes."

"Was he mad that I wouldn't talk to him?"

"No. No, not at all. Don't worry. He understands."

"His name is Jordan, too?" Sarah couldn't read the expression on his face.

She nodded. "But he goes by J.M. That's what all his friends call him in Seattle."

He squinted at her. "What did you talk about?"

Again Sarah knew there was no lying. "We talked about you . . . and your mom."

Sarah had agreed to meet Jordan Mayhew the first time he asked, in Bryn's office. She'd been afraid at first. She worried that if he were anything like Courtney, she'd fall for his manipulations. But since the invitation came through Bryn, and Bryn and Reece and Kramble had all already met with him, she made herself go.

When she'd first faced J.M., her breath caught. Looking into this man's face was like looking into a mirror of Jordan's future. The resemblance was so strong it caused Sarah a fleeting moment of horrified wonder—but then she remembered the unmistakable signs of Mark Kendrick in Jordan's face as well.

She'd found J.M. funny and gentle, although she initially tried to resist feeling anything positive about him; she was wary of her own perceptions of people. She'd been so wrong before, after all.

Bryn helped them get started talking but then mostly just listened, twisting one of her fabulous curls around her finger.

"Look," he'd said, "there's no gracious way to small-talk into this. We might as well jump in. I'm still here because I want to help Jordan if I can. I've already been open about the past, so don't worry about being subtle or making me uncomfortable. He's probably nowhere near ready to talk to me yet, but I wanted to lay the groundwork, you know, suggest the possibility. One of the greatest things that helped *me* was meeting someone who'd lived through the same stuff I had and seeing that they were okay, that they had this good life and people who loved them and all that. Before I met any other survivors, I just thought of myself as damaged goods and assumed that everyone I met could probably tell."

He was completely comfortable when Sarah asked questions about their childhood. He told her how they were never allowed to see any other doctor except their father. Even Courtney's gynecological exams were done by her father, and at a much earlier age than had been needed.

Sarah told J.M. what Courtney had said about hating the doctor she had as a young girl, about being afraid and ashamed. "So I guess that was just another lie, like all her others."

J.M. asked her, "Or was that as close to the truth as she ever came to telling you?"

J.M. hadn't known that Courtney had a child. And therefore had not known about his mother's apparent change of heart. "The only regret I have about not coming to her funeral is that I probably would have met Courtney's son. And if I'd known they had a child, I probably would have been here, gotten involved, tried to keep that kid safe."

"You mean, you suspected that she'd harm Jordan?" Sarah asked.

J.M. opened his arms. "I would have assumed it. I'd met Mark. I wasn't invited to their wedding or anything, and if I had been, I wouldn't have gone, but I met him several times. I tried to stay in contact with Courtney. I didn't blame *her.* I knew she was in denial, I knew she was protecting herself the only way she knew how, but I knew that Mark was a predator from the first time I met him."

Sarah remembered charming, handsome Mark. His movie-star smile. *"How?"*

"He reminded me of our dad. Even Courtney said that. And she and Mark were doing some service project with high-risk kids, all these kids who didn't have parents around or had parents who were crack addicts or working three jobs or whatever, and these kids were always in their apartment, spending the night with them and stuff." J.M. shook his head. "And I saw the way Mark touched these kids. It was so inappropriate. And that was *in front of me,* you know, so I could only imagine—too well, mind you—what was going on when no one else was there. And I talked to Courtney about it, but she was furious and said I was trying to wreck her life again by making up these lies. It was pretty ugly. I even went to the police but wasn't taken seriously at all. After that she rarely had any contact with me. They even changed addresses a couple times without telling me, and I'd have to hunt them down. I guess I always held out this hope that she'd come around, have some breakthrough about her past abuse, and I wanted to be there to help her. So I just peripherally stayed aware of her and her doings. I'd Google her now and then. She accomplished a lot. I was secretly glad about her medical specialty. Relieved she wasn't a pediatrician like our dad. I figured she was safe in obstetrics, working mostly with adults. She wouldn't have any private contact with the infants, you know?"

Sarah was fascinated by J.M. He was married, with no children and no plans to have any. He had an organic farm on Whidbey Island, about an hour and a half away from Seattle. Bryn laughed as Sarah and J.M. went off on a long "riff"—Bryn's word—about heirloom tomatoes.

Sarah had felt good, more hopeful, about Jordan's future when she'd left that meeting. Here in the garden, she told Jordan most of this and assured him, "Your uncle had to go home, but he'll come back to Ohio. He's going to testify at your mother's trial."

And rather than ask any other questions about his uncle, Jordan asked, "They're going to make me talk at her trial, too, aren't they?"

Sarah picked up a tomato plant. "I don't know. Has Reece talked to you about that? He was hoping that Ali's testimony would be enough and you wouldn't have to be there."

"Maybe I want to go." A slight challenge edged his voice.

"Oh." She lowered the plant into a hole and covered its roots.

"Someone has to tell them that she didn't want to hurt me."

"But she did." Sarah tried to keep the words free of judgment. They came out sounding flimsy in the bright sunlight. "Sweetie, we saw it."

Jordan looked her right in the eye. "But that's not—She didn't want to do that." Sarah looked back into his eyes. Light blue. So different from the dark eyes of her children. He seemed to believe what he said. Or had he simply mastered the façade he'd practiced so long?

She thought of the photos she'd seen Saturday night. They all blurred together for her, not like the first ones Nate had discovered. The photos of Jordan and Courtney were eclipsed by her relief that there was a reason for Danny's behavior, something to point to, something to grasp. She tried now to bring those pictures back: Courtney had been crying, tears streaming down her face, a face more anguished than Jordan's own.

Sarah set her trowel aside and asked, "So why did she?"

"He made her. He said she was cheating."

"How was she cheating?"

He ducked his head and looked down at the dirt again, this time burying his other hand. His voice was quiet, almost dreamy, as if he were remembering. "She had to do it on camera, like everybody else. He said it wasn't fair to do it when no one was watching. He—" Jordan stopped abruptly.

The sweat on Sarah's back turned cold and clammy. "Do . . . do you mean that she made you . . . do that sometimes, even when there were no cameras? When it was just you two?"

He kept his head down.

Sarah tried to imagine that scenario. "Cheating," indeed. How surreal, how macabre to argue about when it was "fair" to have sex with your child.

Jordan pulled his hand free from the soil and made a hard-packed dirt ball. He rolled the ball between his palms, his chin still tucked against his chest. Sarah knew he was processing what he'd just revealed. He hadn't denied it. She knew she had to tell Reece and Kramble. And Jordan was smart enough to know this. She sat silently while Jordan rolled the dirt ball from one hand to the other. Minutes passed.

Jordan looked across the yard and said, "Maybe I did the right thing that day. Maybe it was good I got taken away from her, so she doesn't have to worry about anything but getting well right now. See, I think, even with that disk, she might get out, don't you?" It was the first time Sarah'd seen anything childlike and hopeful in his face, and it made her eyes well with tears. "Maybe without him around, she'd be all right, and I'd be allowed to go home." His voice climbed higher, and he took in a ragged breath. "Do you think she'll get out?"

Sarah answered truthfully. "I don't know, hon." He hadn't asked her what she hoped for, which was more complicated. She sucked her cut lip, remembering hurling the rock at the cat. How good that had felt.

He crumbled the ball of soil in his hands and let it sift down between his fingers. He stood up and tilted his head. "Can they make her . . . better?"

She paused. This boy deserved more than sugarcoating, but she couldn't bring herself to say no. "I don't know."

He looked down at his bare feet in the dirt and said quietly, "I hope so."

"Me, too." Sarah wasn't lying. Part of her wished, so much it made her ache, for Courtney to be made well. For her to return as the woman Sarah had known.

And she wished for this boy to get what he wanted. For once in his life, for him not to feel cheated or betrayed or disappointed. But she only wanted this if it were the absolute right thing for Jordan to get his wish. If Courtney actually *deserved* to get him back. And Sarah hurt with her belief that no matter what rehabilitation miracles anyone came up with, she'd never be convinced that this child, any child, was safe with Courtney.

Jordan looked up at Sarah and smiled. Again he had that look of innocent optimism that changed his face completely.

"It's hot," he said, looking up at the sky. He pulled his T-shirt out from his neck and sniffed, then made a face. "I'm gonna go take a shower." He walked to the gate. "Hey, Sarah? Could I—Do I . . . do I still get a tree?"

She grinned and squinted through the sun at him, blinking her burning eyes. "Sure."

"I want the kind Nate has," he said, pointing. He let himself out of the garden and walked up the porch steps. The back door clunked shut, and Sarah exhaled slowly.

They'd made it through another crisis, it seemed. During Jordan's two-day silence, Lila had told Sarah, "No good deed goes unpunished, my dear." Sarah had stiffened at the suggestion. "This is asking a lot of you," Lila had said before she left.

Jordan did ask a lot of Sarah. He asked for more than she thought she and the boys were capable of giving. Over and over he had asked them to give more, be more for him.

And they had.

God help her, he could *not* return to Courtney.

CHAPTER TWENTY-FOUR

Jordan

Jordan stood in the jail's bright white hallway with Reece and hoped he didn't throw up. He kept breathing funny and swallowing too much as he waited for his first visit with his mom. He wished he could visit her alone, but they had all these stupid rules, and he couldn't even *see* her without stupid Reece being there, too. Jordan hated that Reece was allowed to listen to every word they said to each other. His fingers slid across the laminated visitor's pass clipped to his shirt, and he wiped his hands on his jeans. Why had he told Sarah that stuff his dad said about "cheating"? Jordan had known, even as he said the words to her, that he was screwing up way worse than the first time.

It was almost his turn; he knew he'd be in the next group allowed to go to the windows and the phones. With his stomach so funky, he couldn't tell what he really felt. He wanted to run out of this place and breathe some fresh air. But he should be happy to see her. He wanted to be like when he first saw her on the Ladens' lawn. He'd been happy then, right? Well . . . at first, but then . . . why couldn't he stop swallowing? This feeling reminded him of coming home from school, how he'd slip in the side door holding his breath, to find out what mood she was in, how her eyes looked, what she might do.

He realized that it had been over a month now since he'd experienced that don't-do-anything-until-you-find-out feeling. He'd gotten used to not feeling it. Funny how that was just as easy as getting used *to* feeling it. A person could get used to just about anything. In science class Miss Holt talked about how humans adapted to their environments. A-d-a-p-t-e-d. He tried not to swallow again, but he had to.

"You okay?" Reece asked.

Jordan nodded and wiped his upper lip. It was hot in here, waiting on this stupid blue line in this stupid white hallway. And Reece had already asked him that about five thousand times. T-h-o-u-s-a-n-d. Jordan put his hand in his pocket and touched the broken wing he'd stolen from Dr. Bryn. Turns out she knew he'd taken it. She'd asked him what he planned to do with it. He didn't know.

"We're up," Reece said. He touched Jordan's shoulder to guide him forward, but Jordan shrugged off his touch. Reece didn't react. He just pointed instead.

Jordan knew what to expect. Reece had blabbed on and on about how it would work, practically drawing a picture of it, like Jordan was two or something. There were three windows in the visiting area. The visitors sat on this side of the wall, and the prisoners sat on the other, behind thick windows. You had to talk on heavy, old-fashioned black phones—just like in the movies.

A police officer barked out names, reading off a clipboard, directing traffic as this new shift began. "Justin! Window One. Keller! Window Two. Kendrick! Window—" Jordan saw the recognition snap into the officer's face. The officer glanced up, found Jordan, and made eye contact, which he hadn't done for the others. Jordan felt his ears and neck burn hot as the line grew silent behind him. The officer looked curious, then sad. Jordan glared at him. "Window Three, son."

At least Window Three was the farthest from the line. Jordan swallowed hard as he started walking, panicked that he might puke in front of all these people. The room kept going shimmery on him. Was that even a word? S-h-i-m-m-e-r-y.

Jordan sat on one of the metal seats at Window Three, just a round disk attached to the floor by a metal bar. His mom wasn't on the other side of the glass yet, and Jordan felt bad for being relieved. Each window had two seats, and Reece sat in the other one. The way the chairs were attached to the floor, Jordan couldn't scoot farther from Reece. A side partition on the left separated them from the visitor at Window Two. He couldn't see her, but he could hear her. She started her conversation with, "I'm gonna kick your skinny ass, you worthless motherfucker." Jordan was glad that to his right was a concrete wall.

He gripped the edge of the mesh countertop. M-e-s-h. *Stop it.* "Mesh" was such an easy word. Jordan wondered if it was mesh so the guard could see what you were doing with your hands. His mother's hands flashed into his head. *No. No. Think of something else.* The counter reminded Jordan of a table you'd find in an outdoor playground. Or a table at a rest stop. Like that rest stop he and his grandma had a picnic at when she'd come to take Jordan to live with her. Back before . . . Oh, man, he really might throw up.

"Seriously," Reece said softly. "Are you okay?"

Jordan wanted to glare at Reece again, but he was afraid if he moved his head, he'd puke. Plus, if he looked at Reece, he might cry. He didn't know which would be worse or make him feel more like a baby. Tears pushed behind his eyes, and his lunch burned against his throat. He just stared straight ahead through the glass. And, as he did, his mother sat in the chair opposite him.

His heart stuttered in that extra beat that still startled him, and made him gasp.

He studied her face. Her skin was so pale it looked almost see-through, and her dark blue jumpsuit made every vein in her face stand out across her forehead and her throat. Her lips looked Halloween red, even though she wasn't wearing any makeup. She ran a hand over her messy hair—it looked like she hadn't even brushed it—then tucked it back behind her ears. She started to cry. She looked at him but didn't really see him, he could tell.

He picked up his phone. The receiver smelled like bad breath. "Mom? Mom? Pick up your phone."

Jordan tapped the glass, and she focused her gaze. She picked up her phone.

"Hi, Mom." As the words left his mouth, he knew they were too cheery and fake.

Reece picked up his phone as well. Jordan saw his mother's eyes flicker to Reece.

"Hey, there, cookie." Her voice was hoarse, like when she'd had laryngitis one time. She wiped her eyes. Her nails were short and ragged, the skin around them scabbed.

"What happened to your hands?" It was a stupid thing to ask, but he had no idea what to say, especially with Reece—and maybe these other morons—listening to them.

She held the phone between her ear and shoulder and examined both hands, fingers spread wide, as if she hadn't noticed the dried blood before. "Just a nervous habit, I guess."

Jordan wondered what to say next. He knew they only had fifteen minutes, and it had already started, so he took a deep breath. "I think everything is going to be okay, and we can live together again, without *him,* don't you? I think pretty soon we can—"

She closed her eyes, massaging her forehead, and Jordan shut up. She opened her eyes and smiled. He breathed again. "Is Sarah taking good care of you?"

He hesitated, trying to decide if this was a trick question. What would happen if Mom found out what he'd told Sarah about her? He wished he could tell Mom about planting his own tree, the way Sarah had argued with the guy at the nursery who told them it wasn't a good time to plant a dogwood. How sad Sarah'd seemed about the cramped and twisted root-ball on the tree they'd found. How he and Sarah had dug the hole together while Nate and

Danny were at school, patting earth around it. How he'd watered it every day. But . . . he remembered that funny feeling he'd had yesterday as he watered. This anger that bubbled up in him as he stood there patiently holding the hose. This feeling of, *See? I know how to take care of something. Nothing bad will ever happen to this tree.* The feeling had scared him.

He looked through the glass at his mother, who still waited for his answer. "Yeah . . . Mrs. Laden's okay." He wouldn't call her Sarah. Not in front of Mom. He opened his mouth. He knew what he should say, but his lips and tongue wouldn't say it. He had to force out, "B-but I want to live with you again. In our own house, just us."

Her face did a funny shiver, and new tears ran down her cheeks.

Just us. That image of her hands flashed into his brain again. No, this time would be different. "Mom? Don't cry. You'll get out of here. I know you will. Everyone will find out that it was all a mistake." He wondered if the people in line were listening. Maybe not with the woman at Window Two still shouting "motherfucker" every other word.

He smiled at his mom and felt like his face might crack. It *would* be different, just the two of them. Wouldn't it? It would.

Mom's nose ran, and she didn't wipe it. She looked at him as if she'd never seen him before in her life, as if she didn't know who he was. She coughed once, a weird dry-heave sound, like his cat, Raja, about to cough up a hairball. The thought of Raja sent a bolt of anger, then panic, through him. *It was all my fault,* he thought, almost blurting it out loud. *All my fault, not yours.*

To make up for it, he said, "I love you, Mom."

She made a move as if to scoot her chair back, but she had a disk chair, too, and it didn't budge. The abrupt movement made Jordan think she was going to leave. He'd blown it. She dropped her phone, the heavy black receiver hitting the counter with a loud whack that stabbed Jordan's ear. She put her forehead on the edge of the counter, and Jordan watched her back heave as she sobbed.

A guard appeared behind Mom in the window. Jordan put his hand on the window, then smacked it with his palm. The guard looked at him, and Jordan shook his head. "Leave her alone," he said into his phone, even though the guard couldn't hear him.

The guard pursed his lips and looked at Reece, who nodded. The guard leaned on the wall behind Jordan's mom, lurking there, watching her. Jordan didn't like the way the guard looked at her. The guard hated Jordan's mother, Jordan could tell.

Jordan waited a long time while his mother cried. He stared at the top of her head and decided that it *had* to be different if the two of them got to live together again. She wouldn't do those things anymore, not after being in jail and being on the news. And she would always remember how he had defended her and never told the police the truth about her. "Mom? It's okay." The receiver lay on the counter next to her head, so maybe she could hear him. One of her ears was red and scabbed, as if it'd been scraped. He'd gotten used to feeling the passage of time in his guts. He knew just how long a minute could be, and he knew that right now, unlike all those other times, the minutes were clicking by too fast. "Mom? Mom— we don't get very much time."

The guard finally stepped forward and touched her shoulder. Jordan read her lips through the glass. "Don't fucking touch me." She smacked the guard's hand away. Jordan wished Reece hadn't seen that. The guard talked to her, pointing at Jordan, but Jordan couldn't make out the words. After a few minutes, the guard went back to leaning on the wall.

Mom turned back to Jordan. She placed one hand on the glass and, with the other, picked up the phone.

Jordan knew he should put his hand on hers, palm to palm— he'd seen that in the movies, too. He knew it would look good. He could picture himself doing it, but the rushing-water sound filled his head, even though there would be glass between them. He kept one hand on his phone, his other gripping the counter.

"I'm sorry, Jordan," she whispered.

He squeezed the edge of the counter until his knuckles whitened. She shouldn't say that in front of Reece. She wasn't supposed to have anything to be sorry *for.*

"It's not your fault," he said sharply, wanting to remind her. And as he said it, he saw that it wouldn't be different at *all* if he lived with her. She'd do those things she always did, and then she'd laugh and talk as though nothing had happened. But that picture filled him with panic, just like thinking of Raja had. "Everything'll be all right," he promised, needing to believe it. "I can stay at the Ladens' until you're out."

She raised her eyebrows and seemed to wake up out of her weirdness. She drew her hand away from the glass and twisted her hair around one finger. She looked past him, at the bright, white hall behind him. "You shouldn't be here."

His stomach fell away, and if glass hadn't separated them, he might've flung himself at her feet and grabbed her legs, hanging on tight so she couldn't shake him off. "No, I want to. I want to visit you." He hated how begging and whiny his voice came out. *Stop it.* He would *not* cry. She was supposed to say that she wanted to see him as often as she could. And she was supposed to write him letters every day. She only wrote once last week.

"Are you all right?" she asked. "Do the doctors say you're fine?"

He stared at her, hot blood filling his face and ears. They never talked about that. Ever. Even after the first time, the worst time. She'd bring him "medicine," but they never talked about what it was for. She'd just leave what he needed—Epsom salts and the pads—and he figured out what to do with them. He knew that Reece saw that awful, branding heat in his face. He thought his ears might explode.

"What did the doctors say?" she repeated.

"I'm fine," he rasped, sounding like he was the one with laryngitis.

"Do you feel good?"

He nodded. What was wrong with her?

"Are you playing soccer?"

He shook his head. His hot skin itched.

"Why not?"

He shrugged. "I wasn't at school for tryouts, and . . . I dunno . . . I never really liked it."

He thought for a minute she might get mad, but if she was going to ask about his . . . his *body,* he guessed all the rules had gone out the window. He pictured little white strips of paper, with typed rules on them, fluttering out of the jail's window on the breeze. He thought about saying, "I only played because it was part of the façade," but he didn't. "Mom, they say this judge is really big on keeping families together. You'll be out soon, and we can get back to normal."

Mom laughed out loud. "Oh, cookie . . ."

Dizziness made the room go shimmery again. Why was she acting like he'd made a joke? He wished he had the guts to tell her to shut up; she was ruining all his hard work.

Before she could answer, the guard tapped her on the shoulder, and she flinched. Jordan heard the man say, "Time."

Jordan felt he should pull up the tree at the Ladens. He didn't live there; it wasn't his home; that wasn't his family. "I'll come back next week. Write me, okay?"

But she only mouthed, "Bye," and let herself be led away.

Jordan hung up his phone. He had a façade again. A new one. But either he'd gotten soft and lazy in this past month or the façade had gotten lots harder.

CHAPTER TWENTY-FIVE

Nate

Nate sat on the curb in the dark and wondered what the hell had just happened. He had been naked in the same room as Mackenzie, and now here he sat, dressed and alone. Shit. This was the night Nate had been waiting for his entire life. Mackenzie's parents were gone for three days, at a conference in Philadelphia. He and Mackenzie could be all alone in that huge house. They could take their time. No hiding, no hurry, no contortions in a car.

And he'd blown it. He'd fucking blown it.

He felt that concussion-stunned dizziness that came after being blindsided on the ice. He had a sneaking suspicion that he and Mackenzie had just broken up. Shit. They'd broken up because he wouldn't sleep with her. Great. He couldn't wait for *that* to get around. He'd never get another date again. And she probably thought he had some weird obsession with Jordan, something wrong and kinky, bringing up the kid the way he did.

Nate moaned and put his head down on his knees. He was a loser. What a fucking loser. They'd been *naked*. They'd planned it for weeks. They had condoms. There'd been candles. And that warm, honey scent of her that made him dizzy. They'd whispered. There'd been something reverent about it.

The sensation of her bare flesh on his own had produced the same click and hum somewhere deep within him that getting high did. That same slowing down, moving into time that felt deeper, thicker, like moving through water.

Their first time. He had wanted to remember every detail. He'd knelt above her, hardly able to believe that this phenomenal body invited him, welcomed him, totally trusted him.

He'd been *right there*.

And then the damn kid wouldn't stay out of his brain.

Nate had returned Mackenzie's favor from the snow day. He'd licked a line down her belly back to that triangle of red fluff. He'd tasted that metallic tang of her. She put her hands in his hair and squeezed and released her fingers against his scalp.

And Nate had lifted his head abruptly, forcing her to let go—forcing away the image of Mr. Kendrick holding Jordan by the hair. Mackenzie kept smiling, though, eyes half closed, and flung her arms over her head, past the nest of blankets she'd made, her pink-painted fingernails burrowing into the carpet instead of Nate's hair. Nate saw Jordan's fingers clutching handfuls of the white shag carpet. Nate blinked, then looked at Mackenzie, letting her naked body, her smile, draw him back.

The scent and taste of her made him so drunk his fingers felt numb on the condom wrapper. As he finally tore open the foil, his brain kept repeating, *This is it, this is it*. The moment he'd been waiting for. Their first time.

Had the kid even known what was happening his first time? When did he realize? Nate didn't want to, but his mind tried to take him there, tried to imagine the sensation, the logistics. It had to hurt. There'd been blood in the pictures. Nate shuddered and looked at Mackenzie, wanting to see *her*.

Those pictures were a world apart from this, from him and

Mackenzie, weren't they? He and Mackenzie both wanted it. He slid the condom from the foil. So what the hell was he waiting for?

"Nate? What's the matter? Don't you want to?" Mackenzie lowered her gaze from his face, and her forehead crinkled. She could see the obvious fact that he did want to, *yes, yes, yes,* and that he could, but . . . "What's wrong?"

He couldn't speak. His brain screamed, *What the hell are you doing? Don't stop!* Oh, Jesus, he was blowing this big time. But the candlelit room seemed crowded with importance. Because of Jordan he felt this obligation to make the act almost sacred.

"Mackenzie—I . . . I don't think . . . I mean . . . maybe we . . ."

She stared at him. Her eyes glittered with disbelief.

He opened his mouth but didn't know what to say. *You are fucking blowing this, you loser,* he told himself, but when he managed to speak, he stammered, "M-maybe we shouldn't."

"What?" Her voice was tight and furious, which threw him. "Why? What's wrong with me?"

"Oh, no, Kenzie, that's not—"

She stood up and yanked on her T-shirt, which covered that red fluff.

Nate stood, too, feeling stupid, naked and in the state he was in. A sliding-down-the-drain sensation pulled at him. He would never, in a million years, have guessed she'd be *mad.* He was the one who had been pushing. He hadn't even been sure she wanted to until he saw the nest and candles. "Nothing's wrong with you," he said, now scrambling to recover the disaster this was becoming, "I just—"

"We planned this for *weeks.* I was getting ready all day. Do you know how much these candles cost me? I . . . I . . ." she started to cry.

"Mackenzie." Nate felt like a shit.

"You . . . you said—" she started, but her voice pinched itself off. Nate stepped toward her, but she turned away from him and snatched up her panties from the floor. He watched her wriggle into them, her back to him. They'd been naked. And now she was getting dressed. This was surreal, this was . . .

She picked up her shorts and put them on.

"I want to," he said. That was true. Every single second of his existence felt like it led to this very moment. "It's all I think about, but . . . I . . ." He should just tell her the truth. "I keep thinking about Jordan." His face rushed with heat. *Loser. Total loser.*

She blinked, hands frozen on the snap of her shorts. "What?"

"I'm sorry, I just keep thinking about . . . those disks . . . and I don't want to do this, to . . . be with you, with those thoughts in my head."

She frowned at him.

The phone rang. They waited, but whoever it was hung up. They stared at each other a moment, but before they could speak, it rang again. Mackenzie glared in the direction of the phone. No message again, but a heavy slam when the machine kicked on. "What? Did you tell the guys you were coming over here? They figured you oughta be done by now or something? Gee, how generous of them to give you . . . what? Five minutes?"

"Mackenzie—"

"Fine. Go back to the party. If you'd rather get drunk than be with me, feel free. Just don't bother to—"

"Shut up. I didn't tell anyone I was coming over here. I just . . . I'm serious I keep thinking about Jordan."

She sighed, that you-are-*so*-immature look on her face, like that day at school when Nate had pushed Tony and ended up giving that girl a bloody nose.

"I know," Nate said. "I know that's weird. But you never saw those sick pictures. It was twisted. I just don't . . . I . . ."

Her face softened a little.

"I'm sorry. I don't want to hurt your feelings. I didn't mean to. But I don't think I can. . . . I don't want the first time to be . . . I dunno. Don't you want it to be . . . right?"

She didn't look as mad, but she still didn't speak.

Nate picked up his underwear and jeans and put them back on. Putting on pants had to be one of the most awkward, humiliating movements in the world. Mackenzie didn't watch him dress. She knelt and began blowing out candles.

Nate had apologized a hundred times. Damn. It had gone past the point of her feelings' being hurt. She was just being a bitch. He wasn't going to keep saying he was sorry for *not* sleeping with her, for fuck's sake. Mom had warned him things would change if they did it; she hadn't said how they'd change if they didn't.

But then Mackenzie'd really got him when he told her he'd still spend the night. He'd told Mom he was staying at Mowaza's, for the end-of-the-school-year party. "I want to wake up with you," he'd said. Nate reached for her hand. She let him hold it, but it was still and lifeless in his own. He realized she didn't *want* him to stay, that she was going to say no. He felt like he was falling.

"Unless . . ." he said, wanting to put it out there himself. "Unless you don't want me to."

She nodded, not looking at him.

"Oh. Okay." He hated how hurt he sounded. He didn't want her to know. He cleared his throat. "I'll go." He kissed her, to show her he was fine, he was cool. At least she kissed him back.

"You're different now," she said, in a voice he couldn't read. "Since Jordan came to live with you."

A whir rushed through him—blades on ice, speeding in to defend. He pictured himself blocking the kid as he had on those hospital stairs back when they'd been discovered.

"Maybe I am." His voice came out too challenging. He liked to think the change was for the better but didn't say this aloud.

He stood and put on his shirt. "I'll call you tomorrow," he said, as casually as he could.

She nodded.

Her phone rang again as Nate picked up his shoes, slipped out her door, and started walking. A block away he sat on a curb and put on the shoes. *Damn. Shit. Fuck.* He'd blown it. Totally blown it.

Should he go home? Or go back to the party? Mom thought he was at Mowaza's. Nate couldn't believe that Mom had agreed to let him go. It was the first party she'd let him go to since juvenile court. She trusted him again.

Nate snorted. He didn't know *why* she trusted him again. Look at him.

He stood up and started walking the blocks home in the quiet, deserted neighborhood.

He wondered how things could change so fast. How everything could be just fine and then tilt, as if some giant hand had shaken the game board, sending him sliding. Like barely getting used to the idea that his dad was sick before Ali woke him up in the ER waiting area to tell him Dad was dead. Like realizing there were people in the world who got off on doing the things they'd done to Jordan.

Talk about Jordan changing things. In a way Nate had just screwed things up with Mackenzie because of Jordan. Fine. Fuck Mackenzie, he thought, no pun intended. She didn't know. She hadn't seen Jordan's dead eyes, the blood that ran down his skinny leg.

Nate turned the corner onto his street and froze, his heart in the back of his throat. All the lights in his house were still on. It was after midnight. That giant game board tilted again. What was wrong now? He sprinted down the street and burst in the back door. "What's going on?" he asked.

Danny sat at a kitchen island. His eyes widened, and he glanced at Mom, who rinsed lettuce in the sink. She was rinsing lettuce at midnight? Warning bells went off in Nate's brain.

"What's wrong?" he asked. "Where's Jordan?"

Nobody said anything. Mom kept rinsing the lettuce.

"Is Jordan okay?" Nate asked. Why was everyone being so freaky?

"Jordan's fine," Danny said. "Klezmer's gone."

"Klezmer?" Confusion drowned out the warning bells.

Danny nodded, glancing at Mom, who still hadn't turned around. "He wasn't in his hutch when I went to feed him tonight. We looked everywhere." Then Danny shook his head and mouthed to Nate, "You are in big trouble."

Without turning from the sink, Mom said, "Danny, you need to get to bed. We'll look for Klezmer in the morning."

"Okay," Danny said. He shot Nate a look of sympathy before he left the room. Shit. What was going on?

"Did Danny not latch his hutch?" Nate asked, picturing lost Klezmer running into one of the neighborhood dogs. He wondered if the latch had been damaged in some way when Danny took apart the lid to retrieve the hidden disk. Nate could get a flashlight and go look.

"I don't want to talk to you about the damn rabbit." Mom's voice was weary, even if her movements in the sink were furious and precise.

Nate was becoming way too familiar with this down-the-drain sensation. It pulled all his energy into a pool around his feet. Shit. She knew. He slumped on a stool at the island, suddenly too exhausted to stand.

Mom turned from the sink and dried her hands on a dish towel. "You lied to me."

He sighed, then nodded.

She looked surprised. She leaned against the sink, hands on her hips. "Why?"

He wanted to tell the truth. "I don't know."

She laughed bitterly. "Well, that's a good reason. How do you think it made me feel?"

He didn't know how she felt, but he felt like shit. "I'm sorry."

"Yeah? Well, I'm sorry, too. Nate, I need to be able to trust you. You're not making it easy."

He sat in silence. She was right. What could he say? He was an asshole and an idiot. She stared at him, her eyes bloodshot and tired. She looked so old. He knew it was infuriating her that he didn't say anything. "What were you thinking?" she asked him. "No, you don't need to answer that. I *know* what you were thinking. I know where you were, even if no one answered the phone. I thought about coming over, I was so mad at you." She shook her head, and

Nate hated the disappointment in her eyes, behind the anger. "I wanted to storm over there and bust down the damn door, but then I thought, I don't need this. I don't want to further humiliate myself by walking into some sordid little encounter, this trashy little rendezvous you apparently set up—"

"Mom." The words "sordid" and "trashy" hit him like slaps. "It wasn't like that. We didn't—"

"Nate, don't. Why should I believe anything you tell me?"

He paused, then shook his head.

"Can't think of a reason? Neither can I."

She leaned against the sink, arms crossed, staring at him.

Jordan appeared in the doorway but took one look at their faces and backed out of the room.

"I did that for you," Mom whispered, gesturing toward where Jordan had stood. "I was so proud of you, Nate." Her voice began to waver. "God, if only I could make you feel what I did when Tony came to our door."

The carpet was yanked from under Nate's feet. "*What?* Why did Tony come here?"

"To find you. Apparently you told everyone you were coming home to baby-sit?"

Nate buried his head in his heads. "I . . . I didn't want to make anyone lie for me."

"How noble of you," Mom sneered. "He said he left something here. And *that* makes me mad: You know I don't want him here. When did you have him over without me—"

"Whoa. Wait. He hasn't been here since before . . . you know, the police thing."

God, that sounded lame. But it was true. What the hell was Tony talking about?

"He wanted to go down to the basement to get something. I wouldn't let him. Do you know what he's talking about?"

"No."

She stood there, looking beat up and defeated.

"Mom, everything you say is right." His voice came hoarse and whispery through his tightening throat. "I made a big mistake. I'm sorry. I don't know what else to say."

She wiped her eyes on the back of one hand. "I don't know either. I don't know yet what I'm going to do with you. It makes me tired." She turned to face the sink and stood with both hands gripping the edge, looking down at the lettuce. "So . . . go upstairs or something. Give me some time to sort through this and decide. I'm too upset to talk to you."

Nate stood up, only too happy to get out of this kitchen, but he ran into Jordan, who sat at the top of the stairs, his face pale. He'd obviously been listening to their conversation. "What's she gonna do?" he whispered.

Nate shrugged. "Don't worry about it, Jordan. It's my problem."

"What'll she do?" he asked again. He looked almost scared.

Nate paused on the top step. "Hey, it's okay. Whatever she decides, I'll deserve it. I'm gonna lay low, for a while, okay?" He went into the room he shared with Danny and closed the door, glad Danny was downstairs and he could have some privacy for a few minutes.

He stood in the dark. *Way to go, Tony,* he thought. *Thanks a fucking lot.* But Nate knew it was his own fault. He lay on the bed and stared at the ceiling, barely visible in the streetlight through his window. What did Tony want? It seemed like a hundred years ago since Tony had been in this house. Nate had been baby-sitting while Mom worked some party. He and Tony shared a joint behind the garage, then went to the basement to sneak some of Mom's vodka. They'd sat right on top of the bale of straw for Klezmer's hutch. Tony had wanted to leave the weed there, at Nate's, instead of having it on him when he went to the basketball game, but Nate knew for a fact that he hadn't. No way in hell would he let Tony do that. He remembered Tony dumping his whole backpack out, shuffling papers and magazines and Pop-Tarts wrappers.

Some baby-sitter Nate was.

The look in Mom's eyes almost killed him. "I was so proud of you," she'd said. *Was.* Past tense. He put a pillow over his head.

And Klezmer. His eyes burned, picturing the rabbit, so small, lost and loose in the dark. Somehow that felt like his fault, too.

A tap on the door startled him. Oh, man. He didn't have the energy to take any more shit from Mom right now. "Yeah?"

The door opened, and Nate was surprised to see Jordan there in the hallway light. Nate sat up. "Did you find Klezmer?"

"No." Jordan came in but didn't ask why Nate sat in the dark or turn a light on himself. He closed the door behind him and sat on the bed next to Nate. "Sorry I got you in trouble."

Oh, great. Nate felt even worse. "You didn't. It had nothing to do with you."

"But I heard what your mom said. She let me come here because of you."

"Well . . . yeah . . . but that's not why I got in trouble. I screwed up."

Nate listened to the voices downstairs, Mrs. Ripley's bug zapper next door.

"So . . ." Jordan asked. "Did you and Mackenzie do it?"

Jesus, was that just an hour ago? Nate shook his head and wondered if Jordan could see him in the dark.

He figured Jordan could when the kid asked, "Why not?"

Nate sighed. He couldn't tell Jordan the truth—the poor kid had enough issues. "We just . . . didn't. We were going to, but . . . we messed around and—"

"What do you mean, 'messed around'?"

"You know . . . we kissed and stuff."

"Were you naked?"

Blood rushed into Nate's face. "Yeah."

"You were both naked, and all you did was kiss?" Jordan sounded so confused that Nate had to laugh.

"Yeah, but we kiss, you know, everywhere, not just on the mouth." Nate wondered if he'd ever get to do that again. He could see just well enough to watch Jordan touch his own lips with his fingers. He wondered if the kid even knew he was doing it.

When Jordan spoke again, his voice was thick. "Why do you . . . How do you . . . I mean, you do it because you *want* to?"

"Yeah."

Jordan was silent a long time. "Hmm," he said, as if he'd been thinking.

"Someday you'll know what that feels like."

Jordan snorted.

"Hey, you will. Someday. It can be really good if you really love and trust somebody." He wondered what girl might someday be brave enough to take on Jordan's baggage. "Besides, you've got a while before you need to worry—" He stopped. He realized how strange this was: him, a wimpy virgin, sitting there next to this *kid,* just a kid, who'd had more sex than Nate might ever have in his life. Nate thought about Mackenzie lying naked in the candlelight. Jordan'd already been there, done that, and hated every minute of it.

"What do you make her do?" Jordan asked.

Nate winced. "I don't *make* her do anything. We both like it. I wouldn't get off on forcing her to do something. It's gotta be . . . I dunno, it's more like . . . like giving someone a present." Nate couldn't believe he'd said that. Like he was some kind of stud or something, and girls were grateful for his gifts. That was a laugh. Especially now. He tried to explain it better. "Try to imagine, you know, how it would be to completely trust someone and be able to say you wanted to stop, or . . . I dunno, change something, and know that the person would listen to you."

Jordan didn't answer. The house was now so quiet, Nate wondered if Danny had decided to sleep downstairs rather than share a room with the banished son. Nate liked sitting here with Jordan. He wished he could have protected him back then, before any of those people hurt him.

As if reading his mind, Jordan put a hand on Nate's knee, their legs still side by side. He rubbed his thumb on Nate's knee, in a casual, absentminded way. *Wow.* Nate couldn't remember Jordan ever touching him before. This was progress . . . even if—Nate shook his head and grinned. He loved Jordan, but there was no denying it: The kid was weird.

"That's what happened?" Jordan asked. "She wanted to stop, and you didn't get mad?"

Nate wondered if he should let that go. "No," he admitted. "*I* wanted to stop."

An energy changed in Jordan; Nate felt it. Jordan spoke in a tiny, hopeful whisper. "And she loves you anyway?"

Nate paused too long, caught on that hope. The pause made it impossible to lie. "Well . . . I think she's a little pissed, but it'll be okay."

Jordan nodded.

"I mean," Nate tried to explain, "I think it hurt her feelings. I think—"

"No matter what your mom says," Jordan whispered, "I trust you."

A warmth expanded in Nate's chest. "Thanks, man."

"I feel really safe with you." Jordan's voice was pinched, like he was trying not to cry. "You're the best friend I've ever had. I trust you more than anyone."

Nate didn't know what to say, and he didn't believe he could speak right then anyway.

Jordan turned his torso and embraced Nate. The spreading warmth unfurled further, into Nate's face, where it made his mouth twitch and the inside of his nose burn. He felt honored in some way he couldn't articulate. He hugged Jordan back, amazed that the kid let him, seeing all those times Jordan had shrugged off the casual touches of Mom and Kramble and Reece. Nate wished the kid were his brother, and that none of the bad things had ever happened to him.

In the awkward embrace, Jordan's hand fell between Nate's legs.

Nate would've let it go as an accident if Jordan hadn't, quite deliberately, no mistaking it, grasped him.

CHAPTER TWENTY-SIX

Jordan

Jordan's heart pounded so loud he thought it might bust out of his chest like something in an *Alien* movie. Could Nate hear that? He didn't want Nate to know he was scared. The rushing-water sound screamed in Jordan's ears, but he could do this. He could make himself do this. This was different.

It didn't feel different.

But Nate said if you loved and trusted someone . . . And Jordan loved Nate. He trusted Nate. He wanted Nate to know that. And he wanted to be allowed to stay here. And he wanted Nate to know that even if Mackenzie was mad at him, *he* wouldn't be.

And so even though he felt his Other Self trying to replace the one Here Now, and even though the water sound was so loud it actually hurt him, Jordan slipped off the bed onto his knees in front of Nate.

"Whoa! W-what are you doing?" Nate asked.

And Jordan reached his shaking fingers up for the button on Nate's jeans. He knew what to do. He could do it. He could make himself do it. Nate said it would be different if you did it because you *wanted* to.

"What the hell are—"

Jordan couldn't make his voice work. *It's a present,* he wanted to say. *I want to give you a present.*

"Hey, whoa, *quit it.*" Nate smacked Jordan's hands away and stood up, his legs knocking Jordan off balance, onto his butt.

The water gurgling stopped. Jordan's pounding heartbeat stopped.

"Jordan, man, you can't—You don't—I—It's not right."

Jordan scooted away, afraid of the look on Nate's face in the moonlight, afraid Nate might kick him. "B-but . . . you said—"

"No. That's not what . . . No." Nate stood there with his hand on his crotch like he was guarding it.

Jordan had never felt what he felt at that moment. This feeling was worse than any of the other bad things. Way worse. He'd messed it up. He'd messed it up. This was wrong wrong wrong wrong wrong. It had felt horrible to try it, but now that he'd messed it up, it felt even worse.

He got on his feet, backing toward the door. "I'm sorry," he whispered. What had he done? He opened the bedroom door.

"No, wait. Jordan, don't—"

But Jordan slipped out the door. He knew that he had to leave. That he had done something terrible. He went down the stairs and out the back door and through Mrs. Ripley's yard and onto dark streets he didn't know. Running.

Running, running, running until he could hardly breathe. Running until he wheezed for air and thought he'd puke. He wished he could run until he made himself die.

He'd never forget that look on Nate's face. The way Nate had jerked away from him.

Every time he pictured it, he made himself run harder. He ran until his legs felt like they weighed a million pounds. When he could not run another step, he didn't stop moving. He kept putting one foot in front of the other, panting, gasping. He walked all night.

He didn't know where he was. He ducked into bushes or behind cars parked in driveways whenever a car pulled onto the street he walked.

Three times police cruisers crawled right by him.

The sky grew lighter. He snuck through backyards and hid from people letting their dogs out or leaving for work or church or wherever people were going so early on a Sunday. His legs and feet ached, and his stomach growled. He was so thirsty he felt dizzy. Later, as more and more people were out, mowing yards and riding bikes, he could return to the sidewalk and not be noticed. His brain felt slow, like when his mom gave him those shots. His legs went numb, and he kept stumbling. He hoped he looked normal walking around. Or could people tell just from looking at him how horrible he was? Could they tell he'd done that awful thing?

He walked past a woman unloading a car of groceries. She smiled at him as she struggled to her front door with her arms full. Once she went inside, he snatched one white plastic bag from her open trunk and ran. Behind a garage several blocks away, he discovered he'd stolen a can of coffee, a small bag of rice, and two jars of baby food. He slurped down the mushy beets and carrots, then carried the bag with him the rest of the way. He hoped it made him look more natural as he walked along. He took a bunch of wrong turns before he finally made it here to the woods behind his house.

Jordan crouched in the woods looking at the huge house, just as he'd done a million times before. He used to creep into the woods from the driveway after soccer practice and sit here. It would be about this same time, too—around five o'clock, he guessed. He didn't have a watch to know for sure, but the light seemed the same, hitting the back of the house like a giant spotlight, streaming in the back windows and making long shadows from the tree line where he now stood. He'd stare at the house and picture himself inside it, doing the things he had to do, imagining that it was just a movie, that it wasn't real.

Now, though, he watched for a different reason. Two police cruisers sat in the driveway. Two uniformed officers strolled through the landscaped yard, looking at the ground among the weedy, over-grown gardens and fountain. Checking for footprints, maybe? Another officer peered in through the windows of the house.

Then the three stood on the tennis court and talked. They talked for a long time, but Jordan wouldn't move yet. He had all the time in the world. He was never going back.

Jordan leaned against a tree and thumped his skull against the bark. He'd missed something, gotten it wrong somehow. Hadn't Nate said "if you really love and trust somebody"? Jordan had only been trying to give a present, like Nate said. He'd wanted to give willingly to Nate what they had forced of him, to see if it was different. He thumped his head again, harder, and blinked at the sting it caused.

The cops strolled from the court to the driveway and stood talking by their cruisers. Occasionally they shielded their eyes against the late-afternoon light and pointed to the tree line, but no one bothered to come over. Jordan knew they couldn't see him. In those other days, after watching the house, he would go inside and look out the windows at where he'd been, expecting to see the boy in the woods, the Other Self he'd left there. But all you could see, looking in that direction was a harsh, bright light silhouetting the trees.

He still had the grocery bag and was thinking about giving the rice a try when the cops in his driveway finally got into their cruisers and drove away. Jordan stood up. He waited five or six minutes, watching cars move along the road. The first moment that no traffic passed, he slipped from the woods and sprinted the hundred yards or so to the back door. He thought of soccer, and he realized it didn't hurt to run anymore.

At the back door, he knew no one could see him from the road. He peered through the glass at the alarm, but its red eye was shut. He tried the knob. Locked. He looked at the fancy landscaping now overgrown with weeds and selected a long, flat stone that he smashed into the windowpane. He reached through and let himself in.

The second he stepped in the door, the familiar smell—of the carpet, the wood, the cleaners they used, just the smell of *this house*—grabbed hold and shoved inside him. His feet tingled like his legs had fallen asleep as he made himself walk down the hall.

What would happen to this house now? He hated it, the house itself. He wanted it to burn to the ground.

His sucked in his breath. He shouldn't think that. If his mother did okay in her trial, they would live here again. This was their home. He bit his lip and rewrote the sentence in his head—not *if* but *when* his mother did okay in her trial, they'd come home.

"Home," he tried to say out loud, but his mouth felt like he'd already been swallowing the hard, dry rice.

He walked down the hall, to the party room and stopped in the doorway. The statue of the naked boy still stood on the glass coffee table. He'd always wondered, as he looked at that statue, who'd convinced that boy to pose naked.

The fish tanks still held water, but the fish were gone. Had someone taken them away and now they swam somewhere else? Or had they died and been flushed down the toilet? "Toilet" was a tricky word: t-o-i, not t-o-y. He hoped the fish were dead. He hated them, too, and the way they'd watched with their cold, unblinking eyes. U-n-b-l-i-n-k-i-n-g.

The room felt too quiet. Q-u-i-e-t. Even without music and people, there'd always been the sound of the tanks gurgling. G-u-r-g—*Stop it*. Now the tanks stood still, a thin layer of scum across the top of the water.

Jordan stepped into the room, blinking hard to get rid of the words he saw floating in the air. This time he didn't want them. He needed to be *here* instead. The furniture was moved, and the wall closet was open, its shelves empty. Words like "forensics" and "evidence" nudged him, letting him know they were there if he needed something else to look at.

He didn't know he was going to yell. He just did. A deep, growling yell that started in his toes and scraped his throat. He ran and body-slammed one of the aquariums, heaving it over. A nasty algae smell filled the room. Jordan stomped through the murky puddle, then jumped on top of the white couch and wiped his feet all over it, kicking it, trying to rip the cushions. He stepped on the back, and the couch toppled over, flinging him to the floor with a thud that took his breath away and ended the yell abruptly. But he got up, head spinning, and kicked down the statue of the naked boy on the coffee table.

When he kicked it, the boy broke in half instead of shattering. Jordan picked up the boy's lower half and, holding his base and feet, ran down the hall toward the kitchen, shredding the velvet wallpaper with the jagged edges of the statue's severed torso.

In the kitchen he used the boy to smash the door of the microwave and to chip and crack the tiled counters. He battered at the tile until the boy finally crumbled in his hands.

Jordan had cut his left hand, torn open that little crook of his thumb. He squeezed the wound and let blood drop all over the white chips and dust of the statue boy. Then he smeared his blood all over the refrigerator before opening it and breaking all the old, half-empty condiment bottles on the floor.

He ran down the hall and flung open the door to his parents' bedroom. He stomped on their bed, leaving ketchup and mustard footprints. He suddenly thought, What was he doing? Was he crazy? He was as crazy as his stupid, psycho mother. He hated her.

He froze. The entire room shrank. He couldn't believe he'd even *thought* that.

He fled the room as though Danny's "monsters" were after him, then ran to the second floor, his footsteps echoing in the silent house. He went to his old room and slammed the door behind him. His room was neat and tidy, like he'd left it, except his bed was stripped bare. When Reece had taken him to see his lawyer, Rhonda, Jordan had been surprised to see his superhero sheets on a list of evidence.

He sat on the stripped bed, panting, freaked out by what he'd let into his head. His heart refused to return to its normal pace, and his stomach burned. He pressed a hand over his chest and looked around his room, trying to catch his breath.

A chip in the plaster wall caught his attention. The sight slowed his pulse as if someone had sat on his chest. He stood and went to the chipped place.

He pictured his cat's red collar hooked on the nail. Raja's long black body hanging limp, white belly showing. Golden eyes in that frozen expression of surprise. Those inner lids halfway closed. The cat had been dead before his mom hung him up.

Jordan hadn't seen it coming. He knew he was in trouble that day. He knew from the silence in the car all the way home from that school conference. He'd expected the worst, but somehow the worst hadn't included this. That was before he learned that things could always be worse than what he imagined and that it was better to leave room in his head for things he hadn't thought of.

Coming into the house that day, he'd been ready for anything. He thought bones might be broken. But he thought they'd be *his*. Raja greeted them at the door, and his mother had picked up the cat by the scruff of the neck and carried him to her bedroom.

She'd done that. Not his dad.

Jordan remembered chasing after her. Screaming. "No! What are you doing? Leave him alone!" His father had grabbed him and hauled him upstairs. Jordan remembered kicking and punching. He'd seen the bruises he'd given his father later when . . . That didn't matter. What mattered was, his crying mother had brought Raja—dead Raja—up to his room.

His mother had killed his cat.

She'd still held the needle and syringe in one hand as she set the cat in Jordan's lap. She was crying so much it was hard to understand her as she told him she was sorry, that she hadn't wanted to do this, that this hurt her as much as it hurt him. She kept petting the cat in Jordan's lap, stroking the cat's fur as she said that Jordan had to understand, they were different, that their family wasn't like other families, that other people wouldn't accept or tolerate them, that Jordan "needed to grasp" how urgent this was, how *grave*.

Grave. He'd never heard the word "grave" used that way. He'd only heard it as a noun, like when they visited his grandma's grave. When it was a vocabulary word later that year, he learned it meant serious or life-threatening. He'd sat in class and pictured his mother handing him his dead cat. He got the word wrong on the test on purpose. He did it for Raja. It was the only word he ever missed. He couldn't use it without picturing that day.

His mother had killed his cat. She'd hammered in a nail and hung Raja up on Jordan's bedroom wall as a reminder to him. Raja stayed there for three days, until someone took him down while Jordan was at school. He never knew what they did with the cat's body. Looking back, he figured Raja had been taken down because Sarah was coming to cook.

He touched the chip in the wall, leaving bloody fingerprints from his cut hand. He hated his mother for this. Hated her.

"Stop it!" he wailed. He had to stop thinking that. He pulled a piece of plaster from the wall and ground it into the gash in his hand until his eyes ran with tears.

The doorbell rang, and Jordan jerked awake. At first he thought he was having his usual nightmare. Then he realized that his dream had been good —he'd been living like a pioneer in Sarah's bean tepee, a small, safe place where only bugs bothered him—and he truly was in his old house.

The doorbell rang again.

What was real? What had happened? The sky outside was the dark blue of dusk, and Jordan couldn't get his mind to focus. Why was he here?

He half expected his mom's voice on the intercom telling him to come downstairs. But the doorbell rang again, three times in a row, before a silence fell.

No, he told himself. *They're gone. You're safe with the Ladens. Everything is okay.*

Then he remembered that he'd left the Ladens. And why. It wasn't a dream. He really had done that stupid, disgusting thing. Nate hated him.

A banging started downstairs. It sounded like someone pounding on the patio doors. Jordan stood up. His injured hand throbbed, and his neck felt stiff and sore.

He opened his door, tiptoed down the stairs, and peeked into the living room, but whoever had been pounding was gone. Maybe the police were back. How long had he slept?

He slipped into the hallway but froze at the sound of the back door opening. Feet crackled on broken glass.

"Jordan?" a voice called. It was Nate. "Jordan? Are you here?"

Jordan hunched his shoulders and hugged his chest, wishing he could shrink. His face burned hot. Not Nate. He couldn't look at Nate. What should he do? Run? Hide?

The kitchen light went on. He heard Nate say something to himself. He tried to picture the wrecked kitchen through Nate's eyes. He didn't move as Nate came into the hallway and fumbled for another switch. "Jordan? Come on, I know you're here," he said as he groped the wall like a blind man. He found the switch.

Nate jumped when he saw Jordan there, so close to him.

The two boys stared at each other, but Jordan couldn't look Nate in the face. He couldn't stand for Nate to look at him. Jordan dropped his gaze to the floor and wished it would open and swallow him up. He was disgusting.

Nate cleared his throat. "Look, Jordan, I'm sorry. I think I was rude to you, and I didn't mean to be. I—"

"Why did you come here?" Jordan tried to sound mad. "Changed your mind, didn't you?"

He hated Nate's wounded expression. Like Jordan had shot him or something.

"Jordan." Nate stood there with his mouth open, like one of those stupid fish.

Jordan kicked the wall, hard. Pain ripped through his toes and up his shin.

Nate took a step toward him but stopped. "Why do you want to be here? How can you even stand to be in this place?"

Jordan kicked the wall again, twice, three times more, before sinking down to sit on the bottom step of the stairs.

Nate said, "What happened . . . It was . . . Y-you didn't mean anything by it."

Jordan punched the wall this time, heat flashing through his hand. He *had* meant something by it. He'd meant a *lot* by it. And it was all wrong.

Nate's face was red. "I mean, I know what you thought and I . . . I'm sorry. We just . . ."

Jordan stared at Nate's feet and watched them take three steps closer. He wondered how long Nate would wait if he just sat there. What if he never moved or talked again? If only there were a way to undo what he'd done. Unlike those other things, he'd started this himself. He'd actually *touched* Nate, he'd tried to —He put his hands over his face, hardly able to stand it, seeing himself flee the room, flee the house, run someplace where he'd never have to look at Nate again.

"Nobody knows what happened, Jordan. They just think we argued, okay? Nobody knows but my mom . . . and, okay, Dr. Bryn."

Jordan groaned and pressed his fingers against his eyelids until he saw sparks. Sarah. Sarah would think he was some awful freak. She'd kick him out. She wouldn't let Danny be friends with him. He'd have no one.

"My mom didn't tell the police the details. I was there. Seriously, nobody else knows."

Jordan kept his hands on his face. Through his fingers Jordan saw

Nate lean against the wall near him. "Look, man, you just . . . star-tled me, okay? But when I think back to our conversation . . . I mean, Jordan, give yourself a break. I wasn't putting it together in my head, you know? I set you up, and then I freaked out. We . . . we misunderstood each other. Those people messed with you, Jordan. It makes sense that you didn't . . . that you didn't get what I was talking about. It's okay. Really."

No, it *wasn't*. Jordan couldn't believe that Nate would even sit here talking to him.

"Come on. Let's go back."

Jordan shook his head.

Nate sighed. "Jordan, don't you see it's only going to get easier?"

Jordan dropped his hands and looked up. "But it's *not* easier! It's worse! The . . . the . . ." He couldn't even say it. The thing last night made him want to claw off his own face. "I can't do anything right. Danny hates me—"

"That's bullshit. Are you still worried about that disk? He's been working his ass off trying to find you. He *cried* when he found out you ran away."

Jordan felt all his blood run into his toes. "He . . . he doesn't know what hap—"

"I told you, he just thinks we argued. But leave Danny out of it for now. You left because of what happened between you and me. Right?"

Jordan nodded at the floor, seeing himself reaching for Nate again. *Stupid. Disgusting.*

"Then what's the problem? I'm telling you it's okay. It's over. It's forgotten."

Jordan remembered Nate jerking away from him, and his eyes watered. He felt the convulsion in his chest. On top of everything else, now he was going to cry. Shit. Why couldn't he just curl up and die somewhere? "I just . . . I just wanted . . ."

"I know." Nate cleared his throat again. "And it's okay. You should come home."

Jordan's stomach rolled over. "This is my home."

"No it's not. Not anymore. Your home is with us."

"For now," Jordan said. But inside he knew he wanted it to be true. *Stop it,* he thought, pinching the dirty gash in his hand, making it bleed again.

"For now." Nate frowned at Jordan's hand. "Or whatever, okay?"

Nate looked past Jordan toward the party room, and his eyes widened. He walked over to the archway and turned on the light. "Holy shit. I thought the kitchen was bad." He whistled, then turned to look at Jordan. "Nice work."

Jordan lifted one shoulder, wanting to smile.

Nate opened a door in the hallway and stared at the washer and dryer. "Well, well, well, what have we here?" He lifted a huge plastic detergent jug off the shelf. He opened the lid and poured the bright blue fluid on the carpet. Jordan's stomach lifted like he was flying down a roller coaster. Nate looked at Jordan and said, "Oops. Sorry." Then he spun in a circle, letting the detergent splash the wall.

Jordan ducked to avoid getting hit with it himself. "Hey!"

Nate chucked the container down the hall, where it hit the wall and split open, showering them with sudsy blue drops. As detergent splattered him, Jordan felt something rumble up through his belly, an unfamiliar sensation that scared him for a minute. It was out of control like that yell earlier. Only when the sound spilled out of his mouth did he recognize it as laughter.

"C'mon!" Nate said.

Jordan looked at him. After what he'd done last night, here was Nate not hating him, not hurting him, saying he could still stay with the Ladens. Fueled by the crazy laughter bubbling up from deep inside him, Jordan jumped up to join Nate at the laundry closet. Jordan snatched a bleach bottle and took off running, splashing the expensive velvet wallpaper. Nate followed, dumping handfuls of powder detergent on the floor.

They ran into the bathroom, where they emptied the medicine

cabinet, broke mouthwash bottles, squeezed out shampoo, and scribbled with lipstick and soap all over the mirrors and shower walls. Nate wrote bad words, but Jordan just scribbled and drew heavy Xs, pushing hard, smashing lipsticks and buckling bars of soap. The whole time that laughter kept coming. It hurt almost, like bad hiccups, but it also felt good.

Laughing hysterically, they tossed rolls of toilet paper back and forth, wrapping it around light fixtures and furniture, trailing it through the hall, the wrecked kitchen, and out the back door, leaving it draped over bushes and statues and the fountain, all the way to the tennis court, where Nate tossed the last empty cardboard roll over the net.

They faced each other, panting. Then Nate started walking, and Jordan followed.

CHAPTER TWENTY-SEVEN

Nate

Nate didn't want the long walk to end. He wanted to *stop walking*, sure, but he wanted to kick back on the porch swing with a klezmer CD in his Walkman, not deal with all the high-pitched hyperness that was going to come down when he showed up at home with Jordan.

Sure enough, when Nate opened the front door, Mrs. Ripley was in the living room and saw them first. "They're back! Safe and sound!" she called, starting a commotion.

"Where *were* you?" Mom asked Nate, coming into the room with Kramble and Ali. Nate could see the blue veins in Mom's lower eyelids. "I thought *you* were missing, too!"

She hugged him before he could answer. He tried to step away, but she took his face in her hands. When she held his face like that, Nate felt like a giant, so much taller than she was. He tilted his head, pulling away. "Hey, I found him, didn't I?"

Mom tried to hug Jordan, too, but he did his usual prickly routine, sending out signals as welcoming as a damn cactus. Mom settled for putting her hands on Jordan's shoulders and saying, "Thank God you're back. Please don't scare us like that again."

Jordan stared at the carpet.

Danny ran down the stairs, then stopped. "Where did you go?" Danny asked. "Did you get lost?"

Jordan paused a moment, then said, "Yeah, I did."

"I'm glad you're okay," Danny said. The way he looked down at his shoes made Nate believe him.

"I found him at his house," Nate said to Kramble, but the unspoken *I told you so* in his own voice made him feel like a brat. Nate had told the police that's where Jordan would go.

Kramble didn't seem to notice. He stepped forward, out of the kitchen doorway. "What did you do to your hand?" he asked.

Jordan opened his fist and held out his palm, crusty with blood. "I cut it." Ali stepped in closer. So did Mrs. Ripley, trying to see.

"Breaking a window?" Kramble asked.

"Later," Jordan said. "Inside the house."

"He sort of trashed the place," Nate said. Jordan looked at him quickly, like he expected them to get in trouble. Nate smiled and tried to get the kid to relax.

Mrs. Ripley clucked her tongue, but Kramble didn't seem too surprised. "Trashed the place, huh?" He looked at Jordan. "Feel good?"

Jordan shrugged but looked at Nate again, grinning cautiously.

"Can I take a better look at that?" Ali asked. Jordan held out his hand. Kramble stepped away, as if to give them space, which Nate thought was cool. "You could've used a stitch or two," Ali said. "But it looks too late. No big deal. Sarah, you have medical tape? Or Band-Aids? I could butterfly this up for him."

Danny said, "I'll get it." Nate turned to watch him run up the stairs to the bathroom and saw Mackenzie leaning in the kitchen doorway. He shook his head, but, damn, it really *was* Mackenzie. She stood there, in faded jeans and a yellow T-shirt, her hair in a ponytail. He couldn't help picturing her nude in the candlelight. It freaked him out to even have that thought in the same room with his mother. But he remembered telling Mom that he and Mackenzie hadn't—which freaked him out even more. He'd told his mom everything when he'd woken her up to tell her Jordan was missing. He hadn't meant to tell her that part, but it was part of how Jordan had misinterpreted their talk. Nate glanced at Mom. She smiled.

He looked from Mom to Mackenzie, trying to stop the rush of blood to his face. "Hey. Hi. W-what are you doing here?"

"I called for you, and your mom told me what was going on."

Nate saw Jordan shrink, but Nate was sure Mom didn't tell the whole story. "Uh . . ." He felt like a moron, standing between his mom and Mackenzie. What should he say? Why was Mom smiling? Why was *Mackenzie* smiling? He thought he'd ruined everything with her.

Kramble ended the painful silence. "I'm gonna put in a call, let them know Jordan's back." He left the room.

"I should call Reece!" Mom said. "He's still looking, too. And I'll let Bryn know."

Jordan ducked his head and pulled his hand from Ali's. "We need to wash that," she said, wrinkling her nose, as though feeling that sting herself.

Jordan walked into the kitchen and washed the cut himself. Nate followed everyone else. In the back of the small crowd, Mackenzie reached for his hand. "You okay?" she mouthed.

He nodded. "I got in big trouble. For going to your—"

"I know," she whispered. "Your mom and I talked."

"Whoa. What do you mean, you 'talked'?" He glanced at the sink. Jordan had dried his hand, and Ali examined it under the bright kitchen lights. Nate got a glimpse of a deep gash in the fleshy part between Jordan's thumb and first finger. "What did you talk about?"

"Everything," she whispered, her eyes sparkling with a "wouldn't you like to know?" tease.

What the hell did *that* mean?

"Your mom is cool, Nate. We talked a long time."

Nate felt like they'd been looking at naked pictures of him. But that made him think of Jordan, and just that glimmer of what the kid must feel cross-checked him in the chest.

"It's okay," Mackenzie insisted. "She invited me to come over."

Nate wondered if Mom planned on humiliating him by lecturing him and Mackenzie together. But Mom already knew that they didn't . . . Oh, shit . . . what was going on?

Ali taped up Jordan's wound. She made him copy a series of gestures with his hand—making a fist, opening his hand wide, making a thumbs-up sign. "It's a long way from your heart," she joked. "I think you'll live."

Jordan turned his hand over a few times and held it up with a huge grin. "I got this cut when I broke the statue on the coffee table," he announced, like he'd just made the winning goal for the Stanley Cup. Nate wondered if this was the first injury that Jordan didn't have to lie about. He squeezed Mackenzie's hand.

"All right. I've gotta get going," Ali said. "I'm glad you're back, kiddo. These little Houdini acts get old. Don't expect us to be so nice next time." She scanned the room and stopped at Mackenzie. "You need a ride home?"

"She's staying here," Mom said. "Her folks are out of town."

Nate's jaw hurt, he dropped it so fast.

Ali nodded. "Okay. See ya."

"I'll walk out with you," Mrs. Ripley said. "I need to get home." Please. For what? Didn't her entire social life revolve around whatever crisis-of-the-day the Ladens were having?

Ali and Mrs. Ripley headed for the living room. Kramble and Danny followed.

As they left the room, Nate asked, to make sure he wasn't hearing things, "Mackenzie's spending the night?"

Mom's smile bordered on evil. "Yeah, I'm thinking of giving up the catering and running an orphanage."

Mackenzie laughed, but Jordan stood up from the table and said, in a hard, cold voice, "I'm not an orphan."

But he was, Nate thought. An orphan of the living. Nate felt sorry for Mom, who looked like she'd swallowed glass. "You're right," Mom said. "I'm sorry. That wasn't funny."

Jordan turned and walked out of the room.

Mom sighed and tugged on her braid, over her shoulder. "Oh, God," she whispered. "Why did I say that?"

Nate watched Mackenzie pat his mother's arm. Why did he feel as though, in the hours he'd been gone, his mom had built some sort of camp with Mackenzie? "Is she . . . is she really spending the night?"

"It's too scary to be sleeping in that big house all alone," Mom said. "I called and left a message at her folks' hotel, told them she'd be here and to call if they have questions."

"They won't care," Mackenzie said with a shrug. Nate wasn't sure how he felt about that. He had *offered* to stay, after all. "You act pretty weirded out about this," Mackenzie said to Nate. "Don't you want me to stay?"

Mom turned around and busied herself with some fake job on the counter. Nate remembered Mackenzie asking him to leave and thought about throwing that back at her. But, really, this was better. He didn't *want* to break up with her. "No, I want you to stay."

Everyone came back into the kitchen. Shit, why was Kramble sticking around? Why didn't he leave when Ali did?

"Nate, you want to go get some sheets and a pillow to make up the sofa bed?" Mom asked. "Mackenzie can sleep down here."

He left the kitchen, almost grateful to get away and be alone for a minute.

He climbed the stairs and went to the linen closet. As he selected the nicest sheets, flowered ones that his mom put on her bed, he heard a make-your-skin-crawl scratching sound that curled up his toes inside his shoes. Shit, did they have mice? Or was it bats in the wall?

Clutching the sheets in one arm, he poked at a stack of others, expecting to see a small gray body scurry away. Nothing. He tapped the wall. A stronger scratching answered him. Then a thump, like something falling over.

The hair rose on his neck. That wasn't something small in the wall—that was something big behind the linen closet, which meant it was in Nate's old closet, now Jordan's.

Nate opened Jordan's bedroom door. Everything looked normal, but he heard two more thumps. Nate dropped the sheets. He went to the closet. As his hand closed on the knob, the odor hit him. The unmistakable ammonia sting of rabbit pee.

He opened the door, and a very pissed-off Klezmer blinked in the light. The closet floor was littered with his raisinlike droppings and a pool of the tea-colored urine.

"Hey, buddy." Nate scooped up the rabbit, even though its paws were wet with pee. He hugged Klezmer to his chest and stared down into Jordan's closet. A bowl of water sat there, and an empty bowl with dusty crumbs of food pellets in it. The rabbit hadn't been shut in the closet on accident. Why the hell would the kid do something so mean?

Nate carried the rabbit down the stairs. He wasn't sure what he would say, but he knew he couldn't pretend he hadn't found Klezmer. He took a deep breath and remembered the kid reaching for him in that darkened room, tried to remember how Jordan had seen that act as something other than what it was—and he tried to look at this hidden rabbit through Jordan's eyes. What did it mean? What had the kid misinterpreted this time?

As he entered the kitchen, Danny looked up and said, "Klezmer!"

Jordan stared at the rabbit with an expression like he'd just been slapped.

"He was in the *house*?" Danny asked.

Nate nodded.

"Where?" Mom asked.

"He was in Jordan's room."

Everyone looked at Jordan, who still sat frozen, his mouth stuck in that surprised O. Nate wondered if this was the first time Jordan had been caught without a ready lie.

"What's the deal?" Nate tried not to sound mad; he didn't want to send the kid running again. "You knew that Mom and Danny were looking for him. Why would you hide him in a closet?"

Jordan's eyes shone as if he might cry. He closed his mouth and seemed to struggle to form words. When he did, his voice was so quiet Nate hardly heard him when he said, "I . . . I just wanted him to be safe."

"Safe?" Mom asked. "From what?"

Jordan picked at the tape on his hand. "You were pretty mad."

No one breathed.

Mom's forehead crinkled. "I don't understand."

"You . . . you were so mad at Nate, and I was just worried." He tugged the tape off his cut.

Mom reached across the table and gently stopped Jordan's hands. She pressed the tape back into place and asked, "You thought . . . you thought I might hurt the rabbit because I was angry at Nate?" Nate was glad she kept her voice calm.

Jordan shrugged. "I . . . I was wrong. I'm sorry. I forgot he was in there, when I—" He looked up at Nate, and his pale face flushed red. A tear broke free and rolled down his cheek. Jordan swiped at it roughly with his bandaged hand.

Danny inhaled sharply, and Nate turned to him. Danny's eyes widened, and he looked sad. He said quietly, "He probably worried because his mom and dad killed his cat."

Jordan flashed panic. "That was . . . that was just a story."

"But you used to have a cat," Nate said, a chill on the back of his neck shivering through him as it dawned on him what might've happened. "You told me so."

"A cat named Raja," Danny said.

Nate watched Mom's face register this information. Kramble and Mackenzie, too.

Kramble asked, "They *killed* your cat?"

Jordan looked down at his hand and said, "It was just a story."

Bullshit, Nate thought.

The room was so quiet it felt like pressure in Nate's ears.

Danny touched Nate's arm. "Can I hold him?" Nate handed Danny the rabbit. Klezmer butted Danny's chin with his head.

Mackenzie's eyes were pink.

Jordan's stomach growled, loud and demanding, like a small, ferocious animal under the table. Everyone looked startled. Nate laughed. The others laughed, too. Even Jordan smiled. He put a hand on his belly. The kid must be starving, but he'd never say so himself.

Nate saw Mom's face and knew she was thinking of what she could make. He also knew she was nearing forty hours with no sleep, and she looked it. She rubbed her eyes and, without looking at Nate, said, "How 'bout we order some pizzas?"

Nate grinned. "That'd be cool." He opened a drawer and pulled out a phone book. Mom had suggested the pizzas especially for him, he knew. He looked up from the Yellow Pages. He wanted to do something for her.

So he turned to Kramble and asked, "What do you like on your pizza?"

CHAPTER TWENTY-EIGHT

Sarah

Sarah woke at six o'clock. She lay in bed, not wanting to move at first, wishing that if she just stayed still here, time would stop. This day would not unfold.

Courtney appeared in court today for a pretrial hearing.

The actual trial was still months away, most likely, but this was a beginning, a date to mark on the calendar, leading to more dates to come.

Sarah sat up in bed. The breeze from the open window was cool after last night's thunderstorm. It stirred the curtains and moved the wind chimes in Lila's backyard. The faint tinkle sounded hopeful, but Sarah knew that whatever the outcome in this trial, there would be more hurt and turmoil. More loss.

She got out of bed and put on her white cotton robe. The sky was just beginning to lighten as she left her bedroom. Jordan's door stood open, his bed already made. Sarah crossed to the window and peered down into the backyard. A robin gave itself a dust bath in the sandbox. The gargoyle stood dwarfed by the blooming garden it surveyed, the bean tepee covered in white blossoms. Jordan's dog-wood looked forlorn and scrawny next to Nate's tall, seventeen-year-old tree. A tiny flash of movement caught Sarah's eye, and she saw Jordan. There he sat, just visible, inside the bean tepee with the rabbit in his lap. In a matter of days, the vines and leaves would be so thick that she wouldn't be able to see inside the tepee from here.

God help her, please don't let the trial be full of stories like what she imagined. All the scenarios she created to explain what happened to Jordan's cat. She remembered his cat, black and white, just like the rabbit. It had sat in the Kendricks' kitchen window and watched her when she'd cooked for them, and then, last fall, she'd stopped seeing it. She never thought to ask about it. The house was so huge, so sprawling, Sarah just assumed it was bored with her and off prowling elsewhere.

She sat on Jordan's twin bed. The room now looked like his. Her eyes stung as she pictured him packing and leaving. What started today might lead them to that.

Sarah had gone to see Courtney last week, even though both Bobby and Reece had urged her not to. She'd gone expecting to face the washed-out, cadaverous version of her once radiant friend, that version that had snuck into Sarah's home. But a different version of Courtney sat down on the other side of the glass.

Courtney's hair was neatly combed, pulled back into a ponytail, the buttery blond dangerously normal. Her face, though free of makeup, had regained some natural rosiness, and her eyes were confident, almost mocking. "I'm so glad you came to see me, Sarah," she said, as if they were sitting down to lunch at a sidewalk café.

A greenish purple bruise shone from Courtney's left temple, a black scab connecting it to her hairline. She seemed to follow Sarah's gaze and touched the bruise with her fingers. "They think I'm the lowest of the low here," she said as explanation. She unbuttoned her blue denim jumpsuit enough to show Sarah a raw, scraped shoulder. "Each time it happens, I'm actually glad. This"—she waved a hand behind her, at the guards, the prison—"is horrible but easy enough to endure. But this"—she touched her bruised head again—"brings me closer to him, evens out the score."

Sarah's nostrils flared. "*Score?* This isn't about points. You getting hurt doesn't *undo* the hurt you inflicted." Even so, Sarah hated that bruise and what it meant. That didn't fix anything; it didn't change any reality for Jordan.

Courtney leaned toward the glass, touching it with her fingertips. "They've helped me here, Sarah. I can finally stop Mark and keep Jordan safe."

Reece had told Sarah that some sex offenders were so ashamed of their behavior that they were not *capable* of admitting it. But for Courtney to continue to deny it in the face of overwhelming evidence astounded Sarah.

"*I saw the disk, Courtney.* I saw you . . . having sex with your son."

Courtney leaned closer, her nose nearly touching the glass. "I'm *glad* we have that disk. I didn't want to do those things. Mark made me. Do you think I *want* people to see that? Do you think I want to remember that? But I'm willing to put it out there, to show people the kind of life Jordan and I were trapped in."

Sarah remembered Courtney's tearful face in the photos and knew that people would believe these manipulative, cunning words. "But you weren't trapped. I don't believe that. You *chose* to do this, over and over again."

Courtney's mouth convulsed as she fought not to cry. "Sarah, don't do this. You know me, you know I would never—"

"I *don't* know you."

Courtney gasped as if Sarah had punched her.

"I *thought* I knew you. I *miss* you. I miss who I thought you were, but I didn't know you at all. Tell me, Courtney, I need to know." Sarah was surprised to feel tears streaming down her own cheeks, matching Courtney's. "Were you after my son all along? All those years of friendship, all that you did for me, was it only to get close to my son?"

Courtney's forehead wrinkled. "What are you talking about?"

"You touched my son. On top of all the depraved things you did to your own, *you touched my son.*"

Courtney frowned. Damn her, she was good.

"I saw the pictures of Danny. Did you forget about those?"

Courtney blinked. *"Danny?"* Then she laughed, as if Sarah were being unreasonable. "The boys were *swimming*! Those are harmless pictures. Why are you acting like this?"

"Do you know how *lucky* you are your son saved mine? If Jordan hadn't made Danny leave, if you'd harmed him in any way, I'd find a way to hurt you. So help me God, I would."

Courtney's mouth dropped open. "Sarah, I would never hurt—"

"I don't think you can *help* it. I saw your face in that picture, pushing your breasts all over Danny. I saw your face when you were hurting Jordan in my front yard. You're sick. You shouldn't be around *any* children, ever, much less a child of your own."

"I'm getting my son back!" An edge of hysteria hinted under Courtney's still-controlled voice. "I'm earning him back, and I'll take care of him. He's *my* son, don't forget."

"You don't deserve him."

Courtney shut her eyes, squeezing tears down her gaunt cheeks. After a few moments, Courtney looked Sarah right in the eye and said with a sincerity that chilled her, "I will do everything in my power to keep him safe."

Sarah hesitated, a fraction of her heart wanting to open some small part of her willing to pity this sick, beaten woman. But she shook her head, refusing herself to allow it. "You can't keep him safe, Courtney. You know you can't. You'll only do it again."

"No! I only did it because Mark made me. Only once."

"That isn't true. It happened more than once. Lots more than once. Jordan said so."

And it finally happened—Courtney's face changed, and that blank shine hardened her eyes. Just as Sarah'd seen in her yard that day when Courtney dug her nails into Jordan's mouth. That expression made Sarah breathe again.

Courtney jabbed her finger into the glass. "Listen, I'm calling Children's Services! I'm getting Jordan put into another foster home! You're filling up his head with this bullshit and—"

Sarah hung up her phone. Courtney continued screaming, even pounding on the glass. Sarah walked away when a guard on the other side grabbed Courtney's arms.

When Courtney didn't show that hint of her other self, her normalcy was chillingly convincing. It had fooled everyone for years. Sarah understood that Courtney believed what she said—that she loved Jordan, that she'd protect him. That's what made Sarah's stomach flutter this morning, sitting on Jordan's bed, at this stepping-stone to the trial. Courtney might be able to fool a jury, a judge, her attorney.

But Courtney couldn't fool Sarah anymore. And Sarah wasn't sure she fooled Jordan. His insistence that his mother would be all right had become rote, passionless, and although he used to jabber constantly about the trial, since that night he'd run away he rarely initiated any conversation about his mother at all.

Sarah had taken down the photo calendar and shoved it in a drawer. She didn't want to look at that photo of her and Courtney again. Since that day in the jail, Sarah had felt as if Courtney had died, too.

And Sarah was sick of losing the people she loved.

The floor creaked in the hallway, and she started as if she'd been caught snooping through Jordan's things. Nate entered, wearing only blue boxer underwear. When he saw her, he jumped. "Damn, Mom! What are you doing in here?"

"Just thinking. What are you doing?" She looked away from his almost nude body. It amazed her that the chubby, colicky infant she'd once held now possessed a body so athletic and beautiful. She hated Courtney for making her feel squeamish for looking at her own son.

Nate sat on the bed and drew his knees up in front of him as if hiding himself. Sarah knew that he, too, probably experienced this newfound shamefulness. For God's sake, he went to public swimming pools revealing as much as this. "I saw him in the yard," Nate said. "I was going to leave something in here for him. It's no big deal. I just, you know, thought . . ." He opened his hand, revealing his autographed Wayne Gretzky hockey puck.

"Nate! This is worth a lot of money now."

"I know. But what is it, really? I mean, I use it as a paperweight."

"Are you sure you want to part with this? Your father gave it to you."

Lines appeared on his forehead. "Are you mad at me? That I'd give it away?"

"No." She bit her lip, suddenly afraid she'd cry. She managed to smile. "I think your dad would be very proud of you. I am."

He exhaled an awkward laugh. He put the puck on Jordan's dresser. "I'm getting in the shower," he said, and left the room.

Sarah looked at the puck, and an overwhelming need pressed against her chest and throat, so strong it hurt her. She ached for Roy to be here, to see Nate become a person in the world, a person to admire.

Again that sense came over her, that if she sat still here, she could hold back the day. She might not have to take a step closer to letting go of someone else.

CHAPTER TWENTY-NINE

Jordan

A phone rang somewhere in the house. Jordan pulled the sheet up around his ears and tried to return to the dream he'd been having. In it Klezmer and Raja spoke to him in English. The cat and the rabbit had sat at a table eating pie with Jordan's mother, who said she'd just dropped by to tell him she was really sorry and things would be better now. But the phone distracted him. Who would call so early? He opened one eye to check his clock. Six-thirty. Someone had picked it up after the third ring. Probably Sarah.

Sarah. He sat up in bed. Sarah was supposed to go to court today for another pretrial hearing. These stupid meetings went on forever, and Jordan didn't believe that the trial would ever start. He felt something like relief at that thought, which scared him.

He didn't want Sarah to go today, especially since he wasn't allowed to be there himself. They wouldn't let him be in the building if his mom and dad were there. A few weeks ago, the jerks in charge had had this brilliant idea to videotape Jordan talking so he wouldn't even have to be at the trial. Reece was the only one who seemed to understand why Jordan got sick when they set up the lights and the cameras. Really sick, too. He couldn't breathe right, and he'd spent almost half an hour puking in the courthouse bathroom before Reece drove him home clutching a plastic wastebasket in his shaky arms.

He hoped Sarah answered their questions and then didn't stick around today. He wanted to keep these families as separate from each other as possible. It was easier that way, especially since he had no idea what might happen at the end of the trial—if the trial ever started. He had no idea what he *wanted* to happen anymore. Sometimes he thought he did, but his own thoughts scared him when he let them stay in his brain too long. He lay back and put a pillow over his head.

His uncle was supposed to be there today, too. He was back in Ohio. Jordan had finally agreed to meet him yesterday with Dr. Bryn. No one had to introduce them. He looked so much like Jordan's mom. Like his mom had turned into a man or something.

His uncle had wanted Jordan to know he'd like to talk to Jordan if Jordan ever wanted to. He didn't ask Jordan any questions or even stay long—he'd been in Dr. Bryn's office maybe ten minutes—and Jordan liked that. Jordan sort of wanted to talk to him, but he couldn't make his mouth work. What this man had done, what he knew, what they had in common, made Jordan mute.

He hadn't even thanked his uncle for the box of pictures. Pictures of his mom and uncle as little kids, looking like twins of Jordan. Pictures of his grandma. And his grandpa, the one who did bad things to his mom and uncle. He'd wanted to say thank you, but his voice shut off when he saw his little-kid mom in a pink dress, holding a kitten.

Someone knocked on his door. "Yeah?"

Danny stuck his head in. "Guess what? Mom doesn't have to go to court today!"

Jordan sat up. "Why not?"

"I dunno. But I was in her room when the phone rang, and that's what she told me."

Jordan was jealous of the way Danny lay on Sarah's bed and talked to her. Now that school was out, Jordan had seen Danny do it lots of mornings. They just talked and watched Sarah's TV and were all cozy, and it was safe and normal. Jordan felt cheated, watching them. Once Sarah had said, "Come on in," but he walked away.

Why didn't Sarah have to go today? He didn't *want* her to go, but what had changed overnight? So far everything had gone exactly like Reece and Rhonda, Jordan's lawyer, had told him it would. He'd decided this was bad, this change. He had a horrible feeling. That feeling he used to get, like someone was making him wear a coat that was way too tight.

He heard a door open across the hall, and Nate appeared in a pair of cutoff sweats. He yawned and scratched his belly. "Who the hell's calling so early?"

Jordan shrugged.

Danny sat on the end of Jordan's bed. "It was for Mom. She wouldn't let me listen."

Another door opened, and Sarah came down the hall and stood in Jordan's doorway.

"What's wrong?" Jordan didn't mean to sound panicked. He got out of bed.

"Nothing's wrong," Sarah said. "There's just no hearing today."

"Why not?" He tried to take a deep breath, to stop that too-tight feeling.

"I . . . I don't know." He figured he must look scared or something, because she said, "It's probably something silly, like the power's out or something." Yesterday the storms had been so bad they'd lost power for about three hours. "Don't worry, hon. You can go back to bed."

The phone rang again, and Sarah ran down the hall to pick it up in her room.

Jordan looked at Nate, who shrugged.

Sarah's door closed, muffling her voice behind it.

"You guys ready to eat?" Nate asked. Danny jumped up and followed Nate downstairs. There was no way Jordan could go back to sleep now, so he followed, too, even though he knew he couldn't eat. His stomach did somersaults.

Jordan sat at a kitchen island and watched Danny make toast. Nate sat on the island and ate cereal dry out of the box. Sarah came into the kitchen and stood looking at them, her face pinched up, her eyes far away.

Jordan was afraid to ask her. He held his breath.

"Bobby's coming over to talk to me," she said.

That extra heartbeat kicked Jordan's ribs.

"What's he wanna talk about?" Nate asked, and Jordan could tell he was pretending not to care that Sarah had just called Kramble "Bobby."

Sarah shook her head. "I don't know. He wouldn't say. He just said it was important." Jordan watched her finger the wedding ring on the chain around her neck. "He wants to talk to me in private, okay? Do you guys think you can keep yourselves scarce for a while?"

Nate set down the cereal box and sighed. "Whatever. When's he coming?"

"Right now."

Jordan looked at the digital clock on the microwave. It was 7:04 A.M. He had to press a hand over his heart when that extra beat kicked him again.

Even though Sarah said they could stay upstairs, Jordan was glad when Nate suggested they go outside. His fear didn't make him so claustrophobic out here. They'd put Klezmer in the old sandbox and had just started kicking around a soccer ball when Kramble pulled up in the driveway. He got out of the car and paused when he saw them. He gave them a lame wave, but then he walked around to the front door like he wanted to avoid them. Jordan pretended not to feel the goose bumps that ran unwanted fingers up his spine.

Jordan knew that Nate and Danny were thinking about what was being discussed inside the house as much as he was, but no one said anything. Good. It was better that way. The air hung thick and nasty as the sun rose on a haze of humidity from the rains the day before. They slapped at mosquitoes. But they pretended to concentrate on the dumb soccer drills, as if Jordan had trained them for years.

Another car door jerked them to attention. They lifted their heads to see Reece coming in the back gate. Jordan stood.

Reece held up a hand. "Hey. I need to talk to Sarah a minute, okay?" He didn't wait for Jordan to answer. And he didn't look Jordan in the eye as he let himself in the back door.

Jordan tried to breathe the way Dr. Bryn had taught him.

He did okay, until Bryn arrived, too. And then Ali.

Jordan heard the water sound start in his ears. Why was Dr. Bryn here? He didn't have therapy today. He fought the urge to hide somewhere.

"What do you think they're talking about?" Danny asked, his face pale.

Shut up! Jordan wished he could scream. They weren't supposed to talk about it.

"I'm scared," Danny said. "It's something bad. And it's something about Jordan."

"Danny," Nate said quietly.

Jordan wanted to punch Danny. Why'd he have to say that out loud?

The three of them stood, silent, in the yard, Nate's foot on the ball. They stared at the house for what felt like an hour, then jumped as if they'd done something wrong when the back door opened. Reece stepped out onto the porch.

"Jordan?" Reece's voice came out raspy. "Could you come inside? We need to talk to you."

Jordan's heart almost knocked him down that time. "Okay." His own voice sounded far away, almost drowned out by the gurgling-water sound that filled his ears. He walked to the back door. He hated leaving Nate and Danny behind. Going inside with just a bunch of grown-ups brought bad memories back to him. He tried with all his might to shove those memories out of his head.

Reece held the door for him, and Jordan stepped into the kitchen. The four others sat at an island. Both Sarah and Dr. Ali were red-faced and puffy-eyed, cheeks streaked from crying. Pieces of broken china lay at the base of the Laden Table fridge. Dr. Bryn sat with her hands folded. Kramble's face was white and set, like a statue.

Even with the air-conditioning, the house felt more suffocating than the heavy heat outside. Suffocating. S-u-f-f-o-c-a-t-i-n-g.

That sickening anticipation filled him. A-n-t-i-c-i-p-a-t-i-o-n. The not-wanting-it-to-happen fighting with the wanting-to-get-it-over-with.

He stood by the island and waited.

CHAPTER THIRTY

Nate

Nate sat on the edge of the sandbox, shivering even though it was so damn hot. What the hell was going on inside the house? He rolled the soccer ball toward the rabbit.

Danny stood up. "Do you think his parents broke out of jail?"

"No." Klezmer rolled the ball back to Nate. "No way." Nate saw Danny's fear and remembered Mrs. Kendrick sneaking into their house. Nate stood, too, and reached out to pat Danny's arm, partly to comfort his brother, partly to comfort himself. Thinking about that day still made his knees dissolve. "It's okay."

"But maybe something went wrong and they can't have the trial," Danny said. "Like on TV, some kind of technicality or something, and the judge has to let them go."

"No," Nate said, praying it wasn't a lie. He wished he knew what to say to make those lines on Danny's forehead disappear, to make himself stop shivering, but an icy-sharp melting spread through his belly—what if what Danny said was true?

The back door opened, and Jordan stepped out. Nate saw the kid's white face, white as this sun-bleached sand, and that icy sensation spread to his legs, his arms, hurting his chest. Shit. What now? "Jordan?" Nate's voice was tight, his throat thick. "You okay, man?"

Mom appeared in the door behind Jordan, and Jordan stepped off the porch and stumbled, zombielike, to the garden gate. He went in, leaving it open, and headed for the bean tepee, now covered in green vines and white blossoms. He crawled inside.

Nate looked from the tepee to the porch, where Kramble, Reece, and Dr. Bryn now also stood. Danny stepped close to Nate.

Reece and Dr. Bryn followed Jordan and crouched outside the tepee. Reece's voice was low and bedtime-story soothing, but Nate couldn't make out the words. Nate looked back to the porch. Kramble touched his mom's hair, but her legs seemed to fold, and she sat abruptly on the top step. Ali came out the door then and sat beside Mom, putting her arms around her.

Kramble came down the porch stairs and walked over to the sandbox. His eyes were bloodshot, and he hadn't shaved.

"What's going on?" Nate asked him. Nate put a hand on Danny's shoulder and suddenly pictured them posed in a family portrait. He was sure they looked as somber as those black-and-white photos in Grandma Glass's photo albums, where no one smiled. Had all those people been about to receive bad news?

Kramble cleared his throat and hooked his thumbs in his belt. Quietly and matter-of-factly he said, "Jordan's mother is dead."

The colors changed in the yard. Nate blinked hard to bring the grass back to green, the sky back to its hazy white.

Any relief Nate thought he might feel was buried under the memory of Ali waking him in the ER, whispering to him that his dad was dead. Danny's small moan made Nate know he was thinking of that, too. Nate turned back to Kramble. "What happened?"

"She committed suicide."

Nate waited, and Kramble answered the unspoken question. "She opened her carotid artery with a broken pencil." Kramble pulled one hand from his belt and touched his own throat. He stared down at the sandbox, but Nate knew he was seeing something else. He wondered if Kramble had actually seen Mrs. Kendrick dead.

Danny went to Mom on the porch. Nate turned his head to watch him and had the sensation that his vision lagged behind his movement by a full second, just like after his hockey concussion last year. Danny sat on one side of Mom, Ali on the other. Nate turned his head slowly to the garden. Reece sat on the bench under the apple tree, staring at the ground. Jordan was in the bean tepee, and Dr. Bryn sat right outside it. Nate sat down in the sand.

He was kind of glad when Kramble sat down, too, on the edge of the box.

"What did Jordan say?" Nate asked.

"Nothing. He just stood up and came out here."

Nate picked up a handful of sand and let it run through his fingers. He pictured Mrs. Kendrick, with her messy blond hair and sexy arms. Christ, how did you slice open your own throat with a pencil? He felt that draft-on-the-back-of-his-neck sensation. He knew she was dangerous—crazy, even—a person who'd do anything, but . . . he felt he'd underestimated her . . . her *strength*. Maybe . . .

Nate looked up, and Kramble met his eyes. "You think she was trying to protect him?"

Kramble shrugged. "If she was, it was about time."

Nate picked up more sand. He saw Mrs. Kendrick's red, lipsticked mouth. Smelled her minty breath, felt it on his cheek. Her hand on his chest. Her lips on his. The way her kisses made him think of vampires. Somehow he knew that Kramble was someone he could trust. "I . . . I almost slept with her," he blurted.

Nate stared at the sand running through his fingers and didn't lift his gaze until it was gone, his hands white and silty. Kramble's face was open, waiting.

"She used to . . . flirt with me. She'd touch me, but she always made it seem like an accident. I . . . . I kissed her. And she'd invite me over, tell me to come over anytime. I almost went once. I thought about it all the time, but one day I really . . . almost went."

Kramble's face didn't change, but his voice came out hoarse when he said to Nate, "But you didn't."

"But . . . but I didn't tell anybody. I never warned anybody. And . . . and maybe if I had—"

"Nate. What was happening to Jordan had been happening for years. You couldn't have prevented it."

"But I could've stopped it earlier, maybe. I could've, I dunno. I . . . I knew it was wrong."

"Nate, how old are you? Sixteen? Seventeen?" Kramble leaned toward him. "She was an adult, someone you should've been able to trust. She was a sick woman."

"But I—"

"Hey," Kramble cut him off, and said, slowly and distinctly, "You didn't do anything wrong. The crime was hers, not yours."

Those words washed over Nate with hot-shower comfort. He was afraid he might cry. Klezmer hopped to Kramble's shoes and sniffed them, his whiskers quivering.

"You ever told anybody else?" Kramble asked.

Nate shook his head.

"You might want to. That's a lot of bullshit to drag around."

Nate felt better already, having said it out loud. Light-headed, almost.

Kramble reached down to pet the rabbit at his feet, but Klezmer shied from his hand. Kramble shrugged and pulled a pack of cigarettes from his pocket, shaking one free.

"Can I have one?" Nate asked. He *needed* one, almost craved it.

Kramble started to tap out another but stopped himself. "No way," he said, glancing at the porch.

"She won't care," Nate lied.

Kramble narrowed his eyes. "You trying to blow my chances?"

Nate blinked. He knew that Kramble liked his mom, but he never expected Kramble to say anything about it to *him*. Especially not today, not right now. It seemed creepy, after talking about a woman slitting her throat. Nate knew that his cheeks were red. He sat there feeling like an idiot. "You cool with that?" Kramble asked.

Nate stared into the man's face, but Kramble wouldn't look away. "I dunno," Nate said at last. "It's weird. I don't have a problem with you personally, but . . ."

"I understand." Kramble didn't seem offended at all.

Nate scanned the yard again. Nothing had changed. Ali, Danny, and Mom were on the back porch. Dr. Bryn sat outside the bean te-pee. Jordan was inside it. He could hear Dr. Bryn's voice, just barely, over the cicadas that had begun to scream in the trees. Reece still sat on the bench in the garden. "Reece likes her, too," Nate said.

Kramble took a drag on his cigarette. "I know."

"I don't have a problem with him personally either."

Kramble raised his eyebrows and grinned, just a little. "That's good to know."

Nate watched Kramble take another drag. "Just so you know, she hates smoking."

Kramble squinted at Nate as if he thought Nate might be bull-shitting him. "Shit," he said under his breath, and stubbed out the cigarette in the sandbox.

"Hey, come on, Danny and Jordan play in here," Nate protested.

Kramble picked up the cigarette and held it in his hand. He stood up and brushed the sand off his seat.

Nate looked toward the porch again. Mom leaned her head into Ali's shoulder. Ali hugged and rocked her.

Kramble stood there for several minutes more, as if waiting for some way to end his conversation with Nate. When none came, he wandered into the garden and spoke to Reece.

Nate still sat in the sandbox, the sun beating on his head, his shirt sticking to him. After a while the two men left the garden and walked to the porch. Mrs. Ripley came over to find out what was going on. Eventually Ali took his mom inside. Danny followed them. Later that day Kramble and Dr. Bryn left, and Reece sat on the back porch in the shade.

Nate went once to the bean tepee and bent down to look inside. Jordan lay curled in a ball, hugging his knees, staring straight ahead, his face more empty and far away than in those pictures. It scared Nate. Nate reached in and touched Jordan's foot. He didn't respond in any way. "I'm sorry, man," Nate said. "I'm sorry." And he was. He might hate Mrs. Kendrick. But he couldn't even be secretly glad she was dead, because he knew what that felt like for Jordan.

Nate walked away, but he didn't want to go into the house, so he sat in the sandbox and thought about his dad. He thought his dad would approve of their fostering Jordan, but he also knew that they would never have done it if Dad were alive. There wouldn't be room. And he didn't mean room in the house, but that there wouldn't have been room *inside them,* inside their lives. They wouldn't have known they were strong enough to do this.

They wouldn't have needed Jordan.

Danny came outside and sat by the tepee for a long time. But even when he gave up and went inside to eat, and Reece left, Nate stayed in the sandbox. He remembered building sand castles with his dad. Dad got really obsessive and crazy about them, and every summer they had to top one they'd done before. Today, thinking of Dad, Nate stacked buckets, dug moats, and put in flags of dogwood twigs. Klezmer dug a trench in the cool sand under a shaded edge and watched him.

Nate wasn't sure what he'd do when the castle was finished, so he kept at it, making it complicated and elaborate. Sweat stung his eyes, and the back of his neck burned. He stayed in the sandbox until it grew too dark to see his work and fireflies flitted low in the grass.

His mother touched his cheek, and Nate opened his eyes, blinking, to find himself on his side in the sand.

He agreed to go inside, but only after she promised to come get him if she got too sleepy to keep watch herself.

CHAPTER THIRTY-ONE

Sarah

Sarah sat on the back porch in the cloudy moonlight, barefoot, in shorts and a T-shirt. An icy breeze cut through the heavy air, promising another storm. Distant thunder rumbled.

She heard the breeze rattle the bean vines covering the tepee where Jordan still sat. Ali'd crawled in there this afternoon and made sure he was physically all right. She'd finally left, at eleven, after Priah brought them take-out Indian food. Sarah hadn't eaten.

Her first reaction to Bobby's news had been the feeling of being swept away in a strong current. She'd needed to reach out and grab hold of something steady and strong before she was pulled under.

That's what made her cry in the kitchen. That's what made her throw the cups and break them on the fridge. That's what made her scream at Reece when he insisted they tell Jordan right away. How could they tell him this? Who had decided that this was her fate—to add to the heaping plate of misery this boy had already been served?

Who had decided that this was his fate—to survive unspeakable atrocities committed against his body and spirit and to recover, to thrive, only to be handed this? It was sadistic, perverted. The worst act of all that Courtney'd subjected him to.

Sarah replayed that scenario in her head, countless times, the six of them at the counter, silent, until Jordan had been the first to speak. The bunch of cowards they were, they'd made him suffer, stand there and squirm. Horrors must have crossed his mind, because he'd finally asked, "Are they letting my dad go?"

It shocked them out of their shock, in a sense. And then Reece finally said it: "Jordan, your mother committed suicide last night."

The look on Jordan's face haunted Sarah. His first expression had been unabashed, raw fury. But it had vanished under his mask, and he'd walked out the back door.

Another rumble of thunder and blast of wind made her shiver. Nate's sand castle shone blue in a flash of lightning.

"I will do everything in my power," Courtney had promised, looking Sarah right in the eye, "to keep him safe."

Sarah remembered saying, "You can't. You know you can't." Was this Courtney's way to prove Sarah wrong? She hugged herself in the wind, her braid pulling loose.

If someone else had killed Courtney, in an accident, a fight, Sarah knew that some secret, awful part of her would exhale with relief. But for Courtney to end her life herself seemed yet another betrayal of Jordan. She'd let him believe she was trying to regain custody of him. She hadn't even left him a note, an explanation. Just another set of lies ending in an act that had shocked and humiliated him.

"Sarah?" The quiet voice startled her. Jordan stood outside the garden gate. He looked like a little ghost, so pale and fair in the moonlight. Another flash of lightning illuminated his tortured face, and Sarah stood and walked down the steps to him.

When she reached his side, he whispered, "I hated her."

His expression made her skin contract, as if it were suddenly two sizes too small to hold in the rest of her. "That's okay." She tried to remember how Bryn had coached her. "You can feel whatever you feel."

"But . . ." he looked so lost. She ventured to put an arm across his shoulders, but he practically bristled, so she let it drop. He moved close to her side but kept his own arms locked across his chest. The wind rippled their clothes like sails. In the next flash of lightning, Sarah saw the highest castle tower slump over, blown by the wind. A dogwood twig sprang free and flew across the yard. Both gates rattled. She looked at Danny's tree, bowing and waving in the wind. The robin's nest would be demolished.

"I hated her," Jordan said again. He moaned, his whole body trembling. "I wanted her . . . to die." He sucked in a sob, in a hiccupping gasp. "I wished she would."

Sarah took his face in her hands and felt his jaw tighten, his shoulders brace. "Jordan, you didn't make it happen, no matter what you wished. She did this herself."

He pulled his face from Sarah's grasp. "She said she'd try to get better," he spit out. "But she lied. She never wanted me to come back."

The first raindrops stung her face.

"But I didn't want to either," he said. "I didn't want to live with her again. Not really. I just said I did because . . . I *should've* wanted to, but I didn't. I never did. And now, and now—" He hiccupped another sob. "What's going to happen to me?" he whispered as the rain let loose in earnest.

His hair was plastered down in his eyes, and she remembered him standing in the rain at the end of his driveway, that day both of their lives had changed. She wondered which day would stand out as darker for him, ten years down the road.

She looked into that pained, hopeless face and recognized what he was feeling. His world, too, was being swept away, as hers had been in the kitchen those million years ago this morning. She'd needed something to reach out and grab hold of, and she'd had it. Her children, this home, this family.

She couldn't help herself—she reached and pulled him to her in a hug. Far from the stiff recoil she expected, he clung back to her with an intensity that stole her breath. He muffled his sobs with his face buried in her neck, his arms tight around her shoulders, wrapping his legs around her waist, climbing her, even as her own legs folded and she sank to the ground. She held him, the rain pelting her back, her cheek to his drenched hair, wishing she could absorb him, to start all over again the way he deserved.

Over his head she squinted through the rain. Nate's tree roiled in the wind, the branches waving like tentacles trying to catch her attention, the entire trunk bending and thrashing. Jordan's tree didn't bend but leaned, in danger of breaking. But right now she could stake the boy or his tree, not both.

She held on to Jordan.

Danny

Danny saw that they'd let the frosting get fudgelike and cool in the pan, but he didn't want to say so. He didn't want to break the mood. He would sit here with his elbows on this countertop forever. Mom and Nate and Jordan all leaned there together with him, the magnificent cake between them. Everyone was silent, and Danny recognized that they all knew that night of the storm was the end of one part of the story and the start of the next.

They'd gone to Michigan to escape the chaos after the funeral—news trucks driving down the street taking pictures of their home and reporters shouting questions at Mom whenever she went outside or to or from the van. Reece and Bobby had urged Mom to "take the kids and get out of town." *The kids.* Already Jordan was included in that statement.

One day in Michigan, Jordan had found a whole field of raspberries. And he'd filled bucket after bucket to bring to Danny's mother. And Mom had accepted all he brought her, that day and the next, and brought every berry back home to Dayton, the aroma in the van almost overwhelming. She hadn't been able to use them all in a year, but she didn't throw a single raspberry away.

And every time they used raspberry preserves, like today on the wedding cake, they told that story. And they told how Danny and Jordan had eaten the berries right off the bushes, not even bothering to *pick* them, just bending over and pulling the berries off with their teeth. Once they'd looked up, and not fifty yards away a brown bear was doing the same thing.

There'd been the trial for Jordan's father. He and all the other adults in the pornography ring were found guilty and sentenced to life in prison. Jordan didn't have to testify at the trial. He never went, he never watched, and, as far as Danny knew, he had never read about it. Danny remembered the simple, matter-of-fact way Jordan had nodded when Mom told him the trial was over and that his father was going to prison in Lucasville.

Jordan had nodded in that same matter-of-fact way about five years ago when Mom and Bobby told him that his father had been killed in a prison fight. Jordan didn't go to his father's funeral. Danny wondered if anyone had. He knew for a fact—because he'd asked Jordan outright—that Mark Kendrick had never tried to contact Jordan. Ever. There had never been a phone call, a letter, or an e-mail in either direction.

"I've got nothing to say to him," Jordan had said to Danny, when Danny asked if he ever wanted to see his father. "Some things that pass between people . . . you know . . . make words impossible."

Danny looked at Jordan now. Twenty-three years old and leaning on his elbows, shoulder to shoulder with Mom. He looked so at home.

The back door clacked open, and Deborah Ann entered, the woman who would become Danny's sister-in-law within the hour. He checked his watch. Within the *half* hour.

"What are you all doing?" she asked. But she wasn't angry or worried. Only curious. Probably only worried about missing any fun.

"Finishing the cake," Nate told her.

"The cake isn't *done*?" She put her hands on her hips in mock disapproval but moved immediately to the kitchen island. She rested

THE KINDNESS OF STRANGERS

one hand on Mom's back and dipped one finger of the other hand in the frosting, not caring at all about her wedding dress. Danny loved the way Nate smiled at her, loved how happy this woman made his brother. "Oh, my," she said as she tasted the frosting. "That is amazing."

"We should have made it yesterday," Danny said. "That way the preserves could have really invaded the chocolate."

Mom laughed at this. "Like the cake would have survived overnight, with you all in the house!"

Jordan checked his watch. "Shouldn't we hurry?" he asked. He alone looked nervous. Danny knew that Jordan despised any kind of conflict or deviation from a plan. They'd talked about it a lot, in all the therapy they'd had together over the years. Danny always teased Jordan that he couldn't even recommend a movie without feeling guilty if the person didn't end up liking it.

"Don't worry," Deborah told him. "We can be late. I mean, they can't start without *us*. I just wanted to make sure Nate wasn't chickening out."

Everyone laughed, even Jordan. Even if Nate *did* chicken out, which Danny couldn't imagine, the family would beg Deborah to stay. She was one of them already.

Danny moved to the stove to heat water to thin the frosting, and Deborah Ann took his spot at the island.

Jordan was different with Deborah. Danny liked to watch Jordan and Deborah together, because it was like seeing a new Jordan. Danny believed that Jordan saw himself differently when he was around her. Even from the early days of Nate's dating her.

Jordan and Danny met Deborah on their first Thanksgiving home from their freshman year of college. Nate had been seeing her for nearly a year by then and was finally bringing her home to meet the family. At one point the four of them ended up in the kitchen without Mom, and Nate had been ruthlessly teasing Danny because Mom had told Nate that she found condoms in Danny's laundry. It had all been amiable and comfortable. Danny had been pissed at

Mom for telling Nate but not at all embarrassed. They'd gotten raunchy, teasing about bedrooms in the house and where everyone would sleep, and Danny remembered feeling like they were grown-ups. And with no hint of a blush, no hesitation, no nothing, Deborah had turned to Jordan and asked, "So are *you* a virgin?"

Silence crashed down on the steamy kitchen. Jordan didn't blush either. Not anymore. But he did a double take and spread his arms in disbelief. "Hello?" Jordan said. "Are you forgetting something?"

But Deborah only looked confused. She turned to Nate, eyes wide. "What?" she asked.

And Danny watched Jordan realize *she didn't know.* She knew he was adopted. But Nate told them later he didn't plan to tell her the whole story until Jordan felt like telling it himself.

Jordan felt like telling her right then. Danny felt something akin to awe as Jordan stated—quietly, kindly almost—"I was sexually abused as a kid. I haven't been a virgin since I was like . . . seven?"

Deborah blinked and put a hand to her throat. "Oh, God. I'm sorry."

Jordan shrugged.

And what happened in the next moment made Danny know *right then* that Deborah was a keeper. She returned to the playful mood of minutes before and said, with a teasing lilt, "So what about *now*? In your new life?"

And Jordan laughed—really, truly laughed, pleasant surprise twinkling in his eyes—and said simply, "I don't think you get that back."

"Well, you *should,*" she said. Danny would never forget the way she said it. It was so sincere. But she kept it from being too corny by picking up the chocolate-pecan pie Danny had made and carrying it out to the table.

That was the Thanksgiving they thought Mom was going to tell them she was marrying Bobby. But all she announced was that they were going on vacation together the week between Christmas and New Year's. Danny thought they'd definitely get married while they were in Hawaii. But so far they hadn't. Danny wasn't sure why. They'd waited until Jordan and Danny were in college before they even stayed overnight with each other. Now Bobby lived here in the house. Danny liked that. Bobby was a good guy, and Danny didn't want Mom to be alone.

Danny thought Deborah was allowed to ask Jordan things other people couldn't, because she was one of the only people in the family who had no other version of the story. Jordan got to form the story for her.

"Do you know why your mother wanted to be a doctor?" she asked Jordan once.

Danny had flinched. But Jordan looked sad. "I don't know. I really don't. Her dad was a doctor."

"So maybe it's like Nate wanting to be a doctor because his father was." Nate was now the orthopedic doctor for the Detroit Red Wings. Deborah was their neurologist. The team called them the carpenter and the electrician.

"Maybe," Jordan said.

"You both come from doctors," Deborah said.

And Jordan turned up the corners of his mouth, the way he did when he didn't really buy something. Danny could almost see the vibes come off him, saying, *I don't.* Because Jordan sometimes wanted to know everything about his mother, to hang on to her memory, and other times seemed to deliberately choose things that made him seem unlike her. For a while, in high school, he even dyed his hair.

Danny didn't tell Jordan's story. Even when he wished he could. The story belonged to Jordan. Danny knew he was a part of it, and it was definitely a part of him, but it wasn't his place to tell it. Like at college, when Jordan's girlfriend talked to Danny about him. Jordan and Danny ended up rooming together at college. And Jordan started dating this girl. Danny really liked her. Mom and Nate met her once. Kristi. Really gorgeous, petite girl, shorter than Jordan, even. Smart and funny. Athletic. A dancer. Jordan talked about her constantly. He went to see the same dance recital three nights in a row. Danny went once. And Danny knew that Jordan *must* be crazy about this girl, because the concert was terrible.

Jordan and Kristi watched movies in the lounge, they went jogging on the bike path, they went to dinner. Danny saw them once downtown holding hands and called Nate *right then* to tell him, "You will not believe this."

But then one day, when Jordan was at his job in the library, Danny left the dorm to go to class, and there was Kristi waiting for him. She talked him into going to a coffeehouse, bought him a mocha, and said, "You have to tell me: What is going on?"

Danny honestly didn't know. So Kristi told him. She'd dubbed Jordan the "ice prince" to her girlfriends because she couldn't get him to have sex with her no matter what she did. And she'd tried everything. She was at her wits' end. "Is something wrong with him? Is he not into me?"

Danny felt so bad, looking at this pretty girl. "Ask *him*," he told her.

"I *have*," she said. Tears glittered in her eyes. There was nothing Danny could tell her. He wished he could tell her to go slow, to just wait, to be patient, to be really careful, to back off—but he couldn't say any of those things without implying a reason, without opening a door that Jordan obviously had kept shut. All those years in therapy had taught Danny that he couldn't open the door for Jordan.

And Kristi had asked, "Is he gay?"

Danny had wanted to laugh out loud. He thought about telling her, "No, that's *me*," but he didn't tell her that either.

Jordan and Kristi broke up about a week later. Jordan was blue, he moped around the room, and Danny took him out for beers, but they didn't really talk about it. Danny and Jordan didn't have long talks like Jordan did with Nate and Mom. But he and Jordan could hang out for hours, sitting on the Front Room wall, watching people, and Jordan would say something like, "This time was better. I got closer." And Danny would know exactly what he meant. It was like they'd been talking for hours.

Every now and then there'd be some comment, some weird thing that came up and made something pass between them. And Danny and Jordan just looked at each other, like they did in that gym class all that time ago. This look that said, *I know.*

Like this time a bunch of the guys were drinking and Jordan was kind of tipsy—which didn't happen very often; he told a therapist that he didn't like to lose control of himself, which was funny, because then for a while he got drunk a lot and always joked, "This is part of my therapy," to rationalize it. When he was drunk, he spelled a lot. For no reason, just bizarre words. Like, he and Danny would be walking down Court Street and he'd narrate stuff they saw, saying, "That tall girl is wearing chartreuse stockings. C-h-a-r-t-r-e-u-s-e." It got to where the guys would just ask him to spell stuff because it was funny. Anyway, the guys were bragging about how many women they'd slept with. There was some poster in the bar bathroom about how when you slept with someone, you were sleeping with all of their partners, too. Danny wasn't even thinking about Jordan, but the whole time Jordan just sort of fidgeted with the quarters on the table, until Charlie turned to him and said, "Okay, shy one. Fess up. How many?" Everyone laughed, and someone said, "I bet zero."

Danny remembered how Jordan raised his eyebrows in this funny way that said, "Oh, you think so?" And everyone kept teasing him, trying to guess. And he got this faraway look in his eye and moved his mouth like he was counting, and finally said, "Thirteen . . . I think. Maybe twelve, but I'm pretty sure it's thirteen." And everyone hooted and hollered and then got quiet. They wanted to think he was kidding, but Jordan wasn't like that. And when they pestered him, he stuck by it, even turning to Danny to back him up. Jordan had this little glint in his eye, and Danny didn't know how to take it. It kind of bonded them, but it was also weird. Jordan told the absolute truth without revealing a hint of the reality.

And once, only once, Jordan got plastered. Really plastered. He vowed never again, and Danny believed he meant it. But that one time he was really plastered, he told everyone on their hall that he'd been a child porn star.

Danny even had to tell Mom that later. Sometimes just among their family, someone would bring that up. When they did, Jordan would cover his face and groan. They'd all laugh.

"A *child* porn star?" the guys had asked. "You can't do that. Isn't it against the law?"

"Yes," Jordan said solemnly. "It is. My parents went to jail."

And everyone looked at Danny and said, "B–but I thought you were . . . ?"

Danny nodded. "He's adopted," Danny said apologetically.

"But . . ."

There was a year where Jordan told everyone a different story about his parents. Sometimes he made up utter bullshit, but sometimes he touched on parts of the truth. His "family of origin," he called them, had been "mentally ill and unable to care for him." Sometimes he ventured into, "They were abusive, and I was removed from them." Sometimes he was flippant—"They were crazy"—and sometimes he shrugged and said, "I never knew them."

When he wanted to change the subject, he'd say, "I was raised by freaks—and aren't we all, really?"

And Danny thought, *Yeah, sure they were.* Everyone thinks their parents are freaky, but Danny's were safe, kind freaks, and for that he was eternally grateful.

And he was always really happy when Jordan called Courtney Kendrick his "first mother," because he liked what it said about Mom. Jordan usually didn't call Danny's mom "Mom" to her face, although Danny had seen him write it in cards and e-mails (yes, okay, he sometimes read Jordan's e-mails when they were roomies. He was sure Jordan read his, too). But Jordan would tell the guys on the hall, "Our mom sent some cookies," or "Our mom is coming this weekend. Can you get us a table at Seven Sauces?"

When Deborah Ann asked Jordan about his mom, it sometimes made Danny feel nervous. He worried that it would upset Jordan, but he worried more that it would hurt his mom's feelings. Danny's therapist said Danny should let those fears go. Did it upset *him*? And if not, he shouldn't worry. Danny considered: *Did* it upset him? A little? He still wondered about that time, the Kendrick photos. Without knowing it on any conscious level, Danny figured he probably already knew he was different, even then, and feared that there was some flawed part of him, something visible, that had made the Kendricks know he was a target.

Danny brought the boiling water over to the frosting and poured a little in. He stirred, and the group watched him drizzle the frosting over the cake. His brother's wedding cake. Man. He looked at Nate and shook his head.

Everyone was here. Grandpa and G.G. Grandpa Laden. Ali and Priah. Reece and his wife, Lori. Even Mackenzie and her boyfriend. J.M. and Maya. J.M. came to town one or two times a year, and Jordan went out there just as much. He'd spent a whole summer in Seattle once. Danny worried that Jordan might move there eventually. Nate in Detroit was far enough away. He liked them closer, but they all teased him when he said that. "We can't all work in Mom's restaurant," Nate joked, although they'd all spent summers and breaks busing tables there.

"It won't be mine much longer," Mom joked. The Laden Table would end up as Danny's, everyone knew it. He was already pretty much running the show.

Bobby came in the back door. "Okay, people, is this wedding going to happen or do I need to do some crowd control?"

Nate laughed and took Deborah's hand and headed for the door, for the backyard where Mom really had hired someone to make a chuppah from Nate's dogwood tree.

"Wait!" Jordan called. "Bouquet."

"Oh, that's right." Deborah opened the huge Laden Table fridge and pulled out the bouquet. "Danny, thank you. This is perfect."

Jordan cleared his throat. "Excuse me?" he said with mock indignation. "I helped."

"He did," Danny said, grinning. "He insisted on those daylilies."

Deborah turned to Mom. "Later I am throwing this bouquet straight to you," she said.

Mom laughed and turned to kiss Bobby. The kiss lasted.

And it was one of those moments Danny wanted to freeze and keep forever. As he followed everyone out to the yard, he tried to drink in every detail: the chairs with their white covers, the garden in full bloom—the tomato bushes bent heavy with fruit, nearly obscuring the old, green gargoyle—the silver ice buckets twinkling in the sun, the ends of the white linen tablecloths lifting gently in the wind, the pile of wrapped gifts under Jordan's dogwood tree.

A bird sang, and Danny turned his head to search for it. A robin lifted off from Jordan's tree. Danny watched the bird swoop down to the ground, gathering food. No, it wasn't food—it was straw from the champagne crates. The robin carried it back to the small tangle it had begun assembling in the crook of Jordan's tree. If Danny squinted his eyes just right, he could tell that the trunk of the tree still leaned too far to one side, and a thick, gnarled scar—too tough to cut through—protruded from where that limb had ripped away.

But the tree still stood, and a breeze fluttered the leaves on its reaching branches.

Acknowledgments

The Kindness of Strangers has had a long and complicated journey and many people have touched it along the way. Lisa Bankoff made me believe in the book again and found it a home. Claire Wachtel helped me see the book clearly when I'd lost that ability. Thanks to Tina Dubois at ICM, and to Samantha Hagerbaumer, Kevin Callahan, Jennifer Pooley, Sean Griffin, Susan Carpenter, and all the other good people at William Morrow, and to Maureen Sugden, copyeditor extraordinaire.

For their comments and insightful feedback on various drafts of the manuscript, I thank many talented writers I am blessed to know: Suzanne Clauser, Ed Davis, Chuck Derry, Ben Grossberg, Marian Jensen, Lee Huntington, Sandy Love, Rachel Moulton, Nancy Pinard, Julia Reichert, Barbara Singleton, and Ted Weatherup, with special love and thanks to Nancy Jones and Suzanne Kelly-Garrison.

I owe eternal gratitude to Diana Baroni, Molly Chehak, and Liz Trupin-Pulli for their care, professional expertise, and guidance.

Huge thanks to my Hedgebrook sisters, Ted Lebowitz, Butch & Beverly Kittle, Monica Schiffler, and the Topsail Island crew for asking helpful questions.

Dayton Police officer James R. Krauskopf took me for a ride-along (which provided me with enough material for a lifetime of stories!) and helped divert some plot disasters. Montgomery County Sheriff's officer Sergeant David Hale gave me a thorough tour of the Montgomery County Jail. Lieutenant Joe Neihaus of the Kettering Police Department (and fellow writer) answered endless questions with patience and clarity.

My cousin Rhonda Love, former Assistant Public Guardian at Chicago's Cook County Office of the Public Guardian, shared the heartbreaking stories of her job and offered her professional expertise. Julia Levine, beautiful poet and child psychologist, talked me through sessions for my fictional characters.

Anne Lee and Trisha Bennet of the amazing organization Darkness to Light helped check my facts and reinforced my belief that angels do exist. Harriet McDougal, also with Darkness to Light, gave an invaluable edit of an early manuscript. Dr. Sarah Fillingame, Vicki Giambrone, and Susan Brockman of the Children's Medical Center of Dayton, and Libby Nicholson and Denise Jenkins of CARE House all graciously answered questions, provided resources, and gave me tours. Any blunders or implausibilities that remain are mine alone.

Bill Anderson, the best damn pie baker in all of West Virginia, introduced me to the chocolate-raspberry-caramel frosted cake and supplied the recipe.

Thanks to the generous, supportive community of the Miami Valley School.

I am deeply grateful for grants from the Ohio Arts Council and Cultureworks.

My family—immediate and extended, past and now changed, blood and chosen—sustained and nourished me in many ways. I am lucky.

And finally, special love and thanks are due to two dear friends:

Rachel Moulton wins the prize for having read more drafts of this manuscript than any other person. Thank you for the inspiration from your own writing, for the encouragement on the dark days, and for the "Boy Pass."

And Michael Lippert—thank you, Pook, for getting me off the floor, both figuratively and literally.

Darkness to Light is a national nonprofit organization based in Charleston, South Carolina, that seeks to protect children from sexual abuse by placing responsibility squarely on adult shoulders. They educate adults to prevent, recognize, and react responsibly to child sexual abuse. Go online to *www.darkness2light.org* for their free booklet, *Seven Steps to Protecting Our Children,* as a way to begin.